Does it get any better than this?

"Hello."

The voice was low and husky. The pitch managed to convey sleepy male and sexual desire. The voice matched perfectly with the memories playing in her head.

Only the voice sounded more grown-up, more experienced, more . . . Harriet lifted her head, ever so slowly. The voice wasn't in her imagination.

She blinked, parted her lips, and fixed her gaze on the man a step away from her table.

"I didn't mean to startle you," he said, his dark brown eyes taking her in.

"No," she said, her voice barely above a whisper.

"May I buy you a drink?" He leaned closer, looking down at her with a glint in his dark eyes.

Harriet lowered her hands to her lap and pinched herself on the wrist.

This man was the real thing.

Jake Porter.

By Hailey North

NOT THE MARRYING KIND
LOVE: UNDERCOVER
OPPOSITES ATTRACT
TANGLED UP IN LOVE
DEAR LOVE DOCTOR
PERFECT MATCH
PILLOW TALK
BEDROOM EYES

HAILEY NORTH

Not The Marrying Kind

AVON

An Imprint of HarperCollinsPublishers

This is a work of fiction. Names, characters, places, and incidents are products of the author's imagination or are used fictitiously and are not to be construed as real. Any resemblance to actual events, locales, organizations, or persons, living or dead, is entirely coincidental.

AVON BOOKS
An Imprint of HarperCollins*Publishers*
10 East 53rd Street
New York, New York 10022-5299

Copyright © 2007 by Nancy Wagner
ISBN: 978-0-06-058247-0
ISBN-10: 0-06-058247-2
www.avonromance.com

First Avon Books paperback printing: November 2007

Printed in the U.S.A.

10 9 8 7 6 5 4 3 2 1

This book owes its existence to the patience of my editor, Lyssa Keusch; the persuasiveness of my agent, Mel Berger; the loving support of my husband; the generosity of family, friends, and strangers who came to the rescue during and after Hurricane Katrina; and to the keen eye and red pen of my brother Keith.

An author weaves a tale, but it takes a cadre of specialists to produce a book. Here's to Michelle Lesslie, typesetting whiz and photographer extraordinaire, and to all publishing professionals who work behind the scenes to create the miracle of a book.

Chapter 1

West Village, Manhattan

Some things in life are better left alone.

Harriet P. Smith fingered the black and white surveillance photograph of Jake Porter emerging from a Sunset Strip club eight days—or to be more precise, nights—earlier. She studied the flash of a smile, the dark eyes she could paint in her sleep, the quirk in his nose caused by a basketball injury, the protective way he held his arm around the shoulders of the pint-size blonde who walked beside him. Not that the woman mattered one way or the other. For better or worse, it was Jake Porter who held her attention.

And darn it, that had always been true.

And that despite the almost sixteen years that had

passed since the last time she had been within arm's reach of Jake Porter.

It was funny how she always thought of him with both his first and last names. Harriet shoved the photo into the thick envelope supplied by Gotham Investigations, wishing she could discard her dilemma over the man as easily. To be honest, she'd shoved the situation into the recesses of her brain for more years than she cared to count. It was time to quit hiding. She flipped the envelope over and stared at the logo of the firm she'd hired to find Jake Porter.

We Specialize in Discretion proclaimed the script beneath the company name. Well, she sure as heck hoped so. She'd paid a premium for their services, and the last thing she wanted was either Jake Porter or the press finding out what Harriet P. Smith was up to until she had readied herself to come clean.

Harriet eyed the fat envelope. She'd pulled only the one photograph out so far. Shifting from foot to foot, she considered what she might find if she tugged the rest of the items out. The investigator had filled her in over the phone on the highlights. Jake Porter hadn't let any grass grow under his feet. Good college. Better graduate school. He'd turned his MBA to advantage, establishing himself as a rising star in managing creative clients. And he'd founded his own record company. Way back when, at Doolittle High, Jake had been named Most Likely to Succeed and had tied with Harriet for Most Creative. Funny how none of her classmates had credited her with the potential to succeed. But if fame and fortune equaled success, avant-garde artist Harriet P. Smith of the West Village, at thirty-three going on thirty-four, had outstripped every kid in high school who'd made fun of her geeky looks and her penchant for spending more time painting than worrying about boys and clothes. She'd also shed the pounds she'd packed on courtesy of the dreary years she'd spent hating her life in a small town in Arkansas.

Harriet shoved the envelope away from her. It bumped into her cold coffee cup, and dark liquid splashed onto the packet. She tugged one of her paint rags from the waistband of her yoga pants and dabbed at the spill. Staring at the pattern the moisture made spreading into the paper, she envisioned the shapes in a profusion of color and almost, almost forgot all about Jake Porter.

She needed to work. She needed to retreat into the sanctuary of her studio and commune with her canvas. At some point she would know what to do with the information she'd gathered on Jake Porter. The way she knew when one of her massive creations was just right, the way she knew when the color had come to life the way she saw it within her soul, that's the way she'd know when she was meant to contact Jake Porter.

Until that moment came, she'd keep on keeping on. She had to trust she'd know when the time was right to tell Jake Porter he had a son.

Chapter 2

In the City of Angels
Accompanied by a Few Demons

"No deal," Jake Porter said, his voice as cool and calm as always. The man on the other end of the phone had no way of knowing just how pissed Jake was, and just how unfortunate that would prove to be for future bookings at the man's Sunset Strip nightclub.

After a few more threats mixed with promises of riches if only Jake would give in and cut his price for the act, the man hung up. Jake glanced at his calendar on the notebook computer, the only object on his glass-topped desk. Two minutes until Delice arrived. He rose and walked to the wall of windows. The manicurist would finish in just under sixteen minutes. He had a noon lunch booked at his club with some Sony people. That event would take no longer than an hour and a half. Those in the know knew not to waste Jake Porter's time.

Every minute of the day he had scheduled, from his early morning workouts to breakfast meetings, office appointments, luncheons, lawyers, accountants, marketing, publicity, and studio time. Many evenings he spent making the rounds of small clubs, the venues where the good yet unknown artists without a lot of business sense were to be found. He'd made several musicians bigger than big. He aimed to do it again and again.

The door to his office suite swung open. He turned, expecting Delice. Instead, his father stood there, commanding the space yet at the same time managing to look as awkward as hell.

As well he might. What right did he have to barge in without warning? But old habits died hard. Jake Porter, CEO of Philistine Music, could make or break a musician's career with a nod of his head, but no matter his accomplishments, he'd never outrank the Colonel.

Jake snapped to attention. "Sir!"

"At ease, son," his father, Colonel Theodore Porter, USAF-Ret., strode across the carpet, managing to inspect both Jake and the surroundings as he approached. He stopped and stretched out his right hand.

Jake shook hands, looking at his father for some clue to explain his unexpected appearance. Out of uniform now for a few years, the Colonel wore his khaki slacks and crisp white shirt with as sharp a crease and as stiff with starch as any air force uniform he'd donned in his thirty-year career. He had more of a tan than Jake recalled from the last time they'd seen each other, but other than that, nothing had changed. Certainly there was nothing about his father that gave Jake any hint as to why he'd decided to fly from Tampa, site of his last station and his home since then, to Los Angeles. "You're looking well," he said, at a loss for anything else to say.

The Colonel nodded, swung his head and shoulders around, surveying the room, and returned to stand, at ease, in front of Jake. "This will just take a minute," he said. "I know you run a tight ship. Naturally. You're my son." He smiled.

Jake didn't. He did glance at his watch. His secretary would be chatting with Delice in the outer office. Delice didn't like to waste time any more than Jake did. "Anyone can see we're related," he said, almost thinking out loud with the phrase. He and his father had the same dark hair with a tendency to curl that drove them both crazy, same dark brown eyes, same nose except for the telltale signs of an old sports injury that marked Jake's. Aside from their looks, their mannerisms were enough alike to mark them as father and son, a truth that irritated and pleased both parent and child. Jake indicated a pair of chairs in front of the floor-to-ceiling windows. "Time to sit down?"

His father nodded, sat down, and cleared his throat. Jake took the chair opposite. It occurred to him his father had come with bad news. Why else would he appear out of nowhere after an almost two-year absence?

"I have something to tell you I didn't want to put in e-mail or say over the phone," his father said. He looked straight at Jake. "I know marriage isn't your favorite topic—"

Jake laughed. "As long as it's not mine, I can handle it."

"I hope so," his father said. "Because I plan to marry a wonderful woman."

"You do?" Jake couldn't help the surprise that drove his

voice upward. "I mean, *you're* getting married again?" After the horrible marriage his parents had endured, Jake wondered why his father would ever try it a second time.

His father nodded.

"Does Ariel know?" Jake doubted that his mother and father ever spoke but he figured he'd ask the question.

"No."

"I see," Jake said. No, he would not be the one to tell his mother. If that was what his father had shown up to request, he could take a long walk off the Santa Monica Pier.

"I'm not asking you to break the news to her," his father said, almost impatiently. "I haven't even asked the woman if she'll be my wife."

Jake raised his brows.

"I'd like you to meet her," the Colonel said, looking as awkward as he had when he'd first entered Jake's office.

"I'm not sure what I have to do with it," Jake said.

"You are my son," his father said. "I've learned a few things in life, though it's been tough." He looked out the windows as if seeing something there that drew him from the room to someplace in the past, or perhaps to some spot in the future. "Almost like having nails driven into my head." He grinned. "I don't know if you can teach an old dog new tricks, but I aim to find out."

Jake had no idea what his father meant. "I'm not sure I follow you, sir."

His father waved a hand. "Like that, for instance. No need for you to call me 'sir.' I'm not your commanding officer."

Jake almost fell off his chair. Or so it felt, but he knew he didn't budge a muscle or otherwise show any whit of reaction. "No, sir, you're not," he said. "Perhaps I'm not an old enough dog." His entire life had been ruled by his father's military career. His father would be away the majority of the time, but in the months and weeks his father spent at their home billet, Jake certainly had been the good soldier and his father the CO.

"Anyway, I'd like you to meet my prospective wife."

Jake glanced at the door and rose. He'd have to forgo the manicure and race to his lunch meeting. "Is she in the outer office?"

His father stood up. "Office? No, of course not. She's at her home. I'll be there for Christmas and I'd like you to come visit."

"It's the middle of December now," Jake said. And since when had Christmas become important to his father? He could count on one hand the number of times his father had been home for that holiday. Besides, only the day before he'd had his assistant make reservations for a trip for two to the Greek Islands. On the other hand, taking Lilly anywhere right now might be a mistake. She'd been getting damned clingy. She'd also been hinting since the Emmys that she wanted a ring for Christmas. Maybe surprising her with a trip to Greece wasn't such a good idea after all. He could imagine the scene when she realized not only that there'd be no ring for Christmas, but, as he'd told her all along, that there'd never be an engagement ring.

Jake Porter was not the marrying kind.

"I know how last-minute this is," his father said. "That's one of the reasons I flew out here to ask you face-to-face." He paused and folded his arms across his chest. "Please, Jake. It's important to me. To our family."

Jake stared at his size twelve Gucci loafers. He moved his gaze to his father's size twelve Bostonians. Never once had his father asked him to do one single thing that meant something to him in terms of family. Oh, sure, he had chewed his ass if he didn't get good grades or if he stayed out past curfew. But the note in his father's voice was something he'd never, ever heard before.

He would put off Lilly, explain to her she'd have to spend Christmas without him. Taking her to a family event was the last thing he needed to do. "All right," he said. "I'll do it. Tell me where and when and I'll be there."

His father stuck out his hand and they shook, both maintaining a comfortable reserve, but the relief in his father's face was evident. Jake wished he didn't feel a clutch in his gut. He didn't know what to think about the evidence of touchy-feely emotions in his rock-solid, good-old-boy father.

"Thank you," his father said, turning toward the door, his face away from Jake.

"Details," Jake said. "Where does the lady live?"

"Doolittle," the Colonel said.

Jake couldn't keep his jaw from dropping. So much for the pride he held in his ability to maintain a poker face. And talk about a reminder to get all the facts before agreeing to a deal! "As in Arkansas?" he managed to say.

His father nodded and smiled. "Ironic, isn't it?"

Several other adjectives jumped to Jake's mind, but he held his tongue.

"I'll tell you more later," his father said. "I know how you hate to be late, and I've seen you glance at your watch at least once. Fly into Little Rock, Adam Field, the week before Christmas. Send me your travel details and I'll pick you up."

Jake nodded. "Yes, sir," he said, his voice only two shades above a whisper. The last place in the world he wanted to spend Christmas, or any day of the year, for that matter, was Doolittle, Arkansas. But he'd never gone back on his word, and he wouldn't start now.

His father sketched a salute and then where he'd stood remained only empty space.

Jake stared longer than he cared to admit at the space his father had occupied, and then he walked to the wall of windows behind his desk. He dug his hands deeper into his pockets and blinked once, then again. Silky dark hair and soft skin surrounding the prettiest green eyes he'd ever known filled his mind.

He forced himself to gaze at the view outside rather than the image within his brain.

The air was clear, a gift of a rainstorm that had passed through during the morning commute. A few clouds capped the peaks of the Santa Monica Mountains. Jake's offices took up the top floor of one of L.A.'s older highrises. From where he stood at that moment, the city spread out below glistened like the jewels in Harry Winston's swank Rodeo Drive establishment.

On a day like today, it was easy to love his adopted hometown. Adopted? Hell, it was the only place he'd ever lived for longer than three years at a stretch.

As a career military officer, the Colonel had spent his years in postings around the world, stashing his son and Jake's mother in various towns and cities, with friends or relatives, or other military families willing to give them a home. Rarely had he taken his family to any of the locations where he'd been assigned.

They'd been parked, like baggage, in more boring places than Jake cared to remember while his dad went off and fought wars. One day his mother had had enough and she'd walked out.

Ariel Porter had not been cut out to be a military wife. Or a mother, either. She certainly hadn't been the kind of mom who greeted you with milk and cookies after school or knew how to bandage skinned knees.

Jake crossed to his desk and dropped into his leather chair, swiveled his head back, and kicked his feet up on his glass-topped desk. He gazed out the window at the beautiful view, but instead of blue sky and mountain peaks, his eyes filled with an image of a girl with eyes bigger than her face, a girl who was all hands and feet like a puppy not grown into its body. When he thought of Arkansas, he thought of that face. And surely as thunder followed lightning, the next thought that came was the kick to the gut and the voice that reminded him never hand your heart out to be ground into the dirt.

What were the odds of his father meeting a woman he wanted to marry who lived in the backwater of Doolittle? The one time his father had been there, he'd swept into town to collect Jake after learning that Ariel had left their son with a distant relative while she ran off to perform at a folk music tour and lied to him about it. He'd given Jake time to pack his clothes and books and dragged him off to where he was stationed near Berlin, with no chance to let anyone in Jake's world know he was leaving. No, the Colonel couldn't have met anyone on that trip whom he maintained fond memories of and went back in search of. Jake didn't buy that possibility for one minute.

He'd spent that summer in Germany with his father, and then gone to college in the States.

Jake dropped his feet to the floor with a satisfying thud, a sound loud enough to switch off thoughts there was no good reason to revisit.

Time to hustle some business. Time to make more money. Time to take his mind off memories that would do him no good. His voice mail light glowed brightly. Someone needed him. Hell, half the music world wanted to talk to him. So why had he just agreed to spend even one day in Arkansas? He reached for his phone.

He'd given his word, so he'd do his duty. He'd tell Lilly something had come up, and he'd spend a week with his father, and if necessary to keep the peace, he'd pronounce his blessing on his father's intended. Hell, he might even really like her. Any woman capable of helping his father get over the marriage that had been more war than matrimony had to have something good going for her.

But when it was time for their next familial reunion, Jake would make sure he beat his father to the punch. He'd send him tickets to Vail or Acapulco or San Francisco, and they could meet where there was at least something to do other than stare into the distance and not talk in the way Jake and his dad always did. He used to want to break through that barrier, but eventually Jake realized he never would. Maybe grown men and their dads never really talked except in the movies.

Chapter 3

Meanwhile, Back in Doolittle

Martha Wilson grunted under the weight of the box of Christmas decorations her sister handed down from the attic stairs. She lowered the box to the floor of the upstairs hallway and checked her watch once again. "Is that it?"

"One more," Abbie said, and disappeared upward.

She took her sweet time about it. Martha itched to get to her computer. A morning without an e-mail from Ted was as bad as a gray winter day without a hope of sunshine. Her sister had insisted they get the rest of their holiday decorating done first thing. While Martha knew that last year and the year before that and the year before that, going back in an unbroken string, she would have been the one fussing to pull the boxes down, this time she had other things on her mind.

Not just any other old thing. She had Ted on her mind. And in her heart, too, though she almost feared putting that thought into the voice that ran inside her head. With her mouth she'd be talking to her sister same as she always had, yet inside her head these conversations with Ted kept going on and on, louder and more interesting and much more enjoyable than didn't she agree with Abbie that "the preacher's wife was looking a trifle peaked?" and had Martha heard that "Dr. Mike and that young wife of his, the second one, not the ex, were expecting again?"

"Hello!" Abbie teetered on the attic staircase, the giant wreath waving in sync with her movements. "Is it too much to ask for you to keep your mind on what we're doing?"

Martha held out her arms. "Drop it," she said.

"Humph," Abbie said, coming down a few more steps before lowering the wreath. She acted as if it were made of crystal.

"I thought you said there was one more box," Martha said as she backed the wreath to a spot on the hall floor a few feet from the stairs. There, that would show her sister she was paying attention.

Abbie descended the stairs, her spare frame barely making a wiggle on the ladder. "Someone must have thrown out the wreath box." She dusted her hands and then turned and heaved the ladder back into its ceiling hideaway. "Though I can't imagine why. It was perfectly good. Remember we only bought it when we opened the Inn."

"Of course I remember that box," Martha said. "It was such a sturdy one. I remember saying it would be perfect for a playhouse."

"For mice maybe," Abbie said. Then she eyed Martha in a way that made every ounce of her guilty conscience start to quake. "What did you use it for?"

Martha studied her hands. "I gave it to Evelyn across the street when she figured out that cat she'd taken in was a she and not a he and there were five little reasons she was eating so much."

Abbie snorted. "It's a wonder we have time or money to run a business."

"Speaking of which," Martha said, "I think I'll just pop into my room and check the computer to see if we have any new reservations."

"And leave me to decorate, I suppose."

"I'll be back to help in a flash," Martha said. "I wouldn't leave it all for you to do. That wouldn't be right."

Abbie sniffed. She pulled a hanky out of the pocket of her old wool slacks. After wiping her nose, she said, "You leave me alone readily enough these days that it wouldn't surprise me. Look at the way you're always running off to Little Rock. You were never that close to Mrs. Halifax, but nowadays anyone would think she means more to you than your own family."

Automatic words of apology and reassurance died inside Martha's throat, no doubt choked out by her burden of guilt. It wasn't Mrs. Halifax she went to Little Rock to see. She lifted a hand toward her sister's shoulder, and then let it drop to her side. "I'll just take a minute," she said, edging toward the door to her bedroom.

Abbie narrowed her eyes. "Since you've been going to Little Rock you've changed. I declare, six months ago you were the sister I've always known. First it was that computer you brought into the house and that fancy reservation system." She sniffed. "We operated this place just fine for going on twelve years with writing down our guests' names with a pen and paper."

"Different doesn't have to be bad," Martha said, and before Abbie could read her any more lectures she turned and hurried to her room.

She counted to a hundred waiting for the dial-up modem to connect. While she waited, she paced from the wobbly table she'd squeezed in between the chest of drawers she'd inherited from her grandmother and the matching armoire, to the foot of her bed, and back. Abbie called her a fool for stuffing so much furniture into one room, but Martha liked having her things all around her. And after what had happened when she'd ventured online and there met Ted, she thanked her lucky stars every day that she'd crammed the computer right in along with the antiques. Why, reading Ted's e-mails in the corner of the kitchen that served as reservations office would have been next to impossible!

Casting an ear toward the hall, she logged onto the e-mail, and at last she saw Ted's screen name lighting up her inbox. Her heart did that funny thump-thump that she never would have thought it would know. His face filled her mind; the dark brown eyes set off by crinkly lines at the corners when he smiled seemed to reach across the miles.

She clicked open his message.

Dear Martha,

I awoke this morning wondering what was wrong with the world when only yesterday it seemed so perfect, and as I cleared the sleep from my eyes, and made my way to

the kitchen for a cup of coffee, I knew that
what was missing was you.

   I look forward to coming to Doolittle for
Christmas.

                         Yours, Ted

Martha clasped her hands to her chest. "Yours, Ted,"
she whispered.

"Any new ones?" Abbie poked her head into the doorway.

Martha jumped. She couldn't believe she hadn't remembered to shut the door when she'd walked in. But
she'd been so anxious to get to the computer. "Just a minute," she said, clearing the screen and switching to her
Schoolhouse Inn e-mail.

"I still think we did just fine without having to check
that pesky box every day," Abbie said. She pushed the
kerchief she'd wound around her gray hair back a bit
from her lined forehead.

Martha kept silent. She'd started a spreadsheet to track
their reservations and knew darned well their business had
grown since she'd put them onto the Internet. But Abbie
wasn't going to hear anything she didn't want to believe.
Two new reservation messages had come in, along with
the usual string of spam.

She read the first one and found herself clutching her
chest for the second time that morning. She beckoned her
sister over, forgetting in her excitement that Abbie had
sworn never to look at what she called "that pesky little
screen." "You'll never guess who's coming to Doolittle!"

"To Doolittle or to the Inn?" Abbie peered over Martha's shoulder.

"It's Harriet Smith, asking for two rooms for a week." Martha did a quick calculation. "I hope we have the same two open for that many days."

Abbie crossed her arms over her bony chest. "I have to say I'm surprised that she's going to show up, but it does her credit. Olivia must have told her she's having that knee replacement surgery so she can't go to New York for Christmas." Abbie sniffed. "Harriet Smith hasn't been back to town since Donnie died. You'd think she could visit here just once because she wanted to, not out of obligation."

Martha stared at the screen, marveling how Abbie always knew what was going on and wishing yet again her sister wouldn't be quite so judgmental. "It seems odd that she's not staying with family. Her mother and father have that big old house all to themselves. And it's not as if Donnie's mama wouldn't offer them a place to stay. Harriet's son has spent several summers with her on the farm."

"If she stayed at Olivia's, she'd have to play nurse. How do you think that would sit with a woman used to being catered to hand and foot? Besides, if she wants to spend the money, it's more business for us," Abbie said.

"She must be awfully rich," Martha said, visions of the fancy stores she and Ted had strolled past in Little Rock coming to mind. "Charlene doesn't talk about her daughter much, but whenever I go into the shop, I can't help but notice she keeps that book of news clippings up-to-date."

"Rich is nice, but going off and acting like you were hatched and not born into a family is something else altogether," Abbie said. "We all know money can't buy happiness."

"True," Martha said, pretty much stifling the sigh that escaped along with the word.

"Don't tell me you'd change places with a woman like Harriet Smith." Abbie's glare took in the computer and Martha's whole body, almost as if she suspected the machine of having infected Martha.

"No, of course not," Martha said. "Only wouldn't it be interesting to be able to jet to Paris and London and Capetown?"

"All those places are in that clipping book?"

Martha nodded. "She's famous all over the world."

Abbie shrugged. "Her husband's dead, her little boy has probably been raised by a nanny, and she ignores her family, not to mention her hometown. If she's so rich, why doesn't she come see her family more or help out in Doolittle? Not that we need any charity, mind you."

"Maybe we'll get to know her while she's staying here," Martha said.

"Don't count on it," Abbie said, turning away and heading to the door. "If she even sits down to tea with the likes of us I'll eat my apron."

"Just because she's famous doesn't mean she'll be rude," Martha said. "I remember her as a shy little thing. There never was any harm about her."

Abbie snorted. "That stuff she does that she calls art comes out of someplace inside her, and wherever that spot is, it's not shy and it's not pretty. I don't know what makes you remember her like that, because when she was in my biology class at Doolittle High she always had something to say about everything. And every other student managed to do the lab reports the way I told them to, but not Harriet. She always had to do it her way."

"Well, artists are different," Martha said, unwilling to disagree head-on with her sister. "Let me check the other reservation and I'll come help decorate."

"Maybe it's Santa Claus," Abbie said, pausing in the doorway. "Keep this up and we're not going to have any rooms left at the Inn for Christmas."

Martha smiled and opened the next e-mail. As she read, her smile faded.

"Don't tell me someone else famous is coming," Abbie said, moving back into the room.

"Oh, I wouldn't know about that," Martha said, the name Jake Porter ringing in her head. Was she blushing? Most definitely she'd started to perspire. "The name sounds familiar."

Abbie peered at the screen. "Jake Porter? Now where have I heard that name?"

"Oh, I don't think you have," Martha said. "I mean, it's completely unfamiliar to me. Not a common name, either." Abbie was staring at her as if she wasn't making any sense. Well, she wasn't. She was too surprised. It couldn't be a coincidence. Jake Porter had to be Ted's son. He had only one child, who lived in Los Angeles. Why hadn't Ted told her that his son was coming to stay at the Schoolhouse Inn? Or did he not know? Was it meant to be a surprise? She picked up a notebook and fanned at her face.

"You should have stayed on your estrogen," Abbie said, studying Martha a bit too closely for her comfort. "Do we have a room left for him?"

"I think so," Martha said.

"Jake Porter," Abbie said, her voice lingering over each syllable. She tapped her chin with a long finger and stared at the ceiling. "Wait a minute, I stand corrected. Long time ago, there were some Porters who lived around here. As a matter of fact, one was in my biology class."

"Really?" Martha fiddled with the keyboard and tried

not to seem too interested. "Was his name Jake?" Surely Ted would have mentioned to her if he had ever lived in or around Doolittle. And surely she would have noticed him, any day, any year, any place.

Abbie tightened the scarf around her hair. "Yes, it was. He wasn't here long. Maybe half a year, at the end of his senior year. I remember thinking what a shame his family had to transfer him at that time in his life." She rapped her fingers against the edge of Martha's chair. "There are parents out there who just are not responsible. Imagine dumping your child on someone else."

"Is that what happened?" Martha made herself ask that question, but what she wanted to do was to defend Ted. If indeed this whole story had any basis in reality. An air force officer would have to be gone for long stretches at a time.

Abbie shrugged. "Best as I recall. But I do remember the young Porter boy. Mr. Popularity. Good-looking. All the cheerleaders were after him."

Martha could easily believe that, if he were indeed Ted's son. She'd taught in the grade school down the road from the high school so she wouldn't have crossed paths with him.

"What happened to him? I mean, we'd know if he'd stayed in town."

"Funny thing," Abbie said, gazing across the room and narrowing her eyes. "He and Harriet, who of course wasn't a Smith then because that was before Donnie got her pregnant"—Abbie sniffed, as if the very idea were too much for her to reflect upon—"were in Biology Lab together. Harriet was always causing a ruckus, wanting to do things any way other than what I told them to, but Jake Porter did as he was told."

"A nice young man, then," Martha said, feeling pride in a funny sort of way, perhaps on Ted's behalf.

Abbie placed her hands on her hips. "Who can tell with men?"

There wasn't much Martha could say in response to that comment. Nothing she said on the positive side would hold water, and at this point in her life, she wanted to believe in possibilities. "Well, it's all conjecture anyway," she said, pushing her chair back and rising. "This Jake Porter may be a completely different person."

"And I might be a circus clown," Abbie said. "I say things happen for a reason."

Martha smiled. "Maybe he's coming in search of Harriet. You know, tracking down his high school sweetheart."

"You're a silly romantic," her sister said. "If there's one thing Jake Porter and Harriet Rogers were not, it was sweethearts. The two of them acted as if they couldn't bear to stand next to the same Bunsen burner."

"Ooh," Martha said, "that's a sure sign. That always happens in romance stories. First they detest each other and then they can't keep their eyes or hands off each other."

"That might work in books," Abbie said, "but I wouldn't put up with a man who acted out to me."

Martha looked at her sister. "Do you ever wish you'd gotten married?"

Abbie threw her hands up in the air. "Don't be ridiculous. I declare I don't know what's gotten into you lately. What kind of question is that to ask your sister? You've known me all your life, and have you ever once known me to want a man underfoot, interfering with my freedom?"

Martha tipped her head to one side. "If it were the right man, you might not describe it that way."

"That'll be the day," she said.

"Oh, come on," Martha said, amazed at her nerve in teasing her sister on such a subject. About time she got some backbone, especially as she'd yet to break the news that a man she'd met over "that pesky machine" was headed their way for Christmas. "You're not such a sourpuss as you let on. You have a romantic heart under that armadillo act you put on."

"Harrumph!" Abbie turned toward the door. "I leave all that to other people. The ones who have more time than sense."

Chapter 4

A March Down Memory Lane

Harriet paced her studio. Ever since she'd taken Olivia's phone call right after Zach left for school, she'd been unable to concentrate. Naturally she was concerned that Zach's grandmother had to undergo surgery and couldn't come to New York for Christmas as they'd planned. And yes, of course, the two of them would come to Doolittle instead.

She didn't know how those words had come out of her mouth, but once spoken, they couldn't be crammed back in. Harriet would rather have offered to pay for Olivia to have the knee replacement in Manhattan than to return to Doolittle.

Harriet paused in front of a bank of windows. Twelve

stories below, the streets teemed with cars and pedestrians and the constant presence of yellow cabs. The energy pulsed its way upward and onto the ledges and in through the windows.

She tipped her head back and breathed it in.

Harriet P. Smith loved New York.

She liked to pretend she'd been born there, in any of one of the several hospitals she passed by on the East Side. She should choose one and get its name someday. Yeah, right, she thought, pushing away from the window. Invent a little more of her life. Pretend to an even greater degree. Make believe she belonged in the fast lane.

Well, if she belonged anywhere, it was New York. She'd shaken the dust of Doolittle off her feet the year after she'd graduated from high school. The year Zach had been born.

Donnie's father hadn't liked the idea of his son and Harriet and the baby moving so far away. But the first time Donnie's father had ever truly been pleased with his son was when he learned that Donnie and Harriet "had to get married." He'd been so proud of his son for producing a grandson, he told him to name what he wanted as a present, and no matter what it was he could have it.

What Donnie and Harriet both wanted was a life far away from their hometown. Donnie wanted to play music and Harriet wanted to paint. So Donnie had taken his dad at his word and asked for a place to live in NYC and money to live on while they pursued their dreams. In turn, he'd offered to bring baby Zach home at least twice a year, and welcome his parents whenever they wanted to visit.

So Donnie's father bought them an old warehouse in an as-yet-to-be-gentrified area on the edge of the West Village. He'd made a fortune in real estate by keeping an eye on what people would want in the future. Everyone in Doolittle knew that Donnie's family had more money than anyone else, something you wouldn't think from the way Donnie wore the same red flannel shirt and faded jeans and worn-through Converse basketball shoes every day, seven days a week.

Harriet and Donnie had been friends since grade school. Nobody in town thought their friendship went beyond exactly that, but when Harriet turned up pregnant, more than one neighbor said it just went to prove you couldn't tell. Love struck. And babies got made and born.

Harriet crossed her studio to the canvas she hadn't been working on that day. She believed that her art came to her as a gift, and when the spirit flowed through her, the art created itself. Sure, she had technical training, but other than that, she relied on the gift.

Today, ever since that phone call from Olivia, there'd been no space in her mind or heart open to receiving inspiration. She kept thinking of two things: how to break the news to her son that they'd be spending Christmas in a town with a population less than Zach's high school, and second, but not necessarily taking the backseat to the first issue, were all the reasons she didn't want to go. And those reasons could be summed up in two words—Jake Porter.

After she'd left Doolittle and then refused to visit, she'd become an outcast, willingly enough. But there were still times when Harriet wished Thomas Wolfe hadn't been right. But going home again for Harriet caused way too much guilt and confusion in her mind to make such a trip possible, except for the most extreme of situations.

The last time had been for the funeral, five years past.

And now she faced Donnie's mother's surgery. Why,

oh, why hadn't she offered to send flowers and engage a twenty-four-hour nurse?

Nightmare didn't begin to describe that last trip to Doolittle. Not only had it been her husband's funeral, but her father-in-law's as well. Donnie had given in at long last to his dad's entreaties to take a hunting trip together. They'd gone off to the Rockies, both intent on not discussing politics or any of the other topics that divided them, intent on getting along despite neither one knowing how to accomplish that feat.

Harriet often thought Donnie's father doted on Zach so much because with his grandson he had a chance to do things better.

Harriet and Zach had stayed home in New York. Harriet was adamant that Zach not go hunting, no matter how many times his grandfather brought up the subject. The idea of her husband raising a rifle or a bow and arrow at a beautiful deer was bad enough. She refused to let her son learn such things. Donnie didn't care one way or another, but he remained profoundly grateful to his father for his early financial support and for accepting him after so many years of animosity.

He also remained about as angry as a twenty-something could be toward his father. If only he'd been more understanding, Donnie could have and would have told him years ago that he was gay.

But his father refused to deal in any such possibility, even though the only girl Donnie had ever befriended was Harriet Rogers, and everyone in Doolittle knew that no boy in his right mind would be interested in the pudgy, geeky girl who'd just as soon start some stupid debate with you as say good morning. But when it turned out that Donnie and Harriet had a thing for each other and had gone and started a baby before making their way through the church doors, Donnie's dad forgave all.

He wanted a son and a son's son to carry on his real estate dynasty. If there wasn't a Smith at the helm of Lake Doolittle and his other array of properties, what would his life have meant?

So about the time Zach turned ten, Donnie and his dad went off hunting.

And neither one of them came back alive.

No one was quite sure what had happened. Their rented SUV had been found at the bottom of a ravine, high above the hunting area where they'd planned to spend the week. Two deer were strapped to the top, or so the authorities discovered when they managed to right the upside-down vehicle. Both Donnie and his dad died on impact.

Harriet and Zach had caught the first flight to Little Rock. Her father picked them up at the airport. All the way back, all one hour and thirty minutes of the drive, he kept saying, "The Lord works in mysterious ways, but some days it's sure-as-shit hard to know what he's up to."

Harriet had never heard her dad say "shit." She shivered and began her own litany of "things would be okay, they would get through this loss," and inside she kept wondering if Donnie had at long last tried to tell his father the truth about the life the three of them had made. Both of them were excellent drivers. There'd been no sign of another vehicle involved, no evidence of alcohol, no vehicle failure.

The night before the funeral, Harriet sat at Doolittle's only funeral parlor with a red cashmere shawl wrapped around her shoulders. Her mother fussed over every visitor who signed the book and came inside to pay his respects to the two closed caskets. Harriet had refused to have their bodies displayed. For better or for worse, she wanted everyone to remember her husband as he'd been while alive, not the battered remnant of a man she'd been asked to view upon his and his father's bodies being shipped back to Doolittle.

Olivia, Donnie's mother, was coping thanks to some help from her doctor and the pharmacist. Harriet had laced her own coffee with whiskey she'd spotted in the back of her parents' highboy. She wasn't much of a drinker, but getting through the evening's visitation and the funeral the following morning was a feat she had no idea how to accomplish.

She ached for Donnie. He'd been such a dear, sweet man, and clever and funny. Zach looked like he'd never smile again. Harriet held on more for her son than for anyone else, assuring him repeatedly how much Donnie loved him and how much Donnie would be guarding him from heaven. Not that she knew that she believed in heaven one way or another. But she wanted, with a fierce desire, for her son to believe in such a miracle.

Olivia swayed into the main parlor, gazed toward the caskets of her husband and son, and dabbed at her eyes with an embroidered handkerchief. Harriet rose and went to her side.

"We should have left them open," Olivia said.

Harriet kept silent.

"Everyone should see Zach's daddy and grandpa," she said, her mouth quivering. "I've always said he had the Smith eyes and ears. Your mama insists little Zach doesn't look a thing like Donnie but I know better. Why, just last week, before Donnie left with his dad, I was telling him how much Zach's last school picture looked just like my brother Elmer."

Harriet scuffed the toe of her Manolo Blahnik pump against the dreary beige of the funeral home carpet and bit the inside of her lip. After a long battle with herself, she managed to say, "I'm sure you were."

"And if people could only see, they would know," Olivia said, beginning to cry softly. "No one would ever wonder."

Know what? Harriet's blood chilled. She glanced around. Clusters of visitors stood about the room, with only one or two anywhere near the casket, surrounded by flowers and photographs of the father and son in happier times.

Harriet sensed Zach's presence. She looked over her shoulder. Her son, shoulders squared back and chin held high, watched her and his grandmother from halfway across the room. Harriet forced herself to put an arm around Olivia. She whispered, "Don't worry that Zach doesn't look like Donnie. My mother says he favors the Rogerses. Looks don't matter." Harriet tried to calm the fear rising inside her that Olivia knew the truth and was about to spill it in front of everyone. "Donnie loved Zach. All that matters is love."

"Love!" Olivia broke away. Eyes on fire, she stared wildly around, and pointing a finger at Harriet, she cried, "You pretended to love my son and stole him away from us." She caught a hand over her mouth, sobbed, and dropped to a chair. "I'm so sorry," she said.

Harriet leaned over her. Influenced no doubt by the spiked coffee and her own guilt, she said in a voice that only Olivia could hear, "Will you please shut up about Zach's ears and eyes and nose."

Olivia cried harder and shook her head. "It's not right," she said, then again, "It's just not right. "

"Of course it's not right that they're dead," Harriet said, trying to change the direction of Olivia's thoughts.

Olivia lifted her head and looked Harriet in the eyes. Through her tears, she said, "Please don't ruin my memories. Zach is all I have left now."

Harriet pulled away. What did that mean? *Don't let me know what I suspect is true?* She ran a hand over her hair, feeling more like tearing it out. A wave of guilt slapped her, followed by a raging anger. Guilt for being the one left alive, and anger at not knowing what to do. Guilt for being free now—free to move on with her life without the trauma and speculation that a separation and divorce from Donnie would have brought. Anger at herself mostly, and for the boy long gone who'd disappeared and left her to deal with being eighteen and pregnant. She'd done the best she knew how.

She looked back at Olivia. Her heart softened. None of this pain was Olivia's fault. She was such a sweet-natured woman. "I'm so sorry," she said, her voice breaking.

Olivia reached out a hand and squeezed Harriet's arm. She patted her shoulder and said, "I'm not in my right mind. Just leave me sit here a few minutes," she said, dabbing at her eyes.

Harriet turned. Zach continued to watch them, his eyes dark and wide. He started toward them and then paused. Harriet beckoned him. He came up to Olivia. Putting his arms around her, he said, "Don't worry, Gran-O, everything will be okay."

Harriet's heart caught when she heard Zach using his favorite name for Olivia. Her eyes blurred. She wasn't one to cry. She'd yet to break out in tears; not once since she'd gotten the phone call from Colorado had she cried.

Yet now, as she watched her son with Olivia, a sob rose

up within her and threatened to choke its way up and out of her throat. She clapped a hand over her mouth, then breathed deeply through her nose. Turning away, she walked outside, past her mother calling to her to come see Mrs. Gridley who'd come to pay her respects, past the curious eyes of so many, many people she had nothing in common with and never would.

She left first thing the next morning. Only because he begged to do so, she let Zach stay another two days with Olivia. She picked him up at LaGuardia, and as it did after any death, no matter how personal or tragic, life moved on.

As it would move on now, Harriet consoled herself. Zach would adapt to Christmas in Doolittle, no doubt far more easily than she would. Olivia had never said another word about Zach's non-Smith-like appearance since the night of the wake. She hadn't missed a Christmas visit to New York, either, so all in all, Harriet had to reconcile herself to making the trip to Arkansas.

Harriet let herself out of her studio, closed and locked the door behind her, and trekked down the hall that led back to their spacious apartment. She owed Donnie more than she could ever repay. He'd rescued her, given her opportunities she'd never have had without him as her husband, and the least she could do was to help meet, in some small way, his mother's needs.

Later that day, Harriet sat in the sunroom, waiting for Zach. In the distance, echoing across the expanse of the converted warehouse apartment, a door opened and shut. Steps steady and sure advanced on the plank flooring.

Harriet forced herself to turn the page of a six-month-old issue of *ArtWorld*. She'd maintain a casual, cheerful air, and Zach would follow her example. If she buried her feelings about going to Doolittle, perhaps her son would even enjoy the trip. He loved both his grandmothers, though Harriet saw clearly that Donnie's mother was his favorite. Not that she could blame him for that. For years, she'd felt the same way.

Zach stopped, as usual, in the kitchen. The sunroom was at the back of the apartment. On the days when she wasn't lost in her current creation and remembered to check a clock, she settled there so Zach could share how his day at school had gone. It had been quite a tradition with them, but in the past year, Zach had sought her out less and less.

As it should be, Harriet consoled herself. Fifteen was such an awkward age. The longing for adulthood and the glimpses back into childhood clashed in the most painful ways. God only knew how miserable Harriet had been at the same age.

Today she hoped that Zach would stick his head into the room. If not, she'd wait till dinner to break the news. She turned another page in the magazine and strained her ears for an indication of Zach's direction.

She forced herself to look down. A male model, all dark hair and eyes and muscular build, gazed up at her from an ad for sable brushes. She stared at the image of the man.

Another dark-haired man stepped from the page, into the room in front of her.

"So, how's our son?" the image asked, his eyes fixed on her face.

"He's fine," Harriet whispered. "He's a good kid. Smart, athletic, creative."

The image shrugged and spread out his hands as if to say, *Of course*.

He stepped closer, filling the space between the page

and Harriet's face. "When were you going to tell me about Zach? Another fifteen years from now? What's the kid think about you, hiding the truth from him? Think he won't hate you when he finds out?"

"No," Harriet said. "He won't. He can't hate me. I did it all for the best."

"Right," the image said, and disappeared.

Harriet blinked. She gazed across the room and back down to the magazine.

"Mom?"

She swung around toward the door to the sunroom. "Jake!"

Zach stepped into the room, holding a peanut butter and jelly sandwich wrapped neatly in a napkin in one hand and his book bag in the other. "It's me, Zach." He dropped his bag, draped his body into and across an armchair, and took a bite out of the sandwich. As he chewed, he studied her.

"That's what I said," Harriet said.

He finished his bite, took another one that ate up half the sandwich, and shrugged. From around the peanut butter she heard a smothered "Whatever."

"How was school?" Anything to change the subject would do. Harriet picked the first thing that popped into her mouth.

Zach shrugged. "Same old same old."

Talk about a conversation killer. Harriet stifled a sigh. She longed for the good old days when Zach raced home from school, arms outstretched, eager to be swung up by her or Donnie for a hug. He loved to show his artwork. Her refrigerator had been covered in sketches and pictures and photos of Zach in costumes ranging from Marco Polo to Big Foot to Albert Schweitzer. But those days were long gone. Her child had grown up, and given the life Harriet had been living, the appearance of a baby brother or sister would qualify as a second immaculate conception.

Zach finished his sandwich. He wiped his mouth with the paper towel and folded it up, keeping any crumbs from falling on the floor. He was such a neatnik. Harriet had no idea how he'd gotten to be that way. She and Donnie lived as free-spirited slobs; Zach's room looked like it belonged in a military barracks. To keep the peace, Harriet employed a live-in housekeeper.

"What's for dinner?"

Harriet smiled. In some things Zach hadn't changed one bit. He devoured food, and his weight always maintained a healthy range. Donnie had always been on one diet or another.

"I thought we'd order in," Harriet said. "I gave Monique the day off."

Zach glanced around the room, but said nothing. "Pizza's always good."

Harriet couldn't help but smile again. "Sounds fine," she said. She'd order a salad for herself and two large supremes for Zach, to get him through the evening. She tossed the magazine aside. "Your grandmother Smith called today."

"Yeah?" Zach had bent down to fish in his book bag, but he spared a brief glance in reaction to Harriet's words.

"She has to have surgery right before Christmas."

"Awkward," Zach said, pulling his iPod out of his bag.

"A major inconvenience," Harriet said. "So she can't come for Christmas."

Zach nodded. He lifted his earphones toward his head. "Maybe I can go skiing with D. J."

"Maybe when we get back," Harriet said.

"We're going somewhere?" He left one earphone free.

"Doolittle. For Christmas." Harriet sat up and clasped her hands around one knee. "I told Olivia we'd be there for her."

Zach stared at her. "You said that?"

Harriet nodded.

"But you hate the place."

"Sometimes we do for others what's best for them even if it's not what we want for ourselves," Harriet said, picking through her words and trying not to sound preachy.

"You could've asked me first," Zach said. "Give me a chance to be a martyr by choice instead of by conscription."

Harriet stared at her son. "What did you just say?"

He shrugged. "You heard me."

She had indeed. She took a deep breath and placed her hands on the tops of her thighs. Sitting straighter, she said, "Okay, Zach. You may go skiing with D. J. or you may go with me to Doolittle to be with your grandmother. Whichever you choose you may do."

"Have you been hitting the juice?"

"Excuse me?"

Zach circled his index finger around his ear. "I can't believe you just told me I could go skiing."

Harriet couldn't believe it, either. Single parenting was the toughest thing she'd ever done. Donnie would have known exactly what to say to Zach, and Zach would've ended up feeling that he'd come up with the idea to go to Doolittle for the holidays. "What's your choice?"

"Come on, Mom, what do you think I'll say?"

She tipped her head to one side, studying her brilliant, gifted, and obstinate son.

He hoisted his book bag, popped the other earphone

into place, and said, "I guess I can go skiing over spring break."

"Thank you," Harriet said.

"Gotta study," Zach said. "Call me when the pizza's ready, okay?"

"Sure," Harriet said.

He ambled from the room, lost in his interior world. Harriet would have let him go skiing. She never said anything she didn't mean or couldn't stick by. So why couldn't she let out the things she had cooped up inside? What a contradiction.

She tucked her feet under her and meditated on the fact that she had called her son "Jake." Too many signs were pushing Harriet to do what she knew she had to do.

Reaching for the phone, she punched in the number of the investigator. She'd have him arrange a meeting—right after Christmas.

She'd start the New Year with a clean slate or at least a clean conscience. Between tracking down Jake Porter and facing facts with Zach, she sighed, things were going to get a lot stickier before they calmed down.

If they ever did, she added, feeling more overwhelmed by the minute, yet at the same time more resolute.

Chapter 5

Martha and Abbie Visit the Christmas Market

The center of Doolittle remained situated around the town square. Despite the efforts of the state's famous retailer to woo shoppers to the big-box store perched on the outskirts alongside the highway motel, most of Doolittle's citizens gathered every Saturday to patronize the vendors displaying their wares all around the Courthouse Square.

The Saturday before Christmas was an especially festive day. Martha couldn't help but smile at the sight of shoppers bustling around the booths and wandering in and out of the court building itself, which the circuit judge had left open so that people could warm themselves inside and make use of the necessary rooms.

It helped that the judge's wife chaired the Downtown

Doolittle Committee, Martha reflected. She looked about at the crowd and waved to Dr. Mike's daughter Jessica who was at her usual spot with the pull-wagon pet carrier the veterinarian had built for his younger daughter. A black cocker spaniel with big eyes peered out from the wagon.

"Oh, look at that," Martha said, catching her sister's elbow before she could think better of it, and pointing at the dog sitting beneath the *Please Adopt Me* sign.

"What would we do with a dog?" Despite her grouchy comment, her sister walked over to the wagon and took a long look at the animal.

"Hello, Jessica," Martha said. "Only one adoptee today?"

"Yes, ma'am," the youngster said. She rubbed her bright pink mittens together and smiled. "My dad says people are getting a lot better about having their dogs and cats spayed and neutered."

"My, you have a good vocabulary," Martha said.

"I know," Jessica said.

Abbie stooped close and reached one hand toward the dog.

"Would you like me to take her out of the kennel?" Jessica reached for the clasp.

"Oh, no," Abbie said. "We can't even be thinking of bringing a dog to the Inn."

"Why not?" Jessica asked.

"Dogs are messy, for one thing," Abbie said, pulling off one glove and placing that hand against the square bars of the cage. "And for another, our guests might be allergic. And then where would we be?"

"Allergic-schmergic," Jessica said. "My mom used to say she was allergic to cats and that's why we couldn't have any, so we only had dogs. And one day when Daddy had to bring these kittens home, my mom didn't sneeze once." She paused, took a breath, and put her hands on her hips. Her magenta ski jacket rustled with her movement. "I'm glad Stacey never tried to pull a trick like that on us."

"So you don't think the dog would bother the guests," Martha prompted, deciding to keep Jessica on course and not let her begin any comparisons between her mom and Stacey St. Cyr, her stepmother.

Jessica reached for a clipboard hanging on the front of the kennel. "If you'd like to apply to adopt Faustus, I'll need to ask you these questions."

"We're not adopting any old dog," Abbie said.

"What's the first question?" Martha asked.

"Faustus isn't an old dog," Jessica said. "She's a puppy. Have you had any pets before?"

"No," Abbie said.

"We have a cat," Martha said.

"Oh, you and that pesky critter," Abbie said. "What's the next question, and mind you, just because we answer them doesn't mean we're taking this dog."

"Of course it doesn't," Jessica said. "Your application has to be approved."

Martha smothered a smile. This child was so precocious, even more so than her older sister Kristen whom she'd hired to help out at the Inn during the holidays.

"Will you be keeping the dog inside or outside?" Jessica asked, chewing on the tip of her pen and looking at Abbie and then Martha.

"Inside," Martha said.

"Out," her sister said.

They looked at each other. And then Abbie cracked a

tiny smile. Martha winked at Jessica, and the child nodded and made a check on her form.

"Not that we're adding a dog," Abbie said, a frown quickly replacing the smile. "We're too set in our ways to change."

"Oh, no, we're not," Martha said.

"Humph," Abbie said, and took a step back from the dog carrier. She tugged her glove back in place. "We need to get over to Harolene's."

The dog cocked her head. One floppy ear trailed onto the bottom of the kennel. She gave a yelp and held up a paw.

Abbie faced away.

"It wouldn't hurt you," Martha said.

"That's okay," Jessica said. "The match has to be right or we can't let you adopt and I don't think Cra—, I mean, Miss Abbie, is ready for a puppy." She fished in the space where she'd kept the clipboard and produced a pamphlet. "This tells you how to get ready to become a responsible pet owner. Why don't you read this brochure and come back after Christmas? Faustus may have a new home by then, but sad to say, there's always another puppy looking for someone to love him."

Abbie sniffed. She took the pamphlet, though.

It would have served Abbie right if Jessica had come right out with the nickname most of Doolittle called her sister. Crabbie Abbie and Sweet Martha was how they'd been known for as long as Martha could recall.

Martha thanked Jessica and followed Abbie across the square to Harolene's Craft and Hobby. When they pushed the door open and walked through, the cowbell hung on the door jangled, exactly as it had done all the years Harold and Charlene had run the shop. A glance up at the bell confirmed that, as usual during the Christmas season, the bell was wrapped in holly, with a sprig of mistletoe dangling from the clapper.

Most things in Doolittle were exactly the way they'd always been. Martha looked at the mistletoe and thought of Ted. She pictured him standing beside her beneath the kissing green, and a warmth she couldn't pin on the heating system of Harolene's flushed her cheeks. Martha took off her mittens and patted her face. Thank goodness some things in life were changing!

Chapter 6

Departing NYC

Braving LaGuardia right before Christmas—what was she thinking? Harriet pulled her scarf closer to her throat, hugged the folds of her red cashmere coat closer to her body, and glanced over her shoulder to make sure Zach proceeded at a reasonable pace. He no longer would be seen in public walking beside her, another facet of growing up Harriet had come to accept. Harder to accept right at the moment was how much her feet hurt in her new five-inch-heel boots. They'd looked superb and felt elegant in a naughty sort of way when she'd tried them on the week before. But clearly they were not designed for walking.

The traffic had been such a jumble, she'd foolishly told

the limousine driver to stop and let them out a few hundred feet short of their check-in kiosk. Dodging both a crush of travelers and snowflakes that threatened to blind her, Harriet vowed never to land in this predicament ever again. On the other hand, the reason they were running so late was a surge of creative fervor she'd enjoyed that morning in her studio. As irritated as she was at the immediate moment, she was not one to trade punctuality for inspiration.

A toddler dashed in her path, and Harriet jerked her wheeled carry-on to a halt in time to avoid a collision. A woman snatched the child's arm and yanked her away.

"Give a guy some warning," Zach said as he almost bumped into her back. His wheeled bag tipped to one side.

Harriet waited while he righted his case. At last they took their places at the end of the line. Zach blew on his knuckles and brushed snow out of his hair.

"I'll never understand why you won't wear a cap or gloves," Harriet said.

"What I can't understand," Zach answered, pushing his case forward a fraction of an inch as the line shifted, "is why we're flying commercial. You still haven't told me what happened to Weaver."

"Not true," Harriet said. "I did tell you. He had to change his plans."

"Makes no sense," Zach said, eyeing her as if he suspected her of holding back the truth.

Harriet shifted from one heel to the other and sniffed in annoyance as the bald man in front of her stuck a fat half-smoked but now cold cigar into his mouth. She felt like asking him if he wasn't old enough to know better than to try killing himself via that slow route, but held her tongue.

It wasn't that man or the limo driver or even Weaver who had put her into this short-tempered mood. She had only herself to credit for that state of mind. "People often change their plans," she said to her son.

"Weaver takes you everywhere you want to go. He's been hanging around, like, forever. You close your eyes and point to a globe and he puts you on his plane and off you go. So I don't see why we're stuck in this line now."

Harriet bit her lip. She started to count to ten inside her head, and then broke off before she'd reached five. Her son watched her, those big, dark brown eyes of his regarding her steadily. His leather bomber jacket gave his broad shoulders a few more inches. He'd passed her in height last year and then spurted upward a few more inches, so that wearing her new boots she could look him straight in the eye. The way he held himself, his shoulders back, his body at attention, his chest strong, caused yet another flicker of memory to stir to life. If only he did look like Donnie.

"Weaver and I have been friends for quite a while. That's true. He's been great," Harriet said, picking through her words. "He's always been there for me, as a friend. And he and Donnie were the best of friends."

"Yeah," Zach said. "You just said 'friend' three times. So what gives?"

The man in front of them removed his cigar from his teeth and eyed it longingly, no doubt wondering whether he dared light up. Apparently deciding against it, he propped it back in his mouth. The line bumped forward. How could Harriet explain to her son what she didn't understand herself?

"Did you guys have a fight?"

"We don't fight," Harriet said, snapping the words out more quickly than she intended.

Zach shrugged. "Most of my friends' parents argue all the time." He looked away, across the road jam packed with cars and taxis. "I don't remember you and Donnie ever fighting."

"We didn't," Harriet said. "And just to clarify the point, Weaver and I are friends, not lovers." Harriet thought Zach understood that, but perhaps it was better that she said it outright.

He repeated the shrug. "Whatever. Could we just, like, get on this plane and drop the subject?"

Harriet put one hand on her hip. "You don't believe me, do you?"

"It doesn't matter. You can sleep with anybody you want to," Zach said, his voice rising.

The bald man turned his head a quarter to the right.

"This is none of your business," Harriet said.

The man's head snapped forward.

"It matters to me, Zach," she said. "It's important to me that you believe me. When I say Weaver and I are— were—friends, I mean just that. He and I are a man and a woman who enjoy one another's company."

Again, the shrug that drove her crazy. "Cool by me," he said. "So if you're not lovers and you don't fight, remind me why we're standing here freezing our butts off in this line instead of winging it on Weaver's private jet?"

"Because Weaver asked me to marry him," she said.

The bald man turned around. "Mazel tov," he said with a smile.

"The line is moving," she said, waving him forward.

"So why isn't he coming to Doolittle with us?" Zach asked as he lugged his bag another few inches ahead.

"Because I'm furious with him," Harriet said, surprised at the vehemence in her voice.

Zach raised an eyebrow.

"It's complicated, but the bottom line is that he's gone and ruined everything. He told me some cock-and-bull story about having visited a psychic. Supposedly she told him he'd be married within thirty days. So suddenly it occurs to him that he's been in love with me for years and nothing will do but that we jct off to Las Vegas and tie the knot on our way to Arkansas."

"He's not a bad guy," Zach said. "He's been on the cover of *Rolling Stone* three times."

"That's hardly a ringing endorsement for a stepfather," Harriet said. "Besides, I've no intention of ever getting married again."

Zach looked down at his size twelve hiking boots. "Because of me?"

"Oh, no, honey." Harriet said, resisting her urge to reach out and comfort him by patting his shoulder. "It just isn't in the cards for me."

Zach shifted from one foot to another. He glanced down, then up, and said, "It's okay, Mom, if it does happen. I can handle it."

Harriet's heart turned. This time she did reach out. She hugged him, letting him go quickly so as not to embarrass him. "You're a special kid, you know that? Thank you, but after Donnie died, I knew I wouldn't marry again. I have my art and I have you. Plus friends, fame, and fortune. What more is there to life?"

Zach wrinkled his brow.

The man in front of them reached the skycap. He handed his ID to the man, and then paused and turned back. From beneath a pair of bushy silver brows, he looked over at Harriet, a sad smile on his face. "For your sake, I hope you find the answer to that question."

"What do you mean?" Harriet couldn't help but ask.

He patted the left breast of his camel hair coat. "All the money and fame in the world don't mean a thing without your special loved one to share it with."

Zach stared at the man.

"Here you go, sir," the attendant said. "Two bags checked through to Los Angeles."

The man took his papers and tipped the attendant. "I'm on my way home to my wife of forty-nine years," he said. "May you be as blessed."

"Thank you for your sentiments," Harriet said, wishing he'd kept them to himself. "And may you quit smoking." She handed her ID and itinerary to the next skycap, and Zach followed suit. Her son watched the man as he walked into the terminal, a thoughtful expression on his face.

Once they had their bags checked, Harriet and Zach entered the terminal. She tugged off her scarf and gloves. His hands in the pockets of his bomber jacket, Zach said, "Weird being married that many years. I can't even get a girl to like me long enough to tell me her name."

Harriet sympathized with Zach's feelings, but she found it hard to believe her handsome son didn't have girls falling all over him. "You're sure they're not sending you the signals but in a way too subtle to detect?"

"Whaddya mean?"

"What," Harriet enunciated. "What do I mean?" She glanced around, wondering where the nearest Starbucks was to be found. After all the rushing, it turned out their departure had been delayed.

"That's what I said," Zach said, hands still in his jacket pockets.

"Mmm," Harriet said, deciding to skip the speech and

grammar lesson when Zach was opening up over such a personal issue. "Some girls don't know how to let boys know they're dying to get to know them. So they act like they're not interested at all, hoping that will intrigue the guy."

An announcement over the PA system drowned out Zach's response, but she saw him roll his eyes. Harriet sidestepped an overburdened luggage cart. "Some girls chase but that's all they do. They don't actually want to be caught."

Zach stopped. "Either way is stupid. Why can't they just say what they mean?"

Harriet studied her son, wishing for wisdom she didn't possess. "Girls also say that about boys, you know."

"If I liked a girl, I'd tell her," Zach said.

Harriet spotted a coffee kiosk. "Hot chocolate?"

"Muffin sounds good, too," he said.

They got in line and Harriet waited for Zach to say more, wondering if there was a particular girl he was interested in.

"You do have friends who are girls," Harriet said after a long pause in which Zach had revealed zip.

"Sure," he said. "Everybody does."

Harriet ordered their drinks and a blueberry muffin. They found a place to stand at a counter that shielded them a bit from the hustle and bustle of travelers. The noise over the loudspeakers droned on. Parents dragged screaming toddlers along; business types in suits snapped orders into cell phones; a woman draped in a burka fed a baby from a bottle as she walked behind and beside a man in an Armani jacket.

Zach ate and Harriet watched the passersby as she kept an eye on possible resumption of the conversation. She

wished Donnie were there. Zach always talked so easily
to him.

Donnie.

Harriet took a sip of her latte and pondered Zach's
comments. Was he not interested in girls? Was he
confused over his sexual identity? How did a mother
ask that question? she wondered. Darned if she knew,
except to just come right out with it.

She put her cup down on the ledge of the counter.
"Do you like girls in general?"

"Whaddya—what do you mean?"

"Are you attracted to girls?"

"Sure," he said. "That's what I've been trying to tell
you. I like them. They don't like me."

"Oh," Harriet said. "What about boys?"

Zach crammed the last quarter of muffin into his
mouth. After a moment, he said, "Are you trying to ask
me if I'm gay?"

Harriet nodded. "Yes, I suppose I am."

"I guess it's cool that you're okay with the question,"
Zach said. "But no. I like girls."

Harriet nodded. She and Donnie had had many dis-
cussions on whether to discuss with Zach the nature of
their relationship. Right before he'd gone on the fatal
hunting trip with his father, Donnie and Harriet had
agreed that as soon as he told his father and mother,
the two of them would separate. Amicably, of course,
because they truly loved each other.

But Donnie had met someone else and wanted to live
a life true to himself. He'd sacrificed enough years of his
life rescuing Harriet from her adolescent irresponsibility.

Harriet blinked away a tear that had appeared from out
of nowhere.

Zach eyed her quizzically. "You're not sad that I'm not gay, are you?"

Harriet shook her head. "I just want you to be happy," she said softly.

"I could use another muffin," he said.

Chapter 7

Destination Little Rock

Jake had convinced the Colonel to meet in Little Rock later than he'd wanted. The less time they spent together, the less strain it would be on each of them, striving as they always did to muster some semblance of conversation. Lilly, in her sweetly supportive way, had suggested Jake agree to spend the extra days, as his father probably meant it as a gesture of friendship, an idea Jake dismissed with a pat of her hand. She'd taken his decision to spend Christmas out of town fairly well, which had surprised him.

Whatever her reason, Jake had been appreciative that she hadn't thrown a fit about not spending Christmas together. Lilly had told him over dinner last night that she'd booked a week at a spa. Jake had almost relented and invited her along. Lilly couldn't help that she had no family. She was an only child who'd been orphaned at age eight. But he'd concentrated on his steak tartare and agreed with her that a week of pampering sounded fantastic. He'd left her at her door, too, and kissed her quickly on the edge of her mouth before loping to his car.

Jake now found himself aboard a commercial flight nearing Little Rock, Arkansas. He straightened his seat back for landing as requested by Megan, the pretty brunette attendant who'd been showering him with first-class attention, and wondered how many songs had been written around the premise of guilt. He tapped a note into his Palm Pilot to remind himself to have the question researched.

Megan leaned closer and reminded him to stow his electronic device. He did as she asked.

"Will you be in Little Rock long?" she asked, one slim hand resting on the top of the seat in front of him. Her hair swung over her shoulder, and he could see that it would be soft to the touch.

He shook his head.

"Too bad," she said. "It's a fun town if you see it with the right person."

The silver wings pinned to the collar of her blouse caught the sunlight bouncing off the window. The gleam of light on metal shot through his vision. He turned his head, shook it slightly, and rubbed his eyes.

Another pair of wings filled his mind. A six-year-old Jake stared up at his father's uniformed self, bravely swallowing the sob that threatened to unman and humiliate him. "I'll be good while you're gone," Jake said, willing his chin not to tremble.

"Take care of your mother, son," his father said, raising his right arm in a salute.

"Yes, sir," Jake said, pushing his skinny shoulders back and straining to stand as tall as he could as he returned the salute.

His father turned, picked up his kit bag, and walked to the door. Jake's mother, Ariel, stood there, stormy-eyed, one hand on the handle. He bent to kiss her, and she thrust her face away from his. His father peeled her hand from the doorknob, opened the door, and walked through it without looking back.

Jake's mother closed the door and turned to him. "It's you and me, baby," she said. "Time to party."

And then she burst into tears, ran up the stairs to the bedroom, and slammed the door.

Jake didn't see his mother again that night. He opened a can of SpaghettiOs, heated it in the microwave, and spooned it into his mouth while watching cartoons. When he was done, he washed his bowl and spoon, rinsed the can and placed it in the recycling bin, then trudged to the bathroom to brush his teeth.

The next morning he made some toast and took a piece up to his mother. She opened the door to his knock and invited him into the room, where she was sitting up in bed scribbling in a notebook.

He held out the toast. She didn't look up from her notebook. So he stood there for a long, long time. He knew it was a long time because the bread got cold and hard and stiff.

Finally, just when he'd about given up because he had

to pee really badly, his mother lifted her head, a big smile on her face. "Look, baby, Mama's written a new song. Want to hear it?"

He nodded. He held the toast and listened as she strummed her guitar and sang a song that sounded as sad as he felt every time his father left them to go off to fly his plane.

The plane banked sharply. Jake looked up and was almost surprised to see not his mother, but the brunette attendant, still there, still offering herself to him. He glanced out the window, blinked once, and then found a smile for her. "I'm meeting my father," he said, with a shake of his head. "Family duty, you know."

"Sure," she said, and turned away, disappointment in her eyes.

But her disappointment in no way matched the apprehension knotting his gut.

Once on the ground in Little Rock, Jake moved past the passengers waiting to board the outbound leg of the flight and headed toward the baggage claim. He'd not checked any luggage, as he had very few needs for his brief stay in Arkansas, but he and the Colonel had agreed that's where they would meet.

As he walked, he powered on his phone and reviewed the e-mail and voice messages. The music business thrived on crises, and someone had to manage them. He punched in the code for his office and dispatched the three most pressing situations via instructions to his assistant.

He entered the main section of the terminal and was surprised at the modern look of it. He hoped his leather jacket, T-shirts, jeans, and cowboy boots would fit in to whatever activities the Colonel had scheduled. Before he could meet his father, he had one call that only he could handle.

Lowering his carry-on to the floor, he ran a hand over his closely cropped hair. He eyed a *Welcome to the Natural State* sign and wondered at the coincidence of his mother phoning him while he was en route to meet his father.

The connection made, a plaintive voice said, "At last. I thought I was never going to hear from you."

"Ariel," Jake said, referring to his mother by her first name as he'd done ever since he could remember. "What's up?"

"Don't go all stiff-necked on me," his mother said. "I'm stuck in the middle of nowhere and I need a favor."

Jake rolled his eyes. Across the way, a woman with spiky cropped hair paused in front of a kiosk of magazines. She put her hand on the hips of an elegant long red cashmere coat and surveyed the scene. Her face was arresting, an incongruous blend of huge eyes and high cheekbones and a chin that narrowed almost to a point. Not your classic cover model face, but she carried herself with an air of confidence that held more allure for Jake than any beauty pageant norm.

Traveling, Jake concluded. Or if she was a local, Arkansas wasn't the backwoods he'd always thought it was.

"Are you listening to me?"

"Always," Jake said. "If my memory is correct—and it usually is—you should be halfway between Quebec City and Toronto right now." He checked his watch. "You're due on stage in two hours."

"So like your father," Ariel said. "So precise. Such command of detail."

"I don't know what my father has to do with this discussion," Jake said, for what had to be the ten-thousandth time in his life. "You're on a tour promoting your new release, and as producer of that release, of course I know where you are and what your next obligation is."

A long sigh came over the phone. "That's just the point, Jake. It's an ob-li-ga-tion. I am so tired. I just can't do this tour."

Jake tapped his foot. Why, oh, why, he managed his mother's music career, he'd never understand. Why hadn't he refused? Why hadn't he sent her to someone else once she'd become a star? Plenty of people would handle the whims of a star for the piles of money it brought them. But no matter how much money Ariel brought in, the aggravation was always greater than the rewards. But he knew why he did it. She was his mother and he'd been taking care of her since he was four years old, from the first time the Colonel had left on a tour of duty and put him in charge.

"It's sucking the life out of my creative powers," Ariel said. "I haven't written one new line in the past ten days."

"You know that always happens when you go on tour," Jake said, watching the woman in the red cashmere coat. She had her back to him now, perusing the magazine selections. She was tall, but not too tall. He skimmed his eyes down her figure and spotted sky-high heels on her glossy leather boots. Maybe not tall at all, he reflected. A leather bag sat at her feet and a smaller matching one hung over one shoulder. She wore her money in a classy way. Jake was used to the excesses of the music crowd but preferred a simpler style. He appreciated a woman endowed with natural grace.

She selected several magazines and then turned around.

He was surprised to see that she now wore a pair of dark glasses that covered much of her face.

"I just can't do it," Ariel wailed. "Fans drain the life out of me. They're vampires. And they all want something I don't have it in me to give."

Red Cashmere retrieved the bag at her feet. Jake could swear she was watching him exactly as he was watching her. He lifted one foot, of half a mind to go over and take a closer look. She paid for her purchases and slipped them into her bag. If he was going to make his move, he needed to cut his phone call short.

"What if they don't like my new songs?" His mother sounded calmer, despite the insecurity of her question.

"What's not to like?" The woman walked with energy. She exuded sex and power in a brightly wrapped package. Funny how the airline attendant had held zero interest for him, but this woman with the spiky hair and pointy chin had drawn him in from across the terminal.

"It's all so risky," his mother said.

"You'll do just fine," Jake said, answering his mother at the same moment an image of another pointed chin flitted through his mind. All chin and eyes she'd been, too, with dark hair that had reached halfway down her back. But she'd been chubby, not at all like this personification of style. "Besides," he said slowly, "what is life without risk?"

Ariel snuffled and sighed. Well, those noises were both good signs as far as Jake was concerned. It meant his mother was winding up her creative hysterics for this round. He glanced again at his watch. The Colonel hated for anyone to be late. And talking on the phone with Ariel would be absolutely useless as an excuse for tardiness. "Ariel," he said, "I've got to go. I have an appointment."

"You won't cancel the tour?"

Jake shook his head. "Just do it," he said.

"Oh, all right," she wailed, "but I swear this tour is the absolute last one I'll ever do for you."

And she hung up.

The woman in red cashmere had disappeared.

Chapter 8

Rules of the Road

Returning to Arkansas was already proving to be a mistake. Just being in the damn state did funny things to her mind. Harriet gripped the wheel more tightly.

"Mom, are you paying attention?"

Harriet turned her head toward Zach, careful to leave both hands in position. "Of course I am. Why do you ask?"

"You just went through a four-way stop without slowing down."

Harriet hit the brakes.

Brakes squealed behind her, followed by a volley of horn honking.

"I think it only counts when you stop at the intersection," Zach said.

"Very funny," Harriet said, peering into the rearview mirror. Fortunately the car behind her had stopped short of the bumper of her Hummer.

"Seriously, Mom, do you want me to drive?"

Harriet started forward again. "You don't have a license."

"Are you sure you do?"

Harriet ignored her son's comment. "Driving is like riding a bicycle. It comes back after you've been behind the wheel for a few minutes." She smiled reassuringly. Or a few hours, she added to herself. She'd been smart to hire the biggest vehicle available for the drive from the airport to Doolittle. New Yorkers didn't need cars, another one of the many reasons Harriet knew the city was where she belonged.

Yet here she was, far away from the city she'd adopted as her own, and with every minute, getting nearer to the life she'd left behind. Only a week, she reminded herself, as she hit the brakes for a red light.

Zach gave her a sidelong glance and reached for the stereo controls. Some twanging country song filled the cabin, a man's voice bemoaning the loss of the only woman he'd ever loved. No doubt due to his own stupidity, Harriet concluded. Fortunately for her, Zach made a face and switched off the system.

Harriet grimaced and shot through the intersection as the light turned green. Somewhere up ahead lay the entrance to the highway that led south and west toward Doolittle. She'd already had to circle the area twice looking for the correct turn, all the while wishing herself back in New York City.

And face it, all the while fighting her memories of Doolittle—and more specifically, Jake Porter.

Which was ridiculous. She knew it, yet her mind betrayed her. Had Jake Porter given her one moment's thought after he up and left town without so much as a good-bye? She doubted it. But then why should he? He hadn't loved her, hadn't even liked her, according to the other kids at school who'd told her the harsh truth about how they'd dared him to get it on with her.

What would she do if she ever ran into him again? She grinned, though her gesture had nothing in common with humor, as the image of her running him over with the Hummer swam to mind.

Idiot that she was, if she ever did cross paths with Jake Porter, she'd probably melt at his feet exactly the way she had way back when.

She'd been behind the counter at Harolene's, her parents' shop located on the square in Doolittle, where she worked most afternoons after school and on Saturdays. Her brother, one year younger, was excused from store duty on account of his athletics commitments.

Harriet didn't mind the job too much. She usually had plenty of time to read; she knew all the customers, could usually predict which needlepoint kits and paint-by-number sets each one would ooh and ah over; plus her parents paid her three dollars an hour. She had accumulated quite a hoard dedicated to the day she'd leave Doolittle, the dinky little town where no one, but no one, understood the genius of Harriet Rogers.

So there she'd sat on the stool behind the counter. Harriet could still remember the book she'd been reading. She'd picked out *The Color Purple* because of the title and continued to read it even when she discovered it had nothing to do with art. Grief interested Harriet almost as much as art. The daisy-bedecked cowbell on the shop door clanged, but Harriet, engrossed in Celie's pain, read to the end of the page before glancing up to see who had entered.

She marked her place with her index finger. Bigger than life, staring straight at her, stood Jake Porter.

Of course she'd seen him at school. The new guy. Dark eyes. Tough chin. Determined nose. Hair that looked like it wanted to be thick and curly but had been tamed into a buzz cut.

And his smile. He had white teeth that flashed when he laughed. The gaggle of cheerleaders who surrounded him always seemed to come up with things to say that caused that smile to dance on his face.

They were in the same biology class but Harriet had never spoken to him. She couldn't think of anything she would have to say that would make a boy like Jake Porter look at her as if the sun rose and set by her.

He was a senior, too, but he seemed older than the rest of the kids. From his first day at school, in the middle of the semester, he'd taken command. The class project, the class trip, the graduation ceremony motto—his ideas outranked those of the other kids by a mile. And oddly enough, no one resented the outsider coming in and taking over. They all hero-worshipped him.

There was only one project Jake Porter hadn't taken a leadership role in, and that was the father-son pancake breakfast. He'd gone, and helped clean up, Harriet had heard, but he'd been the only senior without a dad. Even Lil' Skinny Dawkins's old man, his beard scraped clean and his hair slicked back, showed up for the breakfast.

There were rumors that Jake didn't have a dad or a mom. Harriet had heard the orphan stories along with the other wilder-than-wild rumors. His dad was CIA, his mother a striptease artist. She had plenty of imagination herself, but none of those stories matched up with Jake's normalcy.

He was too all-American to be from a weird family. On the other hand, Harriet's family was as Beaver Cleaver as you could ask for, and where in the world had she sprung from?

But staring at Jake Porter that afternoon, licking her lips and wishing she didn't have acne all over her chin, Harriet didn't care about his family or her own.

She just prayed she could think of something to say that didn't make her sound like an idiot. But then, Harriet being Harriet, she realized if she fell all over him, she'd be no different from any of the other girls at Doolittle High.

And she prided herself on being different.

So she sat up straight, put her book down on the counter, and gave him a direct look. "What can we help you with today?"

He glanced around, then leaned across the counter the teeniest bit, but to Harriet it felt like her lungs would be crushed if he came any closer. "We?"

Harriet shrugged. "The royal we," she said, hating how prim her voice sounded.

Jake grinned. "You do look like a princess."

Harriet rolled her eyes. "Now that is a lot of hogwash."

He laughed, laid a tanned hand on the counter, and gave her a wink. "You're okay."

She repeated her shrug. Her worn black T-shirt edged off her shoulder. Her white bra strap screamed its presence.

Jake leaned over and slipped her shirt back onto her shoulder.

She froze. "What are you doing?"

"Helping?"

Harriet touched her shoulder and put her hand back in her lap. "Are you looking for art supplies?"

"Poster board." He kept looking at her. He had the darkest eyes she'd ever seen. But when she dared to meet his gaze, she saw one eye was lit by flecks of golden brown. It looked almost like granite sparkling in a black limestone. She'd paint it that way, she realized as she sat there staring at Jake Porter's eyes. She'd paint his eyes, and they'd be like boulders come to life from some light glowing from within.

"Still with me?" Jake waved one hand in front of her face.

Harriet refocused. "Sorry," she said, but she wasn't sorry at all. She loved it when a vision of art came full-fledged to mind. "The poster board is on aisle four."

"Show it to me?"

Harriet pointed to a large numeral posted above the aisle. "Four. It comes after three. The store only has five aisles."

"I need advice," he said, his body close to the counter.

"Poster board is pretty basic," Harriet said. But she slipped off the stool and walked through the break in the counter. "What class is it for?"

"Shop." Jake met her at the end of aisle four. "Mr. Horton's class."

"Oh, him," Harriet said, barely holding back a sniff that said what she thought of that teacher. "He's a nice man, but his ideas are so antiquated. I bet you have to draw a picture of what you made for your final project."

"You know, the kids at school are right," Jake said. "You are smart."

Harriet flushed. "Just buy your poster, okay."

"Hey, what did I say?" He actually looked concerned. "Smart is a compliment."

Harriet stubbed her toe on the floorboard. "Yeah, right." She pointed to the poster board holder. "White or fluorescent? Take your choice, but I know for a fact Mr. Horton prefers white."

"It's nice of you to tell me that," he said, pulling a white board from the stack. "So you're smart and you're nice."

"Thanks," she said, her voice small. What was smart and nice when you were almost eighteen and no one ever called you pretty and the best-looking guy who'd ever set foot in Doolittle was standing right next to you and you knew that nothing you said or did could get him to want to pay attention to you?

"Don't mention it," he said, the flecks in his eyes now almost golden as he smiled at her.

He really hadn't meant to diss her, Harriet realized. Her heart fluttered the way it did when she ran the hundred-yard dash. "You might want some markers, too," she said.

"You're the expert," he said. "Though I need to buy the cheapest ones you have."

Harriet nodded. "I understand." She turned to move down the aisle, then stopped. "You can borrow mine if you want. That way you won't have to buy any. I mean, it seems a shame to buy them when school's almost out. Unless you'd use them for something else, that is." She shut up at last, checked the floorboards again with the toe of her tennis shoe, and wondered why his answer mattered to her.

"I guess it's not so bad that we're here," Zach said.

Harriet jerked her head to the right and just kept from swerving the wheel of the Hummer. She knew intellectually that it was Zach who'd just spoken, but as far lost in her memories as she was, she heard Jake Porter's voice instead.

"I didn't want to come," Zach said. "And maybe I won't want to stay. But it's okay that we're here. I would've felt lousy going off skiing knowing Gran-O was going under the knife." He hunched a shoulder and looked out the window, as if embarrassed by what he'd said.

Harriet yearned to reach over and pat his shoulder and tell him how much she appreciated what a good kid he was. But she couldn't do it. He'd hate it. She had to accept what he'd offered and leave it at that.

Harriet nodded. An eighteen-wheeler blew by her in the left-hand lane. She sat up straighter. "Don't mention it," she said, hearing Jake's words once more in her mind. She winced. Her memories were intertwining with her present. She couldn't afford for that to happen. She needed to remain firmly in the now. "I mean, thanks, Zach. You're a good kid."

He grunted and played with his iPod, back to his normal fifteen-year-old self.

Harriet settled in for the drive, commanding her mind to dwell on her latest canvas, her shopping list, her alphabet—anything but memories of Jake Porter.

Chapter 9

Am I My Father's Son?

"Do you get to this part of the country much?" The Colonel, as was his custom, drove with his hands at the 10:00 and 2:00 position. His gaze moved from the road to the rearview mirror to the side mirrors and back to the road. As was also his custom, he addressed the windshield.

Jake did the same. Watching the oncoming traffic on the opposite side of the four-lane highway, he said, "No, sir."

His father nodded. They drove on in silence.

"I fly to Nashville fairly regularly," Jake added.

The Colonel cleared his throat. "That would be on business."

"Yes, sir."

"Does your mother still live there?"

The question surprised Jake. "She does."

"Does she like it?"

"I guess she does or she wouldn't live there."

The Colonel shook his head, not missing a beat of his steady inspection of the road, front, side, and rear. "Not necessarily so. People live where they do for all sorts of reasons. I can't say that I enjoyed half of the billets I've had."

Jake almost took his gaze from the road to look at his father's face. He'd never heard the Colonel speak one word against any place he or their family had lived during his years in the air force. Curious to see if he would say anything more along those lines, he asked, "What was your least favorite?"

The Colonel tapped his right thumb against the steering wheel. "I spent two weeks in a bamboo cage. That would have to count right up there with least favorite."

This time Jake did turn to look at his father. The Colonel's face was as unreadable as ever, though he did have a downward twist to the right side of his mouth. "You never told me you were taken prisoner."

The Colonel shook his head. "No reason to mention it. Not then. Other than that, I'd say I didn't care for New Guinea."

"Was Ariel with you there?"

His father's mouth curved upward a bit. "Thank goodness, no."

Jake settled back in his seat and returned to watching the road.

"I didn't mean that as an insult to your mother," the Colonel said. "She did the best she knew how to do."

If Jake had a dollar for every time he'd heard his fa-

ther rebuke Ariel for not trying hard enough to be a good
military wife, Jake could've retired before he'd earned
his high school diploma. Something had happened to the
Colonel to soften him. Jake wasn't sure he could handle
the change. "What was the favorite place you've lived?"

"Eugene."

His father had been born there, but Jake and his mother
had never visited his hometown. Jake used to be curious
why they hadn't, but yet again, that had been another
question he'd never asked his parents. A billboard embla-
zoned with *Visit Lake Doolittle* flashed by. Another Best
Western sign appeared and receded. Jake sat trapped in
his silence.

His father cleared his throat again. "I was born on a
farm right outside Eugene. We raised cows. I had my own
horse. I lived in the house I was born in until I turned
seventeen." His father moved one hand from the wheel,
scratched the side of his nose, and then returned his hand.
"That's something you wouldn't know about, living in
the same place. It does something for a kid, that kind of
stability."

And so does not having it, Jake thought, but he didn't
say it out loud.

"I tried to spare you that kind of shock," his father
said.

If Jake hadn't been fastened in by his safety belt, he
might have fallen off the seat. "I'm not sure I follow your
meaning."

"One thing the military teaches you is how to deal with
change." His father pulled into the outside lane and passed
a station wagon pulling a U-Haul trailer.

"I guess you can say that," Jake said. But he wanted to
disagree. Moving all the time taught a kid a lot, especially

not to put down roots or let any one person matter too much. He couldn't say that equated to learning how to deal with the reality of one day you'd be there, the next you might be gone.

The one time he'd broken the unwritten rule of "never look back," he'd been dealt a sucker punch he never forgot.

"You've seen the world," his father said, "and I'm proud of how well you're doing."

"Thank you," Jake said, surprised by the compliment. Surprised? More like stunned. What was up with his father? Sharing his feelings. Wanting his son around for the holidays. Falling in love, and at his age. Whoever his lady friend was, she must have quite a personality to change him 180 degrees. Take for instance his father's invitation—one might almost call it insistence—that Jake meet him here for Christmas.

Christmas had never been much of a focal family event in the Porter household. More than likely, his father would be on duty and his mother scarcely aware that in other households across the world, families were stringing trees with ornaments and stacking mounds of wrapped packages beneath the brightly colored and sweet-smelling evergreen.

Jake shook his head, mocking himself. His life was just fine without any warm and fuzzy traditions. Not that he'd wish his heritage on anyone else. There were good reasons he'd sworn off creating another generation of Porters.

It wasn't like the Colonel to talk about himself, especially with any show of emotion. Jake didn't recall much affection in a demonstrative way from his father, but he didn't think most guys did. It was the moms who usually wanted to kiss and hug their kids. The Colonel was into

salutes and handshakes. When Jake turned in straight A's
in all his classes for his first two years of high school, his
father had given him an antique coin, a silver Walking
Liberty. He'd told him if he earned two more years of
straight A's, he'd give him a gold coin.

That gift had never materialized. By the time the Colonel left on yet another mission and his mother, Ariel,
dumped him off in Doolittle with a relative as distant
to him as Pluto was from the sun, Jake had gotten into
the college of his choice. It was a challenge to make bad
grades at a place like Doolittle High, but he managed to
score a B in his shop class along with a handful of the
usual A's.

The day the Colonel showed up to drag him away from
Doolittle, his father was too occupied venting at Ariel's
unfit mothering to castigate Jake for the lone B of his four
years of high school report cards.

Funny, but he would have had an A in that shop class
if it hadn't been for Harriet Rogers. He'd gone to the
craft shop on the square in Doolittle in search of poster
board for a term project. He'd intended to buy the board,
pick up a marker, and draw the ridiculous schematic the
teacher required to accompany the project. He didn't even
remember what he'd built, but he did remember the out-
come of the poster board purchase.

Jake smiled, remembering the stunned look on the shop
teacher's face when he'd walked into class with a psy-
chedelic pop-up version of a yellow brick road. Harriet
had told him exactly what the shop teacher wanted kids
to do for the project and then described what she would
do. She'd then whipped it up in the store while she dis-
coursed on the lack of imagination in 99.9 percent of the
population.

Jake had watched her, admiring her despite her weirdness. He'd heard from the other kids at Doolittle High that nobody hung out with her, other than Donnie Smith, the richest kid in town and second weirdest next to Harriet. Donnie's problem was he didn't like girls and Harriet's was that guys didn't like her. No doubt, Jake reflected, because she looked them in the eye and told them they were stupid, coarse, and unimaginative.

Jake shifted in his seat, staring out the window at the leafless trees lining the interstate. *Never look back.* That lesson had been ingrained in him from his earliest years. And what had happened between him and Harriet, the only girl he'd ever met that he'd wanted to find again, had cemented it.

It had been years since he'd thought about it, but he could still summon the voice on the phone that had so cheerfully told him Harriet Rogers hadn't worked at the shop since she'd gotten married right after high school.

Never look back.

Jake studied the taillights of the semi they were traveling behind. He read the 800 number interested drivers could call to compliment or complain about the driving habits of the trucker. He glanced at his watch.

"So your mother likes Nashville?"

Jake nodded, relieved his father had interrupted his thoughts. He never knew how to talk to the Colonel, and they'd exchanged more sentences than they usually did just in the drive so far. But damn if talking didn't make Jake more nervous than not talking.

"That's good."

"Yes, sir."

"My parents lost the farm," the Colonel said. "I'd left for college. Dad got sick and Mother couldn't keep things up. The bank took it over. They rented a house, and when I went home the next summer, someone else was living in our house."

"Wow," Jake said. "That stinks."

"They should have told me. I would have left school and gone home to help them."

Jake nodded. His father would have done exactly that. No doubt that's why his grandparents, who had died before Jake was born, hadn't told their son. "I never knew this story," he said.

"No need for you to then," his father said. "There's a McDonald's off the next exit. Hungry?"

"Yes, sir," Jake said.

Chapter 10

Home, Not So Sweet Home

Five years.

Harriet drove past the Gas 'N Go. The man in coveralls leaning against a gasoline pump gawked at her as if he'd never seen a Hummer. She sighed. That gas station looked exactly the way she remembered it, not only from her last visit, but from when she'd been in high school.

Some things never changed.

Thank goodness she had.

"We there yet?" Zach sat up, blinking, and stretched.

"We're in Doolittle," Harriet said. "We'll be at the bed-and-breakfast soon." To get to the old schoolhouse, she would travel the short way into town, through the square, and onto the other side a few blocks. As a kid, she'd ridden her bike that way more days than she could count. Funny how the town hadn't seemed quite so boring when she'd been knee high to a grasshopper.

Harriet braked, a little harder than necessary, at a four-way stop. Where had that expression come from? She shook her head, as if to clear her brain of such hokey sayings. Avant-garde artists who had their paintings hanging in the Whitney and on display at MOMA did not say "knee high to a grasshopper." Leave that to Grandma Moses.

It was just past six, and many of the stores surrounding the square had *Closed* signs in their windows. In Doolittle, people went home for dinner. She circled the square and slowed as she approached Harolene's, her parents' shop. Zach looked out the window. He tugged his earphones free. "There's the shop," he said.

"Yes," Harriet said. "Locked up for the night."

"Weird how everything closes so early," Zach said. "I'd forgotten about that."

Harriet stared at the windows filled with Christmas crafts. A red nose blinked on a make-it-yourself reindeer display. "When I worked there after school," she said slowly, "closing time couldn't come fast enough."

"Did you pretty much sit around and do your homework?"

Harriet drove on through the square. "Sometimes. I didn't have much studying to do, though. Doolittle High certainly doesn't have much in common with your school."

"Is that why you don't know Latin?"

She nodded. "Among other things," she added under her breath.

"So that's why I have to?" Zach said.

"Bingo." Harriet smiled at her son. "Yes, I'm burdening you with all the experiences I missed out on."

Zach made a face. "You could keep the Latin."

"It'll serve you well in law school," Harriet said, clearing the square and traveling along a block of homes. The lights of Christmas trees and television screens glowed through the front windows of all the houses. The lawns were winter barren.

"Who says I'm going to be a lawyer?"

Harriet knew better than to argue this point with her son. For the past year he'd been talking of putting his own band together. She knew it seemed hypocritical when she'd followed her own creative path, but she wanted to protect him from the hardship so common to struggling musicians. Supported by Donnie's family, they had known a life far easier than most artists experienced. "Latin is useful for many things," she said.

"That's a cop-out," Zach said.

She nodded. "Got me there. I'm sure there's some general who said something pithy about the brilliance of knowing when to retreat and when to advance."

Zach started to say something just as Harriet pulled to the curb across the street from the Schoolhouse Inn, but he must have changed his mind. Harriet noticed another car pulling into the drive in front of the Inn. The driver's side door opened at the same time the front door of the Inn did.

"People," she said.

Zach gave her a questioning look. "They're not Martians, if that's what you mean."

"Let's go see your grandmother," Harriet said.

"We're not checking in?"

"Not right now," Harriet said. She drove down the block. "I don't feel like bumping into other guests."

"That's pretty much guaranteed to happen in a house that size," Zach said. "I mean, it's not like the Marriott at Times Square."

"It's difficult," Harriet said, hesitant to discuss her own irrational reaction, yet feeling she owed her son an explanation. "I hate people looking at me and saying things like 'Wow you've changed' and 'Who would have thought little Harriet Rogers would turn out so well.'"

"Yeah," Zach said. "But it's not like you're really famous. Think how awkward it would be if you were, like, Paris Hilton or Justin Timberlake."

Harriet couldn't help but laugh. "That puts me in my place," she said. She smiled at her son, appreciating how much more he was communicating with her. Maybe it was good that they were making this trip together, despite all her reasons not to want to do so. "I'm sure your grandmother will want to see us right away. She goes to the hospital tomorrow."

Zach nodded. Darkness was falling rapidly. "So what about Granlene?"

Harriet took the turn toward the Smith Place, as the sprawling home and grounds were known by all of Doolittle. "We'll see her and my dad before Christmas."

Zach grunted, a sound that managed to convey disapproval to Harriet's self-conscious sense of hearing.

"We're here to support Olivia," Harriet said, sounding defensive even to her own ears.

"Granlene makes good cake," Zach said.

"Yes, she does," Harriet said. "And I ate so much of it when I was a kid I looked like a stuffed pork chop."

"You've got some real hang-ups," Zach said. "I mean, who turns down cake? Maybe you ought to see a shrink." He stuffed his earphones back in place.

Harriet stared at him. She was so intent on doing so that she didn't see the curve in the road, a road that she had once known like the back of her hand. The Hummer hit the dirt and gravel on the side of the road, sending spurts of rock up into the air. Bits of rock pinged against the side of the vehicle.

"There is nothing wrong with me," Harriet said.

"Or your driving," Zach said.

Harriet gunned the accelerator; the vehicle fishtailed and then surged forward. Just to the rear, the squeal of brakes tore through the air.

"Oops," Harriet said.

"At least they were able to stop," Zach said, craning around to check behind them. "Oh, good one, Mom, you almost hit a cop."

Red and blue lights flashed behind them at that exact moment.

"Oh, brother," Harriet said, wanting to say something much stronger but holding back in front of Zach. A cop! Nothing stayed private in Doolittle. The officer would radio in the stop, and every busybody in town would know Harriet P. Smith, née Rogers, had arrived, as reckless as ever.

A beam from a flashlight bobbed outside her window. Maybe the officer wouldn't even ask her for an ID. He probably only wanted to make sure she was okay. Then she recalled that law enforcement in Doolittle had been the domain of the Simon and Wright families for generations. If it was someone who remembered her, perhaps she could talk her way into his good graces. She lowered the window, returned her hands to the wheel, and manufactured a smile.

"Evening, ma'am. May I see your license and registration?"

Harriet swung her head around. That voice did not belong to any Doolittle native. No earthy twang, but a deep baritone that hinted at the Northeast. She lifted her gaze to the man's face. Dark hair, dark eyes, a determined chin, and a no-nonsense expression awaited her inspection.

"You're not from here, are you?" Harriet blurted out, mortified that she sounded as provincial as she had at eighteen.

The man smiled slightly, and he appeared much less stern. He looked, Harriet thought in a flash, like a man who could charm the socks off a schoolmarm. "Not originally," he said. Despite having sworn off dating, Harriet shot a swift glance at his left hand.

A gleaming gold band adorned his ring finger.

Married.

Just as well.

The last place she'd look to meet a man was back in Doolittle.

"And," he said, "I have a feeling that once you produce your license and registration, I'll be able to confirm you're not a Doolittle resident."

"Right." Harriet kept her hands on the wheel. She knew she'd had her license when she rented the car but she had no memory of what she'd done with it. She was more interested in discovering who this man was and why he was a Doolittle policeman. Apparently things were changing in town. "Actually, I am from here. Or rather, I was." She hated admitting that out loud, but small towns tended to look after their own. "Chief Simon is a dear friend of my parents."

A flicker of amusement crossed the officer's face. "Is that so?"

She peered closer and tried to read the nameplate above his chest pocket. Hamilton. "Hamilton," she said, running the name through her memory.

"Yes, ma'am. Chief Hamilton. Pete Simon is retired now."

"Oh," Harriet said, feeling stupider than she felt she ought to. "Of course."

Zach leaned over. "Excuse me. Can we straighten out something here. Did my mom do anything wrong? If not, we'd like to move on. And if so, we'd like to know what the grounds are for your stop."

"Zach!" Harriet threw a warning glance at him, as much good as it did.

"I have every right to ask that question," Zach said.

Chief Hamilton leaned down and looked across Harriet. "That's a good question. Other than carelessly pulling out in front of an oncoming vehicle and almost causing an accident, no."

"Ha!" Zach jabbed a finger across the space between him and the officer. "Almost. That's the point. No accident occurred."

Chief Hamilton nodded. To Harriet's relief, he looked amused.

"So," Zach continued, "no harm, no foul, and therefore no need for the license or registration, correct?"

The officer glanced from Harriet to Zach and back again to Harriet. "Well spoken. I like to see a son looking out for his mother," he said. Then he grinned. "Besides,

I don't need papers to know who you are. And my wife would never let me hear the end of it if I gave a ticket to Harriet P. Smith."

Harriet stiffened. "How did you know my name?"

"You're the talk of the town," the officer said. "There's hasn't been such a buzz since the day I ambled into Doolittle and swept Jenifer Janey Wright off her feet."

Harriet's jaw dropped. She forgot about her annoyance at the lack of privacy in Doolittle. "Jenifer Janey Wright is married? To you?"

He nodded. His eyes lit up his face, in a way that twisted a soft spot buried deep inside Harriet's heart. "Yes, ma'am, she sure is."

Zach shifted in his seat. "Who's she?"

Harriet stared out the windshield, seeing not the gathering darkness, but rather the kindness and comforting shoulder Jenifer had offered her so many years ago. Not knowing whom to turn to, she'd gone to Jenifer Janey Wright. Folks said that Jenifer practically ran the town, but the reason Harriet had sought her out had nothing to do with politics or getting a speed bump put in or a new jungle gym for the park.

She'd gone to her when she'd finally faced the fact that at eighteen and unmarried, she was pregnant and the father of the baby was nowhere to be found. Everyone in Doolittle knew that the same thing had happened to Jenifer Janey Wright, and that when her worthless boyfriend had insisted that she terminate the pregnancy, she'd moved home from college and had the twins.

Harriet's situation had been the same but yet so different. Her family was 180 degrees apart from Jenifer Janey Wright's. The kind of support Jenifer had enjoyed wouldn't have been forthcoming from Harriet's parents.

Harriet ran a hand over her short spiky hair and sighed.

"Mom?"

She jerked back to the present, shocked to hear her son's voice. Her son. Jenifer Janey Wright had given her priceless advice.

"Wow," Harriet said. "I'm very happy for both of you."

"Thank you," Chief Hamilton said. "Coming to Doolittle was the best thing that's happened to me in my life."

"Because you met her here," Harriet said, realizing how wistful she sounded.

"Right," Hamilton said. "And there are a lot of other great things about Doolittle, too."

"Well," Harriet said, ignoring that part of what he had to say, "please give Jenifer my best. I mean, that is, if she remembers me. But it seems she does given what you said about her being upset if you gave me a ticket."

"I'll do better than pass on your hello," Chief Hamilton said. "Come over for dinner. I know Miss Olivia is having surgery tomorrow so that wouldn't be good, so say two nights from now?"

"Thank you," Harriet said, about to accept, but suddenly shy about imposing. "Let's see how the surgery goes."

"If you think Jenifer Janey Wright Hamilton is going to take no for an answer, you and I aren't talking about the same woman," Chief Hamilton said, smiling. "Six o'clock. We're in the house she inherited from her grandmother."

"Like I'm supposed to remember where that is," Harriet murmured, not meaning to sound rude but realizing the minute the words were out, that's exactly how she did come across. Even Zach looked surprised.

Chief Hamilton sketched a salute. "If you don't," he

said, "one of the Schoolhouse sisters will see that you find us." He straightened, then leaned back to the window. "You drive carefully. And find that license." Then he turned and strode back to his car.

"Find that license," Harriet said. "Like I don't know where I put it. This is the most aggravating place." She jerked the car into drive.

"Irritating or annoying," Zach said. "Not aggravating. You taught me that distinction several years ago. It's weird how you talk different here than you do at home."

"I do not," Harriet said, snapping out the words, knowing as she did that she denied the truth Zach spoke.

"You act different," he said.

"Do not."

"Do too."

"Do—" Harriet laughed. "Listen to me. I sound like a twelve-year-old."

"And you don't act like that in New York," her annoyingly perceptive son said. He grinned. "So I guess that's game, set, and match to me."

Harriet leaned over and ruffled her son's short hair. She might have laughed outwardly, but the behavior Zach observed troubled her. She did not want any vestiges of the old Harriet and life in Doolittle hanging about her. She'd spent far too many years away, cultivating her sophistication and success, to slide even her little toe back into the past.

Of course she was grateful to Jenifer Janey Wright. But that they would have anything in common to discuss over a home-cooked dinner she doubted. The encounter would be awkward, the evening endless. No, the less she entangled herself in Doolittle, the sooner she scooted back to where she belonged, the better off she'd be.

Then she thought of the way the officer's face had lit up when he'd spoken of Jenifer Janey as his wife. What would it be like to have a man react that way about her?

Harriet sighed, swung the wheel to turn into the driveway at the Smith Place as, unbidden, the image of another dark-eyed, dark-haired man filled her mind.

Chapter 11

Martha and Ted and Jake and Abbie

Jake's assistant had explained to him that there weren't many choices of accommodations in Doolittle. She'd booked him into the Schoolhouse Inn, knowing full well he'd reject any idea that he stay at the other options, both roadside motels. Her boss was used to the best, and apparently in Doolittle the best to be had was an old school building converted to a bed-and-breakfast and run by two sisters, both retired teachers.

Given the choices and his father's newfound fixation on family togetherness, it wasn't surprising that the Colonel had booked a room at the same place.

"Well, here we are," his father said, making no move

to get out of the car as they sat in the driveway of the Schoolhouse Inn.

Jake reached to open his door.

His father did not. "Thank you for coming to meet Martha," he said.

"You mean your friend?" He couldn't bring himself to say "girlfriend" out loud. It was just too strange.

"Right," his father said. "I hope you two get along."

"I won't embarrass you," Jake said under his breath, and louder, he added, "Me, too." Then he opened the door and cleared out of the car before his father could make him feel any more awkward.

The Colonel climbed from behind the wheel, and the two of them walked up the steps to the broad porch. A swing piled with green and red pillows occupied one side of the door. Rocking chairs stood on the opposite side. Holiday greenery, fresh not plastic, festooned the doorway and the balcony railings. Jake breathed deeply, enjoying the scent. "Not bad," he said.

"Not bad?" His father knit his brow. "It's downright charming."

"Charming" was not a word that belonged in his father's vocabulary. Definitely dotty, Jake reflected, raising his hand to the brass knocker, just as the door whisked open.

A gray-haired woman, all angles and bones, yanked an apron from over her head. She looked vaguely familiar, but Jake couldn't say why. "Come in, come in," she said, glancing over her shoulder and back to them. "It's not like Martha to keep guests standing on the porch. I don't know where she's gone off to."

"We hadn't even had time to knock," his father said, also looking beyond the woman.

"I'm Miss Abbie," the woman said. "Welcome to the Schoolhouse Inn. You must be the Porters."

That couldn't have been too difficult to surmise, Jake thought. The bed-and-breakfast had only eight guest rooms, and he had a feeling there weren't a lot of men who checked in at the same time in Doolittle.

His father nodded. "Ted," he said, extending a hand.

Jake followed suit, though he found it a bit overly friendly. They were paying guests, not family members arriving at a reunion.

"I apologize for greeting you like this," Miss Abbie said, folding her apron and tucking it under her arm. "How did you find your travel?"

"Fine," his father said.

The foyer wasn't too bad. Jake had expected the worst from what his assistant had described as "cozy country chic," whatever the hell that was, but someone had exercised a degree of restraint in the decorating. Christmas greenery continued the theme from outside, with white candles and bows brightening it. An antique washstand and pitcher, a very solid-looking coat rack, umbrella stand, and bench occupied the entry. He let his father conduct the conversation on their behalf and followed along as the angular woman led the way into what she called the parlor.

Jake might be spoiled by his success, but he'd grown up rough and ready. Living on an air force officer's salary wasn't the toughest thing in the world, but it afforded few luxuries. And what extravagances his family had known had been the ones demanded by Ariel, for Ariel.

So he could be comfortable pretty much wherever he found himself, though he definitely preferred Claridge's over Clarion, the Mondrian over Motel 6, Bellagio over Best Western.

He settled into a seat indicated by Miss Abbie, a high-backed Victorian armchair. He'd never actually stayed at a Best Western, though once when Ariel had spent the travel money his father had given her on a new set of guitar strings and an album she just had to have to practice from, mother and son had slept in their car parked behind a Best Western.

Funny how he hadn't thought about that adventure in years. Jake stretched his legs out in front of him, staring at the boots that cost more than many people made in a month and more than some earned in a year. More than some would know in a lifetime.

Ariel had befriended the motel's security guard, so they'd been allowed to stay as long as they kept out of the way. They'd only had to cross the state of Illinois to meet the Colonel in East St. Louis, so Jake wasn't sure how his mother had managed to run out of gas money, nor clear as to why she couldn't call his father and have it taken care of. But his job was not to question; his duty was to take care of his mother. So at age nine, he'd sat wide awake during the night while his mother slept in the backseat of their Plymouth, her arms around her precious guitar.

Later, when he'd been old enough to understand a few more things about his parents, Jake suspected that his mother had preferred playing the gypsy to driving sedately to their new posting.

"If you'll excuse me," Miss Abbie said, "I'll go see what's keeping my sister. Then I'll get your bags in and show you to your rooms. In the meantime, please enjoy the cookies and sherry."

Jake jerked back to the present. His father was staring, not at him, as he would have expected given his prolonged daydreaming, but at the doorway.

Suddenly a light bulb went off in Jake's head. As soon as the older woman had left the room, he sat up and leaned forward. "Your friend," he said, "she's staying here, too?"

"What do you mean?" his normally astute father looked puzzled.

"You keep watching the door," Jake said.

"It occurs to me that I didn't make things clear. She and her sister, Abbie, own the Inn."

"Here we are," Miss Abbie said, barging back into the room before Jake had a moment to prepare himself. A softer, gentler, shorter, and more rounded version of her followed. "Meet my sister, Martha."

Smiling in a shy way, the woman said, "Welcome to the Schoolhouse Inn."

"The Porters," Abbie said.

"Jake," Jake said, rising from the chair and giving her a brief smile.

His father walked forward, both hands outstretched. The woman looked into his eyes, her lips curved into a smile no longer shy at all. His father clasped her hands. "Martha," he said, his voice more like that of a teenage boy who hasn't yet found his pitch.

"Ted," she said, drawing out his name.

"Well, it seems as if you two have met before," Abbie said, darting a glance from the man to the woman, looking not at all pleased.

His father and Martha nodded.

They hadn't dropped their hands.

Watching their intertwined fingers, Jake retreated to the side of the fireplace. He studied the neat stack of wood awaiting a spark of kindling. He wasn't sure how he felt.

Confused, possibly.

Awkward, definitely.

Ready to be somewhere else. You betcha.

He cleared his throat. "I've got to pick up a few things," he said. "Is there a store you can direct me to?"

His question seemed to break the spell between his father and the woman—the woman his father wanted to marry.

"Can it wait? I was hoping to take everyone to dinner. I've made a reservation at the Verandah." His father let go of Martha's hands.

Miss Abbie fussed with her apron. "Dinner? Oh, we couldn't possibly leave. We have other guests checking in this evening. Besides, you're staying at our bed-and-breakfast. It wouldn't be right."

Martha clasped her hands together. "Kristen's here," she said. "She could handle the Smith party."

Abbie took a step backward, her face as horrified as if the devil had appeared in the parlor. "I hardly think that would do." She planted her fists on her bony hips. "If you want to go to dinner with the Porters, Martha, then you run along. With all the weekends you've been gone lately, I've gotten used to doing things on my own. But what we're doing discussing this in front of guests, I don't know."

"I brought it up," his father said. "And Martha and I have met before. You were right."

Martha colored, a rosy wash to her cheeks that did her rather pale complexion good. Jake cast another eye over her. She wasn't bad looking, just different from what he'd expected. She reminded him of his second grade teacher. Never once had she scolded the class. If they acted out, she'd sigh and say she'd just have to make more love in her heart so it would spill out and fold them in. He wasn't sure any of them understood what she meant, but they'd worked extra hard and behaved as best they could just to please her.

Jake's mother resembled a faerie. She'd always been more child than woman, and even now, nearing her mid-fifties, she looked half her age. Acted it, too. And when she wanted something, it wasn't love that overflowed with her. Ariel was all high drama and earsplitting volume.

"Well, well," Abbie said. "Isn't that nice." She eyed Jake's father and pursed her lips as if she'd sucked on lemon and salt without bothering with the tequila. "Let's get your bags in, Mr. Porter."

"Colonel," Martha said. "Ted's an air force colonel. Retired now," she added, possession and pride in her voice.

"I'll get the luggage," Jake said.

Abbie stepped to the door. "I'll go with you and then show you to your room," she said, apparently as eager as Jake to exit the parlor.

Outside on the porch, Abbie paused by one of the rocking chairs. Her jaw worked, and she stared back at the door she'd just passed through. Jake kept silent. He had a pretty good idea that she'd undergone a shock when she realized her sister had met "Ted" before.

Jake figured there wasn't much Abbie didn't know about Martha, or so she thought.

"I'll get the bags," he said, heading down the steps.

Miss Abbie shifted her body around to face him and the car parked in the front drive. "I'll walk with you."

He nodded and waited for her. He yanked his small bag from the trunk along with his father's larger one. The set of golf clubs stashed in the rear of the trunk surprised him. Golf must be another new entry into his father's life.

"You mentioned a store," Abbie said. "There's a drugstore on Courthouse Square or you can go out to the highway to the Wal-Mart."

"Thanks," Jake said. He should have rented his own car and met his father in Doolittle. The way things were, he might as well be a prisoner. "Are there any cabs in town?"

Abbie gave him a sideways look. "Are you the Jake Porter who went to high school here for less than a year?"

They'd walked back to the door and were stepping across the threshold into the foyer. The entryway already felt familiar, as if Jake had been there many times before. Impossible, of course, but the feeling clung to him. "Yes," he said.

"Then you know this isn't a cab sort of town," Abbie said. "You can put your coat on that rack. No one will bother it."

"Right," Jake said, not intending to part with one of his favorite leather jackets. But somehow it seemed the thing to do, so he found himself setting the bags down and stripping off the jacket he'd picked up in Milan last spring.

"The drugstore is an easy walk, and if you can't manage, they'll deliver." She looked him over, up and down. "I taught science when you were at Doolittle High," she said. "I never forget a name."

No wonder she seemed familiar.

"You look just the same, except you've filled out a bit." She halted in front of a door fixed with a brass sign that read in script *Fourth Grade*. She tapped a bony index finger against the side of her nose. "There's something else different about you." She sniffed. "I guess it's what some people call 'town bronze.'"

Jake grinned. Abbie was droller than she'd first appeared. "And what do you call it?"

She shot him a sharp look. "It'll all come out in the wash and I'll tell you then. So what brings you to Doolittle after all these years?" As she asked the question, she pushed open the door and indicated he should enter.

My father wanted me to meet the woman he plans to marry. Jake heard the words in his head but he couldn't say them. Not to that woman's sister, who clearly had no idea what changes were about to be wrought in her orderly life. He felt a rush of sympathy for the bony spinster. He tried to think of the right thing to say.

She stood gazing at him, her hands on her hips, her silvery eyebrows lifted.

"My father," he said, and left it at that.

She sniffed and pointed to the other bag. "I'll take that," she said.

"No problem," Jake said, and hefted the bag. "Show me the way." His mother might have spent her life composing songs and half hoping that each time she checked on him he'd slipped off to some other family more able to care for him, and his father might have spent his years off fighting whatever enemies the state declared as such, but between the two of them, they'd inculcated him with manners. "I've got it," he said.

"I reckon you say that a lot," Miss Abbie said, striding down the hall to the last room, its door tucked just under the stairway that led to the upper story next to a sign that read, *Staff Only. No Guests, Please.*

"Eighth Grade," she said, opening the door to that room. "Martha put your father in this room." She made that sniffing noise again, a signal of disapproval, he felt sure.

"Looks nice," Jake said, glancing around the forest green decor of the room. Four-poster bed, washstand,

velvet curtains at the window; all in all, much more mas-
culine than the yellow, white, and blue that dominated
his room.

"Thank you," Abbie said. "We try to run a respectable
place. And we aim to keep it that way."

"Yes, ma'am," Jake said, wondering if her warning was
meant for him or his father.

Chapter 12

Well, Well, Well, What Have We Here?

When she finally arrived at the Verandah, Harriet requested a table for one in the bar. She remembered from Donnie's funeral that the restaurant, Doolittle's only fine dining establishment, had a wide open floor plan, offering little in the way of privacy. The preferred tables were those along the broad windows overlooking the lake. The bar, however, offered the advantages of being dimly lit and usually thin of company. There weren't a lot of drinkers in Doolittle.

She requested Perrier with lime and a dinner menu, sat back against the upholstered chair, and took a deep breath. The frenzied rush of Manhattan seemed very far away.

Too far.

She'd visited with Olivia and Olivia's sister Amelia, who would be driving her to the hospital. To her surprise, Zach had agreed to Olivia's invitation to spend the night at her house. She had challenged him to a chess tournament. When Harriet said her good-nights, the two of them, Olivia so fair and Zach so dark, had their heads bent over the chessboard.

Harriet sipped the mineral water delivered promptly by the young waiter. Donnie had taught Zach how to play chess. Bubbles from the drink popped and fizzed in her mouth. She sat up straight, pushing the drink away from her. Of course that's why he'd stayed with Olivia. Even more than Harriet, Olivia formed his bridge to Donnie.

She opened the menu but none of the words registered. Her son didn't talk much about Donnie. He kept a framed picture of the two of them on his desk. That photo had been taken on one of their visits to Doolittle, one of the many that the two of them had made with Harriet remaining behind in New York.

Donnie had been teaching Zach to ride. They were both on horseback, in the corral on the Smith Place. Donnie beamed with pride at Zach, an expression mirrored in his eight-year-old smile. He'd been a natural, Donnie told Harriet upon their return. Olivia had sent an eight-by-ten in a sterling silver frame. It had sat along with the other family photos on the grand piano until they'd returned from Donnie's funeral.

Without saying a word, Zach had put away his suitcase, then returned to the huge space they called the living room. Harriet stood looking out the windows at the lights below, wondering how life could go on for so many when it no longer existed for another. She saw Zach's reflection in the window and watched him as, still silent, he approached the grand piano, studied the framed photographs, selected one, and walked back to his room.

She'd knocked later, before going to bed but not to sleep, to check on him. The picture of him and Donnie on horseback sat on Zach's desk, where it had remained.

Five years he'd been dead.

Five years, and Harriet still didn't know what to do about telling the truth.

"Have you made your choice?"

She jumped. A heavy silver fork skittered to the carpeted floor.

The waiter retrieved the fork and apologized for alarming her.

"No, no," she said, giving him a smile. "It's me. I'm lost in my thoughts."

Had she made her choice? Inaction was a choice of sorts, she supposed. But then she remembered her resolution to have her investigator proceed. How easy it was to let that determination slip to the back of her mind. But it wouldn't do. Or would it? Why not leave well enough alone? Donnie had loved Zach.

And what of Zach's birth father? Would he not have loved him just as much?

"I can come back," the waiter said, "but the kitchen closes in fifteen minutes."

Of course it did. Nothing in Doolittle stayed open late. Harriet ordered the first entrée that came into focus, a petite filet, and a salad, and then she looked around the bar. Better for her to live in the moment and avoid the swell of what-ifs and memories that threatened to overcrowd her mind.

She'd draped her red cashmere coat over the empty chair opposite her seat and placed her purse on top of it. She considered digging in her purse for her phone and stepping outside to call her parents before the salad was served. She knew she ought to call them; she willed herself to make the effort. They would know, of course, that she'd arrived. They probably knew she'd been to Miss Olivia's and not yet checked into the Schoolhouse Inn.

In Doolittle, who needed a cell phone?

The waiter arrived with her salad and a replacement fork, so Harriet decided to let things be. Her parents probably dreaded seeing her as much as she did them. No one would know what to say, not that that would keep her mother from talking nonstop, all the while saying nothing and accomplishing nothing other than raising Harriet's fortunately fairly low blood pressure.

Funny how she and her parents had zero in common. Perhaps it would have been like that with Zach and his birth father, too. She'd known him such a brief time, how could she even tell whether any of Zach's traits or mannerisms were similar? One thing she did know, though, in a way that burned itself into her artist's eye, and that was just how much alike they looked. Same build, same dark hair, dark eyes, quirky eyebrows, determined chin. No mistaking the genes.

Harriet lifted her salad fork. She placed it back on the table. She'd definitely been doing too much mind rambling. Why, on the other side of the room, sitting at the bar with his back half turned to her, sat a man who was the spitting image of Jake Porter.

She forced a bite of salad into her mouth. Chewed. Swallowed. She needed to get back to her therapist on a regular basis. Daydreaming was one thing, but seeing hallucinations quite another.

And then the hallucination shifted, turned toward her, and lifted a glass as if toasting her.

Harriet blinked, shook her head, and took another bite of her salad. Really, she had to get a grip.

Chapter 13

Down the Rabbit Hole

Dinner had been interminable. Jake didn't want to be the third wheel, especially not with his father and Martha Wilson. He'd offered his father every opportunity to enjoy dinner with his friend tête-à-tête, but the Colonel had deflected each attempt.

The restaurant wasn't bad; the food and service at the Verandah turned out to be better than Jake had expected, actually. It was the situation that was so damned awkward.

He gave them credit for not carrying on in public. They behaved with decorum, but any fool could see by the way they smiled at each other, the way his father held the door, pulled out the chair, offered her the salt and pepper, and listened to her advice about the menu as if she were sharing jewels of wisdom, that the two of them had it bad for each other.

Jake didn't begrudge his father a shot at love. But he just didn't have any faith in the happily-ever-after ending to relationships. Surely his father had been just as enamored of Ariel, way back when, or he wouldn't have married her. And how long had those feelings lasted?

Jake stirred sugar into his coffee, one level teaspoon. Across the table from him, his father performed exactly the same action. Jake watched the spoon go round and round.

The spoon twirled and flashed in the flickering light of the candle near his father's place. The rounded edges straightened into the sharp slicing edge of a butcher knife, a knife clutched in Jake's chubby toddler hands. He lay in his bed, holding the knife over his face, watching the light play on the shiny blade. Suddenly his father and mother were standing over him, both reaching for the knife, both shrieking and yelling.

Jake watched them instead of the knife. Somehow he understood the screams and shouts thrown back and forth between Mommy and Daddy had nothing to do with him.

He tossed the knife toward a tower of blocks and clapped his hands as the red and yellow and blue wooden blocks scattered to the floor. Meanwhile, overhead, his mother and father went on screaming at each other.

No screaming now, Jake reflected as he watched his father and his bride-to-be. But most of his memories of his parents followed the same lines. Jake sipped his coffee and wondered how long it would be before the couple sitting at the table with him would be exchanging angry and hurtful words.

"We're going to drive around Lake Doolittle Village

tomorrow," his father said. "Would you like to come with us?"

Jake had to ask him to repeat the question.

"It's a planned retirement community. You'd be surprised how many people retire and move to Arkansas."

"It's big business," Martha said. "It helps us out at the Inn, too, when friends and family come to visit."

"And prefer to stay someplace other than with their friends and family?" Jake knew that would be his choice, too.

Martha nodded. She smiled at the same time. She did appear to be a good-natured woman. But what did she and his father have in common?

"I'll pass," Jake said. "Maybe I'll take a walk and visit my old high school. Or go find my old girlfriend." He said it half jokingly, but what was there for him to do in Doolittle? And why not look up Harriet? Perhaps he'd find her saddled with a brood of kids and some hick of a husband and discover that the very special girl he'd thought existed was nothing more than a wishful figment of his boyish imagination.

"I didn't know you had a high school girlfriend," his father said.

Jake looked him in the eye. "No, you didn't," he said, leaving it at that, when he could have added a lot more, like *How would you know when you were never home? And if you'd given me five minutes to say good-bye before you yanked me out of this town, maybe you would have had a clue.* He didn't say it. It didn't matter now.

His father cleared his throat, looked down at his coffee cup and over at Martha. "I wasn't a model father," he said. "As a matter of fact, the more I consider things, the more I realize I did a piss-poor job."

Martha's expression was a cross between shock and sympathy. She patted his hand. "Jake seems like a fine young man. So you couldn't have done that bad of a job."

"He raised himself," his father said.

Those words surprised the hell out of Jake. He'd always known the truth of that, but had never once heard his father admit to it. "Guys," Jake said, "let's drop the subject, okay? I'm sure being a dad or a mom is one of the toughest jobs around. You and Ariel did just fine."

His father shook his head. "We know that's not accurate, but thank you." He drained his coffee cup. "I sure wish you'd go with us tomorrow."

Why had he come to this blasted town for this phony family togetherness torture? "Yes, sir," he said, and finished his coffee. Then he excused himself, said he'd find his own way back to the Inn, and strode to the bar he'd spotted off the entryway upon their arrival at the restaurant.

A man could only take so much. He entered the dimly lit bar of the Verandah, took a seat at the bar, and ordered a Cognac. He stared into the snifter, swirled the glass, and wondered how he'd spend the rest of the night. The bartender, a silver-haired man with a stoop to his shoulders, had retreated to the far end of the bar after he'd served Jake's drink. After a few minutes, Jake caught the man's eye, and he ambled over.

"Yes, sir?"

"Where does a man go around here to listen to some live music?"

The man eyed him. He picked up a clean cloth and stroked the brass railing with it. "Well, it depends."

Jake waited.

"On whether you want to hear some good heartfelt

country and bluegrass or whether you want to have your eardrums blasted into bits."

Jake nodded. "Know what you mean," he said. "I like all kinds, though." He made money from all kinds, too, though one principle he followed was to produce only music and musicians he believed in. He had no hard and fast rules or rulers by which to measure. He simply knew what he liked when he heard it and witnessed the music being made.

And so far, he and his company, Philistine Records, had batted 100 percent with public opinion by following that route, having produced no losing groups or albums. Jake planned to keep it that way.

The bartender put down his polishing cloth and reached for a piece of paper. Taking up his pen, he sketched a map and wrote a few words. He pushed it across the bar to Jake. "You might want to look up these kids," he said. "They call themselves the J. R.'s. I've heard talk about them around here. You can call over there and see if they're playing tonight."

Jake eyed the rough map. He thought he'd repressed all his brief experiences in Doolittle, but he recognized the name. He'd avoided the hall where anyone could sign up to play. After enduring seventeen years of life with Ariel, the last place Jake wanted to hang out was a musicians' watering hole. One crazy musician in the family was enough, thank you.

"The Barn," he said. "What's it like?"

The other man shrugged. "Can't say that I know. Between my day job and this night one, I don't get out much."

Jake nodded. "I'm a workaholic, too."

The bartender looked at him as if he didn't believe him,

not that that mattered to Jake. He folded the paper and put it in his pants pocket. He returned his attention to his brandy snifter, and the bartender wandered back to the other end of the bar.

A waiter entered the room. Jake shifted around on the barstool to look at the other side of the dark area. One of the small tables was occupied by a woman. She had her head down, but something about her made him look twice.

Opposite the woman, a splash of red highlighted the chair, draping over the back and onto the seat.

Red. Red cashmere?

Jake focused on the coat and willed the woman to lift her head.

He picked up his snifter, swirled, inhaled, and paused before tasting the Cognac.

The woman raised her head. Dark eyes swam into view. Pert nose. Narrow chin. Spiky hair that bounced a bit as her head lifted. She looked at him. No, she looked right through him, apparently lost in her thoughts.

Jake hefted his snifter in a toasting gesture, wondering what in the world he'd done right in life to find the beauty he'd spotted from a distance in the Little Rock Airport seated in the same bar in Doolittle, Arkansas. Whatever it was, he vowed he'd do it again if only she proved to be unattached and as enchanting as she appeared.

Never one to rush his fences, Jake turned back in his seat and sipped his drink. He studied the bar mirror until he found an angle that allowed him to keep an eye on the woman. He didn't plan to charge over there, but he also did not want her to slip away.

He simply had to speak with her.

He shook his head slightly. Speak with her? Jake had

to admit it wasn't talking that he had in mind. From the first glimpse of her, he'd been intrigued by the air of confidence and also mystery. Even now, the way she'd looked straight at him as if not seeing him had only made him want to know more about her. She hadn't snubbed him. It had been as if she lived in a different world. He could see her, but could she see him?

Jake almost smacked his forehead. What was wrong with him? Next thing he'd be imagining that she was a magical creature or some such baloney. Jake moved through the day and night with his feet and his mind planted squarely in reality. He left the creative impulses and wacko imaginings to the artists he managed.

Jake Porter didn't make up stories; he balanced the books for musicians who spun tales and sang of them with silver voices. Not for him the uncertainty and the off-balance experiences of the artistic types. Living with Ariel had cured him of any tendency to let his creativity express itself in any way other than investments, funds, and business deals.

The waiter had approached the woman's table. The young man carried away a dinner plate. After a few minutes, he returned bearing a coffee service.

One plate. One cup and saucer. The woman definitely dined alone.

Could it get any more perfect?

Jake smiled. He certainly hoped so.

Chapter 14

Does It Get Any Better Than This?

"Hello."

The voice was low and husky, as if the man had awakened not too much earlier. The pitch managed to convey sleepy male and sexual desire. The voice matched perfectly with the memories playing in her head.

Only the voice sounded more grown-up, more experienced, more . . . Harriet lifted her head, ever so slowly. That voice wasn't in her imagination.

She blinked, parted her lips, and fixed her gaze on the man a step away from her table.

"I didn't mean to startle you," he said, his dark brown eyes taking her in, assessing her reaction.

"No," Harriet said, her voice barely above a whisper.

No, this could not be happening to her. This man standing next to her table could not be real.

"Good," he said, his tone smooth. "May I join you?"

She had it all wrong. Her imagination had gotten completely carried away. Harriet hadn't conjured Jake Porter. She had attracted a man who reminded her of him, a man alone in a bar in the one decent restaurant in town. And she, Harriet, a woman alone, was not at all unappreciative of the hunk who stood beside her, looking down at her with a glint in his dark eyes.

She inclined her head, ever so slightly. There was absolutely nothing to be gained by giving him any idea just how much those eyes and that graceful and athletic bearing interested her.

It pleased her that he didn't disturb her cashmere coat. Instead he pulled a chair from the empty table next to hers. He placed his brandy glass on the table. "May I buy you a drink?"

He leaned closer as he asked the question, not uncomfortably so, but in a way that placed his face and most especially those compelling eyes directly in her line of vision.

One eye was lighter than the other. Golden flecks highlighted the iris.

Harriet lowered her hands to her lap and pinched herself on the wrist. No imagination. No hallucinations. This man was the real thing.

Jake Porter.

Sitting across from her, all grown-up, in the Verandah Restaurant.

She shook her head, pointed to her coffee cup. The last thing she needed at a moment like this was to fuzz her brain with even a sniff of alcohol.

He leaned back, shifted in the chair, getting comfortable, claiming his space. He wore a leather jacket that shouted money, jeans that were far too nice to be called by that name, a natty yet casual shirt that looked as soft as chamois. The watch on his wrist was a Presidential.

"I've seen you before," he said.

Harriet almost stopped breathing. She tipped her head. Then she took a drink of coffee.

"In Little Rock."

She almost spit out the whole mouthful. After swallowing, she said, "Little Rock?"

He reached over and stroked the red cashmere coat. Watching his lean fingers caress the fabric stirred something deep within Harriet that hadn't felt, hadn't lived, hadn't breathed, hadn't lifted its head to dance and sing in oh so long. "In the airport," he said. He leaned closer to the table, swirled his drink in the glass, and stared into it. Then he lifted his eyes and said, "I never forget a face."

Harriet stared at him, her first instinct to challenge that blatantly inaccurate claim. Then she captured control of her reaction. If he didn't recognize her as Harriet from high school, the smartest action might be to let him remain ignorant of her identity. She raised a hand and beckoned the bartender. He whisked over.

"Yes?"

"Another round of whatever Mr.—" She lifted a brow and looked across the table.

"Jake," he said. "Just call me Jake."

She nodded. How she stayed so calm, she had no idea.

"And for you?" the bartender said.

She smiled. "I'd love some more coffee. With cream, please."

"Very good," he said, and moved away.

"You're very polite," Jake Porter said.

Again, Harriet almost laughed out loud. "Polite" was not a word often used to describe her. Quixotic. Quirky. Independent. Those terms came much more readily to mind. "Thank you," she said. Then she formed a small "O" with her mouth, and said, "If that is a compliment?" She shot him a teasing glance, knowing she played with fire, but unable to resist dancing the crazy dance that presented itself to her.

Jake Porter and Harriet P. Smith reunited.

Yet clearly he had no idea of her identity.

Had she changed that much? Or had she never enjoyed enough of a place in his mind that he would remember her? That thought zinged and caromed and caused more than a twinge of hurt.

He smiled and her heart responded.

Well, okay, not her heart. Harriet the artist had long ago mastered anatomy. Her heart lay within the walls of her chest, safely tucked behind her sternum and ribs. The body parts that responded to Jake's smile lay far below and beneath her heart. She uncrossed her ankles and lifted one leg over the other at her knee. She needed all the defenses she could muster against the reactions this man created within her.

He produced a grin that had no doubt slain more women than Harriet could count. His voice even huskier, he said, "It is indeed a compliment."

She licked her bottom lip, almost unconscious of the gesture. The less she said, the better off she would be. Let him think her either hard to get, disinterested, or simply tongue-tied.

When it came right down to it, it didn't matter what Jake Porter thought of Harriet P. Smith.

Not tonight, anyway.

"Traveling through town?"

Harriet nodded. The bartender arrived with a fresh brandy and another cup of coffee and a small pitcher of cream. She thanked him. He stepped back and said, "I recommended a local band to your friend here. You might want to take it in, too, if you're not planning to turn in early. They're quite the buzz around town."

"I'm not very musical," Harriet said. "But thank you."

"They're playing at the Barn," the bartender said. "It's just down—"

"Thank you," Harriet said, cutting him short. "I'll probably make it an early evening."

"Right," he said, and backed away.

"Not musical?" Jake Porter said, turning his fresh glass at the base. "You look like someone who never misses a premiere or fashion week or a gallery opening."

She laughed. "Do I?"

He nodded. "Very cosmopolitan." He made a face Harriet didn't quite understand until he said, "The antithesis of Doolittle. There's no way anyone would take you for a local. And since I first spotted you in the airport, it seems to reason that you're traveling through. Have I got that right?"

A smile fluttered over Harriet's lips. He was so sure of himself. But hadn't Jake Porter always been that sort of guy? He'd come into town, a stranger, a newbie, a kid no one knew and no one would have listened to under normal circumstances. He hadn't attended K through twelve together with all the other kids in their class. He'd walked into the school a stranger their senior year and yet he'd ended up being voted Most Popular and Most Likely to Succeed.

Face it, she thought, his confidence was one of the traits that had so attracted him to her. And vice versa. Harriet Rogers never seemed sure of herself. She had opinions, of course, but in high school she'd never expressed them in a way that roused others to follow her lead.

"I am on the road," she said, pouring enough cream into her coffee to turn it into the perfect color of beige that she loved.

"It's nice that you don't worry about fat grams," he said, observing her doctor her coffee.

She set the cream pitcher down, hard, on the tabletop. "Why should I?"

He shook his head and waved a hand toward her. "You shouldn't," he said. "You're gorgeous, in case you didn't know."

Harriet had no answer. *Gorgeous.* Had he thought so, so many years ago? Or had he had only the challenges of the jerks in her class ringing in his head when he'd charmed and entranced her, convinced her to go to the prom with him? And afterward, after the dancing and sipping the punch that Joey B. had spiked and way, way, later that night, when it was the two of them and the stars and the riverbank and they'd danced and hugged and kissed and fondled and fallen to the ground, to the soft carpet of moss and grass and sand and fumbled, in all their innocence, to a mating that never should have taken place, had he thought her gorgeous?

"Ah," she said, and left it at that.

"What shall I call you?"

That voice. Those eyes. Of course she'd fallen for him. He was the kind of man who screamed sexuality. Not that she'd understood that, not at seventeen going on eighteen. But she'd known, as surely as she'd known that she was an artist, that she wasn't destined to live her life working at an arts and crafts shop in Doolittle, Arkansas, that Jake Porter was anything other than a commonplace sort of guy.

She'd fallen, and she'd fallen hard.

Harriet ran a hand across the spiky tips of her hair. She leaned back in her chair. "Oh, I don't know," she said. She looked him over, wishing she could inhale his scent, gobble up his delicious body, forget about the past and live only in the present. "How about Ms. Smith?"

He grinned. He lifted his glass, saluting her. "All right, Ms. Smith," he said, stressing the name. "You want to remain a mystery woman, I can run with that game. Smith, though, it's far too ordinary. Shall we pick another name?"

She smiled. "Jones?"

He laughed. "You're great," he said, leaning closer.

Harriet demurred and swept her lashes down over her eyes. Jake Porter was on the make, sweeping in to close in on his conquest for the evening. No doubt he'd be on the road again in the morning, the encounter a distant memory by the time he hit the interstate.

Jake Porter, ladies' man.

Had he been intent on wooing Harriet P. Smith, she might have been flattered by his attention. God only knew she was not at all immune to the man. But she was simply a stranger in a strange town. Harriet cast him a sideways glance and wondered whether she could lead him on a merry chase without being caught up in her own danger-ous attraction to him. She lifted her eyes to his face.

And then she hesitated, as the thought that he might well remember her but had said nothing rose in her mind. After all, she hadn't greeted him with a *Well, lookahere, it's Jake Porter.* Was he playing a game, too? She tipped her head, studying him. He gazed back, eyes dark, teasing, inviting her to look her fill.

No. He didn't have a clue. She had no right or reason for that conclusion to rankle her, but it certainly did. She shifted one hand closer to his. "I know I said I wasn't musical," she said, "but what was the band the bartender was talking about?"

"A terrible name," he said. "No market appeal at all. I don't even want to repeat it. They can do better."

"Oh?" Harriet stirred her coffee. "Are you an expert?" Talk about a superfluous question. Her investigator had given her a detailed report of his business successes.

He shrugged. "I know the music business," he said. "There's nothing like discovering a new talent. I swear, it's better than—" He looked away, across the bar, and then back at her, and grinned. "It's amazing," he said.

She actually thought she understood. "You mean it's like hitting on all cylinders, feeling a creative flow that is coming from your heart and your gut and the soles of your feet, shooting out and consuming anything and everything."

"Oh, my God." Jake Porter let go of his glass. He leaned closer, much closer than Harriet was comfortable with. "You understand."

It wasn't a question.

It was a statement.

She nodded.

He leaned back. "You've got to go to the Barn with me."

She sipped her coffee. The Barn was the last place Harriet P. Smith needed to go with Jake Porter. She'd hung out there with Donnie. Despite how much she'd changed, someone might recognize her and call her by name. But perhaps that would be for the best. "Maybe" was all she said.

He took a long swig of his brandy. Harriet eyed his drink, wishing she'd indulged in the same, yet thankful she hadn't. "I take it you're also just passing through town," she said, fishing for any clues as to why Jake Porter sat across from her in the Verandah.

"Yep," he said. "Actually, I'm here on family matters."

"Do you have relatives here?" Harriet remembered only one family member associated with Jake Porter, a distant relation who, when Harriet had appealed to her after Jake's departure, had insisted she had no idea where he'd gone or why he'd left. She had told Harriet that it was beyond her why he'd shown up in town in the first place. She hadn't seen her great-niece Ariel since the girl was knee high to a grasshopper, and why the flighty Ariel had flown in, saddled her with a boy well on his way to becoming a man, and then dashed off, was beyond her.

"Do I have family here?" Jake sat back, seemingly studying his glass. Then he glanced up. "The answer to that question is fairly complicated." A shadow passed over his eyes. He toyed with his glass, then seemed to shake off whatever emotion the question had generated. "Never mind that. Let's go hear that band."

"Right this minute?" Harriet clung to her coffee cup, to the safety of a table between her and Jake Porter. The Barn was a standing-room-only venue. No tables or chairs to protect her from that lean, hard body and those hands that made her hot and heavy just looking at them. How she'd react if he touched her—well, that she couldn't predict.

Jake Porter stood up, towering over her, one hand lifted toward her. "Come on," he said. "Where's your spirit of adventure? Let's go hear that band. They might be the next Grammy award–winning venture and, man, would I hate myself if I passed them up. It would make this trip worthwhile." He took one of her hands in his. "Of course, getting to meet you has already done that."

Harriet slipped her hand free. It felt too good, yet he was just too darned sure of himself for her to go along with that possessive touch. She pushed her chair back, picked up her purse, and rose. "Okay," she said. "I'm in."

He smiled. "That's the spirit. By the way, do you have a car?"

Harriet nodded.

"Good," Jake Porter said. "Because I don't."

She reached into her purse and pulled out a key, thankful that she'd be in control of her escape route. She waggled it in the air. "No problem," she said. "I can drive."

Chapter 15

Harriet Travels Back in Time and Jake Is Right There With Her

The Barn was an old tub of a building on the outskirts of town, opposite the way Jake and the Colonel had driven in. A single light on a lone pole served as illumination of a gravel drive and parking lot where pickup trucks out-numbered cars.

He figured the Hummer driven by the mysterious and gorgeous Ms. Smith & Jones belonged to the truck cate-gory. She had no trouble following the directions the bar-tender had supplied, but more than once Jake wondered what agency had granted her a driver's license. His own style of driving could best be described as responsible. Like his father, he drove with both hands on the wheel, at the 10:00 and 2:00 position. He even used his turn indicators, though most of the drivers he encountered in Los Angeles clearly viewed those switches as vestigial auto organs.

After she failed to slow at two four-way stops, Jake pointed out the next one. She didn't take offense. Instead she smiled in a way that enchanted him even more.

He'd decided to back off on his approach to her. He had a feeling he'd come on way too strong in the bar. Why else would she not give him her name? Yet she'd consented to let him into her vehicle, something many women wouldn't have done. It was almost as if she knew she could trust him.

Jake gazed at her across the space of the Hummer's front seat. She had just backed the car into a space wide enough to berth an eighteen-wheeler turned sideways, but as it seemed to take every ounce of her concentration, he kept quiet.

She felt familiar. It was uncanny, the way he'd spotted her in the airport and, pow—he'd bumped into her at the restaurant. If he weren't so utterly grounded in reality, he could end up thinking something silly like they were meant to run into each other.

But Jake was anything but fanciful. He pursed his lips, pondering the possibility that her presence was no accident. He'd been pursued by many determined musicians, and more than one beauty had gone to great lengths to catch his attention.

The air of mystery was smart. Savvy. Sure to capture his notice.

"Here we are," she said, letting go of the wheel at last.

Jake nodded. As he unfastened his seat belt, he reminded himself not to let his gonads run away with his common sense. He needed to learn more about Ms. Smith

& Jones before he made too many more moves. "Wait there," he said, and climbed out of the vehicle. He might be on his guard, but he never forgot the manners drilled into him.

He strode around the Hummer and reached for the door. As he did, it swung open and she sat there, one booted foot on the running board already.

"Allow me," he said, offering her a hand and lifting her down.

"Why, thank you," she said, still holding his hand and looking up at him.

Even in that funky light from the one glaring bulb, he thought he detected admiration. Or was it plain old surprise? Not a lot of men remembered to treat a woman in a way that told her, in every move, how special she was.

She removed her hand from his. She tossed her head, and the spikes of her short hair caught on the breeze. "That's . . . refreshing."

"You're welcome," Jake said.

"Though I know that's not politically correct to admit," she said, grinning. "Not that I'm one to bother about people's opinions."

He walked close by her side, guiding her on the gravel, avoiding a rough patch here and there. "Somehow I didn't think you were." He wasn't sure where that thought came from, but as soon as he said it, he knew he'd hit it head on.

She shrugged. Her shoulders flowed, easy, supple, sexy. Something kicked in his groin. *Careful, Porter*, he told himself. *Watch yourself. Change the subject.*

She did it for him. A set of double doors that looked like they might actually have been attached to a barn at one time swung open. Light flooded out, causing Jake to blink against the glare. But worse than that onslaught was the noise blaring from within the building.

"If that's the band the bartender was talking about," she said, "I think we should get back in the car."

Screeching protests from the instruments, wailing bellows from the vocalists, angst on a guitar string. Jake shook his head. He'd heard all that same stuff before, over and over and over. It was youth trying to grow up in a world that didn't much care whether it succeeded or not. But music it was not.

"He seemed like a sensible enough fellow," he said. "The bartender, I mean. Let's go in and see who else is on the bill."

She cast a doubtful look at him but continued to match him, stride for stride.

He liked the way she covered the ground. He continued to keep an eye out for her, minding the gravel walkway. Her boots had such skinny heels on them. How did she balance? He shook his head slightly, but even though the mechanics mystified him, he definitely appreciated the effect on her walk.

She swayed, her hips moving in time to a rhythm universal and also known only to her. His blood kicked up a notch. Ms. Smith & Jones was one hot babe.

Before they reached the doorway, he put a hand on her arm. "Thanks for coming with me," he said, gazing into her wide open eyes.

She nodded but said nothing.

He smiled at her. He liked that she wasn't a chatterbox.

But he also hoped that didn't mean she was hiding something from him.

Jake hated surprises.

They walked through the entrance.

A kid with bad acne stared at them. "You guys members?"

Jake nodded.

Ms. Smith & Jones glanced sideways at him but kept quiet.

The kid shrugged and jerked a thumb toward the interior.

A raised stage ranged across the far end of the open space. Jake adjusted his eyes and saw shifting shapes of people standing between him and the stage. Most of them seemed to be talking to one another and not paying much attention to what was going on in front.

Four young men dressed in black were on stage prancing and raging.

Jake grimaced and looked at Ms. Smith & Jones just as she made a similar face.

He smiled and caught her hand.

She didn't try to slip free.

The volume increased; the lead guitarist screeched one last time and fell to his knees.

The room went quiet. A few people applauded. The foursome gathered their things and cleared the stage. The crowd quieted.

"Ah," Jake said, leaning closer to her. "Now we'll hear something quite different."

"How do you know that?" She put her free hand on one slender hip.

He squeezed the hand he held. "Bet?"

She shook her head.

"Do you want something to drink?" Jake glanced around.

"I don't think you can get anything here," she said.

He glanced at her, wondering fleetingly how she knew that. "I'm happy to look if my lady wishes."

She looked down at her feet and then back at him, almost as if she wanted to say something but wasn't sure what or how to say it. "No, thanks," she said at last.

"Thanks for coming out tonight," a woman called from the stage. She looked to be about Jake's age, and for a moment, he could swear he knew her. It was weird, his having lived in Doolittle for such a short time. He'd long ago forgotten most of his stay in the small town. It folded into so many of the other places he'd lived, then been uprooted from. Perhaps that was why so many faces or builds or accents struck a chord in his memory. But surely the woman on the stage did look familiar?

And it wasn't like the woman whose hand he now held. He'd seen her in the airport in Little Rock and her image had been branded on his brain. That was a different sort of memory than a face one had known as a young adult and then bumped into years later.

"Coral," he said, not even realizing he spoke out loud.

Ms. Smith & Jones's hand seemed to freeze in his. "What did you say?"

He shook his head. The last thing he wanted this cosmopolitan beauty to know was that he'd graduated from high school in this Podunk town. "Nothing."

She nodded. Her tongue appeared, just enough to taste her lower lip. He'd noticed her making that gesture before, and it drove him wild.

Where had the name "Coral" come from? Somewhere in his memory the woman's name had lain buried. She'd been the rough girl in class, the poor kid with the ratty clothes, but the one who could handle any instrument, the girl who would've majored in band and gone on to state college if she hadn't turned up pregnant a month or so before graduation. And here she was, running the Barn.

"We have a special favorite tonight," Coral continued. "J. R. is here!"

The crowd went wild. The floor was even more crowded than it had appeared when they'd first walked in.

"Give 'em some love," Coral said, and backed off the stage as four young men walked on.

Guitar. Bass. Fiddle. Mandolin.

A shiver ran down Jake's back. The image of his mother and her group filled his mind. He wanted to raise his hands and cover his ears, but more than that, he did not want to let go of the hand of the woman who stood at his side.

Once they started to play, Jake forgot about everything else. Their music flowed and sang and danced. It cried out with passion and feeling and depth and angst. Yet it sang of hope and the possibility of happy endings. It rang with the optimism of youth and sagged with the sorrow of the aged.

Their instrumentals filled the room, quieting even the most restive of the crowd. And the lead vocalist sang in a way that Jake hadn't heard in a long, long time.

He didn't realize, until they took a quick break, that he'd practically been digging his fingernails into his date's hand.

But she didn't seem to mind.

By God, she seemed to understand just how beautiful what they were hearing was, and how rare.

"Sorry," Jake said, letting go of her hand, but lifting it to massage it slowly.

"It's okay," she said, her voice barely above a whisper. "They're very good, aren't they?"

He nodded. "Oh, yeah." He looked around the large room. "The audience is all young, but this group would appeal to a lot of people."

"This isn't the sort of place people our age frequent," she said with a hint of a smile.

"People our age?" The comment shocked him. Yet when he looked around he realized he did have a good fifteen years on most of the crowd. Funny, but he never felt anything other than young. Young, footloose, and free to do whatever he wanted whenever he chose. Yes, that was the life for Jake Porter.

She shrugged. "School is obviously out for the Christmas holidays."

Jake checked her left hand. No ring, but she sounded like a parent. Well, that didn't concern him. She was traveling solo and the night was young. "I'm going to give my card to them. I'll be right back."

She nodded.

"Don't run away," he said with a wink.

Chapter 16

Selective Memory

Run away? Harriet P. Smith? If she had half the sense she'd been born with, she'd do exactly that. Instead, Harriet eased a bit closer to the back wall, seeking a more shadowed area of the floor. She, Jake, and Coral might be the only ones older than twenty-one in the room, but she preferred to avoid the off chance that anyone would recognize her.

One of the four musicians on the stage remained there, strumming his instrument. The other three had gathered around Jake. A cluster of teens moved between her and the stage and she lost sight of Jake. Just as well. Whatever business he had to conduct had nothing to do with her.

There was only one matter that the two of them needed to discuss. But how to bring that up was still beyond her.

Would he recognize her? Would someone point out to him that his old classmate had walked into the Barn at his side?

Coral, perhaps? Harriet couldn't believe that Jake Porter had remembered Coral and not her. On the other hand, Coral hadn't changed a bit. She was just as plain and frumpy as she'd always been.

Which no one could say about Harriet. But she'd be willing to bet that if Coral got a good look at her, she'd call her by name, which gave her even more reason to shrink further into the darkened fringe. Coral had been kind to Donnie, had believed in his musical talents even as Donnie's father pressured him to hang up the guitar and go into the family real estate development business. She'd also come to his funeral.

The crowd started to call out for the music to start again. "Give us some more, J. R.," cried a youngster in front of Harriet.

She smiled, thinking that if Zach knew about this place, he'd spend his entire Christmas vacation here. But knowing Zach, he'd already been here during the summers he spent with Olivia. He wasn't one to miss out on a music happening.

Just like his father.

Both fathers.

Harriet literally shook her head. She needed to leave, to clear her head and to keep herself from making any more stupid mistakes. If she slipped out now, Jake would no doubt be disappointed that his mystery woman had been lost to him, but he'd get over it, especially in the excitement of discovering the new talent.

She half turned, and bumped straight into a strong shoulder.

"Looking for me?" Jake Porter said, his voice close to her ear.

"Right," Harriet said. "Actually, I was going in search of the ladies' room."

"I can help," he said, putting an arm around her and steering her around the clusters of the crowd toward the opposite side of the room. "I spotted the sign on my way back from the stage."

"Oh, great," Harriet said. If fate intended her to spend just a little more time with Jake Porter, so be it.

When she returned to the main floor, he was talking to a group of young women. They smiled and giggled and jostled for his attention. She hovered on the edge, but he seemed to sense her presence as he turned, held out his hand, and pulled her to his side.

The girls look disappointed and moved off.

"Sorry to spoil your fun," Harriet murmured, feeling desired and protected by the way he kept her close.

He shook his head. "Jailbait. Never fall for it." He inclined his head toward the stage. "They're going to do one more number."

The group broke into a more raucous song, yet the same poetry in motion drove the tune. Jake stood there, a smile animating his face, his booted foot tapping in time with the beat, his arm around her waist.

She was eighteen again, Cinderella at the ball. Jake was holding her close, dancing the last slow dance, the one they played before they turned off the lights and shooed everyone out. Her head lay in the curve of his shoulder, tucked against his neck. They breathed as one, their bodies meshed. Harriet had no worries ruling her head, no shyness reigning in her heart. When that last slow dance ended, it was the most natural thing in the world for her to slip out of the gym with him, hand in hand.

They went to the lake, as did most of the rest of their graduating class. But instead of joining the group building a bonfire and passing bottles around, Harriet and Jake went off on their own.

"Hey," Jake said. "Still with me?"

Harriet closed her eyes and nodded. "Oh, yes," she said. Spring had come early to Doolittle that year, and the air and the ground had thrown off the winter chill. They found a sheltered spot in a circle of trees, out of sight and out of sound of the others.

When he kissed her, she shivered.

Her lips fluttered against the touch of his.

His strong hands came up and around her shoulders and pulled her tight. She made a sound she couldn't recognize. Joy mingled with surprise.

"I've got an idea," Jake said.

She moistened her lips with her tongue. Nothing but nothing tasted like a kiss from Jake Porter. "What?"

"Let's get out of here," he said, turning her in a half-circle as he spoke.

"But this place is—" Harriet just kept from biting her tongue. She opened her eyes. The four walls of the Barn surrounded her, not the wooded sanctuary of Lake Doolittle.

"Too crowded?" He steered her to the door. "You've got that right."

She let herself be drawn to the exit, but she knew she had to get away. She wasn't safe around Jake Porter.

The music spilled outside, following them. The tempo slowed.

Jake pulled her into his arms and led her in a languid two-step on the concrete apron outside the doors of the Barn.

Harriet stiffened and stumbled, tackling his foot with her boot. He only held her tighter.

"Go with the flow," he said, smoothing the back of her head with his hand.

She relaxed about as much as she would if a Doberman pinscher had been vaulting toward her. He slowed, then paused, tipped her chin up to his, and said, "Inside a few minutes ago, you were like a different person. Mellow. I mean, you were melting onto me. Did I do something to make you nervous?"

Harriet gazed into his eyes. Couldn't he see who she was? Couldn't he also remember how magical that night had been? Even later, when the kids at school had told her what they'd put him up to, she still refused to deny what she'd felt with Jake Porter.

More fool Harriet.

She shook her head. Well, Harriet wasn't eighteen anymore. She was all grown-up and she knew how the game of men and women played itself out. She flicked her lashes, pouted slightly, and said, "You don't make me nervous, Jake." There, she'd done it. She'd said his name and not fallen over in a heap of nerves. He'd forgotten Harriet from high school, but she would make sure he'd never forget Ms. Smith & Jones. She traced the outline of his mouth with her pinky finger. "No, you don't make me nervous. You make me hungry."

He pulled her to him, and she felt his reaction, hot and heavy against the front of her body. "Keys," he said.

She fumbled in her bag, handed them over, then thought to object. "You're not on the rental agreement."

He unlocked and opened the door, and before she knew it she was tucked into the passenger seat.

"That only matters if there's an accident," he said. "And there won't be."

"Not if you're driving," Harriet murmured.

"Thanks for the vote of confidence."

She smiled and decided not to mention that she'd already been stopped once. He hadn't had a car in high school but he'd had a driver's license. For prom night, he'd wangled a car from someone, but never told her who had sponsored their drive to the lake. "You're welcome," she said, turning in the seat so she faced him, as best she could with the seat belt that tugged across her body. She stretched an arm out, rested it on his shoulder.

She could be seduced.

Or she could play the seducer.

He kicked an eyebrow up. He pulled out of the gravel lot and headed back away from town, toward the interstate.

She wondered, idly, where they were headed. Not that it mattered.

Chapter 17

A Lovely Evening for a Drive

"Nice car," Jake said. He liked the way her hand felt resting on his shoulder. "What do you drive when you're not on the road?"

"What do you mean?" Her fingers found the first bit of skin free from the leather jacket. He wished he'd shrugged the coat off before climbing behind the wheel. Cool, warm, hot, inquisitive, her thumb tested his neck.

He, Jake Porter, Mr. Man About Town, almost shivered in reaction to her touch. *Easy, Jake, easy.* He braked for a stop sign. "This is a rental."

She nodded. "At home I walk. Or take a cab. Or the subway."

He smiled over at her. "Aha, the woman of mystery reveals herself at last."

She smiled back at him. He gassed the Hummer and shot through the intersection.

"I took you for a New Yorker the first time I saw you," Jake said.

The smile she gave him that time was a little bit crooked, almost as if she didn't believe his statement yet had decided to humor him.

He crossed his heart. "Honest."

She sighed. "I do believe you."

"So you're from the East Coast. And I'm from the West Coast."

"So what are we doing in the middle of the country?"

He shrugged. Reaching up, he touched the back of her hand that caressed his neck. "I don't know, but I'm glad you're here."

She nodded. Said nothing.

"There is one thing I'd like to know," Jake said.

"Only one?"

"You're teasing me." He leaned his head back against her hand. "And does it feel good."

Her laugh started somewhere deep in her throat and ended in a delicious gurgle. "I'm glad," she said.

"But seriously," Jake said, deliberating between turning to the right and driving around until they'd gotten to know each other better or making the left, heading for a motel he'd spotted along the interstate, and getting to know her a whole heck of a lot better.

"Serious. Okay, I'm serious," she said. "What do you want to know?"

"I'd love to know your name."

"I only know your first name," she said.

"Porter." He grinned. "Your turn."

She laughed, but he detected a hint of nervousness underlying the musical sound. There was a reason she didn't want him to know her identity. His smile fading, he said, "Are you married?"

"Oh, no," she said. Her hand stilled, but she didn't withdraw it from his neck. "If I were, I wouldn't be here with you. That may sound old-fashioned, but if it does, that's too bad."

His smile returned. "I can think of one exception to that statement."

"Oh?"

He caught her hand as she was lifting it from where it lay so snugly against his skin. "If you were married to me," he said. The words slid from his tongue. He would've bitten himself to bring them back. Not only did he never joke about the M word, he never even allowed it into his brain. If Lilly had heard him say that, she would've taken it as an invitation; no, worse, a proposal.

The woman beside him laughed. "Oh, I'm not the marrying kind at all."

Relieved yet a little bit annoyed, too, he said, "I was only pointing out the truth of the statement."

"Right," she said. "Of course you were." And then she tugged her hand free from his and placed it back in her lap.

Just as well, because as much as he enjoyed holding her hand, he preferred driving with two hands on the wheel. Later he hoped to have all the time in the world to explore her body with his hands and lips and tongue. "Have you ever been?"

She nodded. "Once."

"Didn't work out?" As if marriage ever did. It was an unnatural state. This dance, this attraction of the unknown, this chase—who needed anything between a man and a woman beyond the thrill of pursuit celebrated by the rush of sex? That and health and business success made a man happy and whole.

She'd turned her head, studying the passing darkness outside the vehicle. Jake didn't begrudge her the silence. He'd lived through the pain of his parents' rocky marriage and divisive split and continued to witness the same patterns of pain over and over again all around him. He could sympathize.

"My husband died."

Jake almost ran off the road, but swerved back. He didn't know what to say, except to apologize for his cynical thoughts, but how could he do that when she had no idea the kind of muck that ran through his head? Good thing, too, or she'd take her car back and kick him out, leave him on the side of the road. "I'm sorry," he managed to say.

Again, she nodded.

"Was he a Smith?"

She looked startled. "Excuse me?"

"You said I should call you Ms. Smith. So is that your married name?"

"Clever, Mr. Porter," she said.

"Elementary," he said, taking a turn that led away from the bright lights along the interstate. He had a fuzzy memory that one of the routes to Lake Doolittle ran this way, but he couldn't trust a fifteen-year-old recollection. But he also didn't mind how long he drove around with

Ms. Smith. The more time he spent with her, the more he liked her.

Which was a hell of a lot different statement than he made about most women, he realized with just a touch of shame at his own sexism. He either did business with women or slept with them. He didn't mix the two, though. He'd seen too many people come to grief engaging in that lethal combination.

"So far we've established that you're from New York, that your last name is Smith, and that you have incredible taste in red cashmere coats," Jake said, halting at a four-way stop at a deserted intersection. He leaned over, pulled her into his arms, and smiled into her upturned face. He touched the high bone of her cheek, ever so lightly, then bent and kissed her. He meant it as a tease, a taste of pleasure to come, an invitation for her to go back to tracing the line of his neck with her sensitive fingertips.

He'd intended the lightest of kisses, a brush of skin against skin.

Her lips were warm and soft and yielding. They quivered at his touch. She sighed, and he caught his breath.

He also grabbed control of himself. Again he smoothed her cheek with the pad of his thumb and then forced his body upright behind the wheel. He checked the intersection and gunned the accelerator. He wanted to move fast, especially after that taste of her, that confirmation that one would not be enough.

He had to have more.

But first he had to know more about her. He was, after all, a practical, logical, well-ordered man.

"Nice," he said, noting that she'd pressed her fingertips to her lips. Good. He wanted her to go on wanting the feel of his mouth on hers. "So, now are you ready to tell me your name?"

She smiled, a dreamy look that tempted him to pull to the side of the road and take her in his arms again. "Cinderella," she said.

Chapter 18

Not Quite Paradise

"So who's the wicked stepmother?"

Harriet gave him credit for the question. Another man might have made a stupid joke about being the prince. Not Jake Porter. Touching her fingertips to her lips, she relived the sensation of his kiss. Every cliché came to mind. Electrifying. Earthshaking. Causing her tummy to do cartwheels. Funny thing, though, none of the phrases seemed to exaggerate the effect he had on her.

No, Jake Porter didn't need to joke about being a prince.

He was. He'd always played that role in her life.

"Another tough question?" he asked, his voice gentle.

She shook her head, reminding herself she'd determined to seduce him. Therefore, a few, perhaps several, perhaps dozens of kisses would be required. If she let one simple brush of his lips against hers rattle her, how would she remain in control? Dropping her hand to her lap, she said, "Are you asking about my parents?"

"Yes."

"I have two. Mother and Father." She moved her left hand back to his shoulder and cast him a challenging look. "Satisfied?"

"Not by a long shot," he said. "But the night is young."

She was pretty sure his words carried a double meaning. Well, that was fine with her. She'd work him up, lead him on until he was panting for her, and then abandon him to his own egotism. He'd indicated he was only stopping in town. She'd be spending the next day at the hospital with Olivia. And until she and her attorneys sent him formal notification seeking a meeting with him, she would banish him from her mind.

"Do they live in New York?"

"What is this? Twenty questions?"

He grinned. "Good idea. Yes or no?"

"No."

"Do they live—" Jake swung off the road into a picnic area. "Let's get comfortable," he said. He stopped, but left the engine running. "Don't want you to get cold."

Harriet caressed his shoulder. "Oh, I'm fine. You can turn it off. If I get chilly, we'll think of some way to warm up."

He switched off the ignition and turned toward her. He made no move, though, to draw her over against him. Harriet walked her fingertips down his arm, and he took her hand in his. He appeared fascinated by her fingers.

He stroked her pinky finger. "Forget about your parents," he said. "What's your favorite color?"

"Now that's a hard question." He might as well have been kissing her finger. The heat of his hand stroking only that one small space of her skin and nerves was sending the most amazing shooting sparks through her body. She wiggled in her seat. "Cerulean blue. Alizarin crimson. Viridian. You'll have to stop me. I could go on and on."

He moved to the finger next to her pinky. "I take it you're an artist."

She nodded.

"That's one yes for me," he said. "That means I get to kiss you."

"You're making up the rules as you go," she said, her heart skipping faster.

"And that's a correct answer for you," he said. "So you get to kiss me, too."

He leaned forward, pulling her onto his lap. He had the seat far enough back so there was plenty of room for her behind the steering wheel. She tipped her face to his, but instead of meeting her lips with his, he kissed the tips of her eyelashes. "You have the most gorgeous eyes," he said, his voice husky.

"Thank you," she said, her lips a pout, her body screaming inside for the taste of his mouth on hers.

He smoothed his fingers across her brow. "Your turn," he said.

Harriet wasn't going to waste a kiss on his eyebrows or his ears or the tip of his nose. She pressed her lips to his mouth, gently, tasting him, breathing him in as much as kissing him. He responded, and she forgot all about tender and teasing as she suckled his lips and found his tongue and circled it in a dance with her own.

And then she pulled back, shocked at her own heat. Shocked and thrilled.

"I like the way you play this game," Jake said, settling her on his lap.

Just how much he liked it was more than obvious. Harriet fingered her puffy lips and realized she was fooling with fire. She'd never been able to think rationally around Jake Porter. "Next question?"

"Any kids?"

"Me?" Harriet pointed to herself.

Jake craned his head around. "See anyone else here?"

"No." She toyed with the collar of his leather jacket. "Yes."

He shifted a bit. He turned her so she was leaning against his shoulder but so they could still see each other. Their faces were only inches apart. "Let me guess. One child."

She nodded. Sometime between his any-kids question and now she'd stopped breathing. She forced a slow stream of air into her lungs. "Why only one?" she asked.

He traced her nose with his hand. "You're footloose and fancy-free. That leads me to assume if you have children, you don't have a brood of them. Also I'd conclude that the kid is old enough to fend for him or herself. And you said your husband is dead, and somehow it didn't seem like that had happened yesterday."

She nodded and captured his hand in hers. "And I thought you were just a pretty face. You're a smart guy."

"A smart guy who gets to kiss you now," he said, and bent his lips to hers.

This kiss was almost chaste, especially after the last blood-heating dance of passion.

He lifted his head and touched the spiky top of her hair. "I like your hair," he said. "Not everyone could get away with the look."

She tossed her head. "It's fun," she said. "There's such a fuss made about long hair. But some of us are much better suited for short. You should have seen me . . ." She trailed off. What an idiot. She'd been about to say, *When I was a kid*.

"I would have liked that," he said. "Long, short. Hey, you could probably carry off bald."

"Not with this narrow chin," Harriet said.

He touched her chin and bent to kiss her there. "I like your chin," he said. "It's rather elfin." He looked into her eyes and then glanced away, as if seeing something in his mind. "It's the weirdest thing," he said slowly, "but I feel as if I know you, and yet I know that's impossible."

Harriet froze. Literally. Here it was, her opportunity to tell him who she was and bare the truth, until she'd emptied out every last hidden corner of the life she'd constructed. She opened her mouth. Closed it. *Say something*, she commanded her vocal cords.

Instead she curled a hand against his shirt and felt the steady beating of his heart. She clung to that, knowing she might not get another chance to be held by him. After he knew the truth, he'd hate her. Jake Porter wasn't the kind of man you lied to, if even by omission.

He shook his head, then pulled her closer. "Impossible, but I would like to get to know you better."

She nodded. "Me, too," she whispered.

"Stay with me tonight?" he asked, stroking her neck.

She nodded again.

He kissed her, settled her back in her seat, fastened her seat belt, and kissed her again.

Then he started the engine.

Harriet had no idea where they'd go next, but she knew wherever their destination, it would take an incredible act of will on her part to deny herself a night with Jake Porter.

The anticipation of the passion he would create in her, naked, skin to skin, flesh to flesh, sex to sex, sent hungry, heated shivers racing over her body.

She was only human, after all.

Chapter 19

Paradise Postponed

Something was wrong. Jake had a voice in his head telling him that things weren't what they seemed to be. There he was, zipping along with this babe, headed to a motel for night-to-dawn sex.

And it would be good. No, not good, better than good. He could tell by the way she kissed that her body would be hot and ready and hungry.

He shifted in his seat. He couldn't wait to take her.

So why did his mind keep sending him these warning signals?

He glanced over at her. She had a hint of a smile on those pouty lips, and she was gazing out the window as if she found the darkness interesting. He wondered what thoughts worked their way through her mind at that moment. Was she thinking of him? Her life back in New York? Her child? Funny, but he wanted to know. He wanted her to share with him.

He lusted after her body but he also wanted to see inside her head. *That's crazy*, he told himself. *You're spending one night with this stranger, the perfect recipe for a guy like you. No entanglements, no expectations. No future.*

What if one night was not enough?

He shrugged. What the hell, he could always see her in New York. He was there often enough for business.

"Are you talking to yourself?" she asked, reaching out her hand again the way she had earlier to stroke the side of his neck.

Jake grinned. "I do that sometimes."

"Me, too," she said. "It's an occupational hazard."

"Oh?" Good, she was going to talk about herself.

"I spend hours alone with myself and a canvas and paints. Some days I forget to eat. Poor Zach learned at an early age to fend for himself."

Something inside Jake chilled and froze and started to die. "Zach's your son?" He managed to ask the question casually enough.

She hesitated. "Yes."

"He doesn't mind?" *Of course he does*, he wanted her to say. What kid understands when his mother disappears into her room and doesn't emerge for days on end? What kid wants to be forced to make his own macaroni and cheese and talk back to cartoons because they're his only company? What kid wants to go to school and have to confess he can't eat lunch because his mother wouldn't leave her music long enough to scrounge around and find twenty-five cents?

Her fingers stilled. "He does and he doesn't," she said slowly, as if seriously reflecting on her response. "When my husband was alive, he was always there. They were such good pals." She sighed. "For the last five years, I've made much more of an effort. And the housekeeper lives in, so he always gets his meals. There's always food for him."

"So at least his body gets fed," Jake said, without realizing he spoke out loud.

"It sounds awful, doesn't it?" She dropped her hand to her lap. "But fifteen-year-old boys don't have much use for their mothers. He's a great kid and he's very well adjusted."

"You don't have to defend yourself to me," Jake said, feeling that's what she was trying to do. "I've never been a parent and I certainly don't plan on bringing any child into existence."

She turned her face toward the window for the briefest of moments, then looked back at him, but said nothing.

"I guess it did strike a chord in me," Jake said, wanting her to understand his reaction. "I practically raised myself, thanks to my air force father and a musician mother."

"And you resent it." It wasn't a question.

He shrugged. "It doesn't matter. It's done and over with."

Her expression said she didn't believe a word of that statement. "Is your mother someone I would have heard of?"

"Ariel Gabrielli."

"Ariel Gabrielli!" She stared at him. "That's amazing. I mean, I never . . ."

He braked for a stop sign and looked at her, curious as to why she'd made that comment.

"I love her music," she said, studying her nails. "When I'm working I play music to fit the mood of my piece. I've used 'Vista Vitale' before."

"It's haunting, isn't it?" Jake accelerated. He didn't know what to make of this woman. "Hey, maybe we have met before."

She lifted her head. "What do you mean?"

"Have you ever attended one of Ariel's concerts?"

She nodded.

"Maybe that's it," he said. "I can't get around this idea that I've seen you before."

"Do you play, too?"

"Excuse me?" His mind was still working on the knot of her familiarity.

"Are you musically talented?"

He shook his head. "I leave that to the people I manage. I haven't a creative bone in my body."

She tipped her head. "I find that hard to believe." She trailed one finger along the top of his thigh. "I bet you're very, very creative . . ."

His body heated at her touch. He put a hand over hers and held it against his upper thigh, not close enough to touch him where he most wanted her to, but still enough so she could sense the fire growing inside his groin. "Let's go find out," he said, taking the last turn that led to the motel he'd spotted earlier.

He'd explore her body and savor her effect on him. When the morning came, she'd get behind the wheel of her Hummer and speed away. So whether or not she was a terrible mother, whether or not she was a crazed creative type that he'd sworn to avoid, none of that mattered. What mattered was two bodies mating, the pleasure of the moment, the offering to the senses.

So what if she intrigued him more than any woman he'd met? So what if she made him want to know more about her? He already knew enough to warn him that after a few nights in bed, he'd be moving on. If there was one type of woman Jake avoided, it was anyone who reminded him of his mother.

Not that Cinderella, as she called herself, seemed crazy.

Not crazy. But she wouldn't tell him her name and she had no explanation for why she was so far outside New York City.

She stroked his leg.

He forgot about any questions or reservations about her character or identity.

"Let's get a room," he said, pulling into the parking lot beneath a neon sign that flashed *Highway Express*. And below that, *Vacancy*.

Chapter 20

The Clock Strikes Midnight

Harriet stared at the flashing motel sign. Suddenly she didn't feel so sexy. Well, she'd accomplished her goal of getting Jake Porter to want to go to bed with her.

And what she should have done was taken advantage of the golden opportunity to reveal the truth of her identity and Zach's.

But how could she do that given the almost harsh way he'd declared he'd never bring a child into existence? How terrible could his childhood have been to leave him with such strong fears about having kids?

Harriet had to believe it was fear. No doubt he suffered the classic anxiety about repeating his parents' mistakes. Harriet had worried about the same thing, especially given her horrible relationship with her own parents and their inability to communicate. And the first time Donnie's dad had ever praised him was when Donnie told him about Harriet and her pregnancy. For two teenagers from dysfunctional families, they'd done fairly well by Zach.

All Jake needed was a chance to see he'd be okay as a dad.

A chance she continued to rob him of.

She frowned.

Jake shifted toward her. "You okay?" His voice was low and gentle.

Harriet started to nod, then stopped. "Not really," she said.

He put an arm around her. "Nervous?"

"I guess you could say so." She'd tucked her face against his shoulder so he couldn't check her expression. The refrain of *Liar, liar* kept running through her mind, and she knew the frown on her face hadn't gone away.

He smoothed the top of her hair. "Me, too," he said. "Not that I'd admit that to just anybody."

She couldn't help but smile. "Well, I hope you don't think that I stop off by the side of the road to get a motel room with just anybody, either."

His hand kept moving, soothing, relaxing, calming. "You mean I'm special?"

Oh, yes, you're special, Jake Porter. Harriet kissed his chest through the jacket. "Don't get a big head," she said.

"Too late," he said, pulling back and tipping her chin upward. He kissed her, and Harriet forgot about her fears and worries and lies. She kissed him back, marveling at how no other man had ever made her feel the way Jake Porter did.

She sighed and wiggled closer to him. She'd cling to him now and pay the price later.

"Before I go in there and get us a room," he said, "there's something we need to talk about."

She stilled. Did he know who she was and he'd only been pretending not to the entire evening? What would she say if he said, *Boo, Harriet Rogers, it's me, Jake Porter?* She took a deep breath and said, "And what is it that we need to talk about?"

He smoothed a finger over her cheek. "Protection."

So surprised was she that she almost blurted out, "What's that?" Instead, she managed a weak "Oh."

She no doubt sounded like an idiot.

"And the thing is," he said, "I'm not prepared, so unless you have what we need here in your car . . ."

Perfect. Harriet had her way out All she had to do was tell him they were out of luck, and she could drop him wherever he'd left his car and she could go to the School-house Inn and get a decent night's sleep. She shook her head.

Jake sat up straight and craned his head around her shoulders. "There's a convenience store at the gas station next door. I'll take a walk over there, if you don't mind sitting here alone?"

She smiled despite the situation. He was so polite. "Maybe we should just, you know, forget about it?"

He looked shocked. "Never," he said. "Having sex without condoms is like playing Russian roulette with no empty chambers."

My, oh, my, Harriet thought, gazing at Jake Porter. "I meant forget about going to a motel. Of course I agree with you on contraception," she said. "You're very intense on the subject."

He shrugged. "It's a personal thing with me."

She looked her question, but she couldn't bring herself to ask him to tell her why.

He glanced across the interior of the car. "A long time ago I got carried away," he said slowly. "I'm not sure why I'm telling you this, but I was young and stupid and ever since that experience, I have been, as you call it, 'intense' on the matter."

Harriet fingered the fabric of her blouse. Would he say more?

"Nothing happened that time," he said. "Or at least that I know about. I was just a kid and so was she and I moved away and never heard from her." He shrugged his shoulders again. "But I never got so carried away that I forgot about protection again."

"Of course not," Harriet said. She was doomed. She wanted to scream out, she wanted to go poof and disappear in a cloud and never have to face Jake Porter again, she wanted to be held so tightly by him that she became as one with him. She also wanted to shake him by the shoulders and demand to know what he meant by saying he'd never heard from the girl, as if the street didn't run two ways.

"I'll just be a minute," he said, grabbing his jacket and climbing out of the Hummer.

Talk about a mood spoiler. Harriet slumped in her seat and watched him walk away. She was screwed. Not even that play on words could amuse her. It was a lesson in telling the truth, a lesson she deserved. If she'd just been honest with him from the first moment in the bar at the Verandah, she never would have gotten so entangled. And she could have revealed all. Now what would he think of her?

Worse and worse.

Yet what about his behavior? She sat up a bit. He'd left town without saying a word to her. One night they'd made love and held each other tight and, goodness' sake, made a baby. She'd never gotten a letter or a phone call. So if he'd been so worried about unprotected sex, he'd kept his worries to himself.

Harriet glanced across the car, across the parking lot to the direction Jake had walked. As she did, she spotted the key still in the ignition. *Go*, she said. *Scoot over, start the car, abandon him here. Let your lawyers handle the truth telling.*

And then he came into view, striding back from the convenience store. He waved a hand and pointed toward the office of the motel. The *Highway Express* sign flashed on and off and on again, illuminating Jake Porter's progress.

Harriet waved back and watched as he passed through the entrance. It was time for her to leave. She pressed the back of her hand against her lips. She could still taste his kisses.

That memory would have to be enough.

She slipped behind the wheel. Holding her breath, she started the engine and backed out of the parking lot.

Chapter 21

Jake Makes a Most Interesting Discovery

The motel was clean and serviceable. A very pregnant young woman stood up behind the counter when Jake walked in. She rubbed the small of her back, winced, and said, "Can I help you?"

"I need a room for the night," Jake said, trying to avoid staring at her bulging belly but not quite able to help himself. He stuck a hand in the pocket of his leather jacket, and his fingers brushed against the foil packet of condoms he'd just purchased.

"Yes, sir," she said, in a twangy accent Jake recalled from his days at Doolittle High. "Would that be just for you?"

"Er, no," he said. "Two adults."

She nodded and punched some keys on a computer. "That'll be $69.99 plus tax. Breakfast is from six till nine and don't be late because we put it up right on time."

Jake nodded. He shifted from foot to foot, wondering if the woman would go into labor that night. She looked about to pop. "Is it your first?" he said, surprising himself.

She laughed. "Oh, Lord, no. I've got two little boys already but this here one's a girl."

"Oh," Jake said, uncertain what to say next. But he'd asked the personal question, so surely he owed a better response than that. "Do you like having children?"

She stared at him, then ripped a paper off the end of the computer printer. "Doesn't everyone?"

He was definitely out of his depth in this discussion. So he simply smiled, nodded, and looked at the paper she'd pushed across the counter at him.

She pointed to the rate, and then said, "Now I need you to write your name and your wife's name and your license plate number right here. Then I'll need cash or a credit card."

Jake wrote "Mr. and Mrs. Jake Porter." He stared at the ink, the words that had flowed so easily from his pen, and knew himself for both a fool and a fraud. "It's a rental car," he said. "I don't know the plate."

"That's okay," she said, "You can just step outside and copy it down and come right back." She handed him a blank piece of paper and sat down behind the counter. "I'm not going anywhere."

Jake took the paper and crossed the lobby. He pushed through the double glass doors and walked across the lot, his head down. He hadn't paid for the room yet. Maybe it was some sort of sign, not that he put any stock in such beliefs.

But something about facing that pregnant woman who assumed everyone wanted to have babies and who assumed that naturally if he were checking into a motel the other party had to be his wife, well, it unsettled him. He was a man of the world, and not one to worry about what other people thought or said about him.

But he was also fairly straitlaced, in a funny sort of way. He'd never rented a motel room to have sex. Oh, sure he'd ended up in strange bedrooms and left the next morning never to see the woman again. He'd carried on brief flings that had burned themselves out before the woman could realize he wasn't going to stick around. He'd dated Lilly for most of the past year, so perhaps he was simply growing up or slowing down.

What was wrong with him, getting all weak-kneed because the desk clerk, whose life had nothing in common with his own, was about to pop out another kid?

Or was it that he wanted better for Cinderella? He didn't want a one-night stand for this woman who'd captured his attention and stirred up long-buried memories.

Jake lifted his head. He looked around the lot. He could have sworn he'd parked the Hummer in the spot where he stood.

Overhead, the *Highway Express* sign flashed. He turned and gazed the length of the parking lot. He marched toward the convenience store. Only a pickup truck sat in front of that shop.

He felt in his pocket and knew before he checked that he hadn't taken the ignition key with him. He'd left it in the Hummer. All that had been on his mind was getting out to buy the protection.

Protection he wouldn't be needing, if the feeling in his gut told the truth. He kicked a stray chunk of rock and watched as it skipped across the blacktop lot. Just in case she'd moved the car out of the front area, Jake headed to the side parking area of the motel.

He saw plenty of smaller cars and a smattering of pick-up trucks.

No Hummer.

He leaned against a light post. So she'd gone. And the funny thing was, Jake liked her even better for having abandoned him there.

He walked back to the office of the motel, slowly, looking around in case he'd been wrong about her disappearance. Inside the lobby, he said to the desk clerk, "Make that a room for one. My, er—better half— has been called away on business."

She blinked, regarded him, and then lifted a sheet of paper and handed it to him. "$59.99 then, and please sign. Cash or credit card?"

He pulled a credit card from his wallet. He could have figured out a way to make it to the Inn where he'd stowed his bag. But a night alone in the Highway Express seemed a fitting enough end to the adventures of the evening. He'd rather be alone with thoughts of what might have been than back at that crushingly cozy bed-and-breakfast, watching his father making sheeps' eyes at the sweet but aging Miss Martha.

He signed his name, paid for the room, and followed the clerk's directions to a room down the hall. The door was next to an ice machine and the soda and candy vending area, but as Jake appeared to be the only guest wandering around, he decided it wouldn't be a cause of disruptive noise. At one point in his life he could sleep anywhere and under any conditions. But lately, and especially this night, with his mind full of Cinderella Smith & Jones and his body still aching for what each of her kisses had hinted at, he thought he might well lie awake until the morning light broke through the striped beige and green curtain over the window air conditioner.

He crossed the room and sat on the foot of the bed. It didn't give a bit. The bed might have been carved for the Flintstones. He stretched his legs out in front of him and studied the tips of his leather boots. They were the best, the leather hand tooled, the last shaped to fit his foot. He'd paid a small fortune for them.

Right now he would've traded his boots and a hell of a lot more to know where the woman driving the Hummer had headed.

Jake leaned back, then sat up again and shrugged out of his leather jacket. The packet of condoms rustled and he pulled them out, fingering the edge of the foil. The smooth surface crackled under his touch. He eyed the wording on the face of it. He fell back on the bed, dragging his feet up on top of the shiny green and beige bedspread. He'd been such a kid when he'd bought his first condoms.

They didn't call it that, of course. "Rubbers" was the term bandied about in the locker rooms, not that Jake believed any of the guys at Doolittle High knew what they were talking about.

And not that he knew anything, either.

But his father, in his appearances in Jake's life during his teen years, had drilled a few things into his head. And above all, if he chose to have sex, he had to use protection.

His father hadn't looked at him as he'd held forth on the topic. Rather, he'd concentrated on a spot on the wall opposite Jake. He spoke in measured tones, as if delivering a lecture at which he expected Jake to take notes.

But Jake had no notion of grabbing a pen. He'd heard all

the stuff his father was talking about, but what he couldn't fathom was that there was a girl he'd want to . . . well, you know . . . do it with.

But that was before his mother dumped him with someone's cousin's cousin in Doolittle, Arkansas, and his classmates dared him to do it with Harriet Rogers.

Way, way, way before.

Jake sighed and sat up. He tossed the packet on the bed-side table.

He wouldn't need those tonight.

He kicked off his expensive boots and set them beside the low chest that supported the television. He took his jacket, hung it up on the metal bar provided for clothing, turned off the lights, and padded back to the bed. He lifted the remote control and switched on the television.

Leaning back against the pillows, the flicker of the television screen the only light in the room, he thanked whatever forces in the universe had driven away the most enchanting woman he'd met in a long, long time.

Taking her here, joining with her on this rock-hard bed covered with the polyester spread dotted with the fuzzy snippets of fabric beginning to pill, would have been a sin.

Jake sighed and changed the channel.

He'd gone to the prom that night, a long, long time ago, with Harriet Rogers, not just because the guys in his class had goaded him to do it, but because he liked her.

Sure, she was different from the other girls.

But then, Jake wasn't like his classmates. He felt older than the rest of them, worn well beyond his years. Anyone who had to raise a parent would feel that way, he reckoned.

But whatever the reason, and maybe there simply was no reason, he liked Harriet Rogers. She'd been kind to him that day in the arts and crafts shop, and she'd also been clever and interesting and diverting.

And what had he done for her?

Taken her to the prom, danced with her, cheek to cheek, taking advantage of the way her body seemed to melt against his, holding her close and dancing her out of the gym and toward the car he'd begged for the evening.

And then they'd gone to the lake.

Jake hit the mute button. His memories shouted inside his head. He had cared for her, truly cared, and when they had kissed, and hugged, and clung to each other, the only thought that had filled his mind and screamed in his blood was to be as close to her as he possibly could be.

He certainly hadn't thought of what his father had termed "protection."

He sighed.

At the last moment, he'd remembered the lectures and pulled out. She'd been so trusting, so innocent, so open to him. He didn't think she even understood what he was trying to save her from.

The vision of the woman at the front desk walked into his mind. Jake winced and hit the mute button again, bringing the television volume to life.

Some things didn't bear thinking about.

Chapter 22

The Road Home

Light showed through the front window. Harriet didn't know whether to be sad or glad. She'd told herself that if the house was dark, she'd drive on by, check in at the Schoolhouse Inn, and fling herself into bed. Not that she expected to sleep, not with all that whirred in her mind and flamed within her teased and tempted body.

How had she had the sense to drive away?

Harriet pulled to the curb in front of the house she'd grown up in. A line of Styrofoam candy canes marched along the sidewalk that curved toward the two-story house. A sleigh pulled by the requisite reindeer including Rudolph with a red glass nose illuminated the dead grass of the winter lawn. Harriet narrowed her eyes, considering the location of the Santa and its entourage. During her childhood, her mother had insisted her father climb to the roof and display it there. Perhaps her dad had finally put his foot down or the roof was too old to hold the weight.

Whatever the reason, the yard was as tacky as ever. Harriet sighed and tried not to see the fake icicles hanging across the porch or the quartet of elves marking each of the front steps. Her mother never seemed to understand that less was more.

Harriet pulled her red cashmere coat more closely around her chest, shivering despite the warmth cast by the heater. Why had she stopped? Some need to do penance?

She hadn't had a bad childhood. When she thought of Jake moving around constantly, never getting to make or keep friends, dealing with a mother he described in what she guessed were fairly restrained terms, she knew she should be more appreciative. Her life had been stable. Two parents. One brother. She'd ridden her bike all around town and gone trick-or-treating without any thoughts of danger.

Yet all she'd longed for was to escape from Doolittle, and especially from her boring family.

She'd done exactly that.

So why come back? Harriet fingered the steering wheel. She laid her chin on her hands and closed her eyes. Her parents would never understand her.

"Harriet, is that you?"

She jerked upright and swung her head toward the front porch. The door stood open, framing her dad in the light from inside the entry. He had one hand lifted over his eyes as if scanning the horizon.

So much for driving away. She might keep her distance but she did not actively try to hurt her parents' feelings.

She turned off the motor and opened the door. Stepping out, she said, "Hey, Dad."

He pulled the front door shut and climbed down the stairs. He wore a red plaid flannel shirt over navy blue pajamas. He'd always worn navy blue, Harriet thought, surprised at the memory. She'd never thought to ask him why.

He came around the front of the Hummer. "We wondered if you'd show up tonight," he said, stopping in front of her. His hair had more silver in it than she remembered, but that wasn't surprising, given that it had been almost three years since he'd visited her and Zach in New York.

Harriet held her arms out to her side. "Well, here I am," she said.

"So I see," he said. He stepped back and gave her a once-over look. "Mighty fine," he said. "I wouldn't know you to call you by name and you're my own daughter." He sighed. "People change when they move away from here."

"Oh, Dad, I've been gone for ages," Harriet said. "I'm no different than the last time I saw you."

"Aye," he said. "Your mother and I were trying to remember yesterday how long that's been."

Harriet reached back into the car for her purse. "I don't see that it matters. I'm here now."

"Let me get your bags," her dad said, apparently willing to let the topic drop.

"Oh, that's not necessary," Harriet said.

"No need for you to haul them when I'm standing right here," he said.

Now how was she going to tell him the last place she wanted to spend the night was in his house?

"Later," she said.

"You always were a stubborn one," her dad said. "It's not like it's going to get any warmer."

"Of course it isn't," Harriet said, feeling a slice of guilt. Here was her dad in his pajamas and house slippers wanting to get back inside the house that she knew would be toasty warm because they always kept the thermostat too high. She'd let him carry in her one suitcase. It would be easy enough for her to tote it back when she left for the Inn. "It's in the backseat."

Her dad opened the other door and pulled the bag out. "At least you got Zach settled in at a decent hour," he said.

"How do you know . . ." Harriet didn't even bother finishing her question. Of course Harold and Charlene knew that she'd already been to Olivia's house and that Zach would spend the night there. The Doolittle grapevine left nothing undisclosed.

What they didn't know was where she'd been in between that stop and this one, or for that matter whom she'd been with. And that was just as well.

Some things in life were meant to remain a secret.

She walked beside her dad toward the house.

"Mickey said you met a nice-looking fellow at the restaurant," her dad said.

Harriet almost fell down the steps. "Who is Mickey?"

"He works with me at the lumberyard. Nights he bartends at the Verandah." He opened the front door. "I guess you didn't recognize him."

"No," Harriet said. "I most certainly did not." She took

a deep breath and crossed the threshold of her parents' house.

The house smelled like it always did at Christmastime. Cinnamon and apple spice. Spruce and peppermint. Cedar and a mingled potpourri that hinted of myrrh and patchouli. The lights of the tree had been unplugged but the silver angel hair glimmered in the light from the reading lamp next to her dad's favorite chair, a ratty old recliner that had sat in front of the picture window for as long as Harriet could remember.

Her dad lowered her leather bag. "Anyways, we figured if the two of you hit it off, it might be late before you got here, so I told Charlene to go to bed and I'd sit up awhile."

Harriet stared at her dad. He'd actually waited up for her. She hadn't even called them to ask about staying at their house. And only the slightest of chances had led her to drive there tonight. Yet her dad would've spent the night in his recliner, dozing off, glancing out the window if any car came by and slowed as it passed.

I am horrible, she said to herself. *Selfish, mean, and cruel*. Then she shook her head. No, she wasn't. They wanted her to feel that way, but she wasn't bad. She'd spent years learning that she was okay. One conversation with her dad and she'd resorted to name calling.

Harriet sighed and dropped onto the sofa. It was covered in a floral print she didn't recall seeing before. Thankfully, a red and green afghan covered much of the pattern.

"I suppose you also know I got stopped by the new police chief," she said, shrugging out of her cashmere coat.

Her dad sat down on his chair. "That's how I knew it was you in the Hummer. Not that the new fellow is one to talk about his business," he said. "But he mentioned it to Jenifer Janey and she called your mother so we'd know you were here."

Harriet nodded. She waved a hand in front of her face. She'd have to open the window in her room. That always used to drive her mother crazy. She complained that it disturbed the heating system. To Harriet's mind, the only thing wrong with it was that it was hot enough to cook a goose.

She smiled, somewhat wryly. Tonight she was the flambéed goose. Stuck in the oven with no escape in sight.

Harriet hugged her knees with her hands. "He's married to Jenifer Janey?"

Her dad nodded. "That's right." He chuckled. "Nobody in Doolittle ever thought that would happen." He gazed across the room, away from Harriet, his face sad. "I don't suppose you've met anyone?"

"No, and you know I've no intention of getting married again."

"Donnie wouldn't want you pining over him. And it wouldn't hurt Miz Olivia's feelings, either, if that's what's stopping you."

Harriet counted to ten inside her head. "How's the shop?"

Her dad shook his head. "Things aren't as good as they could be. Don't get me wrong. I make good enough money at the lumberyard, but you know that store is near and dear to your mother's heart. Some weeks we make money, others we lose a bit." He frowned. "It's those big stores out near the highway that are killing us. But never mind that. We had the good sense to buy the building little by little over time so it's not like we have to worry about paying the rent."

Harriet hadn't known they owned the building on the square. She and her parents never talked about money. It was awkward with her being so much better off than they were. She and Donnie had once offered to help them, and her dad had been so offended that it had taken losing Donnie until he forgave them for even suggesting he should take money from his daughter or his son-in-law.

"That's good," she said, and lapsed into silence. She studied the collection of Christmas trinkets that covered the coffee table. A small village with snow made from cotton stood in the center of the rectangular space. One cut-glass candy dish overflowed with red and green M&M's; another held peppermints. Harriet leaned forward and scooped a handful of the M&M's.

Her dad leaned back in his chair and folded his hands across his waist. "It's nice to have you home," he said, almost as if talking to himself.

Harriet choked on a piece of the candy. She coughed and her dad jumped up. He slapped her gently on the back.

"Easy," he said. "You okay?"

She swallowed and nodded. That would remind her to keep her hand out of the candy dish. "Fine," she said. "Maybe a glass of water would help."

Her dad got up and headed out of the room.

"Harold?" her mother's voice called from the top of the second floor. "Is that you?"

"And someone else," he said.

Footsteps padded down the carpeted stairs.

Harriet coughed and tapped her chest.

Her mother appeared in the doorway, her thin body swathed in a bright pink bathrobe, her hair tucked under a nightcap. Harriet couldn't believe anyone still wore one of those. She had a pair of glasses perched on the end of her thin nose.

"Well, I declare, if it isn't Harriet come home to roost after all this time," her mother said. "Your dad said you would come here tonight but I told him not to count on it. But you know Harold, he stayed up anyway." She peered around. "Where is your dad?"

"Here I am," he said, coming back into the room and handing a cup of water to Harriet.

She gulped a long, cool drink. The candy melted and she felt much better. She set the cup down on the coffee table and then reached for it again. "Hey, this is my mug."

Her dad nodded.

"The one I made in art class in tenth grade." Harriet didn't know why, but the sight of that old piece made her feel positively sentimental. "I almost ruined the kiln that day, firing it way too hot."

Her mother bustled into the room and perched on the edge of the other chair, an overstuffed one done in the same new floral fabric. "Your dad has his Sanka in that every morning. No other cup will do for him. No, sirree, it's that cup ready to go or he'll get up from the table and wash it."

Harriet gazed at the mug. She'd tried for elegant and settled for oversize. She'd done the body of the mug in bright yellow and the handle in red. Around the rim of the mug she'd worked in X's and O's in navy blue. She looked over at her dad. "It's really your favorite?"

He shrugged and sat back down on the edge of his chair. "It does the job," he said.

Harriet nodded. She wanted him to say more, but the

action alone was enough for her. So seldom had she gotten praise of any sort from her parents. Funny how she'd grovel for even a sign that they appreciated her and recognized her talent. She glanced at the picture over her dad's chair. It was the same paint-by-numbers landscape that her mom had done when Harriet had been in fifth grade. The blues had gone gray, the greens had faded to ochre, and any light that the picture had once proclaimed had died from the sunshine that sliced in from the front window.

None of her early paintings hung on the walls. There had been a time when she'd worked to please them. She'd come home from school lugging her latest art project to show them, wanting them to recognize the beauty that she created on the canvas.

They'd nod their heads and say, "Well look at that, and what were you thinking? And is that what they teach you at school these days?" Then they'd huddle over the kitchen table and discuss whether they should go to the parent-teacher conference and ask Mrs. Addison to stick to the basics in art class. Once Harriet had barged in on them and informed them in her most grown-up voice that if they dared go to school she'd paint a mural of them naked on the front of the school.

They'd stared at her.

Her dad's mouth had flopped open and closed, open and closed.

Her mother had run her fingers through her short hair and said over and over again, "She's not my child, I swear it."

But of course Harriet was her child. Harriet had once tried to prove that she wasn't, but had given up after tracking down her birth certificate and the announcement in the local paper. Besides, she looked like her mother and her father.

At least she did now that she weighed far less than she had in her youth. She hated to admit it, but she had the same narrow chin as Charlene and the broad shoulders and green eyes of Harold.

Her mother clapped her hands together. "You must be starved," she said, jumping up. "Let me get you a snack."

Harriet lifted a hand. "I'm fine," she said.

"You look like a twig," her mom said. "Let's see." She spread her fingers and with one hand played with the tops of the tips of the other. "I happen to have a fresh cake. Carrot. It's Zach's favorite, as I'm sure you probably know. I made it special for him, but he won't miss a piece."

Harriet wanted to choke. "I am not hungry," she said, even as her mom whisked out of the room.

"You might as well speak to the rug," her dad said. "She's going to feed you even if she complains all day tomorrow that she was saving that cake for your son."

Harriet stared at her dad. "You understand, don't you?"

He fingered the arm of his chair. "More than you think." He stared across the room, at the spot between the Christmas tree and a tick-tocking cuckoo clock. "She means well, your mother," he said.

"Yes," Harriet said, faintly. "Why do you always wear navy blue pajamas?"

He swiveled his head around, fixed her with his eyes. "Funny you should ask that," he said.

"Oh?"

He ran a hand over his chin. "No one's ever asked me."

"Not even Mom?"

He shook his head and smiled. "Nope."

"Hmm," Harriet said. She didn't know whether she felt uncomfortable or more at ease than she'd ever been around her dad.

"I just like 'em," he said. "No particular reason."

"Like you use my mug every day?"

"That's right," he said, casting a smile on her. "I like my routines, you might say."

"Edward is like that, too, isn't he?" Harriet didn't know why her dad's words made her think of her younger brother, but they brought him sharply to mind.

"Yes, he is." Her dad sat back in his chair. "It's no wonder your mother is forever swearing you're not her daughter. But you are, so there's no need to fret."

"Here we are," Charlene said, bustling into the room with a huge piece of carrot cake with cream cheese frosting, atop a dinner plate. She placed it on the coffee table and tucked a dessert fork and paper napkin next to it. "Dig in," she said, retreating to her overstuffed chair and tucking her electric pink robe around her shins.

Harriet felt she had no choice but to lean forward and pick up the fork. How many times she'd done exactly that, hoping to please her mom by eating the food arrayed on the table at dinnertime. In the long run, her mother had nibbled and tasted and jumped up to get more to serve to everyone else. It ended with her mom the skinny one and Harriet the chunky misfit.

She put the fork back on top of the napkin. "Do you mind if I eat it later?"

"Oh, no, of course not," her mom said. "I cut it special for you. Zach won't mind if there's a teeny piece missing from his cake. He's a good boy. Tell me, how is he

and how were poor Olivia's spirits when you saw her tonight?"

"Optimistic," Harriet said, eyeing the piece of cake as
if it were a poisonous snake. "She has high hopes that the
surgery will leave her feeling much better."

Her mom sighed. "One can only pray and hope, I always say." She turned toward Harold. "I still think you
need to drive over to the Smith Place tomorrow and bring
Zach back here. It's too much on Miz Olivia to have a
houseguest at a time like this."

"He's staying with me," Harriet said.

"Oh, my dear, of course, but it will be crowded," her
mom said. "As it is, I have the twins in your room so you're
going to have to rough it with the babies, and Edward and
Honey will be in his old room. That only leaves the sofa,
and I'm not sure it's long enough for little Zach."

Harriet pleated the fabric of her skirt. "I have a reservation at the Schoolhouse Inn."

Her mother's jaw dropped.

Her dad gazed out the front window.

"Now why ever would you do that?" Her mom jumped
up and went to the window. She twitched at the drapes,
then skipped over and turned off the entryway light. "You
have a room here and that's where we expect you to stay.
Not that you visit often," she said, "but as long as you're
here, it's the way it should be."

"If she doesn't want to be here, don't force it," her dad
said.

Again, the arrows of guilt hit home. "I'm staying tonight," Harriet said, standing up. She bent down, picked
up the huge piece of cake on the plate, and said, "Let's
deal with tomorrow then, okay?"

Her mother fluttered her hands. "That's not a bad idea. But tomorrow comes early. I have to leave for the shop by eight, so if you want your breakfast, you'll have to be up and at 'em well before that."

Harriet nodded. "I'm sure I'll wake up." She crossed the room, picked up her purse, and shrugged her bag over her shoulder. "Good night, Dad," she said softly, and headed for the stairs.

Her feet knew the way. It might have been more years than her son had been alive, but her body knew every creak and indentation of the stairs. She climbed, balancing the loads she carried, and held her breath, wondering if they would insist on following immediately after her.

But no steps sounded, no voices called after her.

Harriet lowered her shoulders, took a deep breath, and walked down the hall to the bedroom of her childhood.

It was the same, yet different.

It was different, yet the same.

The brass bed remained, and her white princess dressing table that she'd gotten as a gift on her eighth birthday. She'd asked for a set of oil paints, and her parents had presented her with the mirrored vanity and pink velvet–covered stool.

Harriet dumped her bag and purse on the floor. The piece of cake she perched on the edge of a bedside table cluttered with framed photographs. She dipped her knees and examined the pictures. None of them were of her. Her two nephews were prominently featured, along with various people Harriet didn't recognize.

She shrugged and started to undress. A baby bed she vaguely remembered took up the space between the closet and the dressing table. It was piled with stuffed animals, most of them newly minted. One caught her eye, and she tiptoed closer.

"Hey, Buddy," she said, lifting up a faded pink bunny with one ear almost torn from the seam that attached it to the head. Harriet held her old favorite to her chest. She breathed in the remembered smells of baby powder mingled with tears. It seemed she had always held Buddy on nights she cried herself to sleep.

She pulled back the coverlet of the double bed and placed the stuffed animal on one of the pillows, though there wasn't much chance of her sobbing her heart out tonight. She'd long since given up tears as they were just too darned exhausting, and she hated the way she looked afterward.

Harriet yanked off her boots and tossed her clothes across the pink velvet stool. She flipped off the light and slipped naked between the sheets. She needed to go to the bathroom but she would wait until she heard the house go quiet. There was no way her mom would understand why Harriet was flushing her precious cake down the toilet.

So she clasped Buddy to her cheek and closed her eyes.

She'd lain in this same bed all those years ago, the night she and Jake Porter had made love. She'd crept in, managing not to wake her parents, hugging her arms to her breasts, whispering over and over in her head all the things he'd said to her, feeling over and over within her body all the magic he'd made for them.

Again this evening Jake Porter had kissed her. After all these years, she'd felt his touch, so gentle yet so fiery on her face, her lips, her throat. She shivered and tugged the other pillow into her arms. Jake Porter ignited something inside her no other man ever had, and she'd walked away from him. What if she had stayed? What if she had claimed one night with him? With a sigh, she turned over onto her stomach and buried her head under the pillow.

It wouldn't have been enough.

She wanted far, far more of Jake Porter than she could ever have.

Yes, everything in this room was different, yet the same.

Chapter 23

The Scrapbook

After a restless night spent trying to get comfortable on a bed that had more in common with a slab of concrete than a mattress, Jake rose early. He handled a lot of business by phone. Arkansas was only a two-hour time difference from L.A., but Jake couldn't help but reflect when he hung up from a call with one of his assistant producers that it might as well have been on another planet.

Life moved so much more swiftly on the coast.

He liked that feeling of nothing standing still.

He dropped to the floor of the motel room and did twenty-five push-ups. He wondered where Cinderella was this morning, and to punish himself for thinking of a woman he would never see again, a woman he wanted and couldn't have, he did another twenty-five.

Panting, he turned over and added sit-ups to the regimen. Who said he'd never see her again? He had ways of finding people. She'd said she was an artist. She lived in New York. How hard could that be?

He laughed at himself. But as he showered and got dressed in the clothes he'd worn all the day before, his mind worked over the possibility of seeking her out.

At the same time, he decided he would definitely go to the square in Doolittle and see if the old arts and crafts store was still there. If so, he'd at least inquire about Harriet from high school. His encounter with the enchanting Cinderella Smith & Jones had stirred feelings within him he'd long ago buried.

And no doubt should leave piled deep under a mountain of other repressed memories.

Growing up as he had, moving so frequently, pining over what was yesterday's scenery made little sense. Most military brats knew what it was to be uprooted every three or four years. Ariel's refusal to live on a base after her one experience on one had led to even more upheaval. Between kindergarten and twelfth grade, Jake had attended ten different schools and lived in five states in the U.S. and two other countries.

Each move, each transplanting of his boyhood and personality had helped him grow new roots, however shallowly planted they might be. And then the next move would come and those roots would be yanked up and new ones have to be started. When it was time, he did what was necessary, soldiering onward as duty required.

When his mother had dropped him off in Doolittle the

latter part of his senior year, she'd shown no concern for his preferences.

Jake let himself out of the motel room, feeling as if he'd escaped from a prison cell, and headed to the front desk. At least for this visit to Doolittle, his father had asked him if he would come. He'd even said please.

All those different addresses, and Doolittle was the only town he'd ever returned to.

Go figure, Jake thought. He handed his key to the desk clerk, a spry old man who reminded him of Jack La Lanne, and asked about walking into the center of town.

The old guy looked him up and down. "It's an easy walk for any man worth his salt."

Jake nodded and verified the right direction, though he was pretty sure he remembered how to get there. That was another thing about Doolittle. It was almost as if he'd been there more recently than fifteen or so years ago.

Silly idea, Jake thought, and stepped out into the bright sunshine of the morning. The air was clear and fresh. He took a deep breath and headed out of the parking lot.

He'd walked about a block when he heard a horn behind him. A pickup truck slowed and then stopped. The passenger window lowered and a clean-cut man, a few years older than Jake, leaned over and called out the window, "Want a ride into town?"

Jake halted. "How do you know that's where I'm going?"

"The direction you're headed. And I'd say that's about a thousand-dollar leather jacket, and those boots don't look like you're planning on hitchhiking down the interstate." The man smiled. "So I'm guessing you were traveling through and your car broke down and you're headed to Ricky's to pick it up."

Ricky must be the local mechanic. Jake couldn't help but grin. He was reminded of how everyone in Doolittle had always known everyone's business. How they must have talked about his parents way back when. No one in Doolittle would dump a kid with a distant relative just to go on a music tour. "Close enough," Jake said. He put a hand on the door of the truck.

"I'm the local vet," the driver said. "Mike Halliday. My office is on the square." He pushed the door open.

Jake climbed in. "Thanks," he said. And because it seemed unfriendly not to offer his name, he added, "Jake Porter. Stranded here, temporarily."

Mike laughed and accelerated. "Well, be careful. The last couple of strangers to get stranded here got snatched up."

Jake looked at him sideways. Was this some kind of *Deliverance* joke?

"They fell in love and ended up living here," Mike said.

Jake laughed. "Don't worry. That's not going to happen to me."

Mike smiled knowingly.

Jake studied the interior of the cab, unwilling to carry that line of conversation any further. He didn't know what in Doolittle appealed to his father or why he wanted to marry a small-town innkeeper, but Jake was confident that nothing but nothing could keep him in such a back-water. And since he wasn't a marrying kind of guy, he didn't need to find any charm or magic potion to protect himself from whatever it was that had gotten to the other people Mike alluded to.

A small pennant hung from the rearview mirror. Jake

focused on it. Tufts. Tufts, as in the Boston-area university, he concluded. He glanced at the driver. "You're not from here originally, I take it?"

Mike shook his head. "Relocated because of my ex-wife so I could be with my kids. Hated it, but loved my kids more."

"Rough," Jake said, glad he didn't have that kind of complication in his life. No, with him it was easy street all the way. All he had to do was enjoy his success, continue discovering more talent, as he'd done with so many before and now with the J. R.'s, and savor the fruits of his labors.

"Yeah, it was till a certain woman found herself stranded here one night," Mike said. "Everyone should have that kind of luck." He was smiling, as if he'd won a prize no other man could ever attain.

A certain woman. Jake pictured the elfin chin; the huge, dark green eyes; the spiky hair; the shy-one-minute, bold-the-next smile of his Cinderella. He wanted her. Bad.

But why?

To love her and then to leave her?

He frowned.

"We're almost there," Mike said. "The square is just around this corner."

Jake nodded. What was he doing, looking up a girl from so long ago when he ought to be taking care of business? He had the number for Jason Rayne, the lead singer of the J. R.'s. He could call him and set up a meeting. This chasing after some memory could do no one any good.

Mike pulled into a head-in parking spot in front of a building with a brightly lettered sign that announced it as Dr. Mike's Animal Hospital.

They climbed out of the truck. The door to the hospital

burst open and a girl who looked like a female duplicate of the driver rushed out. "Daddy, Daddy!"

Mike swung her up in his arms and around in a circle. "How's my Jessica?"

"Good, but you'd better hurry because Miss Marple is about to have her puppies. Mom said I can stay and work with you until three today."

"Good. Say hi to Mr. Porter."

She stuck out a hand, her youthful face beaming with a smile.

Jake shook hands with her.

"Do you have any animals?" she asked with dancing eyes.

He shook his head.

"How very sad," she said. "Well, if you want some, please come see me. I'm in charge of adoptions."

Jake couldn't help but grin. "Yes, ma'am, I will remember that."

The girl ran back inside.

Mike stood there, smiling. "She's quite a kid," he said. "She's grown up in my exam rooms. Her mother hates that she spends all her time here instead of at ballet and dance and drama class, but Jessica has a very convincing way about her." Then he shook his head. "Sorry. Don't know why I said that."

"No worries," Jake said. "My parents were divorced. They spent more time arguing before they got to that point than afterward, though. It must be tough, raising kids."

"Oh, yeah, but I wouldn't trade it for anything," Mike said. "I'd better get to work. If you find yourself with time on your hands, drop by for a visit. Just watch out for my wife. If Stacey finds a single guy like you loose in town, she's likely to set you up with someone."

Jake held up a hand and laughed. "Thanks," he said. *For the warning*, he added to himself.

He looked around the square. Cars were parked in front of several of the shops and a few people milled about in front of the courthouse. The benches sat empty this brisk morning. Jake headed down the street, his feet taking him to the left at the corner.

His feet knew what they were doing, because when he paused and glanced up, he spotted Harolene's, the arts and crafts shop. The windows were crammed with Christmas items. Jake shook his head at a do-it-yourself reindeer, and marveled why anyone would want to complete a paint-by-number *Last Supper*.

A few lights were on in the store, but when Jake approached and tried the handle, he found the door locked. A sign proclaimed opening time to be ten A.M. Jake checked his watch. He had an hour to fill.

LeDru's was right down the street.

Now where had that thought come from?

It was weird, coming back to a place he'd lived before, if ever so briefly. He'd never had the experience of remembering his past. But he'd bet that the coffee and doughnut shop was around the next corner, assuming that it was still in business and hadn't been replaced by a Starbucks.

Jake laughed softly. He'd definitely be willing to bet that Doolittle was the last place the mega-chain would manage to stake a presence.

Sure enough, LeDru's was still there. He pushed through the glass door with gold and black lettering and a Razorbacks sticker and walked into the coffee shop he hadn't entered since he was just-turned eighteen and about to order his first cup of coffee.

A few men sat at one end of the long bar. Two of the five

booths were occupied, most of them by men, one by two women in business suits. Jake breathed in the aroma of the freshly roasted coffee and the cozy warmth of a place that served as a home away from home. The plank floor was worn smooth and the backless stools at the counter looked as if they'd been in place since the Depression.

On a blackboard behind the counter someone had written, "What's the significance of this date?"

Jake took a seat at the counter and considered the question. A very cute redhead approached with a coffeepot in one hand, thick ivory mug in the other. "Hi, there. I bet you'd love to have a doughnut with your coffee. Buttermilk or regular?"

Jake smiled. He'd always loved buttermilk doughnuts. Somehow this woman asking him this question made him feel as if he'd come home. "Buttermilk," he said, giving her a smile.

She put the mug down and filled it with coffee. "I don't think I've seen you in here before."

He wrapped a hand around the mug. "It's been a while," he said, surprising himself with the admission that he possessed a history in town.

"I'd remember if I'd seen you before," she said, with an impish smile.

Jake smiled back, but his heart wasn't in the game. It was a replay of the airline attendant all over again. Maybe he should have a medical checkup.

"My name's Pickle," she said. "Or at least that's what everyone calls me." She slid a small bowl of half-and-half miniatures toward him, along with a glass sugar container with a pour top, and said, "If you need someone to show you around, you just let me know. I've been gone for a while, but I know pretty much everyone in town."

Jake nodded and took a sip of coffee. "Good," he said. It crossed his mind to ask her if she knew Harriet but he quickly decided against doing so. She seemed like quite a talker, and if he asked and then decided not to pursue the stroll down memory lane, she might not keep his inquiry to herself.

Pickle moved off down the row of customers at the counter, filling coffee mugs and chatting merrily with what Jake assumed were the early morning regulars. He had his own morning coffee routine in L.A., cruising through the drive-through on his way to his high-rise office building. No one bothered him with chatter. It was simply give the order, pay for it, and drive away. No one would ever know if you were new in town.

The door swung open, and a young man in a police uniform entered and took the seat next to Jake. Pickle practically skipped over. She brought Jake's buttermilk doughnut on a plate in the same trip.

"Hey, bro," she said to the man.

He said good morning and nodded to Jake.

"He's new in town," Pickle informed him.

The cop looked him over more closely. "Here for Christmas?"

"I guess you could say so," Jake answered.

"Busby Wright," the officer offered him a hand.

"Jake Porter," Jake said, shaking his hand.

He pointed to the waitress. "Pickle's my sister. Watch out for the redhead. That is, unless you're already married."

Jake shook his head. "Thanks for the warning," he said, and flipped a grin to Pickle to take any sting out of his words. No need to hurt anyone's feelings, but the blunt introduction coupled with Mike Halliday's earlier advice gave him good reason to stand at a distance.

Pickle gave him a saucy wink and moved away to serve other customers.

Jake swallowed half his doughnut. "This is great," he said after he'd finished it off.

"Don't mind Pickle," her brother said. "She's not allowed to date anyone for a heck of a long time." He drank some coffee and shook his head. "Poor kid's still getting through her last divorce."

"Last?" Jake hadn't meant to say it out loud but he heard the words as loud and clear as the guy seated next to him.

"She trusts everybody," Busby said, giving Jake a glare.

Jake raised his hands, palms out. "No need to worry about me."

Busby looked him over. "We have a very protective family."

Jake finished his coffee. He should be going. Before he could ask for the check, Busby asked, "Who are you visiting?"

"Excuse me?"

"You said you're here for the holidays so naturally I assumed you meant you are here seeing friends or family."

"I'm staying at the Schoolhouse Inn," Jake said, wondering when, if ever, someone in L.A. had asked him such personal questions over a cup of coffee. Busby kept his gaze steady and Jake felt compelled to add, "With my father. He's, er, friends with one of the women who run the place."

"You've got to mean Sweet Martha. Crabbie Abbie has absolutely no use for anyone born with a Y chromosome."

"She didn't seem that extreme to me," Jake said. "But,

yes, I was referring to Martha." Calling her by her first name didn't seem right to Jake, but he couldn't see adding the "sweet" to her name, either.

"The Wilson sisters turned the old grade school into a bed-and-breakfast quite a few years back," Pickle said, refilling their cups and delivering another buttermilk doughnut to Jake, even though he hadn't asked for it. "They own and manage it and seem to have made a success of it."

Pickle plopped the coffeepot down on the counter and leaned on her elbows, apparently planning to join in their conversation and leave the other customers to fend for themselves. It was more like having coffee with family than at a restaurant, Jake realized. He smiled at the perky redhead. "What about Doolittle brought you back?"

"It's home," she said. "I move away and think I can't bear to come back and then I do, and voilà, I'm back where everybody knows me and loves me, faults and all."

Jake listened to her, feeling as if some invisible force had rolled over and around him and wrapped him up in a net that had no intention of letting him escape from Doolittle.

Ridiculous. What he needed was some fresh air. Pickle wouldn't let him pay for the second doughnut.

"That was on me," she insisted, eyes bright and not so innocent as she regarded him.

Jake thanked her, paid, and left a hefty tip next to the empty coffee mug. Pickle was engaging enough, but somehow she left him feeling almost like an elderly uncle.

The *Closed* sign still faced outward at Harolene's.

Jake hesitated, uncertain, suddenly feeling incredibly foolish. What if Harriet still worked there, all these years later? How awkward would that be? He should've taken the first flight back to L.A. and left well enough alone.

He turned to walk away. The door swung open. A bell jangled. Jake could swear he remembered that sound. He glanced around. A wiry woman with gray hair curled close to her head and a thin-lipped mouth beckoned to him from the doorway. "Yoo-hoo, no need to come back later. I'm just opening the shop."

Dimly he recognized the "-lene" half of Harolene's. What was Mrs. Rogers's first name? Hell, he didn't remember. And why should he?

Drawn almost against his will, he stepped into the shop.

The gray-haired woman practically danced around him, whisking a feather duster over a shelf of dough art kits. "Merry Christmas, and what can we help you find today?"

She seemed either crazy or just an airhead, but Jake sensed she was studying him rather intently.

"Christmas presents?" he managed to say, craning his head around to see if anyone else occupied the store.

"You've come to the right place, especially if your loved ones have an ounce of creativity in their bones." She tipped her head to one side. The duster moved much more slowly, barely skimming the surface of a lone shelf. "You know, I never forget a face. That's what everyone says about me. Charlene, they say, you'd know baby Jesus if he was to fly in on an angel's wing."

"Is that so?" Jake glanced around, seeking an exit strategy. He shouldn't have come here. What had he been thinking? Anyone with a mother this nuts couldn't have turned out okay.

But how unfair was that conclusion? With a mother like Ariel, who was he to judge anyone else? "I mean, that's quite a talent," he added.

She nodded. "It is indeed. And you do look familiar. I just can't quite grasp who you remind me of. Or have we met before?"

Jake considered his options and decided it was the wiser course to leave them open-ended. The evening he'd picked Harriet up for the prom, Charlene had stood at the front door, hopping side to side. She looked pretty much the same now as then. But that night, he'd been spared more than a moment's conversation. Her dad had done the talking, what little there had been, more of an agreement that he wouldn't keep their daughter out late, but neither would he deliver her before the end of the dance. Apparently they had little faith that their daughter could keep a good-looking kid like Jake captivated for an entire evening. "I'm not sure," he said.

"Where are you from?"

"Los Angeles." He was getting used to the catechism directed at him from the other Doolittle residents he'd met thus far.

"And your people?"

"My people?" In his line of work "his people" meant his army of assistants who worked out details of deals and concerts and recording studio commitments and appearances with "the people" who represented all the other parties involved.

She stared at him. "Why, your family."

"Oh," Jake said, realizing he'd somehow lost standing with her by want of his quick uptake of her question. "They're from all over."

She nodded. "Military?"

"Yes, ma'am, as a matter of fact, that's right." Out of habit, he reverted to his childhood training. He probably even straightened his posture, putting back his shoulders and butting out his chest.

"I could tell," she said. "You have that look."

"I've never been in the service," Jake said, not to offer more personal information but to set straight her assumption and incorrect conclusion that he had, indeed, served in the nation's military.

"No, but I'm sure your father was." She wagged a finger at him. "There's no fooling Charlene. You can ask anyone in Doolittle. They'll tell you that nobody slips a slider past my home plate."

Jake stared at the woman's index finger. What had Harriet told him about her mother, that evening so many years ago? Every time her mom did that finger dance Harriet had to fight back the impulse to bite it off. That was it. His own mother drove him nuts, but right at this moment, Jake wasn't so sure that Ariel's creative craziness wasn't easier to endure than Charlene's ramblings.

He retreated a few steps into the shop, lifted a snowman off a shelf, and looked at the price tag, anything to get Charlene to stop talking. The snowman broke into a tinny rendition of "White Christmas."

"It's $19.95," Charlene said. Without missing a beat, she said, "I suppose you're staying at the Schoolhouse Inn."

Jake grunted, unwilling to confirm or deny her assumption.

With the feather duster, she swatted at a three-foot-high Santa's elf made from white clay, bearing a sign that said, *Paint Me Yourself and Impress Your Friends*. "They're full up this week. Sweet Martha was telling me the other day how busy they are for Christmas." She snapped her fingers. "I know who you are!"

Jake jumped. The snowman dropped from his grasp. It hit the wooden floor, bounced, rolled down the aisle, and came up missing the broom and its nose. He moved to scoop up it up, wondering why in the hell he'd followed his impulse to visit the shop. She'd make him pay for the snowman, of that he was certain. The amount was trivial, but getting stuck with a piece of junk rankled.

"You're Ted Porter's son." Charlene was patting the side of her cheek and nodding, evidently pleased with her pronouncement despite his not having confirmed it.

He stared at Charlene. How could she possibly remember him?

"I told you I never forget a face." She'd tucked her arms over her skinny chest. The feather duster swung from one hand. "You might want to mention to your daddy that we don't take lightly to anyone trifling with a lady's feelings. If he doesn't mean to do the right thing by Sweet Martha, he'll have the whole town of Doolittle to answer to."

He just kept on staring at her. It wasn't his place to tell this woman that his father planned to marry Martha. "I'm not sure I follow what you're saying."

"Oh, I'm sure you're playing it close to the chest. And I can't say that's a bad thing. Sweet Martha doesn't like to talk about her personal life, only she mentioned to Kristen's stepmother, Stacey, that she needed extra help because for once in her life she wasn't going to work the entire time and that tied in with a special fellow coming to visit her. She even showed her your father's picture. You're the spitting image of your father. I just can't get over how familiar you look." Charlene swatted at some speck of dust seen only to her. "What else would you like to buy to go with that snowman?"

Jake carried the broken item to the counter in the back of the shop. He placed it next to the register. An old stool sat empty behind the counter right at that spot.

That's where Harriet had been sitting the day he'd walked in looking for shop project supplies. An image of her, book in hand, head down, lost in the story, filled his mind. He could almost hear her voice. A basket of ornaments and one of sachets cluttered the counter. Jake shook his head to clear the memory. "I'll take some of these ornaments, too," he said. "By the way, what's your daughter doing these days?" Did she have more than one? Jake couldn't recall if Harriet had any siblings.

Charlene moved behind the counter. From atop a cabinet covered in paint-by-number kits, she lifted a large padded book. She set it down, carefully, in front of Jake. "I should have guessed you weren't here to buy arts and crafts supplies. Are you a collector?"

Jake glanced at the book in front of him.

A scrapbook.

"Collector?" He had no idea what she meant.

Charlene opened the book. "It never ceases to amaze me the prices some people will plop down for a piece of art." She hung the feather duster on a hook next to the register. "Look at this one," she said, pointing to a photograph of a floor-to-ceiling canvas that sparked a sense of recognition within Jake. "It went for $19,500. Why, you could practically build an entire house for that."

She turned the page. "This one's in the Dallas Art Museum. I've seen it there." She flicked at something on the plastic sheet cover. "Not that I mentioned that to Harriet. She's a funny child. She might be grown, but she still has a way of looking at the world that some folks around here don't quite understand."

Jake studied the picture, entitled *Chaos*; the colors and the energy and the palpable pain in the twisting, shouting figures cried out to him. "I've seen this one," he said, slowly.

"I wouldn't be surprised," Charlene said, sounding satisfied. "But if you're not a collector, why are you looking for Harriet?"

Jake turned the page. A newspaper clipping occupied the top half. "Harriet P. Smith Takes Rio by Storm," ran the headline. A dark-eyed woman with a short, spiky haircut stood between two old men in white suits. He lifted the book a few inches off the counter and stared.

"Smith?"

Charlene nodded. "She married Donnie Smith right after high school. They had one son. Up until this past year I thought I'd never have another grandchild."

"So she has more than one?" Jake asked quickly. Surely the woman he'd met last night had claimed only one kid.

"Oh, no. After Donnie died, Harriet put all thought of men out of her mind." Charlene sighed. "Not too surprising. Even if she is my own daughter and maybe because she is I'm more qualified to say it, it would take a special man to put up with her ways. It's my son and his wife, Honey, who've finally had twins."

Jake flipped the page. Another painting. Another amazing one, he had to admit. But what he wanted was a larger photograph of the artist, Harriet P. Smith.

Because Harriet had to be the same woman he'd met

last night. But if that were so, why the mystery, the pretend names?

He lifted the page to turn it. Charlene slapped her palm over his knuckles and held his hand there. "Wait just a minute," she said, pointing her finger at him. "Are you a reporter?"

"No," he said, eyeing her evenly.

"I've had them come around and lie to me," Charlene said. "Let's see your wallet."

"There's really no need," Jake began, but then thought better of the protest. He wanted to see more pages of that book. She wanted to check him out.

"There, you see," he said after pulling out his wallet. "My California driver's license."

"Porter," Charlene said. "Porter. I've met you before. Oh, I know you think I'm nuts, but like I said—"

"You're right," Jake said. If he didn't tell her she'd keep guessing, and he wouldn't put it past her to drag half the town into her quest until she remembered where she'd met him. "I graduated from Doolittle High School."

She relaxed her grip on his hand and the scrapbook. She narrowed her eyes and looked him up and down, cocking her head to one side as she did so. "My, my, my," she said at last. "Won't Harriet be surprised to see you."

"I'm only here for a few days," Jake said, fishing for more information.

"So's she," Charlene said. "And don't think she'll be back for a long, long time after this visit. First time since Donnie died she's been home." She sniffed. "Not that she calls Doolittle home anymore. But at least she slept in her own bed last night."

Jake didn't know what to say. How had he not known

Cinderella Smith & Jones was Harriet? But then, how could he be expected to recognize the woman when he'd known a girl? "She's changed a lot, hasn't she?" Jake asked as he studied another newspaper clipping.

Charlene shook her head. "Her own mother wouldn't know her. She doesn't eat enough to keep a lizard leaping. And her hair looks like she takes a butcher knife to it. She used to have such beautiful hair. But then I guess you must remember her. I remember the two of you went to some dance together."

Jake nodded. He wasn't going to discuss that date with Harriet's mother. And if he stood here much longer, she might recall a young man who'd called so many years ago over a crackling international connection asking for her daughter.

"Funny how I didn't remember that until right this minute," Charlene said, looking sharply at him. "Well, I suppose if your father steps up to the church with Sweet Martha we'll be seeing a bit more of you. No telling what else might come back to me with a bit more time."

Jake made some noncommittal noise. Even if his father married Martha, would they live in this backwater? His father had globe-trotted his entire professional life. Then he recalled the story about growing up on a farm in Oregon. Maybe the Colonel wanted to return to some version of his roots.

He reached for his wallet, drew out a fifty, and paid for the snowman and the ornaments. "Nice talking to you," he said, "but I've got to be going now."

"Come by the house," Charlene said. "I'm sure Harriet would love to see you. I've whipped up a cake or two. I bake a carrot cake that just about everyone who knows me says can't be beat."

"Carrot? That's my favorite," Jake said.

"That doesn't surprise me one bit," Charlene said. "Harriet's supposed to spend the day at the County Hospital with her mother-in-law. Drop by after dinner tonight. She might be back by then."

"I'll see," Jake said. "But thank you."

She nodded. "On the other hand, she might have hightailed it back to New York." She shook her head and closed the photo album. "You never can tell with that girl."

Chapter 24

Modern Medicine

Doolittle had the courthouse, so why the area residents hadn't built the new county general hospital there wasn't clear to Harriet. She followed the directions she'd gotten from her dad before he left for the lumberyard and made the thirty-minute drive without speeding, running a stop sign, or scraping the curb when she parked the Hummer.

Harriet had very little experience with hospitals. Zach had been born in the old clinic in Doolittle, superseded by the shiny glass and steel building she was now entering. She'd never broken a bone or experienced any illness, and neither had her son.

Donnie, until the car accident that killed him, had also steered clear of medical facilities.

Such were the ironies of life and death, Harriet reflected. She asked an elderly woman wearing a coral jacket and a perky smile for directions to the surgery waiting area.

"Yes, dear," the woman said. "Who are you here to see?" She peered at her over a pair of rimless glasses.

"Olivia Smith."

"Oh, dear Olivia," the woman said. "We've been in the same gardening club for years. Simply years. Gardening is so hard on one's knees. I had my right one replaced a few years ago. Nothing to it, dear, so don't worry." She tch-tched as she typed on the computer keyboard. "Unless you have a weak heart, of course. Let's see. She's in surgery now. You may wait on the third floor. No smoking and no cell phones unless you step outside." She waggled her fingers at Harriet.

Harriet nodded. What defined a weak heart? And how did one get lucky and draw the right lot to end up with a strong one? She pondered the question as she moved down the hall toward a bank of elevators. She thought of using her cell phone to locate Zach, who'd traveled to the hospital with Olivia and her sister, but decided to obey the prohibition. He'd probably be in the surgery waiting area or the coffee shop she'd spotted past the elevator.

She punched "3." She must possess a strong heart. Otherwise, how would she have been able to carry on a fairly rational conversation with Jake Porter last night? And this morning, lying in her childhood bed, coming slowly awake and listening to the sounds of her mother and father getting ready for the day, the flood of emotions and memories had threatened to overwhelm her.

The morning after the prom, the morning after the two of them had been as close as a boy and a girl could be, the

morning after the night they'd passed from boy and girl
to man and woman, Harriet had lain in bed, hugging her
pillow to her tummy. Everything good in life had seemed
possible. Her entire life lay in front of her, sunshine on
every single day of the calendar.

She'd gone to school humming, smiling. It was silly for
the school to require seniors to show up after senior prom,
but it was one of those rules they enforced. You couldn't
get your report card if you didn't make an appearance.

Harriet had gone, not to collect her grades, but to see Jake
Porter. To touch his hand, to watch his smile, to delight in
the way his eyes warmed when they looked into hers.

He hadn't been at school.

No one knew where he was.

But her classmates knew more about him than she did.

When she asked around about him, they whispered,
and then openly they began to laugh at her. Just before
noon, when they were to be dismissed, someone pulled
her aside and explained the joke.

Harriet refused to believe it.

Chin quivering, she debated the rumor. The Jake Porter
she knew would not take her to the dance on a dare, try
to score with her on a dare. No, no, no! She screamed the
denial inside her head even as her body remembered the
feel of his touch, the magic of the way he kissed her and
held her tight.

Her classmates had to be wrong.

She'd known most of them all her life. And very few of
them had ever been her friends.

Donnie Smith, though, had always stood by her. She
went to him, and when he confirmed the rumors, she hung
her head.

She didn't cry.

She simply walked all the way to her house from the Smith Place. She didn't care that a rock had worked its way into her Keds. She didn't care when the rock ate a hole through the top layers of her skin. She didn't flinch when she finally removed the shoe and found a bloody mess.

Nothing mattered anymore.

Yet she knew they could all be wrong. Only if Jake Porter confirmed his guilt would she believe he had acted on a dare.

But she'd never seen him again.

Until last night.

The elevator doors opened and closed and opened and closed and opened and closed.

"Hey, Mom." Zach stepped through the silvery doors and out in front of her. He waved a hand up and down in front of her face. "Yoo-hoo, it's me, your son, remember?"

Harriet stared at him, absorbing the sight of her son, his broad shoulders, his dark eyes, his shock of dark hair. Zach was the living, breathing image of Jake.

"Zach," she said. "Sorry, lost in my head there."

He grinned. "Yeah, you do that a lot. Don't worry. I'm used to it."

"How's your . . . Olivia?"

"Gran?" He motioned with his thumb toward the elevator. "She's in recovery now. They told me that could last for a while so I thought I'd take a walk."

She grinned. "You mean find a snack?"

He grinned back.

"There's a coffee shop down this hall."

"Yeah, it's not bad," he said. "They've got decent pizza."

"Is that what you had for breakfast?" She fell into step beside him.

"Aunt Amelia made scrambled eggs and biscuits. From scratch." He held open the door to the coffee shop, and Harriet passed through. "That was practically the middle of the night, though."

He ordered pepperoni and sausage. Harriet settled on a cup of coffee.

"How was the bed-and-breakfast?" he asked before diving into the pizza.

"I didn't stay there," she said.

He quirked an eyebrow.

Harriet almost blushed. "I stopped to see my parents and one thing led to another." *One thing led to another. Right*, she mocked herself inside her head. That was what was happening with Jake Porter until she'd found the guts to drive away. Guts? It was either the bravest thing or the stupidest action she'd taken in a long, long time.

"I guess that made them happy," Zach said.

"I guess so," Harriet said. Her dad—yes. As to her mother, she could never tell. She'd never understood her or been able to read her feelings or determine if she had any under the constant stream of words, words, words.

Harriet sighed and stared into her weak cup of coffee. She'd have to go back to the Verandah. They did a decent steak and their coffee was almost as good as her house-keeper brewed.

She'd taken her bag when she left her parents' house that morning. Staying there put her on edge, and once her brother and his wife arrived with their twins, she couldn't imagine sleeping in her old room turned nursery. Why they hadn't put the crib in Edward's room she couldn't imagine, unless he and Honey had decided between them that children shouldn't cling.

That would be the sort of thing her brother would decree.

Harriet reached for a spoon and stirred her coffee, even though she had put neither cream nor sugar into it.

"She beat me two out of three games," Zach said.

Harriet looked her question, and then realized what he was talking about. "Olivia. Chess."

He nodded. "She's pretty good." He chewed another few mouthfuls of pizza, and then wiped his mouth with a paper napkin. "I wonder if she'd like to live in New York."

Harriet felt only alarm at his statement. "What makes you say that?"

He shrugged.

She took a sip of coffee.

"I think she's lonely here."

"She has her garden club," Harriet said, thinking of the lady at the front desk. "And her sister. Amelia would hate to lose her. She has her brother here, too."

He nodded, leaned back, and patted his flat stomach. "Yeah. It stinks, doesn't it? I mean, being scattered all over. Not that I want to live here," he said quickly. "I don't mind visiting in the summer."

"Does she still have your horse?"

He nodded.

"I think she's happy," Harriet said.

He shrugged. "You're not around here much."

Harriet eyed her son. "Suggesting I don't know enough to draw a conclusion?"

He glanced across the almost empty coffee shop, then back at her. "Yeah, I guess that's right."

"Good," Harriet said. "Don't back down when you believe in what you're saying."

He grinned, even though he looked a bit shocked. "You're a funny kind of mom."

"Thank you, Zach," she said, feeling more proud of that comment than so many other attributes she'd garnered.

"Maybe I'll get some dessert," he said, and loped over to the counter.

Harriet watched him, her heart overfilling. No matter how many bad decisions she might have made in her life, giving birth to her son continued to be one of the most precious blessings of all. She wouldn't have traded him for anything. If it meant she had to endure a boatload of grief once she had her attorney contact Jake Porter, she'd live through it. As much as she didn't want to share her son, she knew his birth father had a right to know the same joy she'd known, the same worries, the same fears, and the same pride. Having a child was such a precious gift.

Jake might have been adamant last night when he'd said he had no plans to have kids, but surely, once he knew about Zach, he'd change. She had to believe that.

"Want some?" Zach held out a paper cup overflowing with soft-serve vanilla ice cream.

"No, thanks," Harriet said.

He shrugged and attended to devouring the contents. After he had finished, he said, "They had some decent-looking cake, but I'm saving myself for Granlene's. Nobody but nobody makes a carrot cake like she does."

Harriet hoped her guilt didn't show on her face. She'd

had to flush the toilet three times to get that darned piece of cake to disappear. "Do you want to go over there tonight after we leave the hospital?"

"Okay." He collected their dishes and took them away to a bus station atop a trash can.

Things would turn out for the best. That, too, Harriet had to believe. She'd stop to see her parents, but make sure she got away. She really ought to call the Inn and make sure they were holding their rooms. She dug in her purse, pulled out her cell phone, and lifted it to her ear.

"Mom," Zach said, pointing to the phone.

She rolled her eyes, but didn't dial information. "Tell you what," she said. "You go back upstairs to the waiting room and I'll step outside. I just have to check on our reservations."

He nodded. He went up the elevator, and then Harriet walked back to the front of the hospital. She stepped through the double glass doors to another day full of bright sunshine. Taking in a deep breath, she moved a few yards away from the entrance, lifted her phone, and started to punch in "4–1–1."

"I was hoping I'd find you here," said a voice she knew all too well, from just behind her shoulder.

Harriet lowered her phone, turned, and looked straight into the dark eyes of Jake Porter. The gold flecks were even lighter today, illuminating his face in a way she remembered not only from last night, but from a lifetime ago. Harriet blinked. What was she doing thinking about his eyes now? *I was hoping I'd find you here.* That sentence told her that he'd figured out who she was. She tucked her phone back into her purse, wondering to what point his discoveries had gotten. "You were?"

"Now I can't say anything because even though I thought you seemed familiar, I didn't recognize you, so how could I expect you to recognize me?" He smiled, his face alive, his eyes warm and inviting. "I'm the Jake Porter you knew in high school."

Harriet nodded. She couldn't tell him she'd known that all along. He seemed glad to have been reunited. He looked downright happy to be standing there outside the County Hospital, smiling into her eyes. But not to reveal her knowledge was another lie.

He slapped the side of his head. "Now don't wound my ego. You do remember me? You did my shop project for me, well, practically. And we went to the graduation dance together." His voice lowered when he said those last few words.

"Jake Porter," she said. "That Jake Porter. Of course!"

"Whew," he said, grinning. "I don't think I've changed a bit but it is true that you have. You were cute then," he said, "but now you're amazing."

"Thank you," she said, finally smiling back at him. "Especially for saying I was cute in high school. I think we both know that's more than kind."

"I always speak the truth," Jake said.

"Of course," Harriet said, wondering why he'd come to the hospital, worrying over how long it would be before Zach decided to take a walk outside, and marveling at how pleased she was to see Jake Porter, all complications aside. She couldn't help but glance over her shoulder toward the hospital doors. She had no idea how she would handle Zach and Jake running into each other. What was she going to do?

He'd come looking for her.

But what did that mean?

"How's your mother-in-law?" He sounded concerned.

"In recovery," she said. "Thank you for asking."

"Your mother is an interesting woman," Jake said. "To be frank, I haven't thought about high school in a long, long time. But when I was in the shop this morning, I remembered as clear as day you telling me that you wanted to bite off your mother's wagging finger."

Harriet laughed and blushed at the same time. If he remembered that random comment, how much more clearly must he recall the evening of the prom? Or had he forgotten all about it? "She is unique."

Jake grinned. "You've grown tactful as well as beautiful."

"Now don't start puffing me up with compliments," Harriet said, pleased nonetheless.

He leaned a bit closer and skimmed one finger over the back of her hand. "They'd all be true," he said, his eyes darkening, the golden flecks glimmering in contrast.

She pulled back. "I need to check on Olivia," she said. "Thanks for coming by."

He reached for the door. "Do you mind some company?"

Harriet could have dropped through the concrete walkway. Here was Jake Porter, the man who'd haunted her dreams for sixteen years, asking to spend time with her. And she had to turn him away. Today was about supporting her mother-in-law, not about setting her son's life and this man's life into an uproar. She didn't step toward the door. "How about later? Hospitals are so . . . so . . ." she trailed off, having no idea what she meant to say about hospitals.

"Sterile?" He didn't drop his hand.

She nodded.

"Antiseptic?"

"That, too."

"Useful?"

"You could say that."

He grinned. "None of which are terms that apply to you, thank goodness. Want to have dinner with me tonight? Assuming, of course, you're able to take a break from the hospital."

"Dinner?"

"Appetizer, soup, salad, entrée, dessert. Yes, dinner."

"I'm not sure," she said, tempted to say yes but wondering how to arrange matters to make it possible. And safe. Yes, safe for her secrets. She glanced over her shoulder again.

"Tell you what," he said. "Hand me your cell and I'll punch my number in, and if you want to have dinner with me tonight, call me. I can see you're anxious to get back inside."

"I am? I mean, yes, I am."

He quirked an eyebrow at her. "Either you're anxious or you're afraid some boogeyman is coming through that door to get you. You've looked behind yourself more times than I can count."

"I have not!" But of course she had. She slapped her cell phone into his hand. His fingers moved over the face of it, and he took her hand in his as he returned the phone.

He tipped her chin upward. Looking stern, he said, "Call me. I can understand why you ran away last night, because I was a jerk to try for a one-night stand. But tonight is different." His voice lightened. "Hey, it's Jake and Harriet, catching up on old times."

She tried to smile. He bent and kissed her on the lips and then walked away before she could react.

Down the sidewalk, he stopped and turned. "If you run away again, I'll find you. Everyone in Doolittle does know everybody else's business!"

Chapter 25

Sometimes the Early Bird Gets the Grief

Martha rose early that morning. It was a good thing because it took her twice as long to dress as she kept pausing to gaze at the diamond ring Ted had surprised her with after dinner.

Martha applied a soft pink lipstick and smiled at her reflection. She had never been what she or anyone else considered pretty, but this morning she felt downright pleased with the whole wide world, including the way she looked.

And why shouldn't she be? She hummed a few bars of "White Christmas." A miracle in the form of Ted Porter had come into her life, and she wasn't so stubborn or too stupid to accept it.

She headed to the kitchen, wanting to get a head start on the day before Abbie began crabbing at her. With Ted wanting to look around Lake Doolittle, and other guests expected that afternoon, she hoped to ease the inevitable tension the announcement of her planned absence would create.

The lights were already on, the oven going, the kettle atop the stove bubbling away. Martha sighed but put the smile back on her face. "Good morning, Abbie," she said.

Her sister eyed her balefully. "And what's got you so cheerful this morning?" She slapped a pot holder against her open palm, obviously ready for battle.

"Why not be?" Martha reached for an apron, noted the stains on it, and put it back on the hook. She crossed to their walk-in pantry and picked up a new Christmas motif apron. She tied it around her and started a pot of coffee.

Abbie sniffed. "I guess that old one wasn't good enough for you."

"Not anymore," Martha said. She yanked it off the hook and wadded it up. Then she tossed it into the trash. "We're able to treat ourselves nicely so there's no reason to act like we're not worth it."

Her sister glanced downward. "A few reminders of hard work don't spoil a good apron. Besides, we need every penny we make. Speaking of which, Ms. High and Mighty Smith and her son did not show up last night."

Martha eyed the phone. It was too early to call Charlene Rogers and ask if Harriet was over there. And Olivia didn't need anyone bothering her when she was off to the hospital. "I'm sure they're fine."

Abbie checked the oven thermometer. "And so are we because they guaranteed their reservation with her American Express. So we get paid no matter where they spent the night."

"Oh, Abbie, that seems so harsh," Martha said. "It would be for the best if they did spend time with their family."

Abbie glared at her. "You've lost your mind if you think we're not charging them. Who says they're with family? She might have decided it was just too much trouble to come see her mother-in-law and not bothered canceling the reservation."

Martha perched on a stool and pulled a shopping list pad and pencil toward her. She bent her head over it and drew a heart-shaped smiley face. "You sure know how to spoil a person's good mood."

"I suppose it's that Mr. Porter who's responsible for your cheery face."

Martha added a cupid's arrow to the page. "We had a very nice dinner," she said. "We brought you your favorite, too, but you were asleep."

Abbie's face softened. "A petite filet?"

Martha nodded. "Medium rare. Just the way you like it."

Her sister cast a longing eye at the refrigerator. "Well, thank you. I suppose I'll have a taste of it for lunch. That is, if we ever get a minute to call our own today."

"I'm sure we won't be that busy," Martha said. As soon as the words were out of her mouth, she wished she could swallow them back. Her sister hated being told anything was easier or simpler or less burdensome than she declared it to be.

Abbie leaned back against the counter next to the oven. She crossed her arms over her spare chest. "You're such a perky optimist. It's just a little hard to take when I'm the one left to do all the work while you go gallivanting. I bet you're planning on disappearing today, no doubt with that man, and with the St. Cyrs arriving this afternoon, to boot."

Martha quit doodling and looked her sister straight in the eye. There would never be the right time or the perfect place or the appropriately softened mood. Not with what she had to say to Abbie. "That's right. I am going to spend some time away today. Time with Mr.—with Ted Porter."

"So it's Ted now?"

"Yes, it is. And we—"

The phone rang. Martha reached for the portable. The caller ID showed a long distance number she didn't recognize so she assumed it was a reservation call. "Schoolhouse Inn. This is Martha. How may I help you today?"

"Martha, Jake Porter."

She tried to keep her expression noncommittal. Across the room Abbie was loading two pans of muffins into the oven. "Yes, Jake?"

"I hope I didn't cause any concern last night when I didn't return. Of course I'll pay for the night. It was late and I didn't want to call and wake you. I will be staying there for the rest of my reservation."

"Oh, good," Martha said, wondering why he'd phoned her and not Ted. Or perhaps he had. It felt too awkward for her to ask.

"I have other plans for today but I'll be there this evening," he said. "Please give my best to my father, and you two have a nice day."

"Of course." Martha's tongue felt tied in a figure eight. She probably sounded like an idiot. All she wanted was for Ted's son to accept her and not give his father any grief over their getting married. But how to convey that was beyond her, especially with Abbie watching her from across the room. "I mean, I'm sure we will and thank you and you have a good day, too." Whew. She hung up and dabbed at her forehead with her brand-new apron.

"He had a lot to say," Abbie said. "I hope he didn't give you any trouble over paying for an unslept-in bed."

"Not at all," Martha said, somewhat loftily. "He's a very well-mannered young man."

"Well, he's too young for you by half," Abbie said, and laughed.

"Maybe you should go back to bed and get up again," Martha said. Her sister was crabbier than usual.

"Maybe I should." Abbie turned the heat off the teakettle. "This thing's almost boiled dry." She sighed. "Kind of like me, I reckon."

It made Martha sad to hear her sister say that, even though it was pretty much true. "People can change, you know."

Abbie made a face. "You mean the way you've dragged our little bed-and-breakfast into the Internet age?"

"Good example." Martha took a deep breath. "I'm changing." Her heart beat so fast, she wondered if it would trip on itself.

"Is that right?" Abbie opened a cupboard and rooted around on a shelf. "You've got something else new to go with that fancy apron?" She turned around holding a cake stand.

"A-a fiancé," she managed to say after a few stammering starts.

Abbie stared at her face and then at Martha's left hand. "Well, I'll be."

"Ted asked me to marry him and I said yes." There, she'd said the words.

"A man who's been in town less than a day?" Abbie whisked flour, sugar, and oil out onto the kitchen island. "He buys you one dinner and you're his for life?" She plunked a mixing bowl next to her baking ingredients. "Have you gone and lost your mind?"

"I think I'm just beginning to find it," Martha said. The cat scratched at the back door, and she walked over and let it in, daring Abbie with a look to say a word against her. "Besides, I've known him for some time now."

Abbie paused in measuring flour. "So that's what you've been doing sneaking off to Little Rock? You ought to be ashamed of yourself, at your age."

Martha blushed. "I didn't know how to tell you."

Flour sprayed into the air as Abbie dumped several cupfuls into the bowl. "Did you meet him at Mrs. Halifax's house?"

She was determined to be honest with her sister. "We met online."

"In line at a store?" Abbie stared. "You started talking to a stranger and the next thing you know you're getting m-m-married?" Even the word was hard for her to say.

"Online," Martha said. "On the Internet. We met over eBay."

"Now you're talking Greek," Abbie said. "And I've gone and lost count of how many cups I've measured. See if this cake isn't ruined as well as everything else."

"Nothing is ru—" Martha shut up. "I know it's hard to believe. Sometimes I have to pinch myself. You know how I love to collect Blue Willow plates. He had one for sale on eBay and I wrote to him about it and we started talking online and one thing led to another."

"A man who collects plates?" Abbie shook her head. "He looks like he's made of sterner stuff than that."

"It was his mother's and he wasn't attached to it so he was selling it," Martha explained, even though it felt to her that any way she tried to spell things out for Abbie, her sister would refuse to understand. "He knew he'd be moving so he was clearing things up." She sat back down on her stool by the counter. "He's very neat and organized."

Abbie rolled her eyes. She'd smudged flour on her chin.

Martha started doodling again. She'd meant to get started on chores, but nothing else would get done until she and Abbie had finished this discussion. "Don't you want me to be happy?"

"You're not telling me you haven't been happy all these years. I know better. Why, the whole town calls you Sweet Martha." She put her hands on her hips, spreading more flour. "If you were so miserable, how could that be?"

"Oh, Abbie, I wasn't miserable, but I didn't know how much happier I could be." She stood up and waltzed over to the island. "Ted's so wonderful. We talk and talk and talk and he makes me laugh. I feel like a teenager, as silly as that sounds. I'm getting a chance to . . ." She trailed off, unable to put into words what it meant to her to experience life as she'd never known it. And she sure couldn't say anything to her sister about how it made her feel all quivery and alive when Ted kissed her. Martha blushed. "To live life as I've never experienced it before," she finished.

Abbie held her head down, straight over her mixing bowl. Her jaw worked as if it held a wad of Red Man tobacco, something Martha knew her sister wouldn't touch with a ten-foot pole. Abbie wielded a wooden spoon, and then to Martha's horror, tears spilled from Abbie's eyes and dropped into the bowl.

Abbie tossed the spoon into the bowl and dashed at her face with the back of her hand. "Now look what you've gone and made me do," she said. "We'll have to get by with the cookies and scones because I don't have the heart to mix another cake right now." She yanked off her apron just as the cat jumped onto the counter. "You get down from there," she cried, and swatted it with the apron.

The cat dove for the door.

"If you're upset over what I told you," Martha said, letting the cat outside, "I wish you'd take it out on me."

Abbie looked at her. "Well, I hope you come to your senses before you make a mistake you'll regret for the rest of your life."

"I have," Martha said. "I know exactly what I'm doing!"

Abbie nodded. "So when's the wedding?"

Martha took a deep breath. "New Year's Eve."

Abbie's jaw dropped. "*This* New Year's Eve?"

Martha nodded.

"And where will you live?" Abbie asked.

"We're not sure yet."

"Well, don't think he's moving in here." Abbie tossed the apron onto the back of a chair. "I won't have a man bossing me around."

"He's not bossy," Martha said.

Abbie raised her eyebrows so high they looked like they'd go into orbit. "Wait until after the wedding. All men change. Remember what Mother told us."

"If she hadn't been married, neither one of us would be here," Martha said. "Good gracious, why do you have to make everything so difficult?"

"Me?" Abbie slapped a hand against the top of the island. "What about you causing a ruckus and never thinking of anyone other than yourself these days? I knew something had come over you but I never thought for a minute it was a man."

"You make it sound like a man is worse than a Martian."

Abbie snorted. "I've got no use for either species."

"I've never heard you be this harsh," Martha said. "You're good friends with a lot of men. Why, Deacon Martinson and you have played on the same bridge team for years."

"That's different," Abbie said.

Martha shrugged. She didn't want to argue the point. "I'll do the rooms now," she said. "The timer's about to go off for those muffins. And I'm sorry about the cake. If you want I'll make one later."

"Later?" Abbie eyed her with suspicion. "I suppose that means after you and Mr. Porter go off on whatever it is you're planning to do."

Martha rose. "Yes, that is what I mean."

Martha dusted her hands. "If you go through with this, you and I are going to have to sit down and have a long talk about our business." Her mouth quivered as she spoke.

Martha went to her and put her arms around her. It was like hugging a board, but she did it anyway. "Aw, Abbie, I don't want you to be sad," she said. "You'll always be my sister."

The kitchen timer buzzed. Abbie broke free. "I'd better be getting those muffins out," she said, and turned away.

Chapter 26

Family Ties

With Harriet occupied at the hospital and nothing else to attend to, Jake decided he might as well join his father and Martha and the real estate agent showing them around. He met up with them on the square.

"Hop in," called a woman who introduced herself as Mrs. Ball. She was behind the wheel of a vintage Cadillac. Martha occupied the middle of the front seat and his father sat beside her. The agent craned her head around and watched Jake as he climbed into the backseat. "My, if you're not the spitting image of your father."

Jake nodded. That observation wasn't exactly news to him. He stretched out his legs and prepared himself for a long afternoon.

"You missed our tour of Doolittle Village," she said, whipping the car into reverse. "I've been telling your parents that it's one of the country's premier destinations for retirement-age couples. Why, we have people moving here from all over. I sold a house to a man and a woman from Duluth just last week."

Jake started to interrupt the agent to clarify the family relationships, but decided to save his breath.

Martha stared at Mrs. Ball. "Patty, you know good and well I am not anybody's mother so of course we're not Jake's parents. And do you think I care what someone from Duluth likes? I've lived in Doolittle my whole life and if I hadn't loved it, I could have left any time I pleased. I stayed because it's my home and there's no place like it."

Martha's stock shot up.

"I agree with Martha," his father said. "Just looking around inside that development brought back the feelings I used to have when I'd walk onto a new base, and damn if it didn't look exactly like the last one I'd left."

"I thought you wanted to live on base," Jake said, leaning forward. "I thought it was Ariel who insisted on moving out of military housing and living off the economy." His parents had argued the point every time they'd been transferred.

"I did, but that was because it would have given you better structure in your life while I was away," his father said.

"Oh," Jake said, which was pretty much all he could think of to say to that revelation.

"The situation is different now," his father said. He brushed Martha on the shoulder and smiled. "No need to curl up inside a cookie-cutter world."

Jake sat back. Maybe no matter how old one got, understanding a parent never came easy.

"There is a lovely property out along county line," Mrs. Ball said. "It runs alongside the Smith Place."

"How big?" Ted asked.

"The house is only a cottage, I'm afraid, but if you want land, it's sitting on ten acres. With a pond. The Wallaces moved to Florida, and they'd love to have it off their hands." Mrs. Ball swung a sharp right. "We're headed there now."

"Ten acres sounds like a lot to keep up," Martha said, glancing sideways at Jake's father.

"It's only minutes from Doolittle," Mrs. Ball said. "Cra—I mean, your sister won't have far to come to visit you."

"Let's take a look," Jake's father said. "I'd enjoy walking out my door and not seeing the neighbors."

This from a man who'd spent his life crammed into a cockpit. Jake wondered if he'd ever get to know his father.

"Mrs. Ball, do you live within Doolittle Village?" Jake's father asked.

"Oh, not me," she said. "I'll never retire. I love what I do. The Village is perfect for people who want to settle down and relax. Like you and Martha. It's your time to take it easy."

Jake's father made a noise that sounded pretty close to a snort. "We haven't got one foot in the grave, you know."

Mrs. Ball laughed. "I'm saying you've earned the right to kick back and hit a few rounds of golf every morning."

"That would kill me." Jake said.

His father nodded. "Me, too, son. Nine holes every so often is one thing; retreating from life is quite another. Let's hope we like this ten acres."

Martha looked out the window. "We're just passing the Smith Place now."

"I went to high school with a Smith kid," Jake said.

"That would have to be Donnie," Martha said. "You didn't get to stay very long in school here, did you?"

Jake said nothing. Ted shook his head. "Chalk that one up to me," he said.

"What happened to Donnie?" Jake asked.

"He's dead," Mrs. Ball said. "He and his daddy both, killed in a car crash. It liked to have killed Miz Olivia. But at least she has her grandson, when that nutty mother of his lets him visit. Do you know she's in town now?"

"Harriet? Yes, I do," Martha said.

Jake's gut clenched. She'd given her name as Smith. He heard the silky voice in his head. *My husband's dead.* Harriet married Donnie Smith? That made no sense at all.

Mrs. Ball laughed. "Why, of course you know that. I'm sure the only place good enough for her to stay is the Schoolhouse Inn. She's too high and mighty to spend the night with her own family." She sighed. "There was always something a little bit different about that girl."

"Now, Mrs. Ball," Martha said, "it's not right to judge what we don't understand."

Jake leaned forward. "Harriet stayed at her parents' house last night."

Martha swung around to face him. "Well, praise the Lord," she said. "Everyone needs peace in their family."

Jake didn't smile.

"And how do we know that?" Mrs. Ball asked. She pulled off the road onto a gravel lane strewn with pine needles from the trees crowding the passage.

Jake said nothing.

"Well, why shouldn't he? You know what we always say," Martha said. "There are no secrets in Doolittle."

Mrs. Ball turned down a lane overhung with branches. Jake looked right and left, wondering whether it was true there weren't any secrets in Doolittle. From either direction he saw no break in the trees.

"It's about a mile to the house," Mrs. Ball said. "What a trek to get the mail or your paper. Of course, if you want to be all alone, it's got that going for it."

His father nodded, a slight smile on his face.

The tires crunched over the drive. At last they came to a clearing large enough for several cars to park. Beyond that, surrounded by several sheltering trees, sat a small house. The porch that ran along the front and sides appeared to be almost as big as the house. Two oversize rocking chairs sat on the porch.

Nothing could have been more different from Jake's beachfront penthouse condo in Marina del Rey. He half expected his father to suggest they turn around without getting out of the car, but something about that hint of a smile warned Jake that his father would get out and look around.

"Isn't this nice," Martha said, sliding out of the car. His father held out a hand to assist her, and she smiled at him as she accepted his hand.

Jake blinked and glanced away. His shoulders tightened. Watching them made him so damned uncomfortable. Yet he would've performed the same courtesy for a female companion. He'd learned the behavior expected from what his father termed a "gentleman and an officer" at an early age. So it wasn't the Colonel offering his hand to Martha that bothered Jake. It was the way the two of them made those goo-goo eyes at each other.

He'd handed plenty of women in and out of automobiles, but he'd yet to have it mean anything beyond a simple physical transaction.

Jake kicked at a piece of gravel. Sex was like that, too. He wanted something; she wanted something. They agreed to achieve mutual satisfaction and they were able to enjoy the pleasure for as long as the sensations and the afterglow lasted. A guy helped a lady out of a car; she alighted gracefully. It was all part of the dance of male and female.

But this gazing at each other as if the very touch reached into their souls was something Jake couldn't grasp. He had lots of clients who made buckets of money writing about what Jake was witnessing between his father and Martha.

To him, though, that kind of emotion was spoken in a language he'd never learned.

He kicked again, and a spurt of rocks scattered dust. Who needed it anyway? Feelings came and went. Lovers loved and moved on, or were pushed away if they got too demanding, if they wanted more than Jake was prepared to give.

His father held out his hand to Martha and the two of them walked toward the house, talking to each other and smiling as they looked around.

Another rock followed the prior one.

He couldn't remember one time he'd seen Ariel and his father look that much of a couple. But he'd be willing to wager there was a time the two of them had been that much in love with each other. And in their time, that meant they got married.

But at his age, his father had no reason either cultural

or professional to acquire a wife. But maybe reason had nothing to do with it.

"They are cute together, aren't they?" Mrs. Ball's voice broke into his thoughts.

Jake nodded but didn't reply. He hated to admit it even to himself, but what he felt resembled jealousy. But how ridiculous was that? He enjoyed being footloose and fancy-free.

"So I understand you're from Los Angeles," Mrs. Ball said. "We could use some more men in Doolittle. Single men, I mean. Why, after my first husband, Mr. Clark, passed on, I had to go all the way to El Dorado to meet Mr. Ball." She glanced sideways at him. "Los Angeles is just so big and people aren't neighborly the way they are in Doolittle."

"I like it," Jake said. "It suits me." And it did. Everybody was from someplace else. His penthouse occupied the top floor of the beachfront high-rise. He could go home from his office, drive into the underground parking, take the elevator to the top floor, and never speak to a soul. After all day on the phone or in recording sessions or with the media or babysitting clients at lunch, and with his late evenings booked many nights with club visits, he relished the quiet and the isolation.

"Well, if you decide to look for a vacation home here, just whip me an e-mail. In Doolittle, ask anyone and they will tell you, I am Real Estate."

Glancing toward the house, Jake saw that the Colonel and Martha were taking the two rocking chairs for a test drive. "They look at home already," he said, his comment coming out as a surprise to him.

She smiled, no doubt counting her commission. They climbed the few steps leading to the porch. His father had an expression on his face Jake didn't recognize. He studied him as he approached, puzzling out what seemed so unfamiliar.

Contentment.

His posture was as erect as ever, but sitting in that big chair, rocking slowly, his hands folded over his chest, his father seemed at peace.

"Ready to see the interior?" Mrs. Ball asked, jangling a ring of keys.

"You go on in," his father said. "We'd like to speak to Jake."

Mrs. Ball unlocked the door, curiosity evident on her face and in the way she cast one long look back at them before stepping into the house.

Jake glanced from his father to Martha. Something glittered on her left hand. He looked more closely.

She hadn't been wearing that diamond ring last night at dinner.

His father rose from the rocker and stood beside Martha. He smiled at her and at Jake. "We didn't want to wait any longer to tell you. Martha has done me the honor to say she'll marry me."

His father couldn't have looked any happier. Or more solemn. Both emotions seemed to fit the occasion, Jake realized. He stretched out his hand to his father. "I'm happy for you both." And he was.

His father ignored his hand and hugged him. "Thank you, son," he said. He stepped back, cleared his throat, and glanced down at Martha.

Jake smiled at her. "May I kiss the bride-to-be?"

Martha colored up. She nodded, and Jake leaned over and gave her a hug and a kiss on the cheek.

"When's the wedding?" he asked.

"New Year's Eve," they said in unison.

"This year?"

"No reason to waste time," his father said.

No reason to rush things, either. Jake thought of Abbie. "Have you told your sister?"

"This morning," Martha said. "She's . . ."

"In shock?" Jake said.

"Yes," Martha said. "But life is meant to be lived. And I know my sister. Once she chews over this news, she'll end up thinking it was her idea in the first place."

"That's fine by me," his father said. "I don't want our happiness to upset anyone." He looked straight at Jake.

Jake returned the direct gaze of his father. "I may have to return to L.A. and come back by New Year's, but I'll be here for your wedding. That is, if you want me."

"Want you?" Both his father and Martha threw their hands up. "We wouldn't have it any other way."

Mrs. Ball popped outside. "I couldn't help but overhear. Congratulations! Best wishes! Another wedding in Doolittle." She danced over and gave everyone a hug. Jake wouldn't have been surprised if she wasn't already planning who she would tell first.

All of a sudden, images of Harriet filled his mind. He'd enjoy sharing the news with her. The time it took them to traipse through the house, inspect the backyard that sloped down to a stream and pond, drive to town and pick up the other car, and finally make it to the Inn seemed interminable.

Jake checked his cell phone three times to make sure he hadn't missed a call from Harriet.

Not that she would have called this soon.

Not that it mattered either way.

Not that he was fooling himself for a second.

He wanted her to call.

He wanted to take her to dinner.

He wanted to get to know the Harriet of today and listen to her voice and watch the expression on her face as they caught up on what she'd been doing between eighteen and the present. He wanted to learn what experiences had changed her from the admittedly geeky girl to the sophisticated babe of today.

He wanted to see her smile.

More than that, he realized, lacing on his running shoes, determined to go for a run long enough to beat the tension out of his body. He wanted to see her smile at him, with him, and because of him.

Jake shook his head, laughed at himself, and headed outside. He hit the street at a steady lope. He'd been doing PT, as the military referred to exercise, since he was able to tag along with any kid willing to put up with him. Once he discovered the joys of running alone, though, he never looked for a companion to join him.

Running, for Jake, was the perfect thinking time. And on days or nights when his brain had been far too active and he simply wanted to forget it all, running also served as an excellent antidote. Concentrating on each step, each stride, each breath, he could surge forward, literally leaving his thoughts behind him, becoming one with the pavement or the track or the grass.

That was the kind of run he wanted this day. What he needed right now was that mind-blocking union of heart and lungs and muscles doing the work and giving his thoughts a well-deserved break.

And that's what he got, too. A long time later, he returned, walking the last several blocks to cool down. As he approached the sidewalk of the Inn, a pickup truck slowed. He heard a tap of a horn and glanced at the truck and saw that the driver was the man who'd given him a ride that morning. Mike the veterinarian, Jake recalled. The man waved and turned into the Inn's driveway. The passenger door opened and a teenage girl hopped out.

The driver's window lowered. "How's your stay so far?"

Thinking of Harriet, Jake smiled. "Better than I expected."

Mike nodded. "The place grows on you."

Kristen walked around the front of the truck. "I beg to differ with that statement. I can't wait to get out. Hi, I'm Kristen."

Jake glanced from the girl to the man he figured was her dad. He guessed from the lack of reaction that her complaint was a familiar one. "Hi, Kristen. Are you going to college soon?"

"Not soon enough," she said.

"I've got to run," Mike said. "Call me when you're off work, Kristen."

She nodded. Her dad drove off. Jake walked beside her up the sidewalk.

"Where are you from and what do you do?" she asked.

"Los Angeles," he said. "I'm in the music management business."

"Cool. Did you have to go to law school to be a manager?"

"Some people do. I didn't. I have an MBA. That's a master's—"

"Oh, I know all about that degree," Kristen said, a note of scorn in her voice. "It's easy."

She must have realized how rude that sounded. "Oops, I apologize. I'm always speaking first and thinking second. At least that's what my dad tries to tell me."

"Are you planning on law school?" Jake was curious to find such determination in the teenager. He didn't remember anyone from his DHS class who spoke of becoming a lawyer. Hell, half of them hadn't even planned to attend community college.

"That's my intermediate range goal," she said, climbing the steps. "Then I plan to go into the Foreign Service and later work in the State Department. That's where the political action is."

"That's . . ." He had started to say "interesting," but what a lame word to attach to this caliber of goal.

She nodded. "Go ahead. Say it. Everyone else does. 'Oh, Kristen, how interesting. But when will you have time to date and get married and have babies?' I'm surrounded by morons!"

Jake laughed. "I was only going to use the word 'interesting.' Not the rest of that, believe me. You wouldn't hear it from me."

The girl glanced up at him. "You're a lot like my dad. He doesn't say any of that negative stuff, either. It's my mom, mainly, and my stepdad, which is pretty hypocritical of them. I mean, my mom's a lawyer and her husband is in state politics and it's not like she didn't have babies." She made a face. "Not that she would have if my dad hadn't made her have me."

Jake wondered about that statement, but what could he say to that? Folks around here sure were open about their family's private business, in a way he wasn't used to at all. His clients who got their personal lives spread out in screaming tabloid headlines did that as a matter of publicity. In this town, it was different. Not only did they all seem to know the good, the bad, and the not-always-pretty, they seemed to care for one another.

They were on the porch, standing outside the door. She didn't seem to be in a rush to get to work, and Jake enjoyed talking with her, so he leaned against the porch railing. It was a little bit weird to be told he was like someone's dad, but he tried to take that in stride. He'd never wanted to be a parent, but he could see having a bright kid like Kristen would be both challenging and rewarding. "When do you go to college?"

She made another face. "I have the rest of this year and next in high school, unless I can convince my dad to make a real push for the school to let me graduate early. I'm the smartest kid in my class and it's so dumb that I have to sit there when I'm ready for college."

Jake smiled. "Will he do that?"

"We're negotiating," she said. "Speaking of which, part of my strategy is to earn money, so I'd better hop to it." She held out a hand. "It was nice talking with you."

He shook hands. "Same here."

She whisked inside.

His cell rang. Harriet? Jake yanked the phone from the pocket of his running jacket, fumbled with it, and dropped it on the porch. It hit the floorboards, clattered, and bounced down two steps before coming to a stop. Jake snatched it up just as the battery came detached.

"Piece of junk," Jake said out loud. The face of the phone showed solid black. He snapped the battery into place and hit the power on key.

Nothing.

He said a few choice words. Why hadn't he asked for her number? What if she didn't check in at the Inn? *Good thinking, Porter*, he said to himself. He walked back onto the porch and stood there, hands on his hips. The air was pretty darned cold, but Jake was still warm from his run, so he took a seat in the porch swing and considered his options. He'd feel like an idiot calling her parents, but if it took that to track her down, he'd do it.

The last of the afternoon sun was slipping behind the horizon. It was late enough that the call could have been from Harriet, knowing she could leave the hospital.

Or it could have been from a client. Or God forbid, Ariel, in the throes of another fit of creative hysterics.

He had to quit guessing and figure it out. Or forget about the phone, and shower, change, and track down Harriet. He smiled. After all, he was in Doolittle.

Jake jumped up from the swing, whistling a cheerful tune. Running into Harriet again made this trip to Doolittle worth it. He didn't understand why, but he wanted to see more of her. She was a beautiful babe, a sexy and appealing woman he'd been ready to take to bed in a motel only last night, but she was more than that, too.

She was Harriet, the girl from high school who hadn't fit in, the girl from high school who had gotten under his skin in a way no woman had since.

Hell, the first time he'd had sex was with Harriet.

Jake stopped whistling.

How embarrassing was that? He'd been so totally ignorant, so clueless, and to top it off, he hadn't used the condom he'd stuffed under his cummerbund when he'd gotten ready for the prom. Why in the world would she want to see him again? No wonder she'd stranded him at the motel last night.

But she'd been equally innocent. It was so long ago he scarcely remembered the details. Why she'd married Donnie so soon after graduation remained a mystery, but it was one he could solve by asking her. Besides, it didn't matter now. Past was past.

Given the sophistication of her life, she'd grown up sexually as much as he had.

Jake grinned. He hoped to find out if that was true.

But he was happy that if he got to that point, he would do so knowing it was Harriet, his first girl, he held in his arms and not Ms. Cinderella Smith & Jones.

Chapter 27

It Was the Best of Evenings

Harriet stared at her cell phone. Had Jake Porter just hung up on her? Unbelievable. He'd asked her to call, punched the number into her phone as if he owned it, and smiled in a way so self-assured, she knew he had absolutely no doubt that she would have dinner with him.

She was free to do so. Olivia had been resting comfortably and assured them she'd be fine and didn't need a fuss made over her. So Harriet had no compunction about leaving the hospital early that evening. Zach had asked to spend the night at her parents' rather than accompanying her to the Schoolhouse Inn. She'd just been inside to drop him off and now, once again, she sat in the Hummer outside her parents' house.

She had serious doubts about the wisdom of spending any time with Jake Porter, though. So she'd almost made up her mind to call and tell him she was otherwise occupied.

Not that she was, of course. But she couldn't endure a full evening at her parents' house, especially not after her mother had told her at least four times what a fine-looking man Jake Porter had turned out to be, and how she'd known at a glance they had to have met before.

The way she said it, speaking to Harriet but looking over at Zach, made Harriet's stomach tighten and her pulse race. So naturally she hadn't volunteered he'd asked her to have dinner with him.

She started the engine and drove slowly down the block. Lighted Christmas trees showed through the front windows of most of the houses. The sun had set and night was coming on.

It was a time of day Harriet usually loved. She would have spent productive hours creating art that welled up from her soul, and would be winding down to enjoy some time with Zach or an evening curled up reading or a night out on the town with Weaver and the entourage that always seemed to find him no matter where he went.

That was one of the differences between being an artist and being a musician, she reflected as she paused at a stop sign, and wondered whether to head over to the Schoolhouse Inn and check in for a quiet evening or to drive around and around town, wondering why Jake Porter hadn't answered her call. Musicians tended to be surrounded by people, and artists walked through life much more alone.

Unless, of course, you were someone like Andy Warhol. Harriet thought of Weaver. She could call him, see what he was doing. He hadn't meant to upset her by asking her to marry him. He'd been a good friend for a long time, both to her and to Donnie. If she'd wanted to marry again, she could see that he'd be a good husband. He wouldn't hang around the house bothering her to spend time with him, as he was on tour so much of the year. And money would never be a problem.

Harriet wrinkled her nose. Were those the factors that made a marriage good? She and Donnie had gotten along exceptionally well despite the unusual circumstances of their union. They had their own quarters, they parented, they socialized, and they played husband and wife for the benefit of his parents.

In all those ways, they were husband and wife.

But they'd never known the intimacies of a man and woman joined as one.

Harriet sighed and took the turn that led to the street where the Schoolhouse Inn was located. What would be the point in calling Weaver? She wasn't the marrying kind, and there was no use in pretending she was. All her sexual energies went into her art. Even the art critics remarked on that phenomenon.

"Yeah, right," she muttered. She might not be the marrying kind, but there were times she wanted all that being a woman meant. Like last night, for instance. If the man involved in that potential one-night stand had been anyone other than Jake Porter, she would have been tempted beyond denial into the chance of passion sans any complicating factors.

It had been a long, long time for her.

Too long.

She grimaced, remembering how foolish she'd been in

the months after Donnie's death. She'd dated several men and then taken a lover. She never invited him home, not wanting to upset Zach's world. But she'd fallen hard for the older investment banker. He wined and dined her and opened sensual horizons she'd never known. As busy as his schedule was, he never pressed her to spend evenings or weekends with him. Her art began to suffer, though, and she started to pull back from the time she spent with him. Which was just as well, because the day he introduced her to the brunette he referred to as "the other woman in his life," and suggested the three of them become better acquainted, Harriet found it less painful to walk away. She was shocked and hurt, and felt like a naïve fool for believing he loved her the way she thought she loved him.

Not long after that, she started spending a lot more time with Weaver. Safe, reliable Weaver.

Harriet parked on the street opposite the inn. She didn't know why, but she didn't want to pull in too close. It was as if she wanted to be ready for an escape.

Or ready to race off to meet Jake Porter if he returned her call?

No, she had more backbone than that.

She collected her bag, purse, and coat and climbed out of the Hummer. She crossed the street. Light streamed from the windows of the bed-and-breakfast. It looked cozy and welcoming.

Harriet felt her shoulders relax. She'd have a long hot bath and curl up with a book.

She'd reached the sidewalk leading to the inn's front door when she realized there was a man standing in the doorway. He had his back to the street and appeared about to be ready to enter the building.

Through the growing darkness she couldn't make out much detail. But she knew the shoulders, the angle of the head kicked slightly to one side, the long, powerful legs.

Jake Porter.

Had he come looking for her?

One foot on the walkway, she hesitated. She could turn and slip back into the car and drive away.

Alone.

Into a lonely night.

Why should she do that when all she wanted to do was relax, retire for the evening in a room she'd reserved, in an inn where she could remain in peace, quiet, and isolation.

The man in the doorway shifted, his head turned first, and then his body. He'd seen her, of course. He seemed to have radar when it came to her.

Right, Harriet said to herself. *Don't be ridiculous*. Not wanting to be caught running from the scene, she strode toward the inn.

"Now here's an answer to a prayer," Jake Porter said, stepping beneath the porch light fixture.

Bathed in light, he fit that description much better. Only Harriet knew he was no angel and she was far better off regarding him as a devil to be avoided, no matter how great the temptation he offered.

"What prayer was that?" Harriet said. She managed a light, almost flip tone to her voice, which pleased her. Jake Porter didn't need to know how easily he affected her.

"Let me help you with that," he said, reaching for her leather bag.

She found herself letting him take it from her.

"I'm growing fond of this coat," he said, also removing the red cashmere coat from her hands.

She stood there on the porch, not moving into the light, feeling as tongue-tied as she had back in high school.

"So you are staying here," he said. It wasn't a question. He'd known. She hadn't even guessed he might be staying there, but of course it made sense. Doolittle didn't offer many hotel options.

"If they haven't given away my room." *Or if I don't bolt again after finding you here.* "I should go in and check."

"In a minute," he said, drawing her over to a porch swing.

She sat down, wondering what had happened to her self-sufficient, contrary, and independent self.

"How's Mrs. Smith?"

"Resting."

He nodded. He used his foot to set the swing into a gentle motion. "Hungry?"

"I am," she said, speaking without thinking.

He smiled. "Shall we go back to the Verandah?"

"Oh, I don't know," Harriet said. "I'm exhausted from all that sitting around the hospital."

"Do you good." He grinned. "It'll do me good is what I mean."

She laughed. "Now that's honest."

"That's me," he said. "Ask anyone in the music business and they'll tell you Jake Porter is a straight shooter. And I'll tell you I need to shower and change before we can head out."

So she still had time to wriggle out of any dinner plans. "Me, too," she said, starting to rise from the swing.

He put a hand on her forearm. "Did you call me?"

She looked down at him. He sat in a shadow cast by the porch light. "Is that a trick question?"

He dug in a pants pocket and pulled out his cell phone. "Dropped and broke it," he said, with a mournful sigh. "Just as it rang."

Harriet couldn't help but smile. "And I thought you hung up on me."

He stood up. "I would never do that, Harriet whatever-your-last-name-is." He touched the side of her cheek, ever so lightly.

She shivered, in a long, slow move that started somewhere deep inside her and ran down to her toes. He was about to kiss her. She wanted him to. She didn't want him to. She rose to her toes and tipped her chin upward. "Smith," she whispered. "My last name is Smith."

Lowering his head, he dropped her case to the porch, floated the red cashmere coat around her shoulders, and pulled her close. "Smith," he said, heat in his eyes.

The door to the inn burst open. Light from within flooded the porch. A boisterous male voice called, "Joanne, it is not cold out here. Come sit a spell."

"Damn," Jake said, releasing her. He traced the outline of her lips and said, "To be continued."

"Oh, excuse me," the man said, but didn't turn back inside. He stepped toward them, hand outstretched. "Louis St. Cyr," he said. "Don't you just love this place? I meet new friends every time I visit."

"Jake Porter," Jake said, recovering before Harriet.

She took the moment to pull her coat around her shoulders. "Harriet," she said.

"I've met your father," St. Cyr said to Jake. "He's a lucky man to be marrying Sweet Martha. And Harriet with no last name, you're very discreet and I'll respect that wish for privacy, but I must tell you I own two of your paintings."

A slender, silver-haired woman stepped onto the porch and pulled the door closed behind her. "Louis? Oh, you're with company."

"Joanne St. Cyr," Louis said. "Meet Jake Porter and Harriet P. Smith."

"Hello," she said, slipping a leather coat around her shoulders. "If you're the artist, Ms. Smith, Louis isn't going to give you a moment's peace. He raves over your work."

Harriet tried to smile. Praise from strangers made her feel so awkward. In all the years she'd been painting and since becoming well-known, she still hadn't gotten used to the feeling that people who bought her art and knew her art felt as if they owned a piece of her. "Thank you," she finally managed.

Jake stood close to her side, almost protectively. "Are you an artist, too?"

The silver-haired woman laughed, a light, musical sound. "Heavens, no," she said. "I wouldn't have a clue. I'm a dermatologist and Louis is in orthopedics."

Harriet did smile then. "It's a good thing we all enjoy different gifts. My mother-in-law had knee replacement surgery today, and I couldn't face the world without my dermatologist."

Jake slapped his head. "Poor me," he said. "Kristen was right about the uselessness of an MBA."

"You know Kristen?" Joanne St. Cyr asked. "Kristen Halliday."

"The girl who's working here?" Jake asked.

"Yes. She's our daughter's stepdaughter."

"Everyone in Doolittle is still related to everyone else," Harriet said.

"We're from New Orleans," Louis said. "But I like to

get away to Doolittle whenever I can. Joanne does, too."

"Joanne can speak for herself," Joanne said. She smiled. "Since Stacey married Dr. Mike, I write 'time in Doolittle' into my schedule. I'm even thinking of moving here."

Louis raised his eyebrows. "That's news to me, Joanne."

"I don't know why it should surprise you," she said.

Harriet looked from one to the other. "We were just heading inside," she said. "Perhaps you'd like to take the swing?"

Louis held up his hands. "Sorry," he said. "Joanne and I enjoy arguing with each other, but we forget not to do it in front of other people. One of the best things about being divorced for as many years as we've been is that we never hurt each other's feelings."

"I'm not sure I'd say it that way," Joanne said.

Louis laughed and put an arm around her shoulders. "Let's let these young people go on inside and get warmed up."

She smiled and moved over to the swing.

Harriet stepped toward the door.

Louis leaned closer and said, "The moment I saw *Heat* I knew I had to own it. It is the sexiest art I've ever viewed."

Harriet blushed. She'd thrown herself into that painting, literally, rolling and writhing and panting as she body-painted on the canvas. She wasn't known for restraint. Alone in the privacy of her studio it had been an incredible, orgasmic experience. Having the result commented on by this older man made her feel as if she were walking across a stage and everyone in the orchestra pit could see she wore no panties. Fortunately, St. Cyr didn't seem to require a response.

"Now that's a painting I'd like to see," Jake said, walking beside her into the inn.

"Be nice to Kristen and maybe you'll get to know the family," Harriet said.

"If that's a comment that indicates you're maybe just the teeniest bit jealous of the precocious Kristen," Jake said, "you should know Kristen is all of sixteen."

"I'm not the least bit jealous," Harriet said. She walked into the Schoolhouse Inn. "Why would I be?"

"Some questions are better answered by actions rather than words." He turned and pulled her to him. "They robbed me of this kiss a few minutes ago," he said, and before she could react, he lowered his head and brushed his lips against hers.

It happened so quickly she wondered if she hadn't imagined the kiss. But her reaction was all too real. Breathless, she said, "Mr. Porter!"

He laughed softly. "I like the way your eyes sparkle when you're pretending to be indignant."

"I am not," she said. "Pretending, I mean."

"Look, here's Miss Abbie coming to greet you," he said.

Sure enough, a spare older woman approached, a thin smile on her lips. "Welcome to the Schoolhouse Inn," she said. "Mrs. Smith, isn't it?"

"Call me Harriet," she said. She never thought of herself as Mrs. Smith. She hadn't while Donnie was alive, and after his death, the phrase had seemed even less appropriate.

"Harriet," Abbie said, testing the name as she said it. "We've got your room waiting for you. Sherry and tea cakes are being served now in the front parlor. I'll take your bags and show you to your room."

"Did you teach biology?" Harriet asked.

The older woman nodded. "I did indeed. And both of you were in my class, but you've changed so much I almost wouldn't know you were the girl who dressed up our science skeleton like a sideshow freak."

"I'd forgotten all about that," Harriet said. She turned to Jake. "It was Halloween, so that was before you'd come to Doolittle."

A shadow passed over his features. He looked far less carefree than he had only a few minutes ago when he'd sneaked that kiss.

"There's plenty of time to talk over the past," Abbie said. "Did you enjoy your run, Jake?"

He nodded. "I needed it."

Abbie's mouth turned downward. "After traipsing around looking at houses with that chatterbox Mrs. Ball, I should think you would."

Houses? Harriet shot a swift look at Jake. Surely he wasn't buying property in Doolittle.

"I'll let my father and Martha go alone next time," Jake said. "I'll carry Harriet's bag. Which grade is she in?"

"Third." She pulled an old-fashioned metal key out of her apron pocket and handed it to Harriet. "The bath is just across the hall. If there's anything you need, just let us know. Ask for Martha or me. Or Kristen, I suppose."

Harriet was curious to meet Kristen. "Precocious" and "sixteen" weren't adjectives that one heard bandied about a lot in Doolittle. "Thanks," she said, and followed Jake down the broad hall. To the left a large parlor had a fire burning in the fireplace. A man sat reading next to it. He glanced up briefly, and Harriet stopped in her tracks. Jake just missed bumping into her.

She looked from him to Jake and back again. The older

man smiled at her, and she managed to return the gesture and get her feet moving again.

"Was that your father?"

"Yes."

"You look so much alike," she said, her voice trailing off. Yes, they looked as much alike as Zach and Jake did. Something in her gut twisted. She'd kept that man from knowing he had a grandson.

"I'll introduce you sometime, if you'd like," Jake said. "Third Grade. Your key, madam."

"Oh, I can do it myself," Harriet said, working the large metal piece into the keyhole. It caught and stuck. She wiggled it, pulled it out, and started over. The lock didn't budge.

He leaned close and whispered, "Let me know when I may be of service."

Harriet could feel his chest moving up and down with each breath. His body was warm and strong, and she was a fool. She glanced down the hall toward the front of the building and saw Abbie was no longer in sight. She allowed her body to rest against Jake's, only for a moment. She sighed. "I give up," she said.

He placed his hand on hers and lifted the key the teeniest bit. Their hands joined, they turned the key. The lock clicked free and the door swung open an inch or so.

"Voilà," he said, his hand still wrapped around hers. "See how easy it is when one stops fighting it?"

"Right," she said. She tugged her hand free, opened the door, and said, "Thanks for carrying my bag. I can take it from here."

"Harriet, Harriet," he said. "You are one stubborn woman."

"I don't know what you mean." But of course she did.

She placed her hand on the edge of the door, using it to protect herself not from Jake Porter, but from her own desire to yank him by the arm into her room, slam the door shut, and show him just what she wanted from him.

He pushed the door open, walked right past her, and set her case down next to the bed, a four-poster covered in apple green chintz.

"Hey," she said.

"Don't worry," he said. "The door is open, and I never stay where I'm not wanted."

"It's not that," Harriet said. She tossed her cashmere coat and her purse on a double stuffed chair, and then perched on the edge. "I'm taking off my boots now," she said, and proceeded to do exactly that. "You are a very attractive man." She kicked off one boot and ran her eyes up and down his lean body. "Very."

"Gosh, thanks," he said, leaning against the bed and making himself comfortable.

"I have, um, fairly positive memories of you from high school, and I look forward to catching up on what you've been doing with your life." There, that sounded noncommittal enough. She slid her other boot from her foot.

"Over dinner?"

What harm would it do? Harriet nodded. "Okay. Over dinner."

"Would you like the bathroom first?"

"We're sharing a bathroom?" Harriet stared at him. That felt far too personal.

He shrugged. "It's the bed-and-breakfast thing. You know, get to know the other houseguests. Don't worry, I always rinse out the sink after I shave and I wipe down the shower glass."

"You're kidding me."

"You mean you don't?" He smiled. "Somehow I can't see you being a neat freak, but I confess I am. Growing up in my house, someone had to keep order."

"I'm guessing your father demanded it and your mother had no clue so that left you."

Jake nodded. He crossed his arms over his chest. "Something tells me that Martha and my father will be much better suited than he and Ariel ever were."

"They're a couple?"

"Getting married New Year's Eve."

"You said you were here on family matters," she said slowly, remembering that last night he hadn't seemed to want to talk about why he was in town.

"My father wanted me to meet Martha. It's pretty sudden, and I guess he wanted my blessing." He shrugged. "As weird as that feels."

"Maybe he wants you to know his life is going in a good direction."

"And I hope it is," Jake said. "He's a good guy."

Harriet smiled at him, pleased that he spoke well of his dad—Zach's grandfather. "I think second marriages can be especially successful. I mean, lots of times people learn what doesn't work for them in a relationship, and the next time around they look for what they realized they can't live without."

"Is that what you're going to do?" He spoke softly, slipping the question past her defenses.

Almost.

She laughed. "Heavens, no. I'm not getting married again."

"Sorry you had a bad experience." He looked grim. "But the bad do seem to outweigh the good."

For some stubborn reason, she didn't want him to think

she'd had a miserable marriage. But how in the world could she explain to him, of all people, what it had been like? "We were good friends," she said.

Jake raised an eyebrow. "I remember Donnie Smith from our class. You two were friends, then. But I don't remember thinking he was interested in girls."

Harriet flushed. "You didn't know him very long."

"And you knew him all your life." He pushed himself away from the bed. "Always the outsider," he said with a wry smile. "Of course you would know better. You married him and had his kid." He shrugged. "Tap on my door when you're finished in the bath, okay? I'm in Fourth Grade."

And just like that, he strode out of the room.

Harriet kicked a foot at her boots. She'd just added another layer to the lie she was living. And she'd hurt his feelings. She hadn't meant to, and it felt bad, watching him withdraw from her. She sighed and got up from the chair. She'd meant to cry off from dinner, even at the last minute, but after what had just happened, she didn't have the heart to cancel.

But how dangerous a game she played. *Jeez, Harriet*, she said to herself. *He gave you the perfect opening to explain what happened and you let it slip right past.*

Yeah, because I'm a chicken. A big, goofy, guilty chicken headed for the chopping block.

Chapter 28

All One Happy Family

Harriet was definitely not a neatnik. Jake had to pick three towels off the floor and fish the bar of soap from the drain before he could shower. But he enjoyed picturing her standing under the showerhead, naked and glistening with water droplets, so he didn't mind. He had to calm himself down before he could get dressed and join the others in the parlor, where Harriet had said she'd wait for him.

Yeah, because she didn't want to let him back in her room. He couldn't blame her. He'd come on hot and heavy, but she had that effect on him. He'd be the gentleman at dinner, though. No point in scaring her off.

He found it hard to believe she and Donnie Smith had tied the knot. The more he thought of it, the odder it seemed. But the two of them had been friends a long time. They were the outcasts of their class. Perhaps it had made sense for them to join forces.

Not that he found that a good enough reason to get married. But then maybe it made more sense than two people giddily believing themselves in love and only later finding out, after the bills mounted and the babies were crying, that he liked vegetables and she ate only pork and neither one could remember what in the world they'd been thinking when they'd said, "I do."

He knew he was a cynic.

But he'd rather answer to that description than be trapped in misery.

With the way he lived his life, he could always move on. Tonight, if he and Harriet discovered they had nothing else to say after the first course, he would have invested only one evening. Tomorrow, the rest of the world would be there, beckoning.

He'd tried, time and again, to explain that philosophy to women he'd dated. None of them got it. Like Lilly, each one thought she'd be the one to change his mind.

And here he was, going out for the evening with Harriet, who'd laughed at the idea she'd marry again. Talk about kindred spirits.

Could things get any better?

He snatched up his leather jacket, flung it over one shoulder, and, whistling, headed down the hall toward the front parlor.

Voices greeted him before he reached the double doors. He recognized his father's deep tones and the pleasant enough sound of Martha. The bossy baritone of Louis St. Cyr did battle with the low, controlled, and rather patient sound of his ex-wife. Jake knew there had to be a good story there, one someone was bound to share with him. No doubt if he strolled into LeDru's the next morning, Pickle or one of the customers would be happy to fill him in.

He paused just outside the parlor. The one voice he hadn't heard belonged to Harriet. Well, women always took longer to get ready than men did. He wouldn't read anything into her absence.

Stepping into the room, he noted his father waving him over to where he sat on a love seat, Martha by his side. The two St. Cyrs were seated in high-backed chairs on either side of the fireplace. The span of the crackling fire did nothing to deter them from arguing over what sounded like the respective merits of various types of anesthesia.

Before he could say good evening, Abbie whisked into the room. She placed a silver platter of tea cakes on a side table, eyed the tea service, and then lifted a bottle of sherry and a small glass. She filled it and crossed the room to him.

He accepted the glass, not because he liked sherry, but because he felt sorry for her. He figured that would drive her crazy if she knew it, so he smiled and lifted the glass toward her, toasting her.

She waved a hand at him. "Aw, get on with you," she said. "Have a tea cake. I made them myself."

"Thank you, I will." Jake placed a small cake onto a cocktail napkin. "Were you surprised that Harriet remembered you?"

She lifted one eyebrow. "I suppose I was."

"It seems like a lifetime ago," he said. He took a sip of the sherry. "Pretty smooth."

"Wouldn't have it any other way," Abbie said. "You'd best get back over there and spend some time talking to your father. That man has a lot to tell you."

Jake looked at his father. He was holding hands with Martha now, discreetly enough, their joined hands tucked between them on the love seat. He sighed. "I guess they surprised you?"

She snorted. "Have another tea cake."

He accepted one from her. "Some changes are hard to adjust to."

She put one hand to her hip. "Why people want to go and uproot themselves is more than I can understand. Why, I plan to live in this place and run this inn until the day the good Lord calls me to join him in heaven."

"And I believe you will," Jake said. "Maybe your sister wants something different. Not that I understand it," he added.

She shook her head. "I've got to get back to the kitchen. Kristen can't do all the work." She shot a glance at Martha, and with that parting blow she whisked from the room.

Jake held his sherry glass in one hand, a half-eaten tea cake in the other. Abbie, he'd just realized, regarded him as an ally, a fellow sufferer deserted by a loved one. That made him feel even sorrier for her. Jake's life would change very little as a result of his father's second marriage. Abbie's world would be turned on its end.

"Jake," his father said, beckoning him over.

At least he hoped he was right about that assumption.

He finished the tea cake, wiped his mouth with the napkin, nodded to the St. Cyrs, and moved over to his father and Martha. He ignored the chair beside the love seat and remained standing.

"We saw you went for a run," his father said. "I need to do that myself."

Jake nodded.

"We've decided to make an offer on the last house we saw," his father said. "Martha and I have had time to talk things over, and we both know we can't live in one of those boxes the agent showed us in Doolittle Village."

That didn't surprise Jake one bit. "Makes sense. It seemed like a case of love at first sight."

"Sitting on that porch was like coming home." His father smiled at him. "We're also discussing our wedding plans."

Martha was gazing at the Colonel as if he'd been a genie who'd just granted not three wishes, but three thousand.

"New Year's Eve will be here before we know it," his father said. "I'd like you to stand up for me."

"Sir," Jake said, unsure what to say.

"You're still getting used to the idea of our marriage, aren't you?" That was Martha, looking up at him, rather shyly.

"Yes," Jake said, "I guess you're right."

"I know it seems sudden," she said. "But when you meet the perfect person, it doesn't make any sense to wait and live apart and have to get by on phone calls and e-mail when all you want to do is spend every day of your life with the man you love." She blushed slightly and glanced down at her hand joined with his father's.

"I couldn't have said that better," his father said. He rose and put an arm on Jake's shoulder, lightly, as if afraid of being rejected. "And there's no one else I'd rather have by my side than my son."

"Thank you," Jake said, wishing he understood why he felt both honored and a bit at a loss all at the same time. "I'll be there." He raised his sherry glass. "A toast to the bride and groom."

"May we join in?" Louis St. Cyr and Joanne moved

from their chairs beside the fire to stand beside Jake. "Nothing like a wedding to make a man feel young."

Joanne punched him playfully on the arm. "You should know, Louis."

"True," Louis said. "I've been to the altar four times."

Jake shook his head. "Why?"

Louis shrugged. His eyes twinkled, though. "I'm old-fashioned, I suppose. I don't believe in sleeping around."

"Dr. St. Cyr!" Martha looked shocked.

"Well, would you be more horrified if I said I did?" He lifted his glass. "No, don't answer that." He retrieved the sherry bottle, topped off everyone's glasses, and said, "To Sweet Martha and the man who captured her heart."

"That's so romantic," Joanne said.

Abbie hustled into the room.

"Come join us," Martha said. "You don't have to work all the time."

Her sister put her hands on her hips. "Oh, don't I just?"

"Please?" Martha patted the love seat arm. "We're having a toast. Get yourself a glass and put your fanny over here. I insist."

Jake chuckled a bit, then. The command had a way of relieving his tension.

"What's the occasion?" Abbie asked.

Martha pleated her skirt. "They're toasting our engagement."

"Is that right?" Abbie looked anything but pleased.

Jake couldn't help but feel a sense of kinship even more strongly.

"We've definitely decided on New Year's Eve," Martha said.

"I still can't believe you mean this year," Abbie said.

"No one's getting any younger," Louis said.

"It's time for us to leave for Stacey and Michael's," Joanne said, laying an arm on Louis's shoulder. "All our best," she said to Martha and the Colonel, and practically dragged her ex-husband from the parlor.

"I don't care how fine this man seems, you haven't had time to get to know him," Abbie said, frowning at Martha. "And you know what Mother always said. You can't tell a chicken from a rooster until the sun's set more times than you might want to wait, so when all is said and done, you'll be happy when you've held your horses."

Martha looked like she was going to cry.

"That's quite an expression," Jake said. "Mind if I use it? It could come in handy in many a business deal."

She gave him one of her thin-lipped smiles. "If you can put it to use, that's fine by me. I don't see what all the rush is about, Martha. You've gone through the change so I know you're not expecting, so what's the hurry?"

"Abbie!" Martha was blushing to the tips of her ears. "I want you to be happy for me. For us."

Abbie rammed her hands into her apron pockets. "For you. For us. Well, and I ask you, what's to become of me?" Her voice caught and shook. She glared at her sister.

Jake almost reached out and put an arm around her bony shoulders.

But it was Martha who leaped up, letting go of his father's hand, to take Abbie into her embrace. "Nothing's going to happen to you," she said. "We'll still run the inn. I'll come here every day and go home at night. And I'll always be your sister."

Abbie gave a mighty sniff. She kept her hands locked

in the fabric of the apron. "You mark my words. Nothing will ever be the same again."

"But maybe that's not a bad thing," Martha said. "I'm happy in a way I never thought I'd be. Maybe you'll find the same opportunity."

"Ha!" Abbie drew herself out of her sister's arms. "If you think it takes a man to make me happy, you've got another thought coming. I wish you and Mr. Porter happy. I guess I really do. But one woman's dessert is another woman's poison."

"Here, here," Jake said, clapping his hands together, taking care not to drop the sherry glass. Then he lifted it and said, "Here's to those of us who are not the marrying kind."

"I'll drink to that," Harriet said, stepping into the parlor.

Jake turned. She looked fabulous, her tall, slender form moving as if one with the silky knit of a black minidress worn with the spike-heel boots. Clearly she wore no bra. He swallowed, hard, and tipped his glass to her in tribute.

She smiled, a look almost as smooth and hot and wanton as her outfit.

He ceased to worry over his father's rash decision to marry. Who cared? They were on their own.

The sight of Harriet blanked all other thoughts from his head. His body leaped in anticipation, and it wasn't dinner he was relishing, but dessert.

He had to have her.

He couldn't go without tasting her, plundering her, diving into what he knew would be her hot, silky, wet, wanting self.

She'd made it clear she wanted no entanglements. He need have no concerns in that direction. She was sexual sophistication personified. And he could tell she was as hot for him as he was for her. Could a guy get any luckier?

"I'd like to be married at the Doolittle Community Church," Martha said. "And Ted agrees with me."

Church? That was the last thing on Jake's mind. "So that's the plan?"

"Pastor will never allow it," Abbie said. "How's he going to fit in planning a rehearsal and arranging a ceremony with all the work that goes into the children's Nativity pageant and the midnight service? He deserves some time to enjoy the holiday. You'd be imposing to ask him to do it."

Martha had an amazingly stubborn-looking chin, Jake realized.

"I'm going to ask him first thing in the morning," she said. "And if you think he won't be happy and willing to help us out, you don't know Pastor."

Abbie curled her lip. "And what are you planning for a reception?"

"We haven't gotten that far yet," Jake's father said. "But whatever Martha wants is what I want."

"If you're going to up and spend a lot of money at some other place, you'd be better off saving your cash and having everyone back here," Abbie said.

You could've knocked Jake over sideways. He shot a glance at Abbie. She still had her arms banded over her chest and looked as cross as ever. Maybe she couldn't stand to be left out of the event. What the hell? "You arrange it and I'll kick in the money to cover it," he found himself saying before he had time to think it over. "We'll air-drop some caviar and champagne."

"That's nice of you, Jake," his father said, "but we couldn't accept that."

"Why not? Think of it as a wedding present. I'll hustle up the music, too. There's a group I heard last night that could do something special."

"The J. R.'s would be perfect," Harriet said. "Their music touches the heart." She looked from Martha to the Colonel. "It's hard to explain, but it just does. You'll like them."

"J. R. is Rebecca's son," Martha said. "I always said he'd make it big one day, if he'd just put his mind to it. I'd be happy to have them play here, if they'd agree to it. They could set up around the fountain."

"I'll talk to them," Jake said. "Tomorrow." He held out a hand toward Harriet. "Tonight, Harriet and I have dinner plans. So if you'll excuse us, we'll be off."

His father stepped to Jake's side. "Thank you for your support, son," he said.

Jake nodded. He didn't understand his own conflicting emotions. He wanted to be happy for his father. He was pleased that he seemed so much more relaxed with Martha. Yet he didn't trust that goodness would win out over conflict in the long run. "Certainly, sir," he said, falling back on old habits. He turned to Harriet, took in the delicious sight of her. "Will you be warm enough?" he asked.

She smiled at him. "I'm sure I'll be fine."

"The wind is picking up and the temperature is dropping," Martha said. "I'll grab a shawl for you."

"Oh, no, really, it's not necessary," Harriet said.

"It's no trouble at all. I keep some extras on the pegs inside the door."

"It's much colder in New York," Harriet said. "This feels like springtime to me."

"What she means, Martha," Abbie said, "is that she's

not going to be caught dead in a homemade wrap. She'd rather freeze than be unfashionable."

Everyone stared at Harriet. Jake opened his mouth to protest but decided against it. He was curious how Harriet would react to that left jab to the jaw.

She smiled at Abbie, and then she stuck her tongue out at her. "Just because you taught me the difference between an X and a Y chromosome doesn't mean you know what's what." She turned to Martha. "Perhaps you're right. I accept your offer of the shawl."

Abbie laughed. "It's good to see you haven't gotten all hoity-toity. You always did have more gumption than most of the other kids in your class."

Harriet looked surprised. "That's not what you said then."

Abbie shrugged. "Get on with you. Like it or not, I've got a reception to plan. I don't have time to stand here jawboning."

Martha hugged her sister. "We," she said, "we have a reception to plan. Harriet, take any one of the shawls."

At last they escaped the parlor. At the front door, Jake eyed a wooden pegboard painted with pictures of flowers. Harriet plucked a wrap without looking at it, and they walked onto the porch.

They looked at each other and broke into grins.

"Hoity-toity," he said, whispering the phrase into her ear.

"Champagne and caviar," she whispered back. "Doolittle won't know what to think."

"Doolittle won't have to know," he said. "I'm sure it will be a small group. My father doesn't have siblings, I don't, either, and Abbie seems to be Martha's only family."

Harriet started laughing. "I may have been away from Doolittle for years," she said, "but I know there's no way the people of this town are going to let Sweet Martha get married without them being present."

"Oh," Jake said. He slapped his forehead and grinned. "How silly of me. I guess I'd better order extra caviar."

Harriet shook her head. "It would just go to waste. Once someone figured out you were serving fish eggs, they'd complain that you hadn't let the fish grow up to be caught fair and square."

"It is a different world here."

She nodded. "Just think. We don't have to discuss where to go to dinner. If this were New York or L.A., we'd face so many choices. Plus we'd need reservations. Here it's either Sonic or the Verandah."

"Don't forget LeDru's," Jake said.

"So you remember that place?"

"Went there this morning." He patted his stomach. "A waitress named Pickle gave me a second buttermilk doughnut at no charge."

Harriet looked surprised. "Did you say Pickle?"

He nodded.

She shot a saucy glance at him. "If you go to LeDru's again, she's likely to trap you into marrying her. She always was the wild one in the Wright family."

Jake tucked Harriet's hand into his. "Don't worry. I am untrappable. I hate to ask you this, but may we take your Hummer? I'll never again agree to my father picking me up in his rental car."

"Sure." Harriet smiled at him. "The key's in the car."

When she looked at him like that, all relaxed and trusting and soft and touchable, he forgot about his father's hasty wedding and ordering caviar and how many people might show up. He also forgot to question the wisdom of her leaving a key handy for any car thief who might wander by. He tightened his hold on her hand for a moment. "Let's go."

Chapter 29

A Night Out of Time

They never made it to the Verandah. Harriet had asked Jake to drive the Hummer. He had one hand on the wheel and his other on her knee as they approached the Sonic. The drive-in fast-food place was brightly lit and had quite a few cars parked in the stalls where one pulled in and placed an order over the speaker.

They looked at each other and laughed.

"Why not?" Jake said, and swung into the driveway. "I'm not sure I want to sit through a drawn-out dinner."

As he spoke, he circled the flesh just inside her knee. Harriet tingled all over. It wasn't food she hungered for. "When's the last time you went to a Sonic?"

"I have no idea," Jake said. He scanned the menu posted beside the driver's window. "What about you?"

"When I was here for Donnie's funeral," she said, remembering how Zach had cried and cried and the only time he'd cheered up at all was when she took him for chili cheese fries.

Jake turned toward her. "If being here makes you sad, say the word and I'll drive away." He traced the curve of her lip with a fingertip. "The last thing I want you to feel is sorrow."

She trembled. "Believe me, that's not what I'm feeling now."

He brushed a kiss across her forehead. "Good. So may I take your order, my beautiful Harriet?"

"I'm not . . ." She trailed off. She'd been about to protest that she wasn't his. But she'd always belonged to Jake Porter. She'd never given him up in her heart all these many years. Besides, that wasn't how he meant the expression. Clearly her memory hadn't burned so brightly in his mind's eye. *Quit thinking so much*, she ordered her brain. "I'll have a burger, hold the mayo, add catsup and extra pickles. Small fries, no salt. I'll add my own."

He looked amused. "I appreciate a woman who knows what she likes."

She gave him a teasing glance. "This chain puts mayonnaise on their burgers, so if you hate that as much as I do, you'll need to tell them to hold it."

"Hold the mayo? That's the best part." He pressed the red call button and ordered over the speaker system.

"My son is the only person I know who can stand mayo on a burger," she said, speaking without thinking.

"Maybe you can introduce me sometime," he said.

Harriet nodded. This was it. The universe had handed her the perfect opportunity to tell Jake Porter there was something critically important she had to say to him. Forget about how sexy he made her feel and how much she wanted to make out with him. *Tell him. Tell him about Zach.*

He took her hand in his. "Right now," he said, "I'd like to concentrate on you." He traced the lines of her palm with the back of his thumb. "We've got quite a few years to catch up on in a very short time."

She nodded. "We do."

"Why New York?" He continued that seductive skimming of her hand.

"Why L.A.?" She couldn't think with him touching her.

"No fair. I asked you first," he said, smiling at her.

Tell him. Tell him you had to get away. Ask him why he took the other kids up on that stupid, mean dare and broke your heart. Harriet looked at his fingers so gently touching her palm. Had the other kids been wrong? Maybe he'd wanted to be with her and they made it all up. But Donnie had said the same thing, confirmed the dare.

"Hey," Jake said. "I didn't mean to ask a hard question."

She met his gaze. "I know. There's no simple answer. I wanted out of Doolittle. So did Donnie. He was into music and I always knew I'd be an artist. We helped each other escape."

"So just like that the two of you tied the knot."

Harriet looked down at her hands. A car pulled into the space to her right. The driver lowered the window and music blared. "He'd always been my friend. And after you left, I was pretty . . ." She trailed off. Devastated? No, she wouldn't admit to that. "I never heard a word from you."

Jake, his face one big frown, was drumming a thumb against the steering wheel.

"Why didn't you say good-bye?" she asked.

He drummed harder. "My father was so mad at my mom for leaving me he dragged me out of town. We flew to Berlin the next day."

"But you didn't write. Or call."

He shook his head. "Right. And wrong. I didn't write because I didn't know what to say. Jeez, Harriet, I was a dumb teenager. I didn't know whether I mattered to you or not. Hell, you could have been pissed with me for taking advantage of you."

Harriet put a hand over her heart. "You didn't take advantage of me. We both wanted to be together the night of the prom. It was never hearing from you that pissed me off."

"In my world, the rule was 'Never look back.' And you know something, I followed that rule every day of my life except one." He quit drumming and shifted to face her head-on. "That was the day I finally got a chance to make an international call. I got through to your parents' shop."

"When was that?" Harriet's voice trembled. He *had* tried to contact her.

He shrugged. "I don't know. Late July, early August of that summer."

Harriet let out a long breath. She and Donnie had married July 25.

"The woman at the shop told me you quit working there when you got married. So you see—"

A teenager on Rollerblades skated up at that moment, carrying their order. Jake passed two sacks and his drink over to Harriet and paid the teen. He must have given him a hefty tip because the kid said, "Wow, thanks!"

The heat from the sacks seeped into Harriet's hands. What would their lives look like if she had waited a little bit longer?

"Anyway," Jake said, turning the ignition key, "once I heard that news, there was never another reason to look back." He swung the car into the exit lane. "Heck, Harriet, we were kids and it was prom night. Obviously I didn't break your heart or you wouldn't have married Donnie."

Harriet licked her bottom lip. She wanted to protest that statement. But what could she say unless she told him everything right that very moment?

"Don't look so stricken," he said. "I was pretty hurt, to tell you the truth, but look at us now. You. Me." He pointed to the Sonic sacks. "Dinner date."

Harriet found a smile for him. "To living in the present," she said.

"Let's drive to someplace more scenic to enjoy our repast," he said.

Harriet nodded. "Good idea."

Jake exited the drive-in. "Isn't there a park around here?"

"You're right," Harriet said. "It should be ahead on the left."

"It's funny how some things in my memory come back in snippets," he said. "I lived here such a brief time, yet I knew there had to be a park. Let's see, there's one set of swings and a big boulder kids used to jump off of into a sandpit and a couple of benches."

"That's it," Harriet said. "What a memory."

He shrugged. "I didn't recall it until just now. So please don't think I remembered that little park more clearly than I remembered you. I feel that I should have known you the first moment I saw you in the bar at the Verandah. That was only yesterday, and now it seems as if no time has passed between high school and tonight."

"Well, I have changed a lot," Harriet said, willing to cut him some slack. If she hadn't been intent on deceiving him as to her identity, she might have given him a clue or two and he'd have remembered her right away.

"Not in some ways," Jake said.

"Like what?" She probably sounded indignant.

He smiled. "You're still the most fascinating person in Doolittle."

"Oh," she said. "But I don't live here anymore."

He nodded. "Don't protest too much. I've seen enough of the people here in one day's time to believe that the place has a way of luring even the most diehard city slickers into its web."

"Ha!" Harriet pointed. "There's the park."

He pulled off the road. After dark on a chilly December evening, they were the only ones around. He left the engine running to keep them warm. "Unless you want to bundle up and sit outside?"

Harriet shook her head. "No, but let's make this a picnic."

"Okay. What do you suggest?"

She tipped her head toward the backseat. "Hop out and get back in."

"I'll go you one better," Jake said. "Stay there." He slid from behind the wheel, leaped out, and ran around the vehicle to her side. He opened the door and held wide his arms. "May I?"

"Very gallant," she said. She didn't want to dwell on the past and the long list of melancholy what-ifs. She wanted to savor every moment she had left with Jake. She passed the sacks to the floor of the backseat, then slid off the seat toward Jake. Her short skirt hiked up almost to her tush. He reached out and pulled her to his chest, encircled her with his arms, and stepped away from the running board, holding her close.

He kicked the front door shut. "Mmm," he murmured, his voice close to her cheek. "You smell so sweet." He spun around, once, then twice, then one more time.

Harriet was laughing. She was alive and in Jake Porter's arms and she was free from any thought of the past or the future. She clung to him, then kissed him on the earlobe. That felt so good she kept his skin between her lips and sucked, gently, then harder, on his ear.

He drew in his breath in a rush. "Vixen," he said, and swung open the rear door. He lifted her in, on the edge of the seat. Her legs were far enough apart for her to feel naughty and inviting and oh-so-sexy. She lifted her index finger and beckoned to him.

He needed no further invitation. He lowered her to her back and leaned between her legs. Dipping his head, he kissed her on her mouth, her neck, her eyelids. Then with what sounded like a groan, he lifted his body. "I'm a jerk," he said.

Harriet fluttered her eyelids. "That's not what I was thinking," she said.

"I brought you here for a picnic," he said. "Your burger is going to get ice-cold."

"Oh," Harriet said. She could have cared less. And neither could Jake, she'd be willing to bet. Judging by the bulge in the front of his jeans, he had only one main course on his mind.

He held out his hand and pulled her to a seated position.

"Scoot over," he said, moving in beside her and shutting the door after him. "You'll be freezing, too."

"You're not only gallant, you're chivalrous," Harriet said. "And sexy, too."

He nodded. "Don't forget to add modest to the list." He grinned and reached for the paper sacks. "And Machiavellian."

"Why that?"

He quirked his brows. "I've no intention of seducing Harriet P. Smith in the back of a car. She deserves a much more refined setting."

Harriet didn't mind, but it didn't seem like the time to tell him that. They could be sitting in a tree for all she cared, and she would tip her head back and delight in the way his kisses made her hot, then wet, then quivery. "I think you're hungry, Jake Porter."

"Oh, yeah. I am." He leaned forward, suckled her lips, drew her tongue into his mouth. His arms wrapped around her, and her breasts crushed against his leather jacket. The fast-food sacks dropped to the floor.

She drew him down, reveling in the weight of him claiming her body. She opened her lips and offered her mouth and her tongue and her body and soul to him.

He responded, he took over, he led. She was on her back, her arms over her head, the scant fabric of her skirt rising higher and higher with every response her body made to each of his demanding kisses.

He pressed against her, the heat of his need igniting her even more. He shrugged out of his leather jacket, and it joined the burgers and fries on the floor. She spread her legs wide and he surged between them, fitting himself exactly where she wanted him.

Except that he wore those darned jeans.

Harriet sighed and tried to flutter her hands, but with her arms overhead and Jake kissing her mouth, her throat, her breasts, and then her lips, her eyes, her shoulder, then lowering, lowering, lowering his body to where the edge of her skirt skimmed the top of her thighs, there was nothing she could say or do except savor the taste and scent and feel of him.

"Harriet, Harriet," he said, his breath hot on her thighs, warming her where she was already hot and moist and wanting, writhing with needing him to plunge inside her, make her whole, make her cry out and arch against him and never, ever, ever let go.

He raised his head, captured her lips again, and as he suckled her and plundered her mouth, she felt his fingers slip beneath her skirt and brush aside the wisp of a thong that she'd donned that night. He made love to her with his every touch, his fingers as gentle as his kisses could be, and then as demanding as his tongue was, punishing her mouth, then softly healing it with his kisses.

Then he moved his finger inside her, swirled, teased, withdrew.

"Don't leave me," she cried out.

He swallowed her words with his mouth. His finger moved inside her, claiming her as his own, marking her for his body to take and taste and conquer.

She opened her legs wider, pushing up against his hand. She was panting and sweating and crying. He rode with her, teasing, promising, withholding, giving.

When she could stand it no longer, she grabbed his shoulders, cried out his name, and shuddered in release, clinging to him, limp and hot and wet and wanting him all the more for what he had given her.

"Harriet. My Harriet," he said, over and over again, stroking her head, holding her close.

Her eyelids fluttered. She breathed out a long, raggedy breath. "Oh, my," she said. "Oh, my."

She wasn't sure but she thought he was grinning. He looked pretty darned pleased. And before she could put her thoughts back into any coherent order, he'd pulled her up, onto his lap, straddling him. He reached to the floor, lifted his leather jacket, fumbled around in one of the pockets, found something there, and unzipped his jeans.

All the while, he was kissing her face, her lips, her throat, stroking her greedy nipples with one hand. "I've got to have you," he whispered. "Now. Here." He ripped open a packet, sheathed himself in the condom, and lifted her off his lap a few inches. Cradling her, he said, "You're amazing. There's nobody like you, my hot, hot, hot Harriet."

She laughed and gave him a breast to tease through the thin fabric of her dress. He took her nipple in his mouth, puckering her even more. She cried out, and as she did, he pulled her onto his hot and hard and demanding self.

She took him in, wanting him as much as he wanted her, riding him, embracing, giving, driving. She writhed and forgot about anything but the incredible need building up in her all over again, and about what he wanted and what he would demand from her.

He grasped her buttocks with his hands and drew her down, filling her, completing her.

"Jake Porter," she said.

"Yes, Harriet?" He lifted his mouth from her breast and took her lips again.

"I just wanted to say your name," she said, and leaned into him, dancing, driving, surging, her fists beating against his shoulders as he pumped and lifted her against him, then drew her down again. The heat rose within her and she moved on the waves he'd built and this time the climax was calmer, yet even more beautiful, joined as she was with him.

"Harriet, I can't wait," he said. He held her cheeks even more tightly, ramming into her, scarcely breathing. And then he cried out in release. His head fell back against the seat, but he did not let go of her. His arms wrapped around her, drawing her close to him.

He blinked and opened his eyes, and smiled at her. "I really did mean what I said."

She snuggled against his chest. "What was that?"

"I did not intend to seduce you in the backseat of this car."

Harriet kissed the tip of his nose. "Thank you for your lack of restraint."

He hugged her tight. "You are as wild as I thought you'd be."

She played with the collar of his shirt. "So you've been thinking about this for a while?"

"Since about eight-fifty-five last night."

She laughed. "You have not."

"Want to bet?"

"What's at stake?" What a ridiculous question for her to ask. Harriet clung more tightly to Jake, even as she bantered with him.

"On the other hand, you could just take my word on it," Jake said. He shifted around on the seat, still holding her atop his lap. "Where's that shawl? You must be freezing." He wrapped it around her back and hips, then seemed to think better of it. "You can't be comfortable. Let me slide you over so you can stretch out your legs."

"You're so considerate," she said, content to sit on his lap and curl against his chest.

A light flickered. "I'm seeing stars," Harriet murmured. Again, a beam of light bobbed and flickered.

"I don't think that's a star," Jake said, "but I do believe the man outside our car window is wearing a badge."

"Oh, no!" Harriet tugged at her skirt. "And your pants are still down. What were we thinking?"

"That we couldn't wait? Whatever you do, don't get off my lap," Jake said, actually laughing.

A rap sounded on the window. "I can't lower it from here," Harriet said.

"That's okay." Jake reached past her and swung the door open. "Evening," he said, as cool as could be.

Harriet looked into the amused eyes of Eric Hamilton. She was blushing to the tips of her hair.

"Everything okay?" The chief of police was surveying the scene. Beside him stood a young man who looked as if he hadn't spent more than one day out of police academy.

"Sir, do I get to search them?"

Eric shook his head. He winked at them. "I think some-one's already done that, Randy Robert."

"Just enjoying a picnic," Jake said. He lifted one of the Sonic bags from the floor.

Harriet was still blushing. Thank goodness they were in Doolittle and not someplace where the tabloid-mad pho-tographers would have scooped the picture and made a small fortune off it. Yet now everyone would know she and Jake Porter had been making out in the backseat. Be-cause of course Eric would tell his wife and she'd men-tion it to her mother and her mother would ask Charlene who Harriet's friend was.

"I see that," Eric said. "Randy Robert, here's a lesson

for you. If everything is under control, you tip your hat and leave the people alone."

"But, sir, what if the car is stolen? Shouldn't we ask for their license and registration?"

Eric put his hands on his hips. "Do we have any reports of stolen Hummers?"

"No, sir."

"Wait for me in the patrol car."

The rookie saluted and marched off.

Eric shook his head. Jake and he exchanged grins.

"Jenifer and I are expecting you for dinner around six tomorrow evening," Eric said. "Why don't you bring Mr. Porter along with you?"

Harriet stared at the chief of police. "How do you know his name?"

Eric shrugged. "It's Doolittle."

Jake laughed. "Pickle described me pretty well?"

"Yes, she did. Besides, it's my business to know who's new in town. You two behave. Till tomorrow." He closed the car door and strode off.

"Well, of all the embarrassing situations!" Harriet slid off Jake's lap and onto the seat of the car. "And you two acted like best buddies."

Jake opened one of the Sonic bags, drew out a handful of napkins, took care of the condom, and zipped his jeans. "Remind me to throw that out," he said. "Now come back here." He opened his arms and pulled Harriet close to his side. "It is pretty funny. Two successful professional grown-ups like you and me caught making out in a public park."

Harriet realized she was about to start grinning. "Seriously, Jake, okay. Maybe it is funny. But it was so weird, the way you two starting acting as if you had so much in common."

He stroked the back of her neck. "I guess that comes from being so adaptable."

"What do you mean?"

"I call it the chameleon effect." His hand slowed but he left it in place, warm and comforting on her skin. "I moved around so much as a kid that I could walk into any new situation and just absorb whatever was happening around me." He shrugged. "I think you'd find the same thing in a lot of military brats."

"That's how you were able to take over at Doolittle High."

"I didn't exactly take over."

"You did. You organized everything and became the most popular guy in our class. The only thing you didn't run was the father-son pancake breakfast." She glanced up at him. "I guess I understand that now."

"The Colonel didn't even know I was in Arkansas," Jake said. "He'd left my mother and me living off base from Barksdale near Shreveport. When she got an offer to tour with a European folk group, she jumped at it and stowed me with some relative of a relative here." He smoothed the top of her hair. "Never mind that. It's ancient history. But the adaptability does come in handy. It helps me fit in with musicians and managers and fans." He nibbled on an earlobe. "And with one special woman."

With every woman he met, Harriet reminded herself. Well, for tonight she wasn't dwelling on that reality. "I've only lived in two places," she said. "Doolittle and Manhattan. How about you?"

"More than you can count on your fingers—" He lifted

each one and kissed the tips. "And on your toes." He ran a hand around the top of each of her boots, setting up a delicious tickling sensation that ran from her knees up to the still damp flesh between her thighs.

"Mmm," Harriet said. "You know how to change the subject."

He lowered her head onto his lap. Tracing the path of her nose and the outline of her lips, he said, "Our next time won't be in the back of a car."

Next time? Harriet almost quit breathing. What was he talking about? This magical, glorious evening out of time was a one-night stand. A quickie. A hello–good-bye for Harriet, something to cling to in her memory after she'd forever alienated him. And for Jake? What was he doing speaking of a "next time"?

"Not in a car," Jake was saying, "but maybe not in a bed, either." He followed the deep neckline of her dress to the tops of her breasts and drew slow circles with the tips of his fingers.

She trembled and rose against his hand.

He smiled. "Next time we'll start slow. Do you play cards?"

She nodded.

"Good. We'll play strip poker. I get to wear lots of clothes and you, I think, start out wearing that naughty thong you've got on and maybe a bra. Oh, and boots. Yeah, I like this game." His voice had grown deeper, and she could feel his body stirring against her tush.

"A few bad losing hands and all you'll be wearing will be those boots. You'll have to pay for your other losses some other way." He feathered his fingers over her nipples, and she sucked in her breath so quickly she started coughing.

He sat her up, patting her on the back. "Are you okay?"

She nodded. "I'm fine." And then she flashed a quick, shy glance at him. "And horny as hell."

"Ah, the power of fantasy," he said, pulling her back onto his lap, this time sitting up.

"And you say you're not creative." Harriet shook her head. "I bet you have as much imagination and talent as any of the people you manage."

"Wrong on that point," he said. "You know what I'm thinking?"

She knew what his body was thinking, but she said, "What?"

"Time for dinner."

"We can't eat that cold food."

"Harriet P. Smith! I wasn't going to suggest it. Let's sneak into the kitchen at the inn and scramble some eggs."

She cocked her head to the side. "Do you know how to cook?"

"Do I know how to cook? Baby, there are only one or two things I know how to do better."

He kissed her, a slow, deep, sensual exploration of her mouth, her senses, and her soul. When he lifted his head, Harriet touched her lips with her fingertips. "Wow," she said. "I can't wait to taste those scrambled eggs."

He laughed. "You're an imp." He slid her off his lap, ever so slowly, showing her how much he wanted her again.

"And you're a sexy devil," she said. "Tempting me like that."

"Quick. Fire drill!"

They leaped from the car and ran around to the front seats, laughing.

Jake put his hands on the steering wheel, then looked over at her. "I can't remember when I've had so much fun. Thank you, Harriet. I don't know what providence brought you to Doolittle the same time I was dragged here kicking and screaming, but heck, I'm not kicking and screaming anymore."

Harriet kissed her fingertips, reached over, and feathered the kiss over his lips. She couldn't say anything. She was afraid she'd cry, and how could she possibly explain that reaction to the only man who'd ever made her feel this special?

Chapter 30

Only Make Believe

The worst thing about the next day was that Harriet was nowhere to be found. Jake took care of business over the phone, argued with Abbie about his plans to order champagne and caviar for the wedding reception, chatted with Pickle at LeDru's, listened to the J. R.'s, discussed the possibility of a production deal with them, and went for another long run. He went with his father to be fitted for a rented dinner jacket and pants and had to admit the Colonel truly was a changed man.

He couldn't help but think everything he did to fill the day would have been so much more enjoyable had Harriet been with him.

He drove to the hospital to learn from the nurses on Mrs. Smith's floor that Harriet had come and gone.

Jake wasn't keen on going to dinner at the home of the police chief. He disliked getting trapped in situations where the other people had shared history. The old tales would get to being told and he'd sit there, reminded once again that he did not belong. Not there. Not anywhere.

But as six o'clock neared, and he joined the other guests in the parlor and there was still no sign of Harriet, he began to think he might not have to go to dinner. Perhaps Harriet had decided to head over early and leave him out of the picture.

But if that were the case, why had she seconded the invitation? Sure, they'd had fun last night. Jake smiled. More than fun. He stretched his legs out in front of the fire, thinking it was funny how it wasn't just the sex that put that smile on his face. With Harriet, even a trip to a fast-food place turned out to be enjoyable. And after they'd sneaked into the kitchen and he'd whipped up scrambled eggs and toast, they'd laughed like a couple of goofy kids.

"Penny for your thoughts," Abbie said.

Jake jerked his head around. He hadn't even noticed her walk into the room. She was standing next to the tea table, a less than usually grim set to her mouth.

"I guess you caught me daydreaming," he said, rising and crossing to the table. The other couples were talking with one another, and he didn't want her to feel left out. True, she was working, but in a small place like the Schoolhouse Inn, the owners were both staff and companions.

"There's a lot of that going around these days," she said. "Would you like another cup of tea?"

"No, thanks." He glanced at his watch. "Harriet and I are supposed to go to dinner."

She nodded. "I talked to Jenifer Janey this morning when I stopped at the library for a book she had on hold for me. She said she and Eric were having you two over."

Jake shook his head. "Why does that not surprise me?"

She almost smiled. "People like to keep track of each other in Doolittle. It's part of the charm and part of the peskiness."

"That's not a word I've heard applied to the town before."

"Maybe I made it up." She poured a cup of tea and dropped one cube of sugar into it. "Mark my words, if you and Harriet were to make a match of it, there would be people in this town who would know it before you were to admit it to yourself."

"Whoa!" Jake held out a hand, palm facing out. "There's absolutely no reason for anyone to be talking about Harriet and me."

"What's this about you and Harriet?" His father appeared at his shoulder, reaching for the teapot.

Abbie gave him a smile he assumed denoted satisfaction with the trouble she'd stirred up.

"You're sure pesky," Jake said under his breath. To his father, he said, "Harriet and I are going to dinner at the home of some friends of hers."

Martha joined them. "Jenifer Janey Wright Hamilton is the brightest, most capable woman in this town. Why, she practically runs city hall from her desk at the library. But the nicest thing that happened to her, besides having her twins, of course, was the day Eric Hamilton came to town and had the good sense to fall in love with her." She sighed and tucked her hand into Jake's father's arm.

The Colonel squeezed Martha's hand and smiled down at her. The two of them stood there making goo-goo eyes at each other.

"Touching," he said. "I'll see you all later."

"Aren't you waiting for Harriet?" That was Abbie.

"Maybe she changed her mind," he said, half hoping that she had. After watching his father and Martha, an evening spent with two married lovebirds was the last type of torture he wanted to face. He wished he could whisk Harriet away with him, perhaps to St. Tropez or Acapulco or South Beach. They'd get the best hotel suite and spend the entire time in bed. He'd exhaust his desire for her, and then he could return to L.A. and back to life as he knew it.

He turned to walk out of the parlor just as the front door swung open with a bang.

"Now who's that?" Abbie strode out of the room. "Well, whatever happened to you?"

"Oh, nothing that can't be fixed." Harriet's voice sounded cheerful, yet he detected a note of something in her tone he'd not heard before.

He rounded the corner in one long bound. "Harriet?"

She gave him a rueful smile. She was leaning on a walking stick. Her jacket was torn.

"You're hurt!" Jake strode toward her, his arms outstretched. "Tell me who did this to you and I'll rip them apart limb from limb."

She laughed. "Please don't. I did it to myself." She shook her head. She took a step forward and winced.

"Let me carry you."

"Don't be silly."

But she didn't resist when he scooped her up. She sighed

and rested her head on his shoulder. Where she belonged, echoed in his head. *In his arms, letting him care for her.* Jake gave her a stern look. "Tell me what happened."

His father and Martha joined Abbie and them in the front hall. "Dear me," Martha said. "Carry her into the parlor. Shall I call the doctor?"

"I'm fine," Harriet said. "I fell off a horse and twisted my ankle trying to get out of the way so I didn't get stepped on. I'm relieved it's my foot and not my hands."

Jake stood there holding her. He wondered whether she insured her hands, and if so, for how much. Plenty of models did; he imagined artists felt the same about their earning potential. But that was only a fleeting thought. Mainly he wanted to keep her close. And safe. "Why don't I carry you to your room?"

She glanced at him, relief evident on her face. "I hate people making a fuss over me. Thank you."

"If you're sure," Martha said.

"Go ahead, Jake. I'll bring an ice pack," Abbie said, marching off to the kitchen.

Jake felt someone watching him and realized his father had said nothing, but had not once taken his eyes off him. That made him uncomfortable, as if he'd been caught appearing in public with only his underwear on. All he was doing was assisting an injured woman. Nothing more.

"Jenifer Janey will be so disappointed," Martha said. "I know she's looking forward to you two coming for dinner."

"Find me their number and I'll call them," Jake said.

"Whatever for?" Harriet struggled to climb out of his arms. She dropped the cane and it clattered to the floor. "I cleaned up before I drove back. It will only take me a few minutes to change. There's no reason not to go." She quit struggling to get down and met his gaze. "Unless you don't want to?"

I'd far rather take you to your bed and stay there with you. With the audience surrounding him, fat chance he could tell her what he really wanted. "I'm good to go," he said.

She rested her head against his shoulder. "To my room, then, if you don't mind." She looked at him, pain in her eyes.

Jake wasted not another minute striding down the hall. She fished the key out and he opened the door, closing it quickly behind them. "Whew," he said, walking over and lowering her to the bed. "That was like running the gauntlet. Now let's get you more comfortable."

She winced as she stretched out her leg. "I am not used to so many people hovering around me. Even with a live-in housekeeper and a teenager I pretty much feel as if I live by myself. This crew is exhausting." She laid her head back on the mound of apple green pillows.

"Well, I live completely alone. My housekeeper has the good sense to come and go when I'm not in. And as you know, I've got no kids." Jake smiled at her. "So I'm definitely on the same wavelength with you."

Her face had grown even paler.

He leaned over the bed. "What happened? Does it hurt worse?"

She shook her head, closing her eyes briefly. "I—uh—there's something I need—"

A knock sounded at the door. He crossed and returned with an ice pack. He placed it on her ankle. "Poor baby. Now what do you need?"

She looked as if she was about to cry.

"Tell me. I'll make everything okay." He didn't know how, but he knew he would. He couldn't stand to see her hurt. It did something to him, deep inside, twisting some sensitive part of him he hadn't even known he possessed.

"An aspirin?"

He didn't think that was what she'd been about to say when Abbie rapped at the door. "Is that all?"

"For now," she said. "I feel so stupid. Not that I should because I haven't been on a horse in years so how should I have remembered how far up it is to get into the saddle?"

"You mean you fell trying to mount?" He couldn't keep the surprise from his voice.

"Don't rub it in." She turned her head away from him. "Though goodness knows Zach did."

So she'd been with her son. So where was he now? "What happened to your son?"

"Oh, he has no trouble staying in the saddle. I left him at Olivia's to take care of the horses and the other animals."

"She doesn't have a hired hand?"

"Yes, but Zach actually likes being there." She made a face. "I had to coax him from the city, but the funny thing is, once he's in Doolittle, he likes it a whole lot better than I do. He has his own horse at his grandmother Olivia's. When we were at the hospital today she said it would do her a lot more good to know he and I were helping at the house rather than fussing over her at her bedside."

"She sounds like a lively sort." He smoothed her forehead. "I went by the hospital today."

"Looking for me?" She looked stunned.

He shrugged. "Caught me."

"That's kind of nice. I guess."

"Anyone ever tell you that you're one stubborn and independent lady?"

Harriet stuck her tongue out at him. "I'm going to sit up and get ready to go to Jenifer Janey's."

"What can I do to help you?"

"Turn around and look the other way."

"That's no fun."

She smiled impishly at him. "It can be."

"Show me," he said, turning around as she'd directed.

He heard her slide off the bed and hobble toward the dressing table across the room. A rustle of fabric followed. Something, he guessed it was her torn shirt, flew across the room toward him. He caught it. It smelled vaguely of hay and horses but most of all, Harriet's sweet self. He breathed in, his senses sharpening. He started to turn around, cross the room, and bury his face in her lap.

"I bet you're using your imagination right now," Harriet said.

He laughed, and the sound ended in something of a groan. "I'd like to be using your body."

"Seeing things inside the mind heightens the senses," Harriet said, sounding as if she were delivering a lecture on artistic creation. "With practice, the imagined becomes reality."

"That would be nice," Jake said, inching around a bit. There, he could see her in the mirror. Forget the imagination when she was in the room, only a few feet away, her delectable body teasing him. A scrap of lace that couldn't really be called a bra drew his attention to her lush breasts. Jake licked his lips.

"Try it," she said. Leaning on the edge of the dressing table, she drew off her jeans, one leg at a time.

"The most beautiful tush in the world," Jake said, savoring the sight of the bare curve of her fanny, and the hint of a thong, "is what I'm imagining. Sweet and luscious and tantalizing."

"Ooh," she said. "I knew you had a wild imagination."

He grinned. "Let's see . . . black lace. Yes, you're wearing black lace, and just like last night, one of those thongs that cries out for me to slip it aside."

"Jake Porter, are you peeking?"

He placed his hands over his eyes and turned toward her.

She laughed.

He dropped his hands and stepped toward her. He caught her hands and lowered her to the dressing table stool. "Watch that ankle," he said, bending to kiss the swelling. He jumped up, got the ice pack she'd abandoned, knelt beside her, and held it against her ankle.

"That's very sweet of you," she murmured, tipping her head back.

Her breasts arched and almost spilled out of that wisp of a bra. Her legs opened as she worked her ankle around the ice bag. Jake lowered his mouth to her thigh and kissed the silky skin inside her leg, above her knee, just below where he wanted like hell to kiss her. "It may be sweet," he said, his voice almost a growl, "but it's entirely designed to promote my self interest."

"Why is that?"

He lowered his lips to the edge of the thong, breathed against her flesh, tasted her through the silk.

"Oooh," Harriet said, throwing her head back even further, "I see what you mean. Only it's more like *my* self-interest."

He gazed up at her face, so beautiful, so relaxed, so

open to him. "Ours," he said. He repeated the word, wondering when if ever he'd said such a thing. He bent to taste her, pushing aside the panty, his mouth hungry and greedy, and yet at the same time, reverent.

She moved against him, drawing him into her. She panted his name and he took what she offered, all her passion and joy and freedom. She clutched at his hair as she tensed and tensed again and then she cried out. Jake drank her in, inhaled her scent, and sucked her release, holding on to her body and burying his head between her thighs as if he couldn't let her go.

Ever so slowly, he came to his senses, but as he lifted his head and pulled her to him, he realized he'd done exactly the opposite. He couldn't be in his right mind because all he could think and feel was that he couldn't let this woman walk out of his life.

And that was crazy.

Jake Porter did not think in those terms. He nuzzled her breast and stroked her back, willing his blood to slow. He didn't have any condoms, and he might be experiencing an out-of-body moment, but he sure as hell wasn't going to have sex without protection.

"Jake," she whispered.

He lifted his head.

She lowered her mouth and kissed his lips, so full of the taste of her. "Thank you." She trembled and gave him a smile with lips that quivered.

"You're crying?"

She dashed at her eyes. "I never cry."

"Sweetheart," he said, "I didn't mean to make you sad."

She tangled her fingers in his hair. "You didn't. Believe me, you only make me happy."

He tousled her hair. "Good. That's the way it should

be." He studied her face, still willing his own body to calm itself.

She reached down and ran a finger under the edge of the waistline of his jeans. "What about you?"

He took his arms from around her body and forced himself to stand up and take a step back. "There's always tomorrow," he said. "We'd better get to that dinner."

She looked rather wistful. "What if tomorrow never comes?"

"Have faith," he said, trying to grin, all the while wishing he could strip his jeans off and bury himself inside her hot, wet, and willing body.

She touched her fingers to her lips and nodded. "I guess I'd better put my clothes on."

"So you can force me to use my imagination again?" He handed her the pair of trousers she'd left over a chair and helped her pull them on, carried her bag to her side, and then tucked her into the black sweater she held out.

"I like doing it the other way better," Jake said, watching her comb her hair and flick on some powder and apply mascara. "You know, taking off your clothes."

She smiled at him, leaned back on the dressing stool, and snuggled her head against his groin. "You turn me on so much," she said. But again she sounded sad when she spoke.

"Hey, that's not a bad thing."

"No, but it is like eating candy when you're on a diet and you know you have to quit having what's forbidden."

He tugged her around and helped her stand. "We're grown-ups. Nothing we're doing is against the law." He winked. "At least not so far."

She laughed. "You can make me smile even when I'm trying for a downer."

"One of my many talents," Jake said. "Come on, let's borrow some house slippers for you to wear and get this dinner thing over with. It's dessert I'm looking forward to."

She rewarded him with a slow, sweet kiss. He wrapped one arm around her, and she limped beside him out of the room.

Chapter 31

Home Is Where the Heart Is

Harriet's body occupied the passenger seat of the Hummer as Jake drove them to Jenifer Janey and Eric's house. But her mind had returned to the events of that afternoon.

It had happened while she'd been in the corral of the Smith barn with Zach, that searing moment when she'd known she had to tell Jake. Now. Not after Christmas through an intermediary. No more delays.

Harriet had easily agreed to help Olivia by doing something useful. Sitting around in a hospital held zero appeal for her. Unlike her son, she couldn't entertain herself with trips to the cafeteria. But exercising the horses and feeding the chickens and ducks and collecting eggs gave her something to do to occupy her time, if not her mind.

Having a mission to accomplish also kept her away from Jake Porter, especially as she'd been so determined not to let his path cross Zach's.

Zach had led his horse, Zanzibar, and Olivia's horse, Miss Kitty, out of the barn. They had one other horse, Rock 'n Roll, who had been Donnie's. He was getting old now, but neither Olivia nor Zach could bear to part with him. Out in the corral with the other horses, they could hear him whinnying as if to ask, *What about me?*

Zach leaned his head down on Zanzibar's chestnut neck. He stroked his back but didn't move to hop into the saddle.

Harriet had been mounting Miss Kitty and had one foot in the stirrup when she realized her son's shoulders were shaking, as if he was crying. But Zach, crying?

"Zach?"

He didn't lift his head. She paused, undecided whether to get on the horse or get off and go to her son's side. "Are you okay?"

"I miss my dad," he said, his face buried in the horse's mane. "He should be here."

"Oh, Zach," she said, filled with sorrow and even more so with guilt. She missed Donnie, too, but in some ways her life with him seemed so distant. To her son, the pain and loss were so much greater. And because she didn't have the guts to tell Jake or her son the truth, he had to live without knowing he had another father. Jake would never replace Donnie, but if given the chance to rise to the challenge of parenthood, he could be there for Zach, helping him in the many ways only a father knew how.

She turned toward him, twisting her foot in the stirrup, getting her boot stuck, and crying out in frustration. She spooked the horse. Miss Kitty kicked her front feet and then her back, and the next thing Harriet knew, her foot was free but she was lying on the ground with the horse a few yards away, looking at her with an accusing stare.

As was her son. He'd lifted his head, and instead of running to her side, which she expected, he stood there glaring at her.

"Why does everything always have to be about you?" Zach clenched his fists.

"What do you mean?" She tried to get up but couldn't.

He kicked at the ground. "Forget it. You wouldn't understand."

"Well, that is a totally unfair thing to say. How can I understand when you haven't told me what you're upset about."

"I told you I miss my dad." He ground out the words, one at a time. "I'm hurting and you go and fall off the stupid horse. What kind of a mom are you?"

Harriet sat there in the dirt, his words ringing in her head. Her son had a point. Her reaction to his pain had been to focus on her own guilt. She took a deep breath and forced herself to her feet. She hobbled toward Zach, her hand held out.

He turned his back on her.

"Honey," she said, "I'm sorry. I know how much you miss him. He loved you so much and he wouldn't want you to be in pain."

Zach shrugged. "He died. And you fell off your horse. But me, I'm supposed to hang tough." He grabbed a handful of his horse's mane. His fingers working in it, he said, "It must be nice to be grown-up and get to make the rules."

Harriet reached out and put her arms around his shoulders. He didn't fling her away. She held him and kept her mouth shut. Nothing she could say would change anything.

But she knew then that she had to set things right. Zach might well be furious with her for a long, long time, but he had a right to know he had two dads. She couldn't bring Donnie back but she could bring Jake into his life.

"Earlier this evening someone offered me a penny for my thoughts," Jake said, "but I'd say by the expression on your face, I'd better offer you at least a quarter."

"I'm sorry," Harriet said. She stretched her leg, easing the tightness in her ankle, wishing it were as easy to ease the anxiety in her heart for her son, the man next to her, and the others who would be affected when they learned what she and Donnie had done.

"Sure you're up to going out?"

She nodded. She owed it to Jenifer Janey. "Turn right at the next corner," she said. "Their house should be half-way down that block."

The house looked pretty much as Harriet remembered it, an older, rambling, two-story structure with a broad front porch. In the early evening darkness, she couldn't make out much detail, but the twinkling white lights in the front bushes and wrapped around the banister and along the rails of the porch provided a cheerful welcome. A Christmas tree ablaze with white lights filled one broad front window.

"Stay there and I'll come around to help you out," Jake ordered.

She didn't resist. She let him lift her, slowly lower her to the ground, and put his arm around her. They had walked only part of the way to the porch when the front door swung open.

Jenifer Janey ran down the steps, wearing a clingy sweater and flattering jeans. "Harriet Rogers, are you limping?"

She threw her arms around Harriet and captured Jake in the hug as well. "You look like a model," she said, stepping back. "You'd best pick her up and carry her," she said to Jake. "These stairs are pretty steep."

Jake grinned at her. "Nice to meet you. I like the way you think."

"I can make it just fine on my own," Harriet said.

Jenifer Janey shook her head. "Some of us it takes a long, long time to realize it's okay to accept a helping hand."

Jake swept her up, and before she could protest again he was setting her down on a sofa as directed by their take-charge hostess. A fire burned in the fireplace across the room from the Christmas tree. Jake propped her foot on an ottoman that Jenifer Janey indicated he should move into place, and then, also as orchestrated by their hostess, took his seat next to Harriet.

"Eric will be right in," Jenifer Janey said, flipping her long hair over her shoulder. "He and Pooper are in the middle of a heart-to-heart."

"Is that a pet?" Harriet asked.

Jenifer Janey laughed. "Sorry. His real name is Stanley but he got so used to being called by that nickname we finally gave in and let him use it. He's a child we've semi-adopted. He lives with us when his father works offshore, which sometimes turns out to be almost a year at a time."

Jake looked surprised. "That must be a lot of work."

"Not really. My twins are off at college and Eric and I

aren't really planning on having children." She smiled,
rather naughtily. "Though if it happens, we won't be
upset."

Now he looked shocked. Harriet wanted to change the
subject. Reinforcement as to how much Jake disliked the
idea of bringing kids into the world wasn't going to help
her build up the courage to tell him about Zach. "So, Jenifer Janey," she said, "you look terrific."

"You can't possibly have children in college," Jake said.
"Are they your husband's kids?"

She laughed. Perched on the edge of an armchair,
swinging one sock-covered foot that peeked from below
her size four jeans, she didn't look at all like the studious
librarian Harriet remembered. "Oh, no, they're mine."
She glanced over at the Christmas tree. "All mine." She
jumped up. "What can I get you guys to drink? Tea?
Soda? Water?"

Harriet would have liked to ask for a shot of whiskey,
something she rarely drank and didn't particularly like.
She was feeling a great need for some form of anesthesia
to get her through the evening. But perhaps it was for the
best, some form of punishment, that she endure the happiness of her friend and mentor and anticipate Jake's anger with nothing stronger than iced tea and the ibuprofen
she'd taken earlier for her ankle.

"Tea for me," Jake said.

She concurred, and Jenifer Janey left the room.

"How are you feeling?" Jake stretched his arm along
the back of the sofa, just skimming her shoulders.

"I'm fine," she said.

"How can she have grown kids?"

"She was really young when they were born," Harriet

said, keeping her voice low. "The father wasn't in the picture and she raised them herself."

"That had to be rough," Jake said. "He should've been horsewhipped."

"Here we are," Jenifer Janey said, whisking into the room carrying a tray with a pitcher and several glasses. She served them just as the tall policeman entered the room, a skinny boy with large dark eyes at his side.

Eric shook hands with Jake, bent to give Harriet a kiss on the cheek, and introduced Stanley, who followed Eric's example, except for the kiss. "Aw, do I have to do that?"

"Just shake her hand," Eric said.

He did and lowered his small self onto the sofa next to Jake. Harriet suppressed a smile. She had a hard time meeting Eric's eyes, as she kept recalling the scene he'd viewed in the backseat of the Hummer.

Conversation turned to Eric's undercover career, which led to Jake's experiences as a kid growing up in an air force family. The two men hit it off, which Harriet could tell pleased Jenifer Janey. Every so often Stanley would tug on Jake's arm and ask him if he knew how to shoot a gun or drive a truck or fly a plane.

When all three answers turned out to be yes, Jake had entered the superhero category as far as Stanley was concerned. "You know what," he said, "Mr. Eric is really cool, but he doesn't know how to fly a plane."

"Is that so?" Jake looked amused. "Would you like me to give him a lesson?"

"Do you really have a pilot's license?" Harriet was pretty impressed, too. Weaver had his own plane but he had to hire a pilot to get it off the ground.

Jake shrugged. "It's something my father insisted on."

Stanley leaped up. "Yes, a lesson. Right now!"

"Stanley, what did we discuss upstairs before we came to the living room?" Eric asked the question in a gentle and calm voice.

The child rolled his eyes. They danced with laughter. The kid was pure imp. "De-cor-um?"

"Very good," Eric said. He smiled at the child and leaned over as Stanley slapped him a high-five.

Jake was watching the exchange as if he'd never seen a parent-child dialogue conducted on such friendly terms. He looked wistful. Harriet felt the tug at her heart and wanted to give him a hug. He must have sensed her studying him, because he turned away from the child, met her gaze, and smiled at her.

It wasn't until after dinner that Harriet had a chance to talk one-on-one with Jenifer Janey. The guys were cleaning up in the kitchen after insisting that Harriet prop her foot up again. Jenifer Janey curled up on the sofa next to her.

"Harriet, he's gorgeous," she said. "It's like a dream come true. Two high school sweethearts find each other again."

Harriet stared at her friend. "Oh, Jenifer Janey, it's not like that at all."

"What do you mean?"

"We weren't sweethearts, and he only came along to dinner because Eric found us . . ." She blushed and trailed off.

Jenifer Janey patted her hand. "Don't be embarrassed. Eric told me everything. But you two can't keep your eyes or hands off each other. There's a cupid sitting on each of your shoulders. Look, I fought falling in love just as hard if not harder. And look at us now. If I'd let Eric get away I would hate myself."

"But you two met and fell in love. You didn't have any complications."

Jenifer Janey smiled. "Just my own stubborn, independent self. And Eric refusing to believe in truly finding love and family and home."

Harriet couldn't help but laugh.

"What about your son?" Her friend whispered the question. "Do he and Jake know about each other?"

Harriet froze. "Know what?"

Jenifer Janey leaned closer. "Harriet, it's me. Jenifer Janey. Think about it. You told me you couldn't contact the father when you came to see me when you were pregnant. You and Jake went to the prom together. He left town. Zach is the spitting image of Jake. It's two plus two."

Harriet stared at Jenifer Janey. "You knew Donnie wasn't his father and you never said a word to anyone. For someone who knows everyone in Doolittle, that's pretty impressive. And special. Thank you."

"It was important to protect your privacy. And Donnie's and Zach's." She sighed. "Only you can set things right."

"I know. I'm going to tell Jake tonight."

Stanley bounced into the room. "Eric says to ask you if the guys can come in now or are you still talking girl talk?"

Jenifer Janey smiled. "Thank you for asking. Please tell him we need a few more minutes."

"Cool," Stanley said. "Mr. Jake is going to show me how to play my guitar."

Jenifer Janey put an arm around Harriet. "He's going to love being a dad. He's a natural."

Harriet's heart clenched. Jake Porter might be a natural with other people's kids, but what about his own? Would he fight that position or embrace it? She closed her eyes for a moment, and reopened them. She hoped he didn't fight it the way she was fighting her own realization that she was falling, falling, falling hard all over again for Jake Porter.

Forget the present progressive tense.

She was in love with Jake Porter, just as she'd always been.

The telephone rang. Harriet jumped.

Eric must have answered it. His face serious, he stepped into the room, Jake and Stanley right behind him. "Emergency," he said. "Fire at the Wallace property. It's empty right now but the fire department is racing to keep it from spreading. I'm going to get officers out to the neighboring houses and help the force. It's volunteer," he said, which of course Harriet knew but he no doubt added for Jake's benefit.

"Wallace?" Jake said. "Is that a house for sale that's next to the Smith Place about ten minutes out of town surrounded by trees?"

Eric, reaching for his coat, nodded.

"I'll go with you," Jake said.

Eric turned. "This isn't a job for civilians."

"That's the house my father and his fiancée want to buy. It's my duty to help."

Eric looked him over and nodded. "Jeni, you'll take Harriet home?" He kissed her without waiting for an answer and rushed outside.

And before she realized he was moving, Jake crossed the room, kissed her full on the lips, ruffled her hair, and was out the door.

Stanley stood there, hands on his skinny hips, looking forlorn. "Aw, rotter," he said. "Just when I learned the G string."

Harriet and Jenifer Janey grinned. "Go get your guitar and show us," Harriet said. "My son plays the guitar."

So much for telling Jake about Zach, Harriet thought, watching the little boy hustle out of the room.

It seemed she was always waiting for tomorrow. But Jake's immediate reaction to help the firefighters save the house his father and Martha wanted to buy filled her with pride. She blinked back a sudden rush of moisture and kept her head down, certain that Jenifer Janey would pounce on her expression and see right through any excuse she might offer for the emotional reaction.

Clearly Jenifer Janey believed that Harriet and Jake belonged together.

But then, the librarian had always managed events in Doolittle.

You don't live in Doolittle, Harriet chided herself, wishing just for once in her life that she did. Then Jenifer Janey Wright Hamilton would insist on things working out exactly as she predicted.

"Everything will be okay," Jenifer Janey said, breaking into her thoughts.

Harriet lifted her head. She didn't see how, but maybe, just this once, it wouldn't hurt to believe in the impossible.

Chapter 32

Ashes to Ashes

LeDru's made breakfast for all the firefighters, police, and assorted volunteers who'd turned out to try to save the Wallace Place and to keep the fire from spreading through the timbered acreage.

Jake stood alongside Eric and one of his brothers-in-law and Mike Halliday, swigging coffee and downing his fifth buttermilk doughnut. His father was across the room, talking to a couple of older men as if he'd known them all his life. He and Jake had worked side by side during the night, keeping the hoses untangled and the water from the pumping trucks flowing.

His father caught his eye. Jake excused himself and

walked around the crowded tables. His usually immaculate father had soot smeared across his cheeks and forehead. Ted put his arm around him and drew him into the circle. "My son, Jake," he said, pride in his voice. "Jake, this is Pastor Roemer and Harold Rogers."

Jake shook hands. Silence fell. His father clapped him on the back and then lowered his arm. "I was just telling these men what a good fight you put up last night. I was proud to be serving next to you."

Jake stared at his father. Words of praise were few and far between, so rare that he didn't know how to respond. "Sir," he said, "thank you. Same to you."

"You look mighty familiar," Harold Rogers said. "Didn't you go to high school with my daughter?" Rogers. Of course, he was Harriet's dad.

Jake nodded.

"She seems like a fine young woman," Jake's father said. "You must be proud of her and her success."

"We always knew she'd do something with her life," Mr. Rogers said. "Her mother and I didn't quite know what to make of her but after she up and moved to New York, she took a turn for the better. I think having decided to have that baby helped her find what she was made of."

"You mean the child she and Donnie had?" Jake heard his own voice as if it came from a long way away.

Mr. Rogers gave him a stern look. Pastor Roemer folded his hands in front of his chest. Jake's father glanced from one man to the other, clearly puzzled.

"There's no mistaking you two for father and son, Colonel Porter," Mr. Rogers said. "Some families turn out looking so much alike, it's almost like seeing yourself in a mirror." He stuck his hands in his pockets. "Nice meeting you," he said. "That fire might have burned all night, but the lumberyard will be expecting me so I'd better go." He gave Jake another long look and said, "Stop by and see us sometime."

Jake watched him walk away. The man had been sending him a message, that was plain, but what it was, he hadn't deciphered.

"Pastor Roemer is going to marry Martha and me," his father said.

"Nice," Jake murmured, his head full of what Mr. Rogers had said as well as what he'd not said. Not in so many words, anyway.

He needed to get to the Barn. He could call J. R. and reschedule the session, but he wanted to hear them again before they moved forward with any more plans. Running on little or no sleep never bothered Jake, so he asked his father if he could take the rental car for a few hours. The pastor agreed to give Ted a ride to the inn, so Jake said good-bye to Eric and the others he'd worked alongside and headed outside.

He needed to clear his head and think.

Had Harriet been pregnant when she and Donnie married?

And if so, who was the father of her son?

Donnie he could accept, he realized, barreling across town toward the road that led to the Barn. Donnie and Harriet had been pals, two kids who didn't fit in, banded together. Jake had no trouble at all relating to that union. One night they got carried away, Harriet ended up pregnant, and the two of them got married.

But had Donnie *ever* gotten "carried away" with a girl?

He roared into a turn and almost hit a truck. He hit the

brakes, cursed himself, and resumed his usual controlled driving technique.

As long as he, Jake Porter, wasn't responsible, it didn't matter one bit. An image of that long ago night at the lake swam into his mind. He and Harriet hadn't been careful, but surely they hadn't made a baby. If that were the case, even if she'd married Donnie, even if she hadn't known how to find him way back when, she would have told him now.

What difference did it make to him who the father of Harriet's son was? They'd had no claims on each other. Still, in a completely illogical way, it rankled a bit. Harriet mattered more to him than any other woman he'd ever known.

Last night he'd even fantasized about the two of them enjoying a relationship unlike any he'd ever contemplated. Watching Eric and his bubbly-bride wife together had stirred dreams inside Jake's heart. He'd never believed in happily-ever-after. In his mind, he continued to refuse to accept that anyone ever, ever remained in love.

Those two hadn't been married long. What would happen five, ten years from now?

But no matter how cynically he tried to answer the question, he knew in his heart that Eric and Jenifer Janey had something special that would see them over the rough patches that destroyed so many other couples. Look at the way they'd taken in Stanley, or Pooper, as he'd proudly told Jake he used to be called before he'd gotten his first library card and started to spend more time with Miz Jenifer and Mr. Eric, as he called his surrogate parents.

And Jake, a bit grudgingly to be sure, was beginning to

admit that his father and Martha just might have found the same special nirvana in their relationship.

He blinked and looked to the right and then the left. He'd been sitting at this damned stop sign for longer than he could remember. What was wrong with him? No sleep? Nah, that didn't explain anything. Many a night he'd stayed up and run meeting after meeting the next day.

The smoke? The flames?

He shook his head, clearing his vision that had filled with the image of his father kneeling in front of the ruins of the Wallace Place, wiping his eyes and asking out loud how he was going to explain to Martha that their house—the house they'd planned to buy—had burned to the ground.

For the first time in his life, Jake had glimpsed the possibility of a future with a woman. He sat there, at the stop sign, unable to move the car forward, forcing himself to admit what his rational mind laughed at. Harriet Rogers? Harriet P. Smith? Cinderella Smith & Jones?

No, he said. No! He beat on the steering wheel. Jake Porter did not need any particular woman. They were interchangeable. His clients he needed. The stars, the musicians, the recording artists who came back to him over and over again, for one successful project after another—those he needed. He'd admit to that.

But to needing a particular, specific, flesh-and-blood woman—no, he couldn't do it.

To admit to that need would be the end of him.

He licked his lips.

He pictured Harriet as he'd bent over her the evening before, her head thrown back, her mouth an "O" of exquisite pleasure, a sheen of perspiration gleaming on her skin, as he'd brought her to climax.

He bent his head to the steering wheel and beat his forehead against the hard circle of leather-wrapped steel.

A siren sounded behind him, and flashing lights forced his attention to the world around him.

Knuckles rapped on his window. He groaned and lowered the window. Randy Robert MacDougal, the rookie who'd been with Eric the night before last, leered into his view.

"Come on, stranger, I know you've got that woman in there. Chief isn't with me this time, and I'm a-going to run you in."

"Excuse me?" Jake said, in his coolest voice.

The youngster patted the gun on his holster. "Show me that woman."

Jake pointed to the interior of the car. "Take a look."

The officer stuck his neck into the car. If Jake had been a bad guy, the rookie wouldn't have had a breath left in his body.

He withdrew, scratched his head, and said, "Now what have you done with her?"

"If you toddle on over to the Schoolhouse Inn, you'll probably find her there," Jake said. "And if I were you, I'd go back to the academy and take a few more lessons."

"Don't get uppity with me," the officer said.

"Do you know whose house I had dinner at last night?" Jake certainly knew how to play the one-upmanship game. Life in the music industry had taught him many useful lessons.

He tipped his cap back. "Who? Your mama's?"

Boy was he stupid. "Your chief of police. You know, your boss."

Randy fell back a step. "Is that so?"

Jake nodded. He put his hands back on the wheel. "See you later," he said, and sped through the intersection.

He didn't feel at all like his normal self.

He was wired, on edge, on the verge of a discovery. He shook his head, trying to clear his mind. Maybe he was past being able to stay up all night and then function the next day.

He swept onto the gravel drive of the Barn, almost skidded to a halt, and paused for a moment before getting out of the car. The other vehicles in the lot were a mishmash of older cars, mainly American, with two pickups to balance the two sedans.

He shook his head, hoping against hope that he hadn't been wrong about his first impression of the J. R.'s. He hated to raise expectations only to dash them later.

Jake walked into the building, the stare of Harold Rogers still burning behind his eyeballs. He had to clear his mind. He had to concentrate. When it came to business, nothing but nothing got in the way of Jake Porter.

He stepped into the central area, eerily quiet after the noisy raucousness of the crowd he'd heard the other evening. Leaning his shoulders against the wall, he realized just how tired and sore he was from the work all night long of fighting the fire.

But it had been satisfying. Effective. Valiant.

Jake watched the kids at the front, gathering on stage, tuning instruments. How many times had he gone through the same process? How many times had he picked a winner or shook his head and slipped out, sure in his conclusion that the group would splutter and fade into anonymity?

The lead singer, guitar strung across his body, nodded

his head, counted to some unheard tune, and led the group into the first song.

Jake leaned back and listened.

And responded. Hell, who wouldn't? These kids were singing their hearts out and the beat was hypnotic, entrancing, enticing.

"Holy crap," he said under his breath. And then he blinked and tried to focus. The kid playing to the right of the lead singer wasn't the same one who'd been there the first night. The kid who had occupied that position had the brightest red hair Jake had ever seen.

This one . . . this one . . . Jake screwed up his eyes, leaned forward, focused.

This kid could have been him, fifteen years ago.

He blinked.

Same hair. Same jawline. Same way of screwing up his mouth and nose and eyes all at the same time. What the hell?

"Stop!" Jake called out the order and pushed himself away from the wall. He strode forward, very much the executive in charge of production. "J. R., a word with you," he snapped out.

The young man shrugged and walked to the edge of the stage. "Yeah?"

Jake glanced past him to the other guitar player. "I thought I was going to hear your regular group."

J. R. shrugged. "So?"

In spite of himself, Jake had to admire the kid's bravado. "So? So? Who's the baby on the other guitar?"

J. R. barely spared a glance for the performers standing behind him. "He's the new guy. Not bad. Red broke his hand and his parents won't let him sign a deal. Says he has to go to college. This new kid has jammed with us before. He'll do."

"Is that right?"

J. R. nodded.

"If I'm signing you guys to a contract, I expect to be consulted about any personnel changes," Jake said, pointing his finger at the young man's chest.

The young man didn't seem at all intimidated. "Show us the money, and then we'll talk," he said, and walked back to his place on stage. "One, two, three . . . " he said, and they were off, making the most awesome music Jake had heard in a long, long time.

Jake stared at the new guitar player, at the kid who could have been him, if he'd ever given in to the impulse to create music that brought joy and sadness and indescribable emotions to life for anyone within hearing range.

The kid looked as much like him as Jake did the Colonel.

And just like that, he knew what Harold Rogers had been saying to him.

And what Harriet had not said.

Shit! Jake stared, and backed away. He sucked in one deep breath, and then blew it out. "Who is that?" he asked Coral, who was hovering around the edges of the room.

"He's just in town for Christmas," she said. "It's Donnie and Harriet Smith's son, Zach. He plays here when he visits his grandmother during the summer."

Jake stared at the stage. He saw, within his admittedly now fevered imagination, the spirit and energy of his mother, Ariel, there on the stage, demanding everyone's attention, taking over, commanding stage center.

And yet the boy, alone now in the spotlight as someone

behind him seemed to recognize the star potential of the new kid, sang his heart out, making love to his guitar, crying out for all he'd ever lost and for all he'd yet to know.

Jake clenched his jaw so hard he thought it might break.

He had a lot for which to make amends.

But Harriet P. Smith had a hell of a lot more to answer for than he did. If that kid onstage was Donnie Smith's biological son, Jake would spread catsup on his leather jacket and eat it. He asked Coral to tell J. R. he'd be back later, and strode out of the Barn.

He found Harriet in the parlor at the Inn, talking to a tall man clad in purple leather pants and a purple leather jacket and standing with his back to Jake. The man leaned over Harriet, his voice low, too close to suit Jake. Not that he had any intention of pursuing her, the one woman who'd made him think, if only for a moment out of time, that the impossible might be probable.

Not now.

Not unless she had a damned good explanation.

And even then, how could he believe anything she ever said or did? What kind of woman doesn't tell a man he has a son?

The discussion he planned to have with Harriet could not be held in front of another party. He stood in the doorway, annoyed by the other man's proprietary stance, by his very presence, by the long blond ponytail tied with a purple leather strap.

Purple leather.

Jake took a step forward, examining the man more closely. He knew one famous rock and roll legend who used purple leather as his trademark. He'd been told it was a superstition arising from the singer's first album to go platinum. The man had tied his wild hair back during the recording session and afterward wouldn't change what he called his lucky leather. He'd even named one of his albums by the term. *Lucky Leather* had gone double platinum for Weaver. No last name, thank you. Evidently that was another superstition.

But what was he doing in Doolittle? He lived in Manhattan.

Well, duh, Jake Porter, he said to himself. *He's come looking for his girlfriend, the hip artist Harriet P. Smith.*

The hip, lying-in-her-teeth Harriet P. Smith.

He still hadn't asked her what the P stood for. He wondered if he ever would.

He walked out of the room and bumped smack into Lilly, who was supposed to be luxuriating in a spa right at that moment.

"Jakey!" She threw her arms around him. "I've been so worried about you. When I couldn't get you on your cell, I hopped a flight to Little Rock and drove out here." She stepped back. "What happened to you? You've got a black stain all over your forehead." She reached up and brushed it, and her fingertips came away soot-stained. "Ooh." She wrinkled her pert little nose in the way he'd once found so entrancing.

"I was fighting a fire," he said. He heard voices behind him in the parlor growing closer. Oh, great. Just what he needed right now—to be introduced to Weaver the legend and to see Harriet without being able to speak his mind.

"How scary," she said, her pretty blue eyes widening. For such an accomplished attorney, Lilly sure could act like a brainless blonde. That, too, he realized, he'd once found attractive.

Now all he liked were dark green eyes, elfin chins, and pixie-cut hair.

At least Lilly was honest. But he couldn't lead her on. "Babe," he said, "I wish you hadn't come. I'm fine. But you've interrupted your spa vacation for no reason. You probably had to pay for the full week, too."

She gave him a wide-lipped pout. "Oh, I don't mind. Not when I thought you needed me. And as long as I'm here—" She opened her arms wide. "Where's our room?"

Jake shook his head just as Harriet stepped into the foyer.

She stared at him from head to toe, her eyes wide, dark, concerned. In his anger, he'd forgotten she had no idea what had happened to him between rushing out of the Hamiltons' house last night until this moment. She moved closer, raised one arm, and touched his forehead.

He flinched.

"You're hurt," she said.

"That's nothing," he said. Not compared to the hole she'd blasted in his heart. Damn, why had he let her get under his skin, for even a millisecond? "Who's your friend?" he said, nodding to Weaver and wondering if she'd concoct a story about him, too.

"Weaver," she said, rather automatically. "Jake Porter." She backed away. "And I gather you're a friend of Jake's?" she said to Lilly.

"Lilly Zimple," Lilly said, shaking hands, very businesslike. Jake could have hugged her for that, as he half expected her to snuggle against him and announce herself as his baby doll or girlfriend or bride-in-waiting. Why had he put up with that behavior for even a day? When it came to women, he was an idiot.

From now on, he was sticking to business.

"Harriet P. Smith," Harriet said to Lilly.

Lilly's eyes widened. "I know your art," she said, very respectfully.

Weaver was eyeing Lilly like a man in an ice cream shop who thought he had his mind made up to have Cherry Garcia, and then he saw the double white chocolate glazed with pure vanilla and he couldn't remember why he'd ever desired the Cherry Garcia.

Harriet smiled and murmured a thank-you but her eyes were only on Jake. He wanted to throw the other two out of the inn and get down to brass tacks with Harriet. But he saw no reason to alienate Weaver, a man whose business he'd considered going after more than once. With a client as high up the charts as the perennially popular Weaver, who seemed to reinvent himself and his band with each shift of the generational flow, Jake could retire.

But what good would that serve him? Only his work brought him happiness.

"So, Weaver," Jake said, "what brings you to Doolittle?"

The rock and roll icon who could hold a stadium full of fans enthralled kicked the toe of his purple leather boot against a throw rug and cast a wistful look at Harriet. Then he shrugged. "Hell if I know. Porter." He repeated the name. "Hey, my man, aren't you that music biz genius who handles Plymouth to Portsmouth and Beyond?"

"And others," Jake said.

The blond giant spread his arms wide. "Well, maybe that's what the psychic meant."

Harriet was shaking her head.

"Ooh," Lilly said, "you went to a psychic? I wish I could but I'm just too practical to trust in such woo-woo."

They all stared at her. If anyone looked like a candidate for a trip to Sister See It All, it was the petite blonde with the big blue eyes and rosebud mouth and bouncy cheerleader body.

Weaver stared most of all. "Well, I was just trying to tell Harriet why I was here and she wasn't hearing me out. Jeezus, babe, it wouldn't hurt you to listen just once, you know." He gave her a friendly tap on the upper arm and shook his head. "Bitching artist but won't listen to any idea that's not her own."

"That is not so!" Harriet returned his jab, in a touch less friendly style. "But I know a bad idea when I hear it."

Weaver turned down his lips, but Jake noticed he seemed to be laughing with the rest of his face. "Asked her to marry me, and she ran off to Arkansas. Now how's a man's ego to stand that, I ask you?"

"Poor baby," Lilly said. "I can't imagine how you must have felt."

"Relieved," Harriet said. "Relieved is what he ought to be thanking his stars for."

"Well, if you're not in love," Lilly said, "I guess it wouldn't be a good idea to get married."

"It's not about being in love," Weaver said. "Harriet is just plain contrary when it comes to admitting that she has feelings. She puts it all into her art."

"I am not having this conversation," Harriet said. "I don't even know this woman"—she pointed to Lilly—"and you don't know Jake Porter and even if we all knew each other, well, what I'm trying to say is please stop analyzing me."

Weaver drew her into a bear hug and patted her on the back. "It's okay, babe," he said. "I've been trying to tell you for the past hour that I came here to apologize for asking you to marry me."

She pulled back a bit. "Really? Why? Didn't you want to marry me?"

Weaver shook his head. "You ought to be spanked and I hope one day you meet the man who'll do it to you. After you turned me down I found that psychic again to ask her a few more questions and I'm telling you it wasn't easy. She'd taken her cart away and I had to hunt all over to find out where she was hiding. No permit, had to run every time the coppers came by."

"Should be licensed," Lilly said. "It's the law."

Jake remembered why he'd been attracted to Lilly in the first place. It wasn't just her body; it was the way she believed in law and order and structure and always following the rules. He'd thought it made sense to go out with a woman so much like him.

Harriet, now, was the exact opposite. See a rule, bend your way around it, through it, over it. See a flower? Paint it in such a way no one would ever guess the inspiration for the piece had been a daffodil. Get pregnant? Marry a guy who hadn't been responsible and never, ever get around to mentioning it to the sperm donor dad.

He screwed up his mouth. It hurt. *It just plain hurt.*

"Well, I found her. Gave her a Franklin and asked her why you'd turned me down. She said I was working too hard to make it happen and that for someone as creative as I am, I should have had the sense not to pick the obvious choice."

"Gee, thanks," Harriet said. "I agree with the psychic, for what it's worth. We've been friends for too long to ever be married. Not, of course, that I'm marrying anyone."

"You're not?" Lilly sounded so wistful. She tucked her hands together and stared at her ringless left hand. "You mean you never want to get married?"

"You're a professional woman, right?" Harriet said.

"I'm a lawyer. Business affairs with MegaFilms Studio."

"So what do you need a husband for?"

Lilly's eyes opened so wide Jake thought they might pop out of her pretty face. "I don't need one. I *want* one." She glanced over at Jake. He shook his head.

"If you want to get married," Weaver said, "then you shouldn't waste your time dating guys who don't want the same thing."

"Ooh," Lilly said. "You are so right. That is so wise." She fluttered her lashes at him.

He gave a half-shrug. "Thanks, babe. Gotta give credit where it's due, though. That's what the psychic told me when I asked her about Harriet turning me down."

"She sounds smart, even if she does believe in alternate reality," Lilly said.

"I have a feeling she believes in the power of the dollar more than any woo-woo stuff," Jake said. "If every guy who asks her for advice hands her a hundred-dollar bill, she's doing okay all the way to the bank. Maybe I should consider asking her if she needs a manager."

Everyone laughed. There, he'd broken up this discussion about marrying and not marrying, all of which gave him the heebie-jeebies. Somehow Lilly had moved so that she was standing next to Weaver, and Harriet was now closer to Jake. Good. Maybe he could send the two of them off together so he could get Harriet to himself.

"As long as you two are in town," Jake said, "you ought to check out the Verandah. They do a decent steak."

Weaver nodded. "Thanks for the tip. Harriet, what's Zach up to?"

Jake froze.

"He's helping his grandmother with the horses," she said.

"He's over at the Barn," Jake said, keeping his voice light and not taking his eyes off Harriet. "Local music place. The kid is a natural."

"For sure," Weaver said. "He's hung around my band for years, and of course Donnie taught him more than he'd learn at Juilliard."

"You saw him play?" That was Harriet, sounding as if she could barely squeeze the words out of her throat.

Jake nodded. "The J. R.'s want to include him in their lineup."

"That's impossible," Harriet said. "He's in high school. And then he has college and law school."

Weaver laughed. "Babe, do you think I went to college? I wouldn't have gotten that high school whatever it's called if my old man hadn't locked up my Fender until I passed it."

"GED," Lilly said. "That's the name of the test."

Weaver winked at her. "You're smart as well as pretty."

She beamed at him.

"So Zach's fine," Jake said. "Ask anyone and they'll give you directions to the Barn."

Weaver held out a hand to Lilly. "Split with me?"

She glanced from Harriet to Jake, a question in her eyes. "I guess you won't be missing me, will you, Jakey?" she said, but she didn't sound too brokenhearted.

Jake gave her a smile and a brief hug. "Take care of yourself," he said.

"Bye, Jakey," she said, and blew him a kiss.

"Later," Weaver said, and then they were gone.

Jake picked Harriet up and made a beeline to his room, ignoring her protests that she was perfectly able to walk. Limping wouldn't get her there fast enough, and he'd be damned if he'd put up with another interruption.

Chapter 33

To Tell the Truth

Harriet stopped protesting and clung to Jake as he carried her through the door of his room. She knew this would be the last time she would feel his strong arms around her, the last chance to feel his heart beating against her cheek. He had seen Zach and he had guessed the truth.

He dumped her on the bed, paced across the room, stood with his back to her, his shoulders tensed.

"Jake, please," she said, her voice pleading for him to give her a chance to explain.

He spun around and advanced on the bed. He stared down at her, his eyes almost black. She could see none of the golden flecks. "He's my son, isn't he?"

She nodded. She sat up straighter and held out a hand

toward him, whether to bring him closer or ward off his anger she wasn't sure.

"Say it," he said.

"Zach is your son." She whispered the words.

"Son of a bitch." Then he laughed, a sound without any humor. "I guess that's pretty much true." He leaned against the bottom poster of the bed, his eyes fixed on her face. "When were you going to tell me?"

"Last night," Harriet said. "On the way home from dinner."

He gave another bark of laughter. "Right." He took a turn around the room, pacing off the steps around an antique trunk and a walnut armoire and a washstand that held a blue and white porcelain bowl and pitcher. And then he came back to rest in front of where she sat on the edge of the bed. "What kind of woman doesn't tell a man he has a son?"

"A coward," she said. "And also an extremely brave one. What was I supposed to do, all those years ago? You disappeared, no forwarding address. I turned up pregnant." She ran a hand through her hair. "Dammit, don't judge me for what I did! You weren't there."

She could see the muscles in his jaw working. "No, I wasn't. But what about yesterday and the day before?" His eyes widened. "You knew who I was even before I found out who you were, didn't you?"

Harriet nodded. It was a relief, actually, not to be telling lies or protecting half-truths. "Yes, I did. I couldn't not know. Every day since Zach's been born, I've looked at him and seen you all over again, in so many ways."

"Shit," he said. "But you said nothing. Every time I said I'd never bring a kid into the world, every time I asked you about your life since high school, every time I wanted you to share a little bit of yourself—you said not a word about what really happened."

Harriet shook her head.

He swore again, then raked his fingers through his short hair. He looked like he was going to cry. Or curse some more. Or beat her senseless, not that Harriet thought he would. No, he'd disappear and leave her to live a life of guilt-ridden what-might-have-been. And then she knew that no matter what she had to risk, she couldn't let that happen.

She inched to the edge of the bed and stood. He pushed back from her, as if flinching from even the possibility of coming into contact with her. "I think the main question is where do we go from here?"

"Are you nuts?" Jake roared the words out. "Where do we go from here? *We* are not going anywhere. You lied to me, you hid from me the knowledge that I have brought a son into this world, despite me being dead set against that ever happening. You led me on, made love to me as if you and I were two people with no past, no baggage, no—" He broke off. "Does Zach know?"

"Not yet," she said. She was trembling, reacting to his anger and his pain and her own sense of guilt and loss.

"Good. We'll tell him together."

"Now who's nuts?" Harriet glared at Jake. "He's my son and he needs to learn this news from me."

"Right," Jake said, crossing his arms over his chest. "I'd like to be a fly on the wall when you tell him you just never mentioned to him that you didn't get around to letting his father know he'd come into existence."

"It's not like that," Harriet said, bunching her hands into fists. "Donnie loved me and he loved Zach. There's no way he'll hate me for what I did."

"I wasn't thinking of that," Jake said. "I suppose I'm grateful that Donnie married you and that he and his parents took care of you so well. God only knows I couldn't have done the same when I was eighteen. And my father would have skinned my hide. No doubt we would have ended up stuck in Doolittle. Now wouldn't that have been punishment enough?"

"I don't know why you're speaking of punishment," Harriet said. "One of the greatest blessings in my life has been having a child."

"And even though I've never wanted to have one," Jake said, "thanks for taking the experience away from me."

"That is so unfair!" She kicked at his boot. "If you had ever once written to me, or tried to let me know where you were, do you think I wouldn't have told you? I would have begged you to come back and take care of me and the baby, even if what all the other kids in the class were saying was true. But no, Jake Porter was nowhere to be found."

"What were they saying?" He'd dropped his arms to his sides.

"That you asked me to the dance on a dare. They wanted to laugh at me and they set you up to make a fool of me."

Jake shook his head. "They did do that stupid dare, but that's not why I asked you to the dance."

"It wasn't?" She was surprised that at this point in her life his answer still mattered to her.

"I asked you because I wanted to. I liked you. I really liked you." He looked up to the ceiling and then back at her. "I'm sorry."

"What are you apologizing for?"

"I liked you and I got carried away. If I'd remembered to use protection, none of this ever would have happened."

"And Zach wouldn't have been born." Harriet tapped her forefinger against Jake's chest. "Don't try to change what happened. I'm glad he's my son."

"And mine?"

She met his gaze. "Yes."

"Then why the hell didn't you tell me?" He was back to shouting. They stood, toe to toe, his dark eyes boring into her face. "I guess I understand why you married Donnie, but Donnie's been dead for what, five years? I'm not exactly living under a rock. If you'd wanted to find me, you could have."

She licked her lips. Lips he'd never kiss again. What a stupid time to be thinking of that loss. "I did know where you were," she said. "I hired an agency to track you down and after New Year's I was going to contact you."

He put his hands on her shoulders. "Yet you didn't need to wait till then. Not after we happened to bump into each other here."

"No," she said, her voice a whisper.

"I always liked you," he said, his voice full of pain. "You're the one girl who made me want to want more than I ever thought could be possible and dammit, yesterday, last night, fighting that fire, I kept thinking over and over again that maybe, just maybe, I was a hardheaded fool and that maybe love was possible." He broke off.

She waited.

He pushed her to the bed, and before she knew what was happening, he was straddling her, his arms on her shoulders. "Did you have to take that away from me?"

Harriet struggled against his hold. "I did what I had to do," she said.

He pushed her deeper into the plush comforter. "Liar."

She shook her head.

"You did what you *wanted* to do," he said. "It was easier, wasn't it, to let things go along as they had been? And I don't really blame you for that, because you had Zach to think of and maybe he's better off thinking his father was dead than knowing he had a father who was stupid and irresponsible and got a girl pregnant and never came back to take responsibility."

"No," Harriet said. "Well, yes, it was easier. A day passed, and a week, and a month, and a year, and then another year, and I didn't know what to do. But I knew I needed to find you and I can prove that I'd taken steps to do just that."

He shifted his arms. His body ground against hers. Despite her hurt and anger, she reached for him, arching her hips, aching to feel him, to urge him to forgive her, to consider the possibility that they might make everything okay.

"What does the P stand for?" he said, his body hovering above hers.

"What do you mean?"

"You didn't have a middle name. It was a point of pride with you," Jake said. "You told me that the night of the dance."

She grew perfectly still.

"Tell me the truth, please."

She swallowed. "P is for Porter," she whispered. "I took it after I knew I had your baby growing inside me."

"Oh, my God," Jake said, and pulled her tight to him.

Harriet couldn't breathe. He was holding her so close. She didn't know whether he hated her or whether he loved her, but parts of her hoped that the love outweighed the hate. She lifted one hand and stroked, ever so lightly, the back of his head.

He buried his face in her breasts, and then before she realized what he was doing, he was tugging her waistband open, and pushing her slacks down to her knees. She reached for his jeans and yanked the zipper down. She was out of her mind. She had never been so sane. She wanted him even if he hated both himself and her afterward.

He didn't even take his boots off, just lowered his jeans and spread her out beneath him and rammed into her body. His face contorted, his breathing ragged, he plunged into her and demanded that she rise to his need. She cried out, her hands flung out over the top of the silky bed covering, her body rising and arching and aching for his greedy touch. He rode her until she came and came again and fell back limp against the covers, absorbing, receiving, taking, and drinking him in when he cried out and filled her. He fell against her, his cheeks damp with sweat, her own wet with what she knew were tears.

After a long, long time, he stirred and lifted his weight from her. He pulled back, rose from the bed, fastened his jeans, and stood looking down at her, almost in shock.

"What have I done?" he said.

She moved her head slowly from side to side. She said nothing. She had no words to express her feelings. Only on a canvas could she bring forth the emotions of satiation, punishment, and loss.

He backed away from the bed. He frowned. "Forgive me," he said. "Please let me know when you would like to arrange speaking with Zach." And then he turned on his heel and left the room.

His room.

Harriet sat bolt upright. What had he meant, "Forgive me"? And then she realized that despite making such a big deal about using protection, neither one of them had given it a thought.

She hugged her arms to her chest and tugged her pants up around her waist. And then she pulled one of the many pillows on the bed close to her, curled her arms around it, and began to cry.

Chapter 34

What Makes a Family?

Telling Olivia was every bit as difficult as Harriet feared it would be. As soon as she could gather her wits, she slipped out of the inn and drove to the hospital. Her body felt as numb as her mind.

Olivia was sitting up, not in bed, but in a chair. She looked much more like herself than she had during the earlier visits. Harriet kissed her cheek. "You look like you're doing much better," she said.

Olivia's blue eyes twinkled. "They tell me I'm as good as new, if not better. I hope to be riding my horse again in no time at all."

Harriet smiled at her, and giving in to the impulse of the

moment, she reached out and took Olivia's hand. "I need to talk to you," she said, her voice catching slightly.

"What is it, dear? Is something wrong?" She put a hand to her breast. "Not Zach? Say he's okay."

"He's fine," Harriet said. "It's not that kind of news, but I have something I must tell you."

The older woman reached up and smoothed Harriet's forehead. "Then sit down and begin."

Harriet almost cried. "You've been like a mother to me," she said, sliding a hard plastic chair next to her mother-in-law. "Better."

Olivia sighed. "Your mother means well. And she loves you. She just has a difficult time showing it."

Harriet frowned. "She is free to make her own apologies. But never mind that." She hunched forward, not sure where to begin. "It is about Zach," she said. "And me and Donnie. And someone else. I want you to know I'll accept whatever your reaction is, but I also want you to know how much I've loved and respected you."

"My dear, spit it out," Olivia said. "Whatever you have to say, it's better to say it than to keep dancing around it. That's a good way to drive yourself crazy. And you know I've always been as curious as a cat."

Harriet smiled, briefly. "When Donnie and I married, I was already pregnant." There, she'd said it, all in a rush.

"And?"

"And?" Harriet stared at the older woman. "You're so calm. Did you know?"

"You and Donnie told us you had to get married. It happens."

Harriet rubbed her thumb against her knee, cleaning an imaginary spot. A stain. A blot on her life and the lives of her family. "It wasn't Donnie," she said, then lifted her head. "I was pregnant by another guy."

Olivia glanced to her right, out the window at the gray winter afternoon sky. She fluttered her hands, then returned them to her lap. "I see."

Harriet wanted to comfort her, but she felt as stiff as the plastic chair she was sitting on.

"Who?" Olivia said. "Who besides Donnie is Zach's father?"

Harriet moved, then. She touched Olivia's shoulder for the briefest of moments, swallowed back a tear that threatened to spill out, and said, "Thank you for asking the question that way. Donnie is Zach's father. But he does have a biological father, too. His name is Jake Porter."

Olivia gazed at Harriet as if seeing her for the first time. "Why did you and Donnie do what you did?"

"Jake was in our class. He left town before I knew I was pregnant and I couldn't find him. I told Donnie. He was always my best friend. He offered to marry me. I said yes."

"This certainly explains a lot of things," Olivia said, her head tipped to one side, a distant expression in her eyes. "No wonder you were so upset with me at Donnie's funeral."

Harriet grimaced. "Zach looks exactly like Jake Porter."

Olivia brushed a soft lock of hair away from her cheek. "Why now, Harriet? I could have gone the rest of my life not knowing what you've just told me. What happened to break your silence?"

Harriet kept on circling her thumb against her knee. "He's here in town and he saw Zach."

"So your hand was forced?" Olivia sighed. "Perhaps it's for the best. No matter what you've told me, Zach is still my grandson." She fixed Harriet with a fierce look in her eyes. "Don't you dare try to take him from me. He's all I've got left of Donnie, and no matter who his other father was, to me, Donnie will always be Zach's dad." She dabbed at her eyes. "I'm so thankful he had the chance to be a father." And then she broke into a sob.

Harriet dropped to her knees beside Olivia and drew her close. She winced as her sore ankle bent the wrong way, but she refused to give in to a little bit of physical discomfort when the pain she'd caused was so evident in Olivia's reaction. "Donnie was so lucky to have you for a mom," she said. "And I've been lucky, too. I hope you can find it in your heart not to hate me, but the important thing is to help Zach through this."

Olivia lifted her head. She dried her eyes with the hem of a silken bed jacket. "I say we leave everything the same. He comes to Doolittle to stay with me in the summers and whenever else he wants to visit. Maybe it's a blessing, in a way, that he'll have a man's influence, what with Donnie and his dad gone and you not remarried. He's at an age when he needs a man around."

"Jake Porter isn't going to be around much," Harriet said. "He lives in Los Angeles. That's the other side of the country."

Olivia sniffed and dabbed at her dainty nose with a tissue that Harriet passed to her. "I'll have something to say to that. You said the young man is in town? Bring him to see me. I'd like to take his measure, if he's going to be at all involved in my grandson's life."

Harriet smiled. "You're fabulous," she said, her heart full with admiration for the way Olivia was handling the news.

"Porter," Olivia said. "Isn't the man who is courting Sweet Martha named Porter?"

"That's his father," Harriet said.

"Oh, well, then," Olivia said, "he might turn out to be quite acceptable."

"What makes you say that?"

"Amelia told me her good friend Rebecca met them the other night at the Verandah and Mr. Porter is not only handsome, but he treats Sweet Martha just as he ought. The one thing she didn't know was when the wedding is."

"I can tell you that," Harriet said. "It's New Year's Eve at the Doolittle Community Church."

Olivia pointed to the bandages surrounding her knee. "Then I'll have to be out of this place by then. I am not going to miss that wedding." She wiggled her toes. "You may bring Jake Porter to see me here or introduce me at the wedding. One way or the other, I intend to get to know him."

"We haven't told Zach yet," Harriet said. "I don't know how to do it."

Olivia nodded. "Knowing you, dear, you want to do it by yourself. But family is family. We should all be together when we tell him. You. Me. This Jake Porter person. Zach needs to know we all love him." She tapped Harriet on the back of her hand. "Stop fussing with your leg or you'll wear a hole in yourself. Will Jake Porter love your son?"

Harriet thought of Jake stating so firmly that he'd never bring a kid into the world. She heard his voice in her head. But she also felt the tenderness with which he'd helped her when she'd turned up with a sprained ankle, and the caring he'd shown when he'd helped fight the fire.

He'd seen himself in his son at the Barn, no doubt not just in his looks, but in the musical talent that flowed in his own blood.

She felt again his rage when he'd confronted her. He surely wouldn't have been so angry if he'd intended to walk away and have nothing to do with his son. And he wouldn't have insisted on them telling Zach together if he hadn't planned to be involved in his life.

Harriet lifted her hand from her knee. "Yes, Olivia, he will love his son."

Harriet hugged Olivia and left to find Jake. The first place she looked was the Barn. Even before she stepped out of the Hummer, she heard the music coming through the half-open doors.

Gravel crunched underfoot as she made her way to the entrance. She realized the song was one of Weaver's. Slipping through the doors, she spotted Coral, her hair wrapped in a scarf, standing along the back wall. She glanced at Harriet, put a finger to her lips, and jerked her head toward the stage.

Harriet stopped beside Coral.

Jake was there, but not in the audience.

He was on stage, making love to the guitar he cradled against his body. Zach stood by his side, doing the same. They took turns singing into the same standing microphone. And behind them on the drums, Weaver played his heart out. J. R. handled the keyboards.

"Ain't this something special?" Coral whispered. "Right here in my little club."

Harriet knew she referred to Weaver, the megastar. But the most special sight of all was her son and his father making music together, communicating in a language the two of them so clearly and beautifully understood. Harriet dashed the back of her hand across her eyes. Well, if there was ever an occasion to cry, she figured this one ranked pretty close to the top.

Jake could have spent hours talking with Zach and none of the words would have helped create the sort of bond she was watching on that small stage. She blinked and slowly started to comprehend how wrong Jake had been when he'd claimed he had no creative abilities, no musical talents. Liar, she said to herself, smiling for the first time in what felt like days but she realized was only hours.

"Hey," a voice whispered on her other side. Harriet glanced over and saw the bubbly blonde had reappeared. "He's good, isn't he?"

Harriet nodded. She didn't know which "he" the woman meant.

"And the kid is amazing. He looks so much like Jakey. It's such a shame he doesn't want to get married and have babies." She sighed. "He's a natural father. You should have seen him when Weaver and I got here . . ."

Coral leaned over. "Shh. You are listening to music history so either shut your trap or go outside."

Lilly wrinkled her nose. "He's like that with all his clients, like a father, I mean. They all want to do so well to please him. Even Ariel, his crazy mother."

Coral grabbed a push broom and waved it at Lilly. "Out. Now."

Lilly made a lip-zipping motion and Coral lowered the broom. The music grew faster and louder and even more plaintive. Zach put back his head and howled out the refrain of Weaver's paean to lost love. And to her amazement, Jake did the same, letting loose with the vocal cries of passion and pain and loss.

"Wow," Lilly said. "Who would have thought it possible? Jakey Porter sure plays close to the vest."

Coral grabbed her by the arm and hustled her out the door, which she shut and bolted. Harriet smothered a laugh. And the song came to its end.

Coral applauded wildly. Harriet joined her, with more restraint. Once Jake realized she was in the building, would he play again? And then she remembered how upset Zach had been with her when she'd fallen off the horse the other day. *Harriet, it's not always about you.* If playing with Zach helped the two of them get to know each other, she hoped her presence didn't interfere with Jake one bit.

Weaver moved from behind the drums, shook J. R.'s hand, slapped Zach on the back, and said to Jake, "Not bad for a business guy. Give me a call after New Year's, will ya?"

Jake nodded. He said something to Zach, and the two of them moved to the keyboards, huddling with J. R.

Weaver crossed the large room. When he reached Harriet's side, he jerked a thumb over his shoulder. Speaking in a low voice, he said, "No wonder you didn't want to marry me."

"What do you mean?"

Weaver was so tall he blocked her view of the stage and of Coral. "Look, babe, it's okay. I get it now. I knew Donnie didn't play on your side of the street and it's coming together for me. There's enough going on with Porter and your kid to tell me that someday someone will write a song about it." He kissed her on the cheek. "Let me know how it turns out so I can be that guy, okay?"

"You're a pretty smart man," Harriet said.

"I haven't done bad for a high school dropout. But I did

tell Zach he ought to finish school, so I guess you owe me one for that. Now, where's that blond bombshell?"

Someone pounded on the door.

Coral handed Weaver a sheet of notebook paper and a Bic pen. "I'd wet my pants I'd be so thrilled if you'd give me an autograph."

He laughed and scrawled his name.

The pounding came again.

Coral clutched her autograph. "Your girlfriend's outside. She went for a walk."

"Cool. Later. We're off to Acapulco." And like that, Weaver was gone.

"Mom!" Zach jumped off the stage and raced toward her, his eyes aglow, his face beaming. "I'm going to play with J. R. and his band and Mr. Porter is going to give us a recording deal. How cool is that?"

"Very," she said. She couldn't bear to squelch his enthusiasm knowing what she had to tell him.

Jake walked up, a smile on his face, his hand outstretched. "Harriet, how good to see you."

Harriet blinked. She'd expected a continuation of his anger or perhaps cold and distant behavior. "You, too, Jake," she said, somewhat cautiously. He gave her a quick kiss on the cheek.

"I was telling Zach earlier that we'd been friends in high school and only recently bumped into one another."

"Right," Harriet said, finding a tentative smile for Jake and a much more natural one for Zach. She was relieved to find Jake in such a friendly mood. "Only Jake didn't make music like you guys were doing on that stage when he was at Doolittle High."

"Who taught you?" Zach asked, respect in his voice.

"My mother," Jake said, with a shrug. "My father taught me to shoot and how to fly a plane, and my mother forced me to learn to play several instruments."

"Forced you?" Zach sounded shocked. Then he grinned. "Ha. Funny. You're kidding, right?"

Jake grinned back. "Anybody hungry?"

"As a bear," Zach said.

"Shall we get some lunch?" Jake asked. "The three of us."

The three of us. Harriet shivered, both with pleasure and from fear. She was a coward, plain and simple, when it came to emotional encounters. The critics—and her friends—were right. The only way she felt safe showing emotion was within the context of her art.

"Harriet?" Jake said her name and she met his eyes. She read his own uncertainty in them, and her heart responded. She'd rocked his world as he knew it by delivering the news he had a son. She needed to stand by him and help him and her son to accept each other. She needed to do everything she could to make the situation a happy one, and not one that sowed only the seeds of regret and anguish.

"Sure," she said. "Maybe we can get something to go and stop at the hospital. I saw Olivia this morning and she'd like to meet you." She ruffled her son's hair, much to his annoyance. "And she always loves it when you visit."

"Aw, Mom. I'm too grown-up for you to do that. I'm in a band now. But as long as we get a couple of burgers I'm cool to see Gran-O." He looked at Jake. "You'll like her."

They walked toward the door. Jake paused and said

good-bye to Coral. He held the door open for them and said into Harriet's ear, "You told Olivia?"

She nodded. "She wants us to be with her when we break the news."

"I like her already," Jake said. "How's Sonic sound?" He winked at Harriet and she stared back, dumbfounded. What was Jake Porter up to?

Chapter 35

Telling It Like It Is

Jake didn't know whether to hug Harriet or to strangle her. He couldn't remember when he'd been as angry and upset with another human being as he'd been when she'd admitted that the two of them had brought a child into the world. And then his fury had turned against himself, rightly so, after he'd taken her in a rage of want and need and lust and longing and hurt.

He had a son.

Those words had echoed over and over in his head as he took his father's rental car and headed to the Barn. *He had a son*. He hadn't asked for it, he'd set his mind against such a thing ever happening. But now that he'd learned the truth, he vowed to do right by him.

"Zach." Jake said the name out loud. He roared down the streets that led to where he'd left Zach and the rest of the J. R.'s making music that he predicted would make them very rich young men.

He owed it to the child he'd brought into the world to put aside his anger at Harriet. He'd grown up with parents who argued and bickered and never, ever agreed on the small things in life or the large ones. One thing he would not do was repeat that pattern.

He'd swallow his feelings toward Harriet's lies for the sake of his—no, their—son.

Jake had turned into the Barn's parking lot at a speed way too fast. Gravel churned and he had to grab the wheel to keep from fishtailing. He got the car under control, killed the motor, and sat there. He wasn't religious and he didn't believe in anything that wasn't real and concrete and provable. But for a moment, he uttered a wish, a prayer, an invocation, to whatever powers might exist.

Please don't let me let him down.

And then he'd gone inside the Barn and Weaver had been there and they all started jamming. Zach asked him if he played. He started to say no and then he looked at the dark brown eyes of his son. He saw, for the first time, those golden flecks that mirrored his own eyes.

Something inside him stirred and then broke free and he grinned and reached for a guitar, something he hadn't done in years. "Yes, I play," he said to Zach. "Do you know Weaver's 'On the Ropes'?"

Zach had picked out the opening bars and crooned the words made famous by the legend in purple leather. Jake fell in with him, and from that moment on, they made music together.

And here they were, the three of them, headed to Sonic.

"Hey, penny for those thoughts," Harriet said.

He smiled and turned into the fast-food place. And sure enough, both he and Zach ordered their burgers slathered in mayo. Jake thought he'd never tasted a better burger than the one he ate as they drove toward the hospital.

They pulled into the parking lot. Zach loped ahead, which suited Jake. "I take it she wants us to tell Zach when she's there to reassure him?"

Harriet nodded. "I am sick with worry about what he'll think."

"You've put it off a long, long time. I should think this must be a relief to you."

She looked at him, those big, dark green eyes so beautiful yet so distant. "I guess it is, though I hate to admit that." She tugged on her shoulder bag. "I don't know that I'm ready to share Zach."

He nodded. He'd expected her to start to realize she would no longer hold center stage in their son's life. "I want what's best for him. That's my interest."

"Thank you," she said, wetting her lips with the tip of her tongue.

That gesture almost undid him. He might be mad as hell at her, but at that moment he wanted to pull her close and hold her tight and never let go. Jeez! He must be nuts. Want a woman who'd kept this secret for so long? He glanced at her again, at the way she held her chin up to meet whatever challenges lay ahead, at the way she squared her shoulders, at the way she walked as if she were challenging the world.

"Do you want to be the one?" Jake asked.

She nodded. "I need to do it."

"I understand."

She stopped. She stamped her foot. "Why in the world are you being so nice? It's driving me crazy!"

He nodded. "Figured it would."

"You beast," Harriet said, the corners of her eyes crinkling in amusement. "You don't mean that."

"Look, what happened, happened," he said. "Let's make the best of it."

She seemed to find the button on her blouse fascinating. Finally she lifted her face. She looked so sad, it was all he could do to keep from putting an arm around her to comfort her. "I don't deserve you," she said. "You're reacting so well and I've made such a mess of it."

"Well, don't go and get all boo-hooey on me," Jake said, "or I won't be half as nice." He started walking again and guided her forward, moving slowly to accommodate her sprained ankle.

She laughed. He smiled down at her, and found it very difficult to stay mad, even though he knew he had every right to.

They made their way into the building and up the stairs to Olivia's hospital room.

"So you're Jake Porter," the lady in the chair said, extending a hand.

Jake bent over her. He almost felt as if he should kiss her hand. Instead he admitted to being Jake Porter.

"Olivia Smith," she said. "Zach's grandmother."

He nodded. Harriet moved closer. Zach was looking out the window, drumming on the broad sill that was almost covered in vases full of flowers.

"Zach, the three of us have something important to tell you," Harriet said.

She wasted no time, Jake thought. But that would be

Harriet all over again. Once she'd made up her mind, she acted. He supposed all these years she simply hadn't decided to break open the secret.

"Yeah?" He turned to face them, then his face clouded. "I hope you're not going to gang up on me and say I can't play with the J. R.'s."

Harriet shook her head. "It's not about the band. It's about you and me and Jake and Donnie. And Olivia."

He shrugged. "Shoot."

"A long time ago," Harriet said, fussing with her collar, then putting her hands together and parking them in her lap, "when I wasn't much older than you are now, I cared—a lot—for a young man. We made love without, um, protection—"

Zach was looking down at his boots. "Gosh, Mom, I don't need the facts of life lecture. I've only talked to Kristen twice, if that's what this is about."

"Kristen?" That was Jake. "You mean the girl who's working at the inn?"

Zach shrugged. "Yes, but I don't know what hanging out with Kristen has to do with you. Hey, what's this about?"

"It's not about Kristen," Harriet said.

Jake couldn't help but feel a bit nervous about how relieved Zach looked at that news. He'd have to have a talk with Zach, he thought. Jake Porter having a father-son talk? How unbelievable was that?

"It happened before Donnie and I got married. I got pregnant with you, Zach," Harriet said, "and the man wasn't Donnie."

Zach lifted his head. He stared at her and then at Jake. "Say what?"

"Jake's dad had come to town and snatched him away,"

Harriet said. "He never knew. Until now. Donnie wanted to marry me, knowing I was pregnant. And that's what we did."

Zach looked at Olivia. "Gran-O, is this true?"

She held out her hand. Zach took it. She nodded.

"Well, shit," Zach said. "Wow."

Harriet stepped forward. Jake caught her by the shoulders. "Give him a moment," he whispered.

She halted, leaned back against him.

Zach looked at Jake. He lifted his hand, pointed a finger, and said, "You look like me. How weird is that?"

Jake nodded.

Zach ran a hand through his hair at the exact same moment Jake lifted his hand to make the same gesture.

They broke into nervous laughter. When the sounds trailed off, they all stood there. Jake figured no one really knew what to say. Goodness only knew, he hadn't words equal to the situation. As determined as he was to stay calm and emotionally level in front of Zach, he vacillated between wanting to strangle Harriet and sit down and discuss in a rational manner how best to handle their now-joint responsibilities.

After a few more minutes of quiet, Olivia said, "Zach, I just learned this earlier today, and the one thing I demand is that you remain my grandson in every sense of the word."

Zach stuck his hands in his jeans' pockets. He eyed Jake. "You're still going to produce our music?"

"Why not?"

"None of this stuff about me staying in school and not joining a band?"

"Hey," Harriet said, "that is a completely separate discussion."

Zach laughed. "Still my mom, aren't you?"

Harriet burst into tears. "Oh, Zach, can you forgive me?"

He dragged one hand out of his pocket and patted his mom on the back. "Sure, cool, just don't drown me, okay?"

And again they all laughed, and to Jake's relief, there was less tension this time. Maybe things would work out. At least he and Harriet agreed on one important issue—he had no intention of letting his son drop out of high school to play in a band.

Chapter 36

Exploring a New World

"I meant what I said about keeping things as normal and peaceable as possible for Zach," Jake said.

"Naturally," Harriet said, kicking the Hummer into reverse and spinning out of the driveway of Olivia's house. She'd felt a need to be in control so she'd climbed behind the wheel when she and Jake headed out of the hospital to drop Zach, at his request, back at the Smith barn.

She didn't blame her son for preferring the company of horses to that of humans right now. He'd taken the news fairly well, but she sensed the storm clouds building. Seeing Jake as a music producer who could help him achieve stardom was one thing. Viewing him as a man who might weigh in with his mother against those very plans could prove troublesome.

"I can do it in front of him," Jake said, his brow furrowed. "But it's a lot to adjust to."

Harriet nodded. "I understand."

"No." His jaw worked. "I don't think that you do. I defy anyone to understand what I'm feeling." He shrugged. "It's good and bad and maybe one day I'll turn out to be thankful. But no one should have to walk on stage at this point in a kid's life."

"He likes you," Harriet said. She had to remain hopeful that good would come of sharing the truth.

"He doesn't even know me," Jake said. Swinging his body around in the seat, he said, "Dammit, you could have hired an investigator years ago. It's evident you and Donnie were never hard up for money. Why the hell didn't you do it sooner?"

"It didn't seem fair to Donnie," Harriet said.

"You know something, Harriet? I think that's another one of your lies. Donnie might have welcomed a chance to live his life without the layers of pretense you two concocted. No, I think I know why you never looked for me."

Harriet slowed the car. She didn't want to hear whatever it was Jake had to say. She pulled to the side of the road. A pickup truck loaded with four hunting dogs zoomed by.

He leaned over and brushed a surprisingly gentle hand across her cheek. "You were afraid, weren't you?"

She swallowed. "Why do you say that?"

Jake lowered his hand. "I remember Harriet Rogers from Doolittle High. Awkward, unlovable, unpopular Harriet. Harriet who didn't fit in with her family or with

the other kids. With Donnie you were safe—in an arti-
ficial life maybe. But staying there kept you safe from
being hurt by a guy you cared so much about you made a
baby with him."

Harriet tipped her forehead onto the steering wheel.
She would not cry.

"You're afraid to be loved, aren't you, Harriet?"

She lifted her head and rubbed her eyes. "I can love as
well as the next person."

"That's not what I said." His voice was soft and low.
"You can dish it out but you can't take it."

"I don't know what you're talking about."

"If you let someone else love you, that means you give
him the power to quit loving you, the ability to inflict
the kind of emotional pain you depict in your art but shy
away from in your life."

Harriet shook her head. "I thought we were talking
about how to deal with you being in Zach's life."

"Harriet, I'm not trying to hurt you, but if you try to
change the subject, I'm going to be tempted to reach over
and shake you by those beautiful shoulders of yours,"
Jake said.

"If you're not trying to hurt me," Harriet said, "please
quit psychoanalyzing me." She twisted in the seat. "I
may be afraid of letting myself get hurt, but I do have
feelings. Maybe you should see a shrink. Look at the
way you and that Lilly woman dealt with each other. I
mean, come on, she and you had to have some history."
Harriet tipped her head to one side, "'Ooh, Jakey, what's
that on your forehead? Jakey?' And then she waltzed off
with Weaver and you didn't even blink. Who's the mal-
adjusted one here?"

"Hey, that's hitting below the belt," he said.

She stuck her nose in the air. "You've probably never loved anybody in your life."

He turned his head and stared out the window.

Harriet waited, hoping in a foolish, lost way that he'd deny her statement. She knew what she wanted him to say, but when no words came, she pulled back onto the road.

They were almost at the inn when Jake looked over at her. "I apologize if I hurt your feelings. I won't bring up personal issues again. Let's just find a quiet place to sit down and figure out how to handle things with Zach."

"What do you mean by 'things'?"

"Money. Custody. Visitation. Or to start with, introducing him to his grandfather."

Harriet squealed around one of the corners of Courthouse Square. "I don't need any money. You can visit when you're in New York. And I guess we should tell your father and Martha when we reach the inn."

"My, my," Jake drawled, "don't you make things sound simple?"

"The emotional issues are tough," she said, "but at least the other details don't have to be."

"I don't consider my involvement in my son's life a detail." He bit the words out, and they hung in the space between them.

Harriet jerked to a halt in front of the Schoolhouse Inn so hard that her head snapped back and forth.

"Clearly I'll be the one giving Zach driving lessons," Jake said as he got out of the car.

Harriet slammed her door. "Not necessary. The school does that."

Jake walked around the front of the Hummer. Arms crossed, he looked down at Harriet. "You didn't make the baby by yourself and now that I'm in Zach's life, you'll have to get used to sharing decisions."

Harriet stomped her foot. Then, annoyed at herself for giving in to such a childish gesture, she turned on her heel and strode toward the porch. As she bounded up the steps, the front door opened. To her dismay, out walked Ted Porter and Martha.

She stared at this older image of her son, formulated a greeting in her head, opened her lips to speak, and then stood there as gawky as the Harriet of old.

"We're serving eggnog tonight," Martha said. "For Christmas Eve."

Harriet managed to curve her open mouth into a smile of greeting just as Jake overtook her. Harriet hadn't even known it was the twenty-fourth.

"Perfect timing," he said. "Do you two have a few minutes?"

Harriet felt both Ted and Martha's appraising glances and flushed. If they were expecting to hear another happy announcement of two people finding love, she hoped they wouldn't be too disappointed. She indicated the porch swing, and the four of them moved over but no one sat down.

No one spoke, either. Harriet's arm brushed against Jake's. She looked up at him. He lifted a hand and repeated that Zach-like gesture of running it over his hair.

"Is something wrong?" Jake's father asked.

"No," Jake said. "Harriet?"

So he wanted her to break the news. Fair enough. She'd

do it, and then let him tell her parents. Perhaps it would be easier that way. "Mr. Porter," she began.

"Ted," Jake's father said, and smiled, the corners of his eyes crinkling the way his son's—and his grandson's—did.

"Thank you," she whispered. Then she raised her voice to a normal tone. "Jake and I knew each other in high school. We hadn't met again until the other day, here in Doolittle."

Martha smiled. She'd clasped her hands together, clearly anticipating a romantic tale.

"We have a son together. He's fifteen and Jake met him for the first time today."

Jake's father looked as if he couldn't decide whether to horsewhip them or hug them. "Fifteen and you'd never been to see your son?"

Jake shook his head. He said nothing.

Harriet couldn't believe he would let his father get the impression he'd neglected his own kid. "Mr. Porter—Ted—Jake didn't know because I didn't tell him."

The older man focused his stern gaze on her. She didn't flinch. "It was wrong of me, but don't blame Jake. He left town the morning after we . . . went out," she finished, unable to say "made love." It might have been love to her, but what had it meant to Jake?

"I see," Ted said.

Olivia had said the exact same words. Harriet heard the echo of her voice in her head. *Please let him embrace my son.* She glanced over at Jake, standing there tall and silent, awaiting his father's judgment. *And please give him the love to forgive his son for not living up to his expectations.*

To her surprise, Ted took a step back and sat down in the swing. He put his head in his hands. Martha laid a hand on one shoulder. "Ted?"

Jake's father lifted his head. "I owe you a bigger apology than I can possibly give," he said. "If I hadn't dragged you out of town the way I did, you wouldn't be finding this news out now."

Jake said nothing. Despite how angry she'd been only minutes earlier, Harriet wanted to comfort him the way Martha was comforting Ted. Simple contact. A touch. A connection of flesh to flesh. But Jake stood there like a statue.

His father rose from the swing. Harriet wondered what he'd have to say to her. He might blame himself for whisking Jake away, but he knew as well as they all did that she could have found him sooner.

"I always wanted a grandson," he said. "You two couldn't have given me a better Christmas present."

"Sir," Jake said, "thank you for taking the news so well."

Ted reached over and clasped Jake by the shoulder. "If you don't quit calling me 'sir' I'm going to send you to bed without supper."

They smiled then.

"When do we get to meet him?" Ted asked.

"He's at the Smith Place," Harriet said.

"Of course," Martha said suddenly. "You and Donnie married right after graduation. Now it makes sense. Oh, Ted, Zach is a wonderful child."

"Fifteen is more than halfway to a man," Ted said, looking at Harriet. "I'm glad you didn't pussyfoot any longer, young lady."

Harriet nodded, relieved to be spared any greater re-criminations. "I can pick Zach up and bring him back here."

"We," Jake said. "We'll go together."

She opened her mouth to protest, then shut it. It wouldn't do any good. If she left without him, Jake Porter would no doubt jump on the running board.

Chapter 37

Mirror, Mirror

Jake borrowed Ted's rental car to drive them to the Smith Place. To his surprise, Harriet didn't argue. She was probably as relieved as he was to have passed the hurdle of breaking the news to his father, and equally as anxious to be on their way back to ask Zach to come to the inn with them.

"It's a lot to expect a fifteen-year-old to adapt to," he said out loud as they entered the sweeping drive.

"Or anyone," Harriet said softly.

Jake pulled to a smooth stop, turned the engine off, and looked at Harriet. She had her head resting against the back of the seat and her eyes half shut. He realized he wanted to hug her close and tell her everything would be all right. "Harriet," he said, reaching a hand toward her.

She jerked upright, her hand on the car door. "I'm ready." And before he could say another word, she was out of the car.

He sighed and followed her. What could he expect? He'd yelled at her, accused her of being afraid to love, and reminded her of a self she'd worked so hard to put behind her—why would she expect him to offer comfort?

"The barn is out this way," she said, striding ahead of him.

In a few steps he'd caught up with her. In silence they crossed the broad lawn, found the path around the house, and approached the barn. The big doors stood open but Zach wasn't in sight.

A bicycle lay on its side near the doors.

Harriet paused. "Maybe he has a friend over," she said, pointing to the bike.

Jake glanced past the barn to the pasture. A few horses grazed there. The trees dotting the area had long ago dropped their leaves. A pale winter sun hovered just over the horizon. The only sounds were a few bird cries.

"It's peaceful here," he said, speaking in a low voice.

Harriet nodded. "It's so different from New York."

"And L.A." Jake took a deep breath. "No rushing around."

Harriet smiled. "That would drive you crazy in less time than it takes me to speak this sentence."

He grinned. And then another sound joined the calls of the birds in the big tree off to the side of the barn.

Laughter? Giggling, whooping laughter. A girl's voice coming from the barn, joined by the deeper tones he recognized as Zach's.

His son's.

He paused, hearing that word again in his mind. He had a son.

A shriek, louder, brought Harriet's gaze up to his. "Let's go," she said. "He's having a good time. We can tell him later."

"There's a girl in there," he said, leaning closer to her ear to speak. "A girl. A boy. A barn."

"So?"

"You're not, um, concerned?"

She shook her head, a touch of sorrow glinting in her eyes. Jake did touch her then, gently, on her arm. "Wishing it were us?"

Harriet's cheeks colored a sweet pink.

"I like it when you get hot and bothered," he said.

"I am not."

He grinned, and then remembered he was a dad and had to be responsible. "We'll pick this thought up later," he said. "Right now we need to deal with Zach."

"There's no need to deal with anything," she said. "He's fifteen and having a good time, and after the news we've given him, we should be thankful."

Shouts of laughter rang out. A girl dashed out of the double doors, followed by Zach, who caught her around the waist and tickled her ribs. She giggled and swung around to face him.

Jake opened his lips to call out Zach's name, but before he could speak, Harriet had clapped a hand over his mouth. The girl moved slightly, and Jake recognized Kristen.

"Hey, Zach," Harriet said in a light voice, "we dropped back by."

Zach and Kristen froze and turned toward them. Zach dropped his hands to his sides and blushed furiously. Kristen smiled at them, not at all shy.

"Give a guy some warning," Zach said, shooting a look over at Kristen.

Harriet nodded.

Jake decided to follow Harriet's low-key approach, but he felt a lot more like marching Zach over to the side of the barn and delivering the same father-son lecture his own dad had given him. But he could see just how stupid and embarrassing and awkward that would be. One, it would be ineffective and get him off completely on the wrong foot with Zach.

"Thanks, Harriet," he murmured. "Hi, Kristen."

She gave him a wave. "What's up?"

"Apple stock," he said.

She laughed. To Zach, she said, "This guy's okay."

Zach looked at him and gave Jake a shy smile. "Yeah."

Jake went mushy inside, a feeling he wasn't at all used to. He kicked the toe of his boot in the dirt. He wasn't sure what to say, but somehow instinct took over. "You guys hungry?"

Zach's eyes lit up. Kristen nodded.

"Sonic?" he asked.

"Sounds good," they said together.

Harriet smiled at him as if he were the smartest guy in the world. They fit Kristen's bike into the trunk of the Lincoln and drove off.

Several hours later, they'd not only introduced Zach to his grandfather, but shared their news with Harold and Charlene Rogers. They left Zach there, dropped Kristen at her house, and made it back to the inn, where all was dark.

"Whew," Jake said, opening the front door. "What a day."

Harriet tiptoed beside him. "It's not one I'll ever forget."

He bent and kissed the top of her head. "Me, either."

She stilled.

"Walk you to your room?"

She nodded, and they moved down the broad hall side by side. He opened her door for her but made no move to invite himself in. He wasn't sure if she looked disappointed or relieved. "Merry Christmas," he said, and crossed to his own room. What was happening to him? The Jake Porter he knew would've tried to score, especially with a woman as passionate as Harriet P. Smith.

P as in Porter.

Procrastinating, provoking, passionate Harriet, who'd carried the secret of their son for all these years. There could be no one-night stands with Harriet.

Jake stepped inside Fourth Grade and closed the door behind him.

It wasn't every day a man became a father.

Chapter 38

I Do, I Don't

Nothing would do for Charlene Rogers but that she have everyone over for Christmas Day dinner. Jake, Zach, Harriet, Ted, Martha, Abbie, Edward, Honey, the twins, and Olivia, just out of the hospital, Olivia's sister Amelia, and Harold made up the group gathered around the dining table. Abbie had been reluctant to accept the invitation, feeling someone should stay at the inn, until Ted told her he'd stay behind, too. The other guests had family in town and wouldn't miss them one bit, he'd insisted.

So Crabbie Abbie, not looking nearly as grumpy as her nickname implied, sat between Jake and Harriet, a seating maneuver Harriet felt pretty proud about. Jake being polite and friendly grated on her more than the anger he'd expressed when she'd first admitted the truth about Zach. She could have been anyone else at the table given the even-handed manner he exhibited toward her. But to her dismay, Jake gave no hint of the passion and heat and desire he'd so clearly felt for her before he'd learned the truth about Zach.

It rankled.

Harriet played with her fork, moving pieces of a slice of pumpkin pie back and forth on the dessert plate. Around her the conversation buzzed. Her mother had finally quit hopping around and talking a hundred miles a minute. She had one of the twins on her lap, attempting to feed the toddler a spoonful of Gerber pudding.

Harriet put her fork down. She was through pretending to eat to please her mother. Beside her, she heard Abbie and Jake discussing the plans for the wedding reception. On her other side, Honey was describing teething to Zach, who looked like he wanted to ask to be excused. He'd muttered something earlier about being invited to Kristen's house for dessert, but he'd taken a generous slice of pumpkin pie. Not that that meant he couldn't eat again, Harriet thought, smiling.

She loved her son so much. Her problem was that she also loved his father, for all the good that did her. She sighed and looked down the table. Her dad was watching her, a look of concern on his kindly, worn face. She smiled at him. Then she heard her mother's voice and froze.

"I knew from the minute I saw him walk into the shop the other day that Jake was flesh and blood to Zach," Charlene was talking to Ted Porter, but she might as well be addressing the table with a megaphone.

Harriet shrank into her chair. Everyone at the table knew about Jake being Zach's birth father, but did that mean they had to discuss it? Her shoulders twitched and she yearned to be anywhere but stuck at that table. And then she felt a warm hand on her back, just below her neck. Only one man's hand had that strength and sensitivity and warmth, that ability to make her believe that everything would be okay.

She glanced across Abbie at Jake. He was smiling encouragement at her, even as he reached across the back of Abbie's chair to touch her.

"We do have a strong family resemblance," Jake's father said. "I said this to my son privately and to Zach, but I guess it's appropriate to say to everyone here how thrilled I am to have become a grandfather." He lifted his ice tea glass toward Zach. "Anytime you want to learn to fly a plane, you just let me know."

"Cool," Zach said. "Maybe Weaver will let me take his for a spin."

Everyone laughed, even Harriet, despite her tension.

Charlene gazed around the table, a smile hovering on her mouth. "Well, well," she said, "it's good to see how things have turned out. You know we never understood you, Harriet, but we always loved you."

Harriet stared at her mother. She didn't know why, but she wanted to cry. Maybe it was because her mother never said those three words to her? Jake's hand soothed her shoulder. She looked down the table at her mother. "I love you, too," she said, very softly.

"Too mushy for me," Zach said. "May I be excused?"

Harriet said yes at the same moment Jake did. Surprised, she turned toward him. It was so hard to get used to sharing the parental role with him. And they had so many things to work out. Jake had made it clear he planned to be in involved in his son's life, which meant she'd have to find a way to live with him in hers.

He pushed his chair back. "Thanks, Granlene," he said. "Hey, Jake, can I get a ride over to Kristen's?"

Jake dropped his hand from Harriet's shoulders. "Sure."

And like that the two of them loped out of the house. Harriet stared at the piece of pumpkin pie. She lifted her fork, then dropped it.

To her surprise, Abbie reached over and patted her on the forearm. "Change takes a lot of getting used to," she said. "Did I tell you I'm thinking of adopting that pesky dog Jessica Halliday was trying to push on me last week? She calls it Faustus, but I don't know what kind of a name that is for a self-respecting cocker spaniel. I'm thinking of changing it."

"To what?" She should be happy that Zach asked Jake to drive him, she scolded herself. Instead she felt like an orphan.

"Madame Curie," Abbie said.

Harriet smiled at her former science teacher. "Perfect," she said, glad someone could be happy.

Honey started clearing the table. Harriet was hopeless in the kitchen, but she needed to do something to take her mind off mourning the way Jake had gone from hot to lukewarm toward her. She stood up and offered to help. She couldn't blame Jake for despising her for keeping the truth from him, but she didn't know how she could stand to be around him in a co-parenting situation if he kept up his bland politeness.

She was in the kitchen, scrubbing the last pot, when she sensed Jake walk in. She'd chased the others out, preferring to be left alone. They had wheeled Olivia into the living room. Harriet could hear the rumble of voices as she worked at the kitchen sink, a place she hadn't stood in so many years, performing a chore she'd almost forgotten how to do.

He picked up a dish cloth, reached for a roasting pan, and started to dry it. She glanced sideways at him, at the dark brown eyes, the bump on his nose she longed to kiss, the strong mouth, short dark hair, and lean, powerful body. She sighed and scrubbed harder at the practically spotless pot.

"I had a talk with Zach about the importance of finishing high school versus performing with the band," he said. "I told him the J. R.'s could record next summer. That will give them time to work out their material. He can fly here when school is out, practice with them, and I'll book the recording in Nashville. I do a lot of work there."

Harriet stared at him, unable to believe what she'd heard. "Excuse me?"

"He agreed. He said you'd skin him alive if he dropped out of school."

"He's right about that," Harriet said. "But what right have you to plan his life without discussing it with me?"

He stared right back. "I'm making up for lost time."

She slammed the scouring pad into the dishwater, splattering her silk top and Jake's designer T-shirt. "That is a low blow! You can't just walk into our lives and take over."

He set the roasting pan on the counter. He folded the dish towel in half and draped it over the dish drainer. The line of his jaw grew rigid. "Harriet, remind me what the P in your name stands for."

"Don't change the subject!"

"Say it, please," he said, his voice low and calm, at least in comparison to her shouting.

"That is none of your business," she said, knowing she sounded like a sulky six-year-old.

He reached out and turned her to face him. "You meant it when you told me it stands for Porter, didn't you?"

She looked into his eyes, wishing with all her heart he wasn't reminding her of that sentimental action now when she was mad at him and wanting him all at the same time. "Yes," she said, her voice a whisper.

"Would you like to make it your last name?"

"What?"

"Instead of your made-up middle initial, it could be your new last name," he said, still holding her.

"Are you proposing to me?"

He nodded. "I guess I am."

"Why?"

"It makes sense," he said. "Zach needs the stability two parents could give him. He's a great kid. You and Donnie did a wonderful job. He's probably too old for any bad influence from my crazy background to screw him up. Like I said, 'It's sensible.'"

Harriet tugged free from his touch. What about love? What about desire? What about Harriet the woman and Jake the man? "I married once for the sake of my son," she said. "And while I appreciate your concern for Zach," she said, speaking slowly so as not to break into tears, "the answer is no. Besides, you and I both know you're not the marrying kind."

She tried to laugh, to turn it into a joke, but her voice caught in her throat. She grabbed the dish towel, dried her hands, and walked as quickly as she could out the back door, made her way around the house, jumped into the Hummer, and sped away.

Chapter 39

Get Thee to the Church

Jake let her go. It wasn't until the next morning he learned from Abbie that Harriet had checked out of the inn.

He almost dropped his coffee mug. "She what?"

Abbie nodded and gave him a stern look. "You're not supposed to know this, but she's gone to stay with Miz Olivia." She sniffed. "I don't know how much of a nurse she'll be, but at least she's trying to help, and I'll give her credit for that."

More likely she was intent on avoiding him, Jake thought, but kept that to himself. She sure had a habit of running away whenever someone proposed marriage to her.

First Weaver. Now Jake.

So he spent his time hanging out with Zach, who gave him a horseback riding lesson and later played a few songs he'd written. The next day Ted invited both of them to join him for a golf lesson. But Zach's favorite treat turned out to be when Jake offered to take him to the nearest small airfield in El Dorado and rent a two-seater for an hour. He made sure to ask Harriet's permission, over the phone. He could tell she wanted to protest, but he assured her he'd never do anything to put their son in danger.

At the end of the hour, Jake added flying lessons to the list of things he planned to give Zach. He'd made up his mind that Harriet could avoid him as much as she pleased, but she couldn't prevent him from getting to know Zach and providing for him.

For that week, Jake left his business-first world behind. But every day he couldn't help but think how much better each experience would be if he could share it with Harriet, too.

Obviously Harriet didn't feel the same way.

When the evening of his father and Martha's wedding arrived, Jake was relieved, frustrated, restless, and annoyed. Harriet had refused to speak with him when he'd phoned Olivia's house to see if he could pick them up. He had half a mind to borrow Ted's car, race over there, and demand she get in.

But he'd already decorated it with tin cans Abbie had saved. He and Zach and Kristen had cut holes and tied them onto the bumper of the Lincoln with colorful strips of cloth Abbie had produced after a hunt in the attic. They'd also written "Just Married" in soap all over the back and side windows. Getting into the spirit of the occasion, Kristen had added lots of hearts and cupid's arrows. They'd arranged separate rides to the church for Ted and Martha and hidden the car behind the Doolittle Community Church.

So Jake had to be content with leaving Harriet to find her way to the ceremony. He knew she'd show up because she was bringing Zach to his grandfather's wedding.

It wasn't until the ceremony was under way that Jake spotted Harriet. Standing beside his father, watching Martha walk down the center aisle of the church, Jake caught sight of Harriet in the back pew. She sat alone, on the edge of the seat, as if she might flee at any moment.

Zach was in the front pew, seated beside Olivia and the Rogers clan.

Of course Harriet hadn't joined them.

She still didn't feel as if she belonged.

Anywhere. To anyone.

Jake's father stretched out his hand to Martha. They smiled into each other's eyes and turned to face the minister.

"Dearly beloved," the minister began, but Jake didn't hear the rest of the words. Instead, he heard himself accusing Harriet of being afraid to let someone love her. He thought of the last few days, of her hiding away from him, hurt, scared, mad? He should have gone to her, broken through the door and past the wall of emotional defenses she'd constructed around her heart.

He hadn't done that. The time he'd spent building a relationship with Zach was good and necessary.

But Harriet needed him, too.

She needed to know she was surrounded by love, love she didn't need to run away from. Even her mother, who'd admitted she didn't understand her daughter, loved her. Clearly her dad did, too. And Olivia. And Zach.

And what about you, Jake Porter?

Did he love Harriet? He lit up every time he saw her. When she smiled, he felt happy. When she was sad, he wanted to hold and comfort her and take away her worries. When she made him angry, he wanted to rage, yet when he got it out of his system, he desired nothing more than to kiss her, cherish her . . . love her.

"You may kiss the bride," the minister said.

A collective ooh and ah swept across the nearly full church. Jake took the opportunity to glance at the back pew.

Harriet was slipping out, heading for the door.

All he could do was stand there and watch her go.

Or not.

There were advantages to the way things worked in Doolittle. Jake offered his arm to Abbie, and they followed Ted and Martha down the aisle. At the back of the church, he hugged his father, kissed the bride, and slipped into the crowd of well-wishers. He'd spotted Eric and Jenifer Janey and he made his way toward them.

It didn't take them long to understand what Jake wanted. Eric whipped his radio out of his jacket pocket, contacted Busby who was on patrol, and soon had the report Jake wanted. Harriet's Hummer had been sighted turning onto the road that dead-ended at the lake. Something twisted inside Jake. Jenifer Janey gave Jake a quick hug and whispered into his ear, "Don't let her get away."

He sketched a salute and headed out of the church.

Chapter 40

Full Circle

She hadn't known where she was headed. She'd only
known that she had to escape the church.

There was only so much loss Harriet could endure.
Watching Jake at the altar and wishing with all her heart it
had been the two of them joining hand in hand in front of
that minister—and knowing it would never happen—was
more than Harriet could handle.

She drove blindly, yet more carefully than usual. She
came to a full stop at every intersection, didn't skid when
she turned onto the lake road, and even used her signal
indicator when she pulled off to the side.

Kicking off the black satin heels she'd purchased in El
Dorado the day before, she reached into the backseat of

the Hummer, fished in her suitcase, and pulled out her boots. She tugged them on and stepped out of the car.

She was packed and ready to head for the airport as soon as Zach finished at the reception, a fact she hadn't mentioned to Jake.

Harriet pulled her red cashmere coat around her and trudged toward the bluff overlooking the lake. Instead of saying good-bye to Jake, she'd come here, she realized, to say good-bye to the past.

She found the sturdiest of the trees that lined the small hill and sat beneath it. Out of the breeze, it wasn't cold. Closing her eyes, she breathed in the crisp air.

And remembered a night long ago.

They'd been kids. They'd made a baby. A wonderful son. She had to cling to the good and learn to live without what her heart wanted. Jake had said she was afraid to be loved. Maybe he was right.

But maybe he was wrong.

Because she believed that Jake did love her.

He was just too stubborn to admit it, to himself or to her.

Harriet sighed and opened her eyes.

That's when she heard the clattering noises coming from near where she'd parked. She craned her neck and saw a sedan pulling off the road near the Hummer.

She narrowed her eyes. Trails of tin cans clunked and clattered behind the car. She saw writing all over the windows, making out "Just Married." That did look like Ted's rental car. But how embarrassing to be caught here at the lake if the two of them had decided on a quick getaway and romantic tryst.

She looked around and saw no place to hide. Scooting around the trunk, she shrank back against the tree.

She heard a car door slam.

Only one.

She heard footsteps.

No voices.

She closed her eyes, trying to make herself invisible.

"Harriet."

She scrunched her eyes more tightly closed. That could not be Jake's voice.

"It's me. Jake."

He must have bent down. She felt his hand brush her hair, ever so lightly.

Harriet let her lids flutter open. He was sitting back on his heels, face to face with her. The golden flecks in the dark brown of his eyes gleamed. "You took your father's car?"

He shrugged. "Sometimes a man has to do what a man has to do."

Her heart leaped at his words, but she lectured herself not to read anything into the phrase. "Why are you looking for me?"

He sat down on the ground, close but not touching. "Remember when I said you were afraid to let anyone love you?"

Harriet glanced down at his hands, so strong and tender, then back to Jake's face. "I remember."

"You're not the only one with that diagnosis."

"What do you mean?" If only he'd reach out and put his arm around her.

"I knew what I was talking about because I could've been describing myself. Mr. Never Look Back. Keep running and you'll never know what you might be missing." He took in a sharp breath. "Harriet, I've missed you. All week I kept wanting to share my thoughts, my feelings . . . damn, it's not like me at all."

"Zach told me you two were spending a lot of time together."

"Harriet, this isn't about Zach. It's about us."

"There is no—"

"Don't say it." Jake placed his palm lightly over her lips. "Please don't say there's no 'us.'"

"What do you mean?" she tried to say through his fingers.

He moved his hand, bent his head, and kissed her.

She wriggled backward, only to find the sturdy, unmovable trunk of the big tree blocking her retreat.

He kept on kissing her. Then he stopped and she wished he hadn't.

"Harriet, I need you," he said, reaching out and pulling her to his chest.

"Need isn't love," she said.

"Gosh, you're stubborn."

"It's a trait that's served me well," Harriet said. Maybe she should kiss him. She tipped her head, explored the line of his lips with the back of her thumb, and then drew his face to hers.

The kiss was deeper, needier, greedier. Jake groaned and Harriet suckled his tongue, aching for him to admit he felt for her what she did for him.

He pulled away, looked into her eyes, touched her puffy lips. "Harriet P. Rogers Smith, I've never told any woman that I loved her. To love is to lose. But today I figured out that to run away from love is a much worse loss."

"Oh, Jake, I know what you mean," Harriet said, cupping his cheek.

He kissed her fingers. Then he worked his way up her wrist to the sleeve of her red cashmere coat. "I love you," he said. "Wow. It feels so good to say that."

"You can say it again," Harriet said.

He gathered her to him. "I love you, Harriet." And then he kissed her. After their kiss, tracing circles on the back of her hand, Jake said, "I only hope that one day you'll feel free to say those words to me."

Harriet stared at him. "Do you realize where we are?"

He glanced around. "At the lake. Or to be more precise, at exactly the same spot where we were the night we conceived our son."

"You do remember," Harriet said.

He nodded and held her hand more tightly.

"I loved you then and I love you now, Jake Porter."

He kissed her again, lowering them to the ground, cradling her body so that she lay atop the length of him. "Harriet, please say you'll marry me."

He was asking her for all the right reasons. For love. For sharing the risk of whatever might come to them in the future. She took a deep breath, gazed into his eyes, and said, "Yes. And yes. And yes."

Then they were laughing and kissing and rolling in the mounded leaves. It was prom night all over again. They were young and carefree and full of joy. They used her red cashmere coat as a blanket, and snuggling beneath it, they sealed their promises heart to heart.

Next month, don't miss these exciting new love stories only from Avon Books

Untouched by Anna Campbell

An Avon Romantic Treasure

When Grace Paget is kidnapped, she believes it can't get any worse—until she finds herself imprisoned with a mad man. Declared insane and at the mercy of his uncle, Sheene trusts no one. But to escape this deadly web, he and Grace must put their fears aside; for their only chance at survival is each other.

Satisfaction by Marianne Stillings

An Avon Contemporary Romance

Georgiana Mundy has everything: fame, fortune—and a stalker that she would do anything to defeat. As long as "anything" doesn't include former detective Ethan Darling. The man sees too much and Georgie isn't sure how far she's willing to go in this dangerous game of life, death . . . . and love.

To Wed a Highland Bride by Sarah Gabriel

An Avon Romance

James MacCarran, Viscount Struan, must marry and sets out to find a wife of his own choosing. Elspeth MacArthur is beautiful, intriguing, and delightful—but not nearly as biddable as he had hoped! Will these two strong-willed people continue to butt heads . . . or will they find that they have the strength to embrace what they have been given?

One Knight Only by Julia Latham

An Avon Romance

Anne Kendall is a lady's maid impersonating a countess at the request of the king. Traveling with Sir Philip Clifford for safety, Anne is protected from everything—except when it comes to matters of the heart.

Avon Romances

the best in
exceptional authors and unforgettable novels!

DISCOVER ROMANCE *at its*

SIZZLING HOT BEST FROM AVON BOOKS

Avon Romantic Treasures

Unforgettable, enthralling love stories, sparkling with passion and adventure from Romance's bestselling authors

AVON

978-0-06-124086-7
$13.95 ($17.50 Can.)

978-0-06-082481-5
$13.95 ($17.50 Can.)

978-0-06-087608-1
$13.95 ($16.50 Can.)

978-0-06-088955-1
$13.95 ($17.50 Can.)

978-0-06-082972-8
$13.95 ($17.50 Can.)

978-0-06-123221-3
$13.95 ($17.50 Can.)

Visit www.AuthorTracker.com for exclusive
information on your favorite HarperCollins authors.

Available wherever books are sold, or call 1-800-331-3761 to order.

ATP 1107